CREATURES OF LIGHT

By Emily B. Martin

Woodwalker
Ashes to Fire
Creatures of Light

CREATURES OF LIGHT

EMILY B. MARTIN

HARPER

VOYAGER

IMPULSE

An Imprint of HarperCollins Publishers

Cover art and map by Emily B. Martin.

CREATURES OF LIGHT. Copyright © 2018 by Emily B. Martin. All rights reserved. Printed in the United States of America. No part of this book may be used or reproduced in any manner whatsoever without written permission except in the case of brief quotations embodied in critical articles and reviews. For information, address HarperCollins Publishers, 195 Broadway, New York, NY 10007.

Digital Edition JANUARY 2018 ISBN: 978-0-06-268883-5

Print Edition ISBN: 978-0-06-268897-2

Harper Voyager, the Harper Voyager logo, and Harper Voyager Impulse are trademarks of HarperCollins Publishers.

HarperCollins is a registered trademark of HarperCollins Publishers in the United States of America and other countries.

FIRST EDITION

18 19 20 21 22   HDC   10 9 8 7 6 5 4 3 2 1

To Caitlin

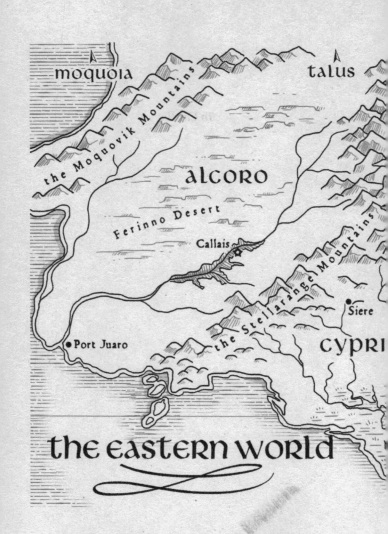

moquoia

talus

the Moquovik Mountains

ALCORO

Ferinno Desert

Callais

the Stellarange Mountains

Siere

• Port Juaro

CYPRI

the eastern world

lumen
lake

the
SILVERWOOD
mountains

the Beacon

the Palisades

Blackshell

Lampyrinae

Wyddroan

WINDER

Sunmarten

PAROA

Matariki

Lilou

samna

CREATURES OF LIGHT

PROLOGUE

Colm Alastaire clutched a stitch in his side, his lungs burning from hours of sucking in the cold mountain air. His beard was thick with hoarfrost where his breath had frozen on it, turning the normally reddish hairs icy white. He was almost to the crest of the Palisades, having started up the towering escarpment just before sunset. Now it was the deep part of the night, the almost-full moon hanging low in a winter-clear sky. It lit the massive freshwater lake at the foot of the cliffs with stark silver, the islands black against the glow. Despite the alien beauty of his home country down below, he didn't pause to admire the view. He had a mission to accomplish, and if he wasn't safely back at Blackshell by midmorning, Mona would have questions he couldn't answer without lying.

He was going to be doing enough lying as it was.

He adjusted his cloak and continued on warily, aware that his wheezing breath and the crunching of his boots on the snow would give him away to any sharp-eared Silvern rangers. He didn't want to run afoul of a Woodwalker's scouting party, as that would mean getting dragged even farther up the mountainside to the Silverwood palace, and there was no way he could keep his trip a secret if the Royal Guard had him in custody. No, he had to make his rendezvous, or everything would be ruined. Despite the fatigue in his legs and the numbness in his toes, he picked up his pace, making for the dark line of leafless trees, still as statues in the windless night.

"I could shoot you in a thunderstorm with my eyes closed."

He skidded to a halt on the icy rock, his heart rate spiking. She was standing so still at the edge of the trees that his gaze had passed over her as part of the landscape. But there she was, her feet spread on the snow, the moonlight glinting off the silver pin on her lapel. Despite her cloak covering the rest of her uniform, that pin and the double band of fringe on her boots communicated her office—a Woodwalker, a steward and protector of the Silverwood Mountains, charged with keeping interlopers like him from harming the forest and its residents. Another glimmer of silver across her brow betrayed her other title, one she took to with significantly less fervor: Queen of the Silverwood.

"Honestly," she said. "Do you have to *try* to make that much noise?"

His alarm ebbed into relief, and he bent double with his hands on his knees, his chest heaving.

Despite her chastisement, she unwrapped her cloak from her shoulders and produced two flasks—one with lukewarm water meant to refresh him after the long, painful struggle up the Palisades in the dead of night, the other with corn whiskey to chase away the chill.

He took a grateful draw at both canteens, spluttering against the whiskey. "Where are all your scouts?"

"I sent the party that patrols the ridge down to Hellbender Bottoms to break up ice dams," she said. "Not their typical assignment, but they're smart enough not to ask questions. There's nobody on the Palisades tonight except us."

"Did anyone see you?" he asked.

"Did anyone see you," she muttered. *"Did anyone see you, you who snuck a rowdy bunch of cutfoot divers through the middle of a populated mountain range."*

"I'm serious, Mae. I don't want word getting back to the lake."

"We'll pretend we're having an affair," she replied.

"That's not funny."

"Oh, sure it is. Think of the look on Mona's face."

"Think of the look on Valien's," he admonished. "What would he say?"

"I'd say get on with it, or take it somewhere else,"

mumbled a groggy voice from under the trees, making Colm jump again. "Leastwise, let a man get as decent a sleep as he can in below-freezing temperatures."

"Val never did like sleeping outdoors," Mae admitted as the king shifted in the darkness behind her, trying to bundle his bedroll around his exposed ears. "It always made him testy." She raised her voice slightly. "That's what comes from having a scented pillow under one's pretty face since infancy."

"He came with you?" While her voice rose, Colm's dropped to an urgent whisper, his breath clouding before his face. "Why?"

Mae looked back at him. "I know you have reason to believe otherwise, Colm, but I don't actually enjoy lying to people—least of all my husband. Besides, we hadn't camped together in over a year—we missed the good old days."

There was something that sounded like a soldier's curse from under the blankets.

Colm shook himself. He couldn't worry about Valien—the king had far more loyalty to his wife than to the queen of Lumen Lake, and if Mae requested a secret be kept, Valien would take death over giving it away. Dismissing his unease, Colm reached into his quilted tunic and pulled out a thick packet of parchment, weatherproofed with beeswax.

Mae's gaze fell on it—and now she was the one who hesitated before ultimately taking it. She looked warily at the inscription on the front and cleared her throat.

"Colm . . . are you sure about this?"

"Yes. Positive. You know what it could mean."

"I don't like getting wrapped up with Alcoro." She looked up at him, the moonlight two pinpricks in her sharp brown eyes. "And certainly not behind your sister's back."

"Mona wouldn't understand," he said, ignoring the massive twinge of guilt in his gut. "I'll tell her—eventually. But not yet. Trust me."

"I guess I'll have to." She tucked the parchment into her own tunic. "I'll send it with a rider as soon as we get back to the palace."

"Thank you."

"But you know that it could be weeks—maybe months before it gets there?" she added. "We're not even sure where she is. We're not even sure if she's . . ."

Still alive, Colm finished for her in his head even as he fought against the tightness in his chest.

"I know," he said. It had been eating away at him since his sister and Mae had returned from their disastrous trip to Cyprien. "But it can't be helped." He nodded out at the lake, as if offering it as proof of his—probably ruinous—convictions, and he drew in a breath. "Queen Gemma needs to know about the cave."

CHAPTER 1

Treason.

The story of my life.

At least, most of my life.

Early on, it was a blissfully unknown concept, a blank space in my childhood. But then, one day, it morphed into a looming, shadowed specter and abruptly devoured everything I'd taken for truth.

It had hung around, that word—*treason*—for years, slowly decaying, but occasionally popping up at important crossroads, dragged out of the closet like an unwanted gift I couldn't get rid of. Something to be pored over, poked, prodded. The same questions, asked again and again. I was relieved, then, when the whispers of *treason* went largely silent in the past few years.

Until five weeks ago, when I betrayed the Seventh King and the country of Alcoro to our enemies.

I knew it had been five weeks because my cycle had come and gone again, and because of the tick marks I was keeping on a sheet of parchment tacked over the cramped writing desk in the equally cramped study of this cramped place the guards all called the Retreat but was really just an elaborate prison.

The Retreat had been built six generations previously to house a prince who had killed a rival over an academic spat. Since then it had become a place to put members of the royal family who had strayed outside the lines of propriety—a senile queen with a penchant for removing her clothes in public, a sickly princess who suffered from narcolepsy, a king who liked to release his anxiety by setting fire to his belongings.

And now me.

It was three miles outside the city, at the end of a lonely track on the canyon rim. It was a single story, made of whitewashed adobe with pudgy corners and consisting of a kitchen and dining area, a little study, a washroom, and a bedroom. There was a courtyard that was almost twice as big as the footprint of the house, and it would have been comparatively pleasant if not for the twelve-foot high wall that encircled the perimeter, blocking any view of the canyon or surrounding sagebrush flats. A straggly cottonwood tree grew in the middle of the yard, along with some sage and a single prickly pear. I'd heard the narcoleptic princess had planted beds of wildflowers during her tenure here, but I couldn't say for certain myself, as everything was cloaked in snow.

I shivered at the diamond-paned window in the study, my face reflected in the rippled glass. Of the five weeks since the disaster in Dismal Green, I'd spent three of them here. The first week I had spent in a cell in Bellemere while my folk put all their effort into tracing Queen Mona, Queen Ellamae, and Rou Roubideaux, hoping to recapture them before they could leave the country. The second week I'd spent locked in a carriage as it bumped along the Alosia River and over the Stellarange Mountains. From there it was down into the capital city of Callais, where we bypassed the dungeons deep in the bowels of the palace and headed directly here, which told me they either hadn't made up their minds about hanging me or couldn't spare the time.

I'd had only one visitor since arriving here—a clerk, who came to take a written statement on everything that had happened since we'd left the dock in Port Juaro in October to sail to Lilou. She was vaguely familiar, but I couldn't recall her name, which surprised me—I thought I knew most of the clerks at Stairs-to-the-Stars. But I suppose I'd never interacted with the one in charge of prisoners. She'd seemed to be freezing the whole time she was here. She'd hunched over her clipboard behind thick spectacles, with the sleeve of her nondominant hand pulled over her fingers and her hair engulfed in a woolen cap. I'd offered to stoke the fire in the little cast-iron stove, but she just shook her head and continued scratching at her parchment. I spent what seemed to be a relatively short time dictating considering all that had happened—the meeting with Queen Mona and Queen Ellamae in Lilou, the attack on the ship, the abduction by the Roubideaux brothers into the swamp, the string of rooms I was locked inside, the confrontation on the banks of Dismal Green. The clerk made only nominal notes at each point of interest before nodding and declaring she needed to inspect the villa to make a security report. One of the guards accompanied her as she tottered around the periphery of the wall, poking at places where the adobe was crumbling and inspecting the cottonwood tree to be sure none of the branches could provide an escape over the wall. She drilled the guard on their schedules and watch posts. She spent a great deal of time studying a little tile fountain at the back of the yard, dry and buried in snow, which might have held lilies or reeds on some distant sunny day. Satisfied, it seemed, she made a few more notes and left without a word or glance in my direction.

That was ten days ago. The only other human presence in this forsaken place were my guards and the cook who came in every other day to prepare stew and cornbread. The leftovers I was merely to place outside, covered, to be reheated and eaten the next day.

It would be no secret to say my spirits were lower than they had been in a very long time. Even with the disastrous events that had occurred in the past year, at least I had had a job to do, a tacit understanding of my role and responsibilities.

And at least I wasn't utterly alone.

I spent the time writing, documenting the details the prison clerk had glossed over in her report. How Lyle Roubideaux had shown me his notes on incendiary technology that made our chemists and engineers look like children tinkering with sticks and string. How his brother, Rou, had been unfailingly kind to me, almost enough to make me forget I was his country's prisoner and political leverage. How Queen Mona had sewn impeccably stitched collars onto my shifts to hide my neck. How Celeno had stared at me, stunned, after I'd thrown the flash grenade that let her and Rou escape down the river.

I left out my wondering if he was ever going to bother looking at me again.

When I finished that, I turned to journaling my daily events, but most of that consisted of *washed*, *ate*, *journaled*. I tried to read, but there were only a few books in the villa, all religious texts, full of theorizing and postulating on the Prophecy of the Prism, which itself was stitched into a thick tapestry that was nailed into the wall of the bedroom.

WE ARE CREATURES OF THE LIGHT,
AND WE KNOW IT IS PERFECT.
THE SEVENTH KING OF THE CANYONS
WILL RISE TO BRING
THE WEALTH AND PROSPERITY OF
A THOUSAND YEARS.
PEACE SHALL COME FROM WEALTH.
I AM A PRISM, MADE TO SCATTER LIGHT.

Beneath the archaic cyphers were the two pictorial images, one of a human figure, which most assumed was the Prism himself, and one of a six-pointed star, which had been adopted as our national symbol. My fingers itched whenever I looked at this tapestry— whoever had sewn it had made the star slightly lop- sided, and if I'd had a needle and thread, I'd have ripped out the stitches to get it right despite my un- derdeveloped needlework skills. As it was, I tried in large part to simply ignore the tapestry, a reminder that at present, I was still in the ongoing process of failing my hopes and plans in every possible way.

I longed for my inks and sketchbooks. My mind was trapped without them, stuck in a place even jour- naling couldn't shake. I tried sketching with the quill and found it maddening, the ink never lasting long enough to get a good stroke. I attempted to fashion a brush out of frayed strings from the tapestry in my bedroom, but it was crude and left sloppy lines. So I settled on charcoal, conserving my few precious nibs for sketching only. The results were smudgy and flat, but it was infinitely better than nothing.

But none of these meager activities were enough to fully distract myself from my predicament, and more often than not, I sat idle in the little study, staring blankly out the window at the frozen courtyard. Time was slipping away, bit by bit, filling me with the same anxious dread I'd carried with me in Cyprien. That country was rebelling, fighting back, but Alcoro's military presence was more organized and better armed than theirs. If my folk managed to regain their hold, any number of consequences could follow, each one with a potentially higher death toll than the first. My thoughts often landed on the shocking bit of news Queen Mona and Rou had given me in the bayou—that the sudden Cypri uprising was in large part thanks to an impending military draft designed to muster a force to march against Paroa. Control the ports, control the trade. Control the coast, control the arteries of wealth to and from the Eastern World.

The thought made my stomach go sour. I'd fought that draft—I'd stalled and harangued and petitioned our council to abandon the idea. But Celeno had been ill all that time, fragmenting my focus and adding a layer of tension to the council's proceedings. It didn't help that there seemed to be constant whispers, nudges toward approving the draft. I knew where they must be coming from, but the Prelate never made her arguments in the open, instead weaving them skillfully into prayer and Devotion and readings from the Book of the Prophecy, adding to the building conviction that this truly was a steppingstone in Alcoro's divinely guided path.

Still, I'd managed to convince Celeno to call instead for an attempt at diplomacy in Lilou. At least, I thought I had. It was only after talks with Mona and Ellamae had literally gone up in flames that I realized he had given his approval for the Cypri draft without my knowing.

And now, every day that passed seemed to add to some phantasmal death count—if Alcoro regained control of Cyprien, it would only fuse the need to spread our control up the coast, spilling blood and wasting lives in all three countries. And if Alcoro *didn't* regain control of Cyprien, who knew what measures the council and the Prelate would deem appropriate. We would be cut off from the main trade routes, facing our own dwindling resources and the looming threat of an unfulfilled Prophecy—it made for dire possibilities. A ruinous last-ditch military effort at the least, with a distinct probability of civil war.

The thought constantly made my head spin, leaving me dizzy and dismayed at my dwindling options.

Yes, I was very, very short on time.

I was in just such a state on my tenth day, gnawing my lip and watching the clouds gather in what promised to be a full-fledged snowstorm. I was wondering whether I might find some success in penning a letter somehow disguised as an academic query to my old biology tutor—all my other requests to send letters had been ignored by the guards—when I heard the rattle of keys and the creak of the wrought-iron gate out front. I looked back over my shoulder as the door to the villa opened.

Who would be coming in now?

One of the guards from the perimeter wall appeared in the doorway.

"You have a visitor," he said. He stepped aside, and like a ghost from the shadows, the Prelate stood on the threshold.

Shaula Otzacamos possessed the innate ability to make me feel like I'd misspoken even before I opened my mouth. Her steely gray hair was pulled back in a tight bun under her star band, a plain one set with three flat glass beads, unlike the overlarge faceted one I still wore despite my imprisonment. Her fur-lined cloak was black, with none of the heavy embroidery that was popular in court. In fact, the only embellishment besides her star band was a large, polished prism that hung on her chest.

None of that mattered, though. She could have been wearing a burlap sack, and she still would have radiated authority.

She flicked her hand at the guard. "Leave us."

It was a mark of her influence that he gave a short bow and disappeared. When the clerk was here, even with her royal seal and badge, a small cadre of guards had shadowed her the whole time. Once he was gone, Shaula flicked her eyes over me, my gray skirt and bolero, my only slightly darker gray sash. Her gaze fell on the writing desk, and her lips tightened at the littering of charcoal sketches. She looked back to me.

"So," she said.

So, indeed.

"The guards tell me you sit and draw all day," she said.

It beat simply sitting.

She looked at the nearest sketch—the tile fountain out in the courtyard. It had an interesting spiderweb of cracks radiating out from where the grotto behind it was pulling out of the adobe—probably why the clerk had inspected it so closely for structural weakness.

"You always did take after your mother," Shaula said.

When my old tutor, Ancha, said the same thing, she said it with warmth, almost reverence. "You have your mother's skill, and all her guts, too," she'd say, poring over an illustration of burnished-gold hornets that I'd run the risk of catching in my aerial net.

"I got stung," I'd told her.

"Obviously," she'd replied.

Shaula did not examine my work with the same admiration. "I should never have allowed this to continue."

That was a bit surprising. Sketching broken fountains was hardly heretical.

She shifted the fountain sketch to a page of cicadas I'd detailed from memory—I'd illustrated enough of them for my thesis to be able to replicate them without a reference. "You've clearly had a closer connection to your mother than you let on in any of your audits."

That, on the other hand . . .

Treason, treason, treason.

I found my voice, usually so scarce in her presence. "I have no loyalty to my mother," I said, falling back on my most basic line of defense, repeated with every accusation. "I haven't had contact with her since I left home to come study in Callais."

Shaula shook her head. "Whether or not you've exchanged letters with Rana has never mattered less. Your own actions have betrayed you, not hers." She set down my sketches and looked me squarely in the eye. The little study had never felt so small. "What do you have to say—what could you *possibly* have to say for yourself—regarding the events in Cyprien?"

I bit the inside of my cheek. The scene played out again—Lyle Roubideaux, dying on the riverbank. His brother, Rou, stricken. Queen Ellamae, unconscious. Queen Mona, enraged. Celeno, holding the crossbow.

The flash grenade in Lyle's pocket, and the way it lit the night like the surface of the sun when I flung it to the ground.

"There have been four independent testimonies," Shaula continued when my silence persisted. "Three from the guards, and one from the king himself. None of them provide a single shred of evidence to suggest you might have acted accidentally, or out of confusion. You intentionally released an incendiary grenade meant to blind your own folk and allow our enemy queens and the Cypri rebel to escape. We have failed to recapture them."

I wasn't surprised. I had a feeling the queens and Rou had managed to escape up the waterways before my folk ever made it down to Lilou. Even if they hadn't moved so quickly, Queen Mona could easily get past a blockade. That I knew for a fact. No wonder I hadn't been tried and hanged yet, if my folk had been spending all their time hunting for them.

"Do you have any inkling how significant your actions were?" the Prelate pressed. "Do you have any idea what it means not just to have lost such valuable captives, but to spur them to unite against us?"

"I know more would have been lost by bringing them here," I said.

"Lies and treason, Gemma." *Treason, treason, treason.* "With the queens of Lumen Lake and the Silverwood as leverage, we could have peacefully negotiated a treaty that would have ushered in the fulfillment of the Prophecy."

By subjugating the rest of the East, I left unsaid.

"Instead," she continued, "we're facing an uprising in Cyprien. The king barely made it back across our border. Many of our folk are still in the country, unaccounted for. Paroa knows our intentions to take the coast. Queen Mona is forming an alliance unlike any the East has seen in centuries—*against Alcoro*. War could have been avoided. Lives could have been saved. Look at me!" Shaula yelled, and I looked up, startled. *"Do you realize what you've done?"*

Silence flooded in. I sat frozen in the hardback chair, shivering from the penetrating cold and mute under her rage. She stared at me with steely, glittering eyes, and I was reminded, once again, just how little she looked like my mother.

She drew herself up, her nostrils flaring slightly. "They've set your trial for next week."

I forced my tongue to work. "Is Celeno back in Callais?"

"Yes."

"Will he come see me?"

Her face gave a brief spasm of anger. "Will he come see you, Gemma? The king does not want to see you. The king has no reason to see you. Perhaps the only good thing that has come of this is that he finally has stopped believing you're his personal savior, ready to swoop in and save him." She shook her head. "I anticipated many ends, Gemma, but not this one. I thought you and he would be unstoppable."

I made myself brush aside the shame she was trying to bury in me—at least I had experience with that. "I need to talk to him—there's something I need to tell him."

"And I'm sure you'll be able to say it at the trial."

"Then may I speak to the council?" I asked. "At least Izar?" Izar was lead councilor, and consistently my closest political ally. He would be the most likely to listen to my case and fight for my plans, so carefully laid and so close to destruction now.

"Councilor Izar is ill," Shaula said. "He's been confined by a debilitating stomach virus. We're not even sure he will be able to attend your trial."

My panic flared. "That would leave only six on the council." Three of whom were fervent devotees to the Prophecy, and one who often swung their way with enough persuading. Izar had been my one hope—if not for a lenient sentence for myself, then at least for one last attempt at a diplomatic alternative to full-fledged war.

"I have the authority to break a tie in trial, should there be one," Shaula said.

I managed to bring my whirling mind to a coherent thought and looked up at her. "Celeno still has to approve the sentence they decide."

"I expect to have his signature in hand by the end of the week," she agreed.

I stared at her. "Before the trial?"

"He was a witness, Gemma—not just that, but a victim of your actions as well. He needs to hear no evidence or argument. He's made his decision."

Her tone made her implications clear. My fingers clenched.

"Let me speak to him," I said. "Before the trial."

"No."

"Please."

She gazed at me silently for a moment, her lips pressed together in a thin line. "Once again, you assume that my loyalty is to you, Gemma. That was your very first mistake. My loyalty is to the Prophecy, as yours was supposed to be. You have always seemed to believe you could shape the world to meet your needs. It should come as no surprise that you're reaping the consequences of your selfish beliefs now."

I cut my gaze away, my face hot, my throat constricting in a familiar way. I blinked several times.

Shaula recognized the warning signs, too. She lifted her chin. "You have no right to cry."

That I had never been able to help when I cried had never made any difference to her. It was an instant, involuntary reaction to stress of all kinds, from everything as small as a botched illustration to as large as the ruination of my country and my life along with it. I ran my knuckles under my eyes.

"If I cannot speak to Celeno, and I cannot speak to my council, may I at least send a letter?" I asked.

She turned, arranging her furred cloak around her with an air of finality. "Of course not."

"Has there been any mail for me?"

Her face flickered with a look of disgust at my persistent and naive questioning. "Enough. You still cannot seem to grasp that you're facing trial for treason. If you had any sense, you would dispel with the notion that you have any autonomy left to you, and you'd spend your next few days in sincere penitence. For my part, I am done with you, Gemma. Your mother's heresy was a blight to our family, and your betrayal is no different. I consider you no more my niece than I would any other common traitor."

She left the tiny room with a sweep of her cloak. As she made her way back to the guarded door, she said over her shoulder, "A clerk will be in tomorrow to take your statement."

I looked up from my hands as the door swung closed.

That made no sense.

A clerk had already taken my statement.

I woke to find myself falling out of bed.

I thrashed, as one does, expecting the hard collision with the floor at any moment. But it didn't come. It took me a few groggy seconds to realize that I had stopped halfway, supported from behind by something that felt alarmingly like a human body.

"What?" I croaked.

"Quiet," whispered a hoarse voice, barely audible over the whistling wind outside—the snowstorm must have gotten worse. The person behind me hefted me to my feet, flung a cloak around my shoulders, and then clamped a hand over my forearm. Struggling through my muddled thoughts—was I dreaming?—I lurched forward as I was hauled toward the bedroom door.

The hallway was freezing, which I quickly realized was because the door to the courtyard had been left open. A snowflake blew into my eye.

I snatched at sense and dug my heels into the tile floor.

"Wait," I said. I gripped the person's hand on my forearm. "Stop—let me go!"

"Quiet," the voice said again. Though muffled, it sounded like a woman. Her head was covered with a dark hood and scarf.

I pulled against her hold. "Let me *go*!"

She hissed at me. "Do you want out of this place or not?"

"I—"

"Then do as I say. Stop fighting. We're going straight across the courtyard." She jerked me out into the swirling snow. The wind sluiced over the wall to the compound, rattling the naked cottonwood tree. I stumbled in her grip, my feet sliding on the frozen gravel.

"Did you put shoes on me?" I gasped.

"You always were a sound sleeper."

We flew across the little space toward the cottonwood. She pushed me against the trunk, my back flat against the bark. I sucked in a breath of frozen air, still trying to sort out what was happening. Should I scream?

She released my arm and took up a wide-legged

stance. She cocked her hand back behind her head, and with a powerful lunge, flung something toward the wall of the compound. The moment it left her fingers, she dove to where I was standing, flattening herself against me and slapping her palms over my ears.

The world went yellow-white. A grinding blast shook the air, followed by a wave of rolling heat. I yelped, the sound lost to the crash of a cottonwood branch as it plummeted to the ground just a few feet away.

The woman pulled back and returned her grip to my forearm. Dazed, I followed her out of the lee of the tree to see a smoking hole in the compound wall, right where the cracked tile fountain had been.

People were shouting somewhere behind us, but we were already at the pile of rubble. I slipped on the loose chunks of adobe and pushed her hand off my arm, preferring to climb out under my own power.

I followed the hem of her black cloak, stumbling over snowy sagebrush. I knew the canyon must open up somewhere to our right, but it was invisible in the swirling storm. I hoped my liberator—kidnapper?—knew where she was setting her feet, or else our last memories would involve soaring downward to the River of Callais.

We didn't run for long. A tumble of rocks loomed up in the gloom, where a mule was tethered to a twisted old juniper, its ears flat against its skull at the commotion.

"Up," the woman said.

I set my toe in the stirrup and slung my leg over the mule's back. The woman loosened the mule's tether and vaulted up behind me. With a sharp kick, she urged the animal into a canter across the open flats.

I crouched low over the coarse mane, snowflakes stinging my eyes. The wind roared off the canyon rim, whipping my cloak and slicing through my nightclothes. It was impossible to make out anything beyond the buckled drifts of snow as they raced by, and I knew the mule couldn't see much better than I could. My stomach flipped as the mule stumbled over a ditch, finding its footing on the far side.

"Of all the nights!" I shouted, my fingers clenched in the mule's mane.

". . . this is the one they won't be able to track us!" she finished for me.

I gritted my teeth—I supposed I couldn't disagree with that.

We circled away from the compound, heading toward the distant main road, though there must have been a mile of open sage flats between us and it.

"Are we going to the coast?" I called.

"Let's hope they think so," she answered.

After thirty minutes of tense riding, we reached a gradual dip in the land. A shallow, rocky creek wound along its base, and the woman directed the mule into its course. We picked our way upstream, frigid droplets splashing my calves. My toes were just going numb when the woman nudged the mule back up the bank. I wanted to ask what the purpose of that uncomfortable activity was, but I could hazard a guess—if the snow didn't succeed in covering our tracks, our pursuers would have to guess which way we had turned, and they would likely pick the direction of the main road. Instead, we climbed back out of the river's hollow on the same side we had started, and with a nudge to the mule, we took off back toward the distant canyon.

The night was later than I thought. By the time we were nearing the rim again, the sky in the east had started to lighten to a dull, sunless gray. The snowfall didn't abate—a blessing and a curse. As we neared the canyon, the woman dismounted and led the mule among the rocks to prevent us from cantering right out over the rim. She stopped several times, occasionally scrambling up a boulder to peer into the distance. I shivered on the mule's back, wrapped in my now soaked cloak. Finally, the woman seemed to find what she was looking for, and she took up the reins of the mule to lead it to the very edge of the canyon rim. A broken, narrow track led down, hugging the wall.

"Right," she said. "Off. If Checkerspot slips over the edge, there's no sense in losing you both."

Numbly, I slid from the mule's back. My boots were frozen and heavy as iron.

The woman gestured down the little track. "You go first."

"No," I said.

She stood before me, her hood still up, her mouth covered by the black scarf. A patch of frost had rimed over the fabric from her breath. The faint dawn light revealed very little of the rest of her, washing out the colors of her skin and eyes and wisps of hair blown loose from her hood.

"I'm not going any farther," I said, "until you tell me who you are."

Not because I didn't already know.

Because I wanted to make her show me.

She sighed. "Honestly, Gemma?" She pulled the hood away from her face and loosened the scarf from her mouth.

I stared into the face of the prison clerk.

Or, more accurately, my mother.

CHAPTER 2

Gone were the thick spectacles and woolen hat, revealing a dark gray braid shot through with silver. Her sepia skin was darkened and spotted by work in the sun, and a simple glass star band—not unlike her sister's—perched on her head, in need of polishing. I couldn't see the canyon-wall brown of her eyes, but I could see their angular catlike sweep—I'd gotten their shape, but not their color, apparently favoring my father's dark blue instead.

She let me search her face, and I wondered what differences she was noticing in my own.

"I thought I might have to fake a scar, or a birthmark, to keep you from recognizing me that first day," she said drily. "Turns out I shouldn't have worried."

"I haven't seen you in sixteen years," I said, more defensively than I meant to sound.

"I suppose not." She gestured down the little track. "Shall we continue?"

"Where?" I asked.

"My house, of course."

She must have seen the struggle on my face, because she said, "Our twirly house is long gone, Gemma."

"*No.*"

The word broke from me and hung there, childish and plaintive. She lifted an eyebrow, and there—*there*—was the echo of Shaula in her face. I cleared my throat. "I mean, no, I'm not going down the track. Why don't you give me the mule, and I'll ride to the coast?"

"Because we want them to *think* you're going to the coast. There's a highly reliable source in Teso's Ford who's about to see you ride past on the main road, and first thing tomorrow, your name will appear on a register at an inn in Port Juaro."

"Not very bright, am I?" I asked.

"My hope is that it buys us a few days," she said.

"Days for what?"

She waved again at the track. "Come on, Gemma. I'm too old to be out running all over creation in the snow."

"What about blowing up walls and breaking out prisoners of the crown?"

She gave me a push. "Hot fire. Hot coffee. I'll tell you everything then."

Reluctantly, I took the first few steps down the path, keeping one hand on the wall to my right. The snow continued to fall, and footing was slippery. More than once I sent a shower of rocks tumbling down the sheer slope below, and soon my nerves were as raw as my windburned cheeks. The mule snorted and champed its bit as it picked its way behind us. We scattered a herd of bighorn sheep, the lambs bleating as they scrambled nimbly after their mothers.

The wind died down the lower we headed into the canyon, and the air warmed slightly. I had never envied folk living down the cliff walls during the summertime, missing out on the fresh breezes up on the rim, but during the winter, it was far more protected and pleasant. Still, I was only dressed in my nightgown and traveling cloak, and soon my feet and hands were chapped and numb.

"How much farther?" I asked over my shoulder.

"Just over this rise," she said automatically.

I stopped and turned around, my fists on my hips.

"What?" she asked.

"That's exactly what you used to say when we were coming back from in the field," I said.

"So it is," she said.

Blowing out a breath of frustration that hid the twinge of nostalgia in the pit of my stomach, I turned back around and stormed on ahead.

It wasn't over the next rise, of course. It never was.

It was a full hour before the little track joined a bigger one, still hugging tight to the canyon wall but wide enough that two mules could walk abreast.

"Up," my mother said, pointing to the switchback that led back toward the top of the canyon.

I was surprised to find that we were back in the settlement below Stairs-to-the-Stars, though the palace was well out of sight high up on the rim. Folk throughout the canyon built their homes in the natural overhangs that cut into the walls, splitting Callais into neighborhoods known as *hobs*. Some of these hobs were sprawling, complete with gentle grassy areas and stands of trees; others were squeezed into crevices so tight the houses looked more like swallow colonies all stacked on top of each other. At this hour and in these conditions, only the earliest risers were up, yawning as they slogged through the snow to teetering communal woodpiles. While they didn't seem interested in us, I pulled my hood farther over my head all the same, covering my ornate star band.

The snow was just beginning to ease up when my mother called tiredly, "Whiptail Hob."

I looked up at the side road switchbacking up the canyon wall. Gathering my last shreds of energy, I started up the climb, my thighs burning. We passed through a stand of junipers clinging stubbornly to the rocks and a little stony creek that chattered down the cliffside. Finally, puffing and panting, we reached the shelter of the overhang. Whiptail was one of the smaller hobs, but not as densely packed as some, home to perhaps three dozen individual houses. There was a common space in the middle, home to a little copse of aspen trees, their black-and-white mottled trunks stark against the snow. A few goats wandered the common, nibbling frozen twigs.

My mother's house was at the very edge, where the angle of the rock floor became too sharp to build any farther. While it meant her roof tapered almost entirely to the ground at the far side of the house, it also gave her the rest of the sloped shelf all to herself. Four squat beehives sat past her door, flanked with straw for winter insulation. She wasn't the first inhabitant; faint petroglyphs scratched into the stone ceiling told of the families who had lived in this house for generations—images depicting occupations, hardship, joyful events, and many, many women having babies.

My mother led Checkerspot into a hay-filled awning. A fluffed-up sage grouse fussed at her from its roost in the loft. My mother responded by poking underneath it and coming up with a single speckled egg.

"Breakfast," she said, beckoning me to the little door in her lopsided house.

I ducked through the opening, knocking a braid of wild onions hanging next to the lintel. One dropped to the floor, and my mother scooped it up and set it on the scrubbed wooden table with the egg. She unhooked her cloak and tossed it over the back of a chair.

I could see why she had kept her long sleeve over her left hand in her disguise as the clerk—her prison tattoo peeked out from the hem, the ink muddy. *M* for Mesa, followed by a line of little crosses to mark the years of her sentence.

"Smaller than our twirly house, of course," she said, filling a tin pot with water from the dipping barrel. "And no willow brush creek, but the view's not bad—oh, great Light, are you crying?"

My palms jumped to my face, my breath slipping between my fingers. Moon and stars, just that *smell*— that musty scent of preservative from the insect vials, the hint of dried sage bundled in the rafters, a touch of beeswax, all underlined by the smell of adobe and woodsmoke . . . the tears had sprung almost instantaneously. They'd blurred my first glimpse of the room, but as they fell I took it all in—the narrow shelves scooped out of the adobe walls, holding crates of collection vials, wooden specimen cases, and spreading boards. Sketchbooks were stuffed in every gap; a few loose illustrations were tacked to the walls, ruffling quietly in the breeze from the open door. My breath cracked again, my tears slipping between my palms and my cheeks. I heard the tap of the pot being set down on the table.

You have no right to cry, Shaula had said.

"I'm sorry," I said thickly.

"Oh, please, Gemma, crying used to be like sweating for you. It came as easily as your laugh. There's no reason to be sorry." My mother put her hands on my elbows and guided me into a chair by the table. "Sit down. Here."

She pressed a handkerchief into my hands, and I blotted my face with it. When she was sure I had a handle on myself, she picked up the pot again and hooked it over the hearth, stirring up a few coals until they caught the bundle of tinder. Dusting her hands off, she took down a rickety little field stove.

"So," she said. "Let's start with first things first."

"First things first," I repeated numbly. I wiped my nose. Then I straightened and said a little louder, "First thing is . . . *what on earth are you doing here?*"

"Oh, I was more interested in how you take your egg."

"How long have you been in Callais?" I asked.

She checked the edge on a knife and started slicing the little onion into coin-thin pieces. "Four years now, I suppose."

"By yourself?"

"Well." She waved vaguely to the cases and vials of dead insects. "Depends on what you mean. But no, not entirely. I have my research team."

"What research team?" I asked. "I read all the natural science pamphlets that come out. Your name isn't ever in any of them."

"No, of course not. I don't release my work to the crown. Hand me that skillet, will you?"

My mouth dropped open. "You don't release your

work to the crown? That's . . ." *Unheard of.* "That's treasonous."

"Yes, we always were alike, you and I."

"We're not alike."

She wiped the last of the onion from her knife. "You even use my hatching technique in your illustrations."

"We're *not alike.*"

"*The skillet, Gemma.*"

I reached up for the dented little thing and yanked it off its peg. She took it and set it on the stove. I watched in frustrated silence.

"Some people," she said, rummaging in a battered old field pack, "would have said 'thank you' by now. I'm no filly, to be breaking into guarded prisons."

"How *did* you get in?"

"Ladder."

"Just like that?"

"The guards had a blind spot on the canyon side," she said, removing a metal tin from her pack. "They detailed it to me quite nicely."

"And the grenade?"

"One of the Cypri's."

"Lyle Roubideaux?" I asked.

"Yes, him. His work made it to Callais a few weeks ago." She opened the metal tin and poked around inside. "Every engineer and chemist in the place has been pressed into developing the weaponry detailed in the report. The chemical bombs—the ones that burn on water, the ones that light damp wood like hay in a drought, and the ones that cause temporary blindness—Alcoro has control of them now. Isn't that a comforting thought?"

Her tone suggested my same reaction—the prospect of being armed with such unprecedented weapons was terrifying. I shook my head. "How did you come by them for your own use? Did you break into the labs like you did the Retreat?"

"No. One of the chemical engineers is part of my old group of rabble, though she keeps it secret to maintain her position. She smuggled me a few devices to use, and she's the one laying the false trail to Port Juaro—at significant risk to herself, I might add."

I clenched my fists on her handkerchief. Several beats of silence passed as she selected a paper-wrapped object from the tin. Finally I blew out a breath. "Thank you."

She snapped the tin shut. "Was that so hard?"

"A little," I said hotly. "It may come as a surprise to you, but you popping up for the first time in sixteen years wouldn't have been my first choice for rescue. You threw me away as a child for your own political agenda. You conspired against Alcoro. You almost ruined my own future." Or at least, she'd tried, before I completed the task for her.

She pulled out a pair of pliers and stuck the little paper-wrapped object in the head. "Good thing my sister picked you up, so she could do it instead."

My fists trembled and clenched on the handkerchief. I could conjure no love for Shaula, but I surged with the irrational need to defend her anyway. "At least she took me in. At least she cared for me, sent me to lessons, gave me a bed—what is *that*?"

With a crunch and flare of sulfurous smoke, my mother had clamped down on the paper object in her pliers, and it had burst into flame. She held it to the rim of her field stove, lighting the burner. "Fire capsule." With the stove lit, she held the flame in front of her, studying it appreciatively. "Coxa—my friend in the labs—came up with them. Highly useful in the field—no need to shower everything in sparks, or carry a tinderbox."

I blinked at the bright spot of flame. "What's the mechanism?"

"Glass beads of sulfuric acid and potassium chlorate. When they're crushed, the chemicals mix and ignite the paper."

I pushed my chair back and picked up the metal tin. I plucked one capsule out and examined it. "No flint or steel at all?"

"Nope."

"Incredible."

"I know."

"Do they store?"

"For a few weeks."

"How long do they burn?"

The flame at the end of her pliers puffed out, leaving only the trace of sulfur smoke. I looked up and was startled to find our faces less than a foot apart. I stood back from the table, still pinching the capsule in my fingers. She slowly set down the pliers.

A beat of silence flickered past.

"You left me," I said, a little quieter. "You said, *stay right here*, and then you left."

She sighed and tapped the ashes left on the pliers into the hearth. "I didn't mean to, Gemma. I didn't expect them to arrest me. They'd let my friends go, and I hadn't done any more than they had. If I had known, I never would have left you at the twirly house. You *do* remember the twirly house, don't you?"

I flushed. I was still having trouble keeping the memories at bay in this tiny kitchen. "Of course I do."

"How we built it together, mixing up the clay and straw from the river, and how we molded funny faces into the walls?"

I remembered the days of squishing the cob together and building up the walls, watching our house grow bit by bit. I remembered collecting baskets full of smooth river stones and embedding them in meandering swirls. There wasn't a straight line in the place—it was all curves and rounded corners. My mother built it that way on purpose.

"Nothing in nature is straight except the horizon," she had said as we molded the arch over the front door. "No boxes, no lines." We had named the resulting lopsided, wandering structure our twirly house.

I had loved it with a fierce, deep-set devotion.

"I remember molding the horned beetle by the back door," I said.

She laughed—a sound that unexpectedly brought back a wash of other memories. I abruptly looked away, gripping the handkerchief.

"We were happy together, Gemma," she said, still smiling. "We had a garden. We grew beans and acorn squash. We had an avocado tree, and a goat named Boots. I wrote articles for the *Journal of Sciences* and illustrated texts for other biologists. You used to help me ink the colors."

"That's not all you did," I said stoically. I had forgotten about Boots.

"No," she said almost thoughtfully. "It's not all I did."

"You were meeting in secret, you were collaborating with dissenters. I remember people coming to our house at night—I used to sit around the corner of the hall when you thought I was in bed."

"No, I knew you were listening," she said. "What did you hear?"

I took a breath. "I didn't understand all of it. But you didn't agree with the Prophecy. You thought it was harming Alcoro."

"Not quite true," she said. "What does the Prophecy say?"

"*We are Creatures of the Light* . . ."

"No," she interrupted me. "What does it *say*—not

what do we say it says. You've spent your adult life in Callais, and most of that in the palace. I'm sure once you were crowned they started engraving the Prophecy into your star bands lest you somehow forget it. But I know, amid all that, you've seen the actual petroglyphs themselves."

She opened a field journal and tore out a piece of paper. She uncorked a traveling bottle of ink and dipped a quill, carefully blocking out several lines of text on the paper.

When she was finished, she turned the paper around. She had indeed copied the old petroglyphs verbatim, complete with all the breaks and patches where the glyphs had worn away over time.

> WE ARE CREATURES O . . . HE LIGHT,
> AND WE KNOW IT I . . . PERFECT.
> . . . THE SEVENTH KING OF THE CANYONS
> . . . ILL RISE TO BRING
> THE WEALTH AND PROSPERITY OF
> A THOUSAND YEARS.
> PEACE SHALL COME FRO . . . WEALTH . . .
> I AM A PRISM, MADE TO SCATTER LIGHT.
> S . . .

Underneath were the two familiar images: the human figure, with the head partially faded, and the six-pointed star.

"What does the Prophecy say?" she asked. "In

short, we have no idea. I'm one of those dissenters who believe we can't fully know what it originally said based on the fragments that are there."

"But there are experts," I said. "People who have studied the Prophecy for centuries, who've written and debated and theorized on what it means."

"Yes, like my darling sister," she said, popping the cork back on the ink bottle with a smack of her palm. "Let me tell you about people like her, and the ones who came before her—things are never as simplistic as the Prelates make them out to be. The Prophecy doesn't exist in a void. It has been intimately tied to the economy and policy of this country since it was first transcribed from the rock."

"You think I'm not aware of that?" I said as she returned her attention to the field stove. "I am—*was*—the queen of this country. I am *intensely* aware of the effect of the Prophecy on our economy and policy. It dictated every decision we made in the council room."

"It's not a one-way street," she said, drizzling oil into the skillet. "It goes the other way, too. Decisions made about the Prophecy are *always* influenced by secular motives. Why do you think Lumen Lake became the target of the Prophecy?"

"Because it was revealed to the Prelate."

She rolled her eyes to the ceiling. "Yes, by fasting and imbibing hallucinogenic tinctures—forgive my recurring heresy, but *I've* had hunger visions before, and I wouldn't base my political strategy on them. But perhaps I'm too cynical, and the Light really did whisper the name of Lumen Lake in the Prelate's ear. You can't really think that was their *only* motive, can you? You don't suppose it had anything to do with the death of an aging monarchy and the ascension of a child queen to the throne? You don't suppose it had anything to do with the wealthiest nation in the East suddenly under unstable control? The plan to take Lumen Lake first started circulating when Queen Myrna Alastaire died and her eleven-year-old daughter Mona was crowned in her place. You don't suppose *that* influenced the Prelate's stratagem at all?"

"That's . . ."

"Treasonous, yes, I know—you must stop being surprised. Why do you think I was locked away in the Mesa prison? Alcoro is rooted in the Prophecy. We've thrown so much money and effort to ensure its fulfillment that any whisper we might be following the wrong agenda is enough to strike terror into a Prelate's heart." She shook her head. "But those whispers exist for a reason, Gemma. And that's the main reason I needed to get you out of the Retreat. There's something you need to know."

"What's that?"

"There's another Prophecy."

The words sounded alien, like they shouldn't exist in the common Eastern tongue. I tested them myself. "*Another* Prophecy? You've found one?"

She cocked her head, the grouse egg poised over the rim of the skillet. "You don't sound astonished beyond belief."

I swallowed. "I've heard there might be more. I mean, you dissenters are always claiming there are other fragments, bits here and there that disprove the one in Callais. I've done a lot of reading on the claims folk have made. Most of them are questionable at best."

My mother snapped the egg against the skillet and poured it over the sizzling onions. "There have always been claims, and probably a few of them have been true. But this one is definitely real."

"Where is it?"

"It's . . . well, first, you have to understand my current work." She pointed to the little door in the far wall—one I had assumed led to a bedroom. "Take a look in there while I finish breakfast. Try not to let in too much light—it disturbs them."

Puzzled, I got up from the table and went to the door. I turned the knob and cracked it open, poking my head inside. The room was windowless, being made up of the last usable space under the hob's overhang, and the ceiling sloped down almost to the floor. But the room wasn't pitch-dark, as I'd have expected. It was filled with a blue-white glow, reflected in clear beads dangling like strings of gems. I blinked a few times, trying to make sense of what I was seeing.

"*Arachnocampa luminosa,*" my mother said over my shoulder. "Fungus gnat larvae."

Packed along every wall were glass cupboards, as one might store fine pottery in. The cupboards were filled with clusters of glowing points of light, illuminating the eerily beautiful strings of beads hanging down toward the ground. I eased farther through the door to better take in the sight, trying to block the morning light in the kitchen.

"Glowworms," I said.

"In the Mesa prison," my mother said behind me, "my closest companions were the rock spiders that lived in my cell. I had ample time to study them, and when I was released, I looked for related species on the talus slopes up in the Stellarange Mountains. They led me, eventually, off the mountaintops and inside the mountains themselves. There are caves there—did you know that? The Range is riddled with them. And they're not empty. The tunnels in the lower elevations are filled with *Arachnocampa*. So a few of us formed a research team. I've fallen in with *geologists*." There was undeniable excitement in her voice as she rattled the skillet over the stove.

"These are mucus?" I asked, tapping the glass near a dozen strands of shining beads.

"Mucus on silken threads." I heard her take the skillet off the heat and come into the room behind me. She wiped her hands on her trousers and pointed to the larvae, hanging in little hammocks from the ceiling of the cupboard. "Each one makes dozens. Their glows act as lures. Any insect drawn to them—even flying adults of their own species—become tangled in the snares. They ingest the silk to draw up their prey, and then—supper. And, Gemma . . ."

She moved to another cupboard, this one shining brighter than any other. "They *change their glow* depending on when they last ate. The hungrier they are, the brighter their light." She took a screened box from the top of the cupboard, filled with a soft ruffling sound. Carefully, she opened the glass door of the cupboard and shook out the box. Out fluttered a cloud of meal moths. She closed the door.

The little brown moths fluttered haphazardly around the glass cupboard, blind. Almost instantly, they began careening into the beads of mucus, the threads swinging as if in a breeze. The effect was immediate. The glowworms' shining lures began to writhe as they slid from their hammocks and started pulling up their threads.

"I've got months of data collected," my mother said as we watched the larvae draw in their prey. "I've got three separate papers drafted. What a presentation this could make to the board of biologists! The *Journal of Sciences* would be at my feet. I could get grants, funds, research power to conduct further studies. Speleothems, extremophiles, fossils . . . there are a hundred different opportunities represented in those caves. But I refuse to let a whisper of them reach that Prelate of yours."

I forced my fascination with the insects back to the

subject at hand. "What's Shaula going to do with a bunch of bioluminescent larvae?" I asked.

"It's not the larvae that worry me. Though, funny enough, they bear a similar resemblance to her own student work."

I looked up in the dim light. "What work? Shaula was a scientist?"

"She took after our parents just like I did. She was a biologist, only instead of insects, she fell in love with myriapods—particularly a funny little millipede that luminesces. It glows, just like these." She tapped the glass with her fingernail. "Little creatures of light."

"She always gave me the impression she didn't approve of the sciences . . . or at least, me taking them up."

"She made a hard pivot once she got interested in the Prophecy." My mother gazed at her glowworms, her fists on her hips. "Funny—she and I *do* have a few things in common, don't we? A background in crawling things, and a fascination with the Prophecy. Only I get thrown in prison, while her word gets waved around as law."

I gestured back at the cabinets to try to refocus the conversation. "If it's not your research you're worried about, why not release your work to the crown?"

"Because it's not what we discovered, but *where*. We're still not sure of the extent of the cave system," she said, taking a small, curved object off the top of the cabinet. "I've only been as far as the *Arachno-*

campa, but two others on my team mapped several other, longer passages, and in the farthest ones, they hit water. Flooded corridors, underground lakes. They brought back this."

She handed me the object. It was hard and subtly ridged, the curved surface forming an irregular bowl. I squinted at it. The inside of the bowl sheened in the glowworms' light.

A mussel shell.

My heart made a strange, erratic leap, and I looked up. "You think the caves go all the way to Lumen Lake?"

"It's an educated guess right now," she said. "It's going to take a lot more surveying to be sure. But no mussel is going to survive in a sterile groundwater reservoir or a glacial pool. They need sun-fed nutrients, which means there must be outlets somewhere. You can understand, then, with the mania to secure Lumen Lake under our own banner, why we might be hesitant to let this information slip to the Prelate?"

I looked back down at the winking mussel shell, casually flashing the wealth of Lumen Lake in its mother-of-pearl interior. For years the Prelacy had preached that the lake was the key to fulfilling the Prophecy of the Prism—that Alcoro's greatness would finally be realized by controlling the pearl trade, the basis of wealth in the Eastern World. My mother was right—offering an alternate course, besides the long, tedious, and now carefully watched route up the Cypri waterways, would be too good an opportunity to pass up.

I looked from the shell to the glowworms, and back to my mother. Things started to lock into place.

"This Prophecy," I said. "It's in the cave?"

"Yes," she said. "And we're going to find it."

"Wait," I said. "Find it—haven't you already found it?"

There was a sizzle from the hearth of a pot bubbling over. She waved me back into the kitchen. Still clutching the mussel, I followed her. She swept the boiling water off the fire and streamed it through a strainer of coffee.

"Sit," she said. "Cream or honey?"

"Both, please." I sank back into my chair. "Mother—you *have* found this Prophecy, haven't you?"

"Tureis did," she said, swirling cream into the tin cup. "One of my team. He's the only one to have seen it. He and his partner's supplies ran out before they could make a second trip."

"But . . . he wrote it down? Or made a rubbing?"

She made a show of choosing which jar of golden honey to pull off the shelf, poking among the identical containers.

Ignoring the question.

"Mother."

"He tried to write it down," she said, selecting one of the jars. "But like most folk, he was never taught Archaic Eastern. He tried to form the cyphers as best he could, but it's not a particularly readable transcription."

She dug in her pack and handed me a battered page ripped from a field journal. I turned it over to see a wobbly mess of charcoal marks, some scratched out, some misshapen to the point that I couldn't tell if they were scratched out or not. A pictorial symbol was below the meandering lines of text—a starburst, with eight uneven points, not six like the Prophecy in Callais.

I looked up. "This man is part of your research team?"

"I admit he's a crap hand at transcription," she said, prying the cork out of the honey jar. "But he's an expert caver—practically a roach, ready to wriggle into any crack that looks big enough. He does the scouting, and then maps places of interest for the rest of us." Holding the open jar of honey in one hand, she used the other to pull out a thick oilcloth pouch from her field pack. She shook it until I was afraid she'd fling honey over everything—I took it from her and slid out a roll of thick parchment. I flattened it on the table—it was the strangest-looking map I'd ever seen, like a ball of string had been dipped in ink and flung down on the paper. Routes crisscrossed and branched and disappeared, labeled with names like *Broken Way*, *Slick Climb*, *Belly Crawl*, and *the Squeeze*. I shuddered, feeling the invisible press of dark walls.

"The petroglyphs are off the River of Milk, a dry streamed of calcite deposits," she said, nodding to the note on the map. "A two-day trip from the cave mouth. And we'll go there and see them ourselves, Gemma."

She stirred honey into my coffee and set it down in front of me. The scent was tantalizing after the long, cold night and weary few weeks. But I didn't drink it right away. I stared first at the unreadable transcription, and then at the map, my gaze traveling along the route to the alleged Prophecy and beyond, to the farthest reaches, where the lines abruptly ended. Slowly, I looked up at her.

"Taking me to see them isn't going to accomplish a single thing," I said. "I've been arrested."

"You're still the queen."

"Only because they haven't stripped my title yet," I said. "I'm awaiting trial. They won't listen to a thing I say. They won't believe me."

She cleared her throat and scooped the fried egg out of the skillet. "No, I suppose not. Hm."

I watched as she laid the egg over a thick slab of cornbread and gave it a sprinkle of salt. She set it down in front of me, and the steam curled temptingly toward my nose. But I frowned up at her.

"You don't want me to see them," I said as it came together in my head. "You want *Celeno* to see them."

She held up her hand. "I never said that."

"You want me to *take* Celeno to see them," I said.

"I never said that, either. Eat, before it goes cold."

I looked down at my plate. She'd made the exact same breakfast we used to eat together in our twirly house. A blob of goat cheese melted over the egg, and the slivered onions were crispy and caramelized. In the summer, we used to eat our eggs over avocados we'd plucked from our tree. In the winter, on cornbread, or a thick slice of roasted squash.

I eyed her. "What about you?"

She sat down across from me with her own battered tin cup. "I run on black coffee and spite. Go on."

I picked up my fork and pierced the egg, letting the just-right yolk soak the cornbread. "It's not possible, you know."

"What isn't?"

I took a flavorful bite. "Kidnapping the king."

"I don't know that *kidnap* is the right word . . ."

"I'd have to get him out of the palace," I said, chewing. "He, the most guarded person in the country, perhaps the Eastern World, out of a place where he's constantly watched. There are never less than four guards with him at all times, and more often it's twice that, plus his attendants and the odd court noble or two. And that's if it's during the day—at night he takes a poppy tincture so strong he sleeps senseless until morning. I once accidentally shattered a clay jar on the hearth, set fire to my skirt, and shrieked like a ghost owl, and he didn't even twitch."

My mother sipped her coffee thoughtfully. "They give him poppy just to sleep? Why not stick with valerian?"

"He used to take valerian, until his anxiety got so bad it didn't work anymore." I waved a hand, unwilling to be deterred. "Anyway, that's even assuming I could get *in* to the palace. I'm an enemy of the crown and now an escaped prisoner. There's no side courtyard or cellar door that's not watched, and my face is on a half-dozen portraits inside."

"A real conundrum," she agreed, taking another sip.

Suddenly her placidity irritated me. I set down my fork. "It's not a 'conundrum,' it's flat-out impossible. You're suggesting something that can't be done."

"I haven't suggested anything," she said. "I'm telling you there's another Prophecy. You're the one trying to drag the king along with us."

"Because they won't listen to me!" I said. "I'll be arrested without a second thought if anyone recognizes me, and nothing I say will make a difference. There's no point in going if Celeno doesn't come, too—unless you'd rather bring Shaula along."

She grimaced into her coffee. "And hear her preach the petroglyphs as sanctified truth the whole way. Tell me, does she still do that thing where she recites her own theorizing as if they're words of the earliest Prelates?"

Yes, she does.

I pressed my lips together as I speared the final precious sliver of cornbread—I'd been saving it to mop up the last bit of yolk. "A better option would be for you to go document the glyphs in the cave, with rubbings and identical copies, and put them into a formal presentation to present to the council."

She was silent for a long time as I finished the cornbread and took a generous sip of coffee, sweetened with just the right amount of honey from her beehives. I wondered if she still hummed to her bees as she lifted out the golden combs.

"Gemma," she finally said. "I'm sure I don't need to detail to you that I have very little faith in the structure of our government anymore. They locked me up for next to no reason—took years of my life away for charges that were questionable at best. They took *you* away, and they molded you into what they wanted. They gave you something to fear."

"I'm not afraid of you," I said flatly.

"I'm not talking about myself," she said. "I'm talking about you. They made you fear yourself."

"That doesn't make any sense. I'm not afraid of myself."

She stared me in the eye for a moment, her scratched and calloused fingers curled around her tin cup. Then she stretched out her hand.

"Let me see," she said.

Heat flared in my ears and neck. "See what?"

She twitched her fingers. "Come on."

I didn't want to. I *wouldn't*. We had other things to talk about. How had we arrived here? We had the future of Alcoro to discuss.

But . . .

I peeled my left hand off my cup and placed it in hers.

She pushed back my sleeve. I was still wearing my nightshirt from fleeing the Retreat, and the sleeve was loose. It slid back easily to reveal the place where the ordinary desert-brown of my skin gave way to the dark, mottled mark, purple-red. I winced as she pushed my sleeve farther, baring more of the stain.

"It's darkened," she said.

"Yes." I couldn't tell if the word was audible or just a rasp. Oh, how I'd watched it with horror over the years, praying the color wouldn't deepen any more, that somehow the mark might miraculously shrink. But it had grown with me, covering my left arm, shoulder, and neck, and running down the front and back of my torso, splitting me in half. Even as my breasts and hips had developed and I'd outgrown my childhood skirts and boleros, it had adapted with me like a terrible exoskeleton I couldn't shed.

"You remember what we used to call it?" she asked.

I fought against the tightness in my throat. "My palette."

Just the right color! I'd giggled as she'd tickled me with her paintbrush, pretending to swirl up the pinky-purple to use on her page. I'd liked it then. No one else I knew had such a mark. It was unusual, and interesting.

My mother had always had a high regard for the unusual and interesting.

She brushed both her thumbs over my wrist, a small, gentle gesture that brought a sudden sting to my eyes. I looked away and rubbed my other fist over my cheeks. My mother sighed and pulled my sleeve back down.

"All the long sleeves and collars, Gemma."

"It's *winter*," I said, hoping I sounded indignant.

"It wasn't on your wedding day. Nor on the handful of other times I've seen you from a distance. Do they ever let you wear short sleeves? A collar that doesn't come to your chin?"

I withdrew my hand from hers. "It wasn't only up to them. I was always in the public eye—I didn't want the stares."

"Is that why you tiptoed, too?" she asked, her palms facedown on the table. "Is that why you flitted and slipped in and out of the king's shadow? Is that why you never spoke at public gatherings, or appeared alone?"

"He has a title beyond just 'king'," I said. "He's supposed to bring about action himself—otherwise it doesn't carry the will of the Light. I knew that going in. I knew that when he asked me to marry him. And I was fine with it—you know I was always happier with just you than with crowds of people. It was no different as queen."

She pursed her lips but held her silence, her gaze

flicking over my face. I took a long swallow from my coffee cup, eventually just letting the liquid wash against my sealed lips.

She sighed and rubbed her eyes, suddenly looking tired—and old. My coffee slopped against my mouth—my mother was *old*. She'd aged sixteen years since we'd last shared eggs and cornbread around the breakfast table. And she'd been out all night, running around—was she going to get sick? Was she hurt, and not telling me?

I set my coffee back down and shifted in the silence.

"The egg was very good," I said. "Thank you."

She didn't reply, only staring distantly at my empty plate, her cheek on her fist. After a moment, she heaved another sigh.

"Gemma," she said heavily. "I don't pretend to know what went on up in those towers, you locked away in the world of the Seventh King. But I'll tell you what it's like down here in my world. If I went into the cave and brought back rubbings of the petroglyphs, it would simply be dismissed as another dissenter's desperate attempt to disprove the Prophecy. Not only would no one take it seriously, but I'd probably be thrown in prison again, just for good measure. You're right. We need the king to come—we need the weight of his testimony, and we need him to see it with his own eyes. And because of that, *I* need *you*."

"You're just doing this because you want to see the

Prophecy finally disproved," I said a little too bitterly. "You just want to finally be vindicated."

"A little," she admitted. "Part of me would have no greater pleasure than to see Shaula utterly gobsmacked for the first time in her life. But that's not the whole reason. Alcoro's in trouble. *You're* in trouble. And this is the one thing I have to offer that might potentially help you. I love you. You're still my bug."

The childhood name hit like a shock, and dammit, the tears practically leaped from my eyes. Why did this always have to be my body's first reaction? I wiped at them with both palms. I kept wiping even after I'd rubbed them away, grinding the heels of my hands into my eyes until my vision went red. I held them there and let out a deep, thick breath that was half-groan.

"There's no possible way," I finally said. I lowered my hands slowly to the wood, resting them palm-down in a mirror of hers. She watched me with a slightly sad look, one edged with barely concealed disappointment.

I blew out the last of my breath. "Except maybe one."

The corner of her lips twitched in a smile.

CHAPTER 3

I lay on my stomach, peering into the dark overhang and clutching a stitch in my side. The climb up to the crawl space under the laundry had been steep and perilous. The snowstorm two nights ago had buried the upper canyon in deep snow, and the trail, already poorly defined as it was, was completely invisible. I'd made the best guesses I could, but it had still taken me twice as long as it would normally have to climb to this little-known place. I glanced skyward, where the golden-white walls of Stairs-to-the-Stars soared into the late afternoon sky. This task still seemed no less impossible than it had yesterday morning in my mother's little kitchen, but our plans had been laid, and the only options were to go forward or waste the opportunity. I drew in a sharp breath of winter air and ducked to look back under the overhang.

One side effect of being an entomologist is that you quickly get used to crawling around places any sane person would avoid. When I first arrived at Stairs-to-the-Stars as a wayward child, my aunt wasn't sure what to do with me. It was Ancha, the palace exterminator, who remembered working with my mother and offered to continue my basic science lessons in exchange for an extra pair of hands in her work. For years I picked through trash middens to gather cockroaches for pesticide tests and slithered along storm drains to break up mosquito pools. Even when I moved from pest control into my advanced studies, frequenting undesirable places was still a necessity. I remembered sweating in the sun until my long sleeves and high collars were soaked while I prized cicada exoskeletons from their summer perches. I recalled moving hurriedly through mountain lion country at night in search of stag beetles, banging a stick against my canteen to keep the cats away. I never minded the work—I could often tune out the most unpleasant surroundings, and even found some exhilarating, like the lion country. Admittedly, that was after I returned home in one piece.

This time, though, rather than me hunting the specimens, the specimens were finding me, no matter how hard I tried to avoid them.

Here's the thing about tarantulas. They're docile. They don't like to bite humans, and even if they do, nobody's ever died because of it. I've encountered tarantulas as much as the next Alcoran who spends any time at all moving among the crevasses of the canyon. It's not uncommon for each house in the hobs to have a resident tarantula or two. Nobody thinks to get rid of them—they keep down pests.

However, here in the space beneath the laundry, there were *hundreds* of them.

They scuttled away from me, surrounding me with a constant clicking and tippling of little claws on the grit. I eased forward on my stomach, crawling arm over arm through the narrow space. The laundry was situated above a natural crevice under the foundation, which had presented a problem for generations of pest controllers. Because it was over a crevice, it wasn't shaped out of straw and adobe like the rest of the palace. The floor and pillars were all wood.

And where there's wood, there are termites.

I paused, brushing silk webbing from my lips. One panicked tarantula the size of my palm was scuttling backward, lifting its forelegs in a defensive display.

"Calm down," I muttered, spitting webbing off my tongue. "I said *calm down*. I'll be out of here as soon as I can find the grate. Hush—don't you stridulate at me." The hissing spider twitched backwards, waving its claws menacingly.

I slid forward some more, navigating through the space by the faint light filtering through the crevice opening behind me. I'd already passed three termite traps laid at the base of the wooden pillars that held up the floor above. These baits had always needed routine checking, and Ancha had often sent me crawling in rather than trying to squeeze in herself. It was hardly my favorite task—she knew I despised small spaces and never made me go farther than the fourth pillar. But because of my numerous trips to this place, I knew something that I'd never have thought would serve a useful purpose.

"There must be a way in," my mother had said the day before, trimming a quill, clearly preparing to begin a long and winding list of all the ways one might sneak into the palace. "Something nobody's thought about . . . we're always told all the sewers have grates, but if one of them were loose . . ."

"There's the grate in the crawl space under the laundry," I said.

She'd looked up at me, her quill poised above her page.

I'd fidgeted. "So they can replace the termite baits."

She'd stared a moment longer, smiled, and lowered her nib to her page. "All right. Step two."

But it wasn't *quite* that simple. The grate existed because nobody was expected to do what I was going to try to do—crawl to the farthest pillar. The dirt beneath me sloped up to meet the floor above, and by the time it reached the final pillar, there was less than a foot of headspace. Ancha had sawn the hole in the floor to allow a person to reach down and replace the baits from above, so I wasn't even sure how I was going to bend my body to fit through the opening—it was barely shoulder-width, and there'd be no room to sit up until I could wiggle the grate free.

And that wasn't even contemplating what came next. I couldn't help but feel that the plan my mother and I had thrown together was a patchwork quilt with too many loose threads. What if I'd misjudged the timing of the laundry schedules? What if someone recognized me? What if I couldn't get into our rooms before Celeno's physician gave him his evening dose?

What if I couldn't get him *out*?

I dragged myself forward again and promptly cracked my forehead on a joist. I paused, rubbing the spot. Two coin-sized tarantulas skittered away. Mother had had me describe the space as well as I could remember, making a sketch from my memories.

"There's headspace for maybe fifteen feet," I'd said over the scratching of her charcoal. "Then it narrows past the fourth pillar. Between it and the fifth, the space drops to maybe eleven, twelve inches."

She'd nodded. "Rattlesnakes?"

"I've never seen them inside. But there are tarantulas."

"Oh good. You'll feel right at home."

I did not feel right at home, but it wasn't the spiders' fault. It was because now the space barely cleared the top of my head, even before I reached the fourth pillar. I shivered. I hadn't factored in how much I had grown since making this crawl as a skinny, knobbly girl. I could handle the shoulder-height crawl to the first few termite baits well enough, where there was still daylight and moving air, but being pressed in on all sides, squeezed by the darkness . . . I fought down a wave of dread and lowered my chin so it almost scraped the ground. I pulled forward again. Another tarantula hissed at me.

"I'll cut you open," I threatened in its direction. "I've picked apart invertebrates tougher than you."

I reached the fourth pillar and the bait trap laid at its base. This was the point where everyone else would turn around, weaving up and then back down through the palace to access the final one. Before I lost all wiggle room, I took a breath and turned over onto my back. Wood dust and grit rained down on my face, and I squeezed my eyes shut. Now came the real test. If the space got too narrow, I'd have to slither all the way back out and come up with a way to make contact with my mother, who was probably lurking near the public livery, waiting to acquire mules and meet me at the Stone Tree, the ancient petrified trunk on the outskirts of Callais. Of course, the longer we waited, the more likely it would be that the royal guards would pick up my trail—not out to the coast like we'd hoped they'd believe, but right here under their noses.

I felt little claws in my braid and made a hasty swipe—a tarantula tangled up in my hair was where I drew the line. That was a surefire way to get a bite to the face or worse, their little barbed hairs stuck somewhere vulnerable, like my eyes or lips. Hurriedly I pulled myself forward again, using the joists above me for leverage.

The space narrowed further. It squeezed. When I slid under the next joist, a button on my coveralls popped free, and I consciously tried to will away my flaring panic. I breathed shallowly, both to keep my chest from expanding too much, and to avoid sucking in a stream of dirt filtering through the cracks above. Another pull, and then one more. Blindly I reached behind my head for the next grip, and then I felt it—my fingertips poked through the metal grate.

Oh, it was going to be tight. The round lip of the sunken termite bait underneath me ground into my back as I forced my body under the grate. My cheek squished against the lattice, and hurriedly I put my palms against the metal and heaved. The grate only rattled—it was heavier than I remembered. Biting back my dread, I wiggled for a better position, my elbows braced against the ground, and pushed again. With a stubborn groan, it slid an inch or so, one corner shifting up to rest on the wooden floor. I spit hair and dirt from my lips and pushed again, feeling the satisfactory slide as the grate lifted free and slid across the floor.

A tarantula hissed again close by, but I couldn't tell where it was. Regardless, I had no space to fend it off now. I wiggled until I could lift my head and shoulders through the narrow opening, and then thrust my arms one at a time until they were splayed out on the laundry floor. Like a butterfly splitting a chrysalis—only a lot dirtier and less graceful—I heaved myself through the hole, first my torso, then my waist, and finally my legs.

I crawled onto the floor, sweaty and panting. I shook my head to release the cloud of dust in my hair, and down thumped a renegade tarantula. It backed up and waggled its claws, clearly furious that I'd snagged it in my braid. I ignored it, straightening and peering across the gloomy laundry room. It was warm and steamy, sharing the space with the furnace to give ready access to hot water. Wide tubs sat in a line, and drying lines ran from one end of the room to the other. Hurriedly I stripped off the grimy coveralls I was wearing, revealing the nearest approximation to a palace laundress' attire as I could remember.

My skin prickled despite the heat, thanks to the unfamiliar feeling of air against my bare forearms and neck. The laundresses who worked in these sweltering rooms spent their days stirring vats of simmering water and lye. Their uniform was the only one I could think of that would have short sleeves in the winter months. And it was the lack of sleeves or a high collar that would be my best disguise. Nobody in the palace knew about my wine stain. Nobody except Celeno, and Shaula, and my physician. I turned my arms, setting the inky purple skin against my sandy brown, and my stomach twisted. Folk were going to stare. But I hoped they'd stare at my mark, not my face.

I wiped at my hair again, nudging my mother's simple star band as I did so. It was the only real option—I certainly couldn't wear my golden band with the three faceted diamonds, and wearing nothing on my head would stand out more than my wine stain. I nudged it one last time, drawing some fortitude from having it on my head, and then bundled up the coveralls.

The hitchhiking tarantula was still sizing me up, its forelegs in the air. On an impulse, I dropped the coveralls over her and scooped her up. She let out a muffled hiss.

"You come along with me—I might need you." Carefully I replaced the grate and tried to brush away the tracks of dirt I'd left. Hopefully the palace termite baits would be on nobody's mind.

I sought out a laundry tub of rinse water that didn't have lye in it and cleaned the grime from my face and neck. I threaded out my braid and shook as much of the dust from my hair as I could before tying it back again, remembering to pull out a few wisps in imitation of spending long hours in the steam. A spotty pane of glass hung on the wall near the staircase, and I peered hard at my reflection. Pulling out my mother's field illustration kit, I used some of the ink to redden my cheeks and spot them with dark freckles. I was reminded a bit of Queen Mona, though she managed to wear hers with elegance and artistry, while mine looked more like a speckled grouse's egg. Still, they added to my disguise, along with the work-worn cheeks. At this point, there was nothing I could do but hope it would suffice.

I packed away the kit and piled my coveralls into an empty basket, trying not to squash the tarantula. I arranged a clean bundle of cloth over it all, hoisted it onto my hip, and wound through the tubs to the laundry door, pausing to listen up the stairwell. No sign or sound of anyone, which was fortunate for me—other palace attendants might pass off an unfamiliar face, but the laundresses themselves would know I wasn't one of them. My heart in my throat, I slipped through and padded up the stairs.

So I'd made it past step one of our plan. I was inside the palace. And now that I was, the next step loomed before, a terrifying obstacle. Our plan hinged dramatically on one factor—I needed to be sure Celeno's physician and attendants assumed he had taken his usual evening tincture of poppy and herbs . . . without him actually taking it. The only time he was left in relative peace was when he had slipped into his listless, drugged sleep—otherwise he was under almost constant watch. If I tried to spirit him away before he took it, someone would find out within minutes. If I couldn't get to him in time, I'd never be able to wake him up. But there was a problem.

Several problems, actually, each of them vying for the spotlight as the worst, most terrifying problem of all.

Celeno's poppy tincture was locked in his physician's case, each dose set into labeled vials. The case, in turn, was locked in the physician's office. The office I thought I could get into, if I could convince a palace guard I was bringing clean bandages, but the bag . . . there were two keys to open the case. One was on a chain around the physician's neck.

The other was in Shaula's apartment.

I'd never had the courage to make an argument over why Shaula had the only spare key to the drugs constantly administered in Celeno's daily regimen. Others passed it off as being the ultimate safeguard— there certainly couldn't be a spare key in our royal apartments, no matter how well hidden, lest Celeno uncover it and have access to the case. And for some reason it was deemed inappropriate for a councilor to keep it. And clearly *I* couldn't have one—at least, it was clear to everyone else. So it resided with the Prelate.

I stood in the hallway, gnawing my lip. I'd already dismissed the idea of retrieving the key from around the physician's neck. Rastaban knew me intimately— *very* intimately, as he also served as my physician, though I required less attention than Celeno. But he'd treated me for illnesses before and examined me to determine my reproductive health. He knew my face, and my wine stain, and the rest of my body as well. There was no way I could even get close to him, let alone remove and then replace a chain from his neck without him noticing.

That left Shaula's apartment. The thought made my blood freeze, and I tightened my grip on the basket. Getting into her rooms would be much trickier, and much more dangerous. I hadn't yet concocted a good reason for me to be there if I was found by a passerby, and if I was found by Shaula . . . my stomach clenched.

Now, I reminded myself. *That's why you have to go now.* It was dinnertime. The Prelate would accompany Celeno to dinner, then guide his evening Devotion, then see to the administration of his poppy tincture, and only then retire to her rooms. It was now, or never.

I had only taken two steps down the hall when someone turned the corner up ahead of me—another servant, dressed in groundskeeping attire and heading in my direction.

I suddenly flushed with uncertainty. How did servants interact with each other? Did they nod? Smile? Ignore each other? Was there animosity between different vocations? I warred with my distant memories, trying to determine how I should react, forcing myself to keep moving forward. He got closer—I could make out the emblem on his jacket. In another heartbeat, he'd entered that awkward sphere that demanded interaction. Before I could make up my mind, he offered a short, perfunctory nod. With a mixture between a gasp and a gulp, I nodded back.

And then we'd passed each other. I exhaled.

Relax, I chastised myself. *Acting like a frightened pika will only make you stand out more.*

I tried to behave more nonchalantly with the next few people, and when I relaxed enough to summon the right kind of distant pleasantness, I finally noticed the furtive stares. Gazes slid from my face to my bare arm clutching the laundry basket. Some lingered; some flicked quickly away. This flustered my newfound courage, and at the next few encounters I hurried past with my head down.

I knew the steps to Shaula's apartment well—they were off the Prism's star courtyard, where Celeno and I used to do Devotion once a week. But I'd never actually been inside the apartment. I hadn't seen her personal rooms since she was an acolyte, where she occupied one of the stark little cells on the adjoining hall with barely enough space for a cot and desk. There had been no space for me to share such a place, of course, so once I came into her care, I lived in another acolyte cell at the far end of the hall. The dramatic jump from that tiny space to the royal apartments had unnerved me for months after I'd married Celeno—I spent much of the time edging through our private halls, trying to take up as little space as possible.

I reached the corridor to the Prism's courtyard all too quickly. The wing was shaped like a T, with the courtyard and Shaula's apartment at either end of the cross hall, and the long stem lined by acolyte cells. I crept past the small, plain door that had once been mine and toward the turn at the end that would take me to Shaula's apartment. Everything was quiet and still—the acolytes took simple meals in their own dining room one hall over and then would retire to their rooms to read and pray for the rest of the evening. I needed to be out of this wing before they finished. Picking up my pace, trying not to jostle my laundry basket, I turned the corner for the Prelate's apartment.

I nearly halted in my tracks—there was a guard outside the door, something I should have factored in but hadn't. I forced myself to keep going rather than stand in dismay in the middle of the hall. She stood crisp and impassive as I approached.

"Yes?" she asked.

"I have the Prelate's laundry," I said, trying to inject confidence into my voice.

"I haven't seen you before."

"I'm new," I said hesitantly.

"Since when?"

"Last week."

"Do you have a note from Chara?"

Was Chara in charge of the laundry? "No."

The guard shook her head. "Bring me a note from Chara saying you're a new hire."

I licked my lips. "She'll be angry at the delay."

"That's no fault of mine. I can't let you into the Prelate's chambers if I've never seen you before. Go get a note."

I dipped a resigned courtesy and retraced my steps back around the corner. Once out of sight, I stood, chewing my lip and thinking furiously. What to do? Wait for guard change? Forge a note? Would the guard know Chara's handwriting? Find a way to scale the three stories up to one of the Prelate's windows?

As I stood vacillating, the door at the end of the acolytes' hall swung open. The sharp clip of boot heels was instantly familiar to me, and my heart rate spiked in terror. My aunt strode smartly up the hallway, her eyes on a sheaf of parchment in her hand.

I nearly melted in fright. Ears ringing, mouth dry, I glanced along the acolyte cells lining the hallway. Without waiting to second-guess my timing of the acolytes' dinner, I turned the handle of the nearest one and slipped inside.

I let out a breath, shaking from head to foot. The little room was unoccupied, and there were no personal effects inside beyond a quill and parchment on the desk, and a spare pair of unadorned boots under the cot. I hadn't mistimed the acolytes' dinner—but I had not expected Shaula to show up here mere moments before the court dined. She would be expected to lead the prayer—what had drawn her away? I leaned against the door, listening to Shaula's heels *clip clip* off the stone. When I was sure she had turned the corner, I cracked the door and put my ear to the opening.

"Unlock the door, Gienah."

"Yes, your Reverence."

"And come inside, I need to give you a missive for the captain."

I heard the lock click and the door open.

I didn't hear it shut.

Heart in my throat, I eased out of the acolyte's cell. I tiptoed to the corner and peered around. The door was cracked.

Suppose I could slip inside. Suppose they had gone into a separate room. Suppose I could dive for cover—under a bed, in a closet—and wait until they had left. Suppose I could then make a search for the key to the physician's case.

Suppose they were standing by the door and saw my face appear in the crack like the stupidest of criminals.

Cursing myself and every person that came to mind, I tiptoed to the door. I held my breath, straining to listen. I heard my aunt talking to her guard, but her voice was muffled, as if in another room. I set my fingers lightly on the door handle.

If I didn't get myself hanged before the night was over, I'd be pleasantly surprised.

I peeked into the room. It was more spacious and elegant than the acolytes' plain cells, but it could hardly be called opulent. Two doors led off the sparse foyer—one stood open, showing the edge of a writing desk. My aunt's voice filtered from within. My gaze flicked over the rest of the foyer—there was a low couch and two hardback chairs around a hearth, a coffee table, and a large tapestry of the Prophecy on the wall, finer than the one in the Retreat. The couch was too squat to hide under, so my gaze traveled to the second door in the wall. Praying it was a bedchamber with either space under the bed or a large wardrobe to hide in, I slipped into the foyer, crossed the space with my heart in my throat, and opened the door.

It was a bedroom, but the bed would be no good—it was narrow and set against the far wall, making the space underneath clearly visible. But I was granted a tiny slice of luck—instead of a wardrobe, there was a curtained alcove built into the adobe wall. Shifting my laundry basket, I hurried to it and let the curtain fall behind me.

It was only as I shoved stiff black skirts and boleros aside that I wondered if Shaula had also come to dress for dinner, but I couldn't change my mind now. I wedged myself into the back of the alcove, my nose filled with the funny scent of almonds hanging about her clothes. I curled into as tight a ball as I could in the corner, tucking my feet under my skirt, the laundry basket balanced on my knees. The tarantula twitched under the fabric.

I must have been sitting against the wall separating her bedroom from the office, because I could hear her speaking to her guard. Her words were just muffled enough that I couldn't make them out, but I recognized the firm agitation in her voice. I shifted to find a more comfortable position, and something hard poked into my shoulder. A cloth shifted free. I blinked a few times—there was a new shadow on the wall. Or, rather, a new source of light. The room beyond was gray in the winter twilight, and the curtained alcove almost completely dark, but shining on the whitewashed wall beside me was a faint slice of light.

I shifted and plucked at the fabric, and it slid off a wooden crate. Something rustled in the darkness. Something *alive.* Half-alarmed, half-curious, I peeked through the metal screen that rested over the top.

Millipedes.

It was a box of millipedes.

They were glowing.

I squinted in the half-light, peering at the eerie luminescence they were giving off, a dim green-white. They crawled over one another, hundreds of little legs waving and reaching. Several sat on a damp sponge, taking in moisture. Some clustered around a dish of cornmeal. This wasn't just a box of the creatures—it was a habitat, meant for them to thrive.

Here, in my aunt's bedroom.

My mind drifted back to my mother's words in her little house in Whiptail Hob, how Shaula had taken up their parents' profession but dropped it to pursue the life of an acolyte. So why did she have a cage of her old study subjects shoved in her closet? Millipedes weren't popular as eccentricity pets, like stag beetles or mantids. And anyway, she wasn't displaying them as if they were meant for show, despite their unusual luminescence. I nudged the box slightly, making the glowing bodies shift and curl. Again the wash of almond scent hit my nose. It was their defense mechanism, I realized. They released a strong-smelling liquid to deter predators.

Why does my aunt have them here?

I leaned back from the box, my mind whirling. Only then did I realize the voices from the far room were traveling—circling out into the foyer.

Getting closer.

I scrunched up into a ball again, hugging my knees to my chest, squashing the basket of laundry. The tarantula hissed.

Shut up! I thought fiercely.

My aunt's clipped footsteps moved across the floor of her bedroom. "—haven't gotten a response."

"Councilor Izar is still unwell, then?"

"Quite so, though the healers suggest he may be recovering. Still, we can't afford to wait for his health to return. I need you to deliver that warrant to the captain, along with the suggestion to split up his forces."

"They haven't found the queen along the coast?"

"I have my doubts about the validity of that trail," my aunt replied. "I don't want the generals to waste their time, not now that we've got a foothold back in Cyprien. With four of the provinces back under our control, our ground troops need to focus on retaking Lilou, not shuffling our feet over the queen. With the king's signature on the warrant, there needs to be no uncertainty once we've recaptured her."

"Shall I take it now?"

"No, stay here until I send another guard to relieve you. I won't leave my door unwatched. I would take it myself, but I'm expected at dinner—poor timing, but at least the king has given his signature."

With a sound like a death rattle, the rings on the alcove curtain slid back, and I could swear everything in my body—head, heart, lungs—stopped functioning. I could see the toes of her polished black boots under the hanging overskirts. Behind her, the room was still dim—she hadn't turned up a lamp. She rifled among the garments and slid a bolero off its hanger.

"Chara is late," she murmured absently.

"A laundress came," said the guard. "I didn't recognize her. I sent her away to get a note."

My aunt sighed and slid the curtain closed. "We have more important things to worry about than a new face in the laundry. Next time just let her do her job."

"Yes, your Reverence. I'm sorry."

"Go ahead—return to your post. Make sure the captain gets that warrant."

"Yes, your Reverence."

Two pairs of boot-steps left the bedroom. They made their way across the foyer. The door creaked on its hinges. Then it shut.

My breath streamed out in a low hiss. I stayed frozen where I was, squashed against the millipede cage, the tarantula squirming under the laundry. Clearly things were moving quickly, both within Alcoro and outside it. Four of the six Cypri provinces back under our control . . . how long could the other two hold out? How long before we reestablished our strategic position in the waterways and made the leap to seize the Paroan ports?

And what warrant had Shaula finally gotten Celeno to sign? What had he agreed to? She didn't believe I had fled to the coast, as my mother had intended. That meant we had to get this thing done tonight—it had to be now.

When I was positive that both of them had left the room, and that nobody was coming back in for something they forgot, I let my legs uncurl. I shifted forward and crawled out from under the Prelate's stiff black overskirts. My body felt loose and wobbly, as if undone by the terror of imminent discovery. I knelt on the floor of the bedroom, trying to stir up enough courage and ignore the fact that I was now effectively locked in this apartment by the guard outside the door.

I rose to my feet. The light from the narrow, diamond-paned windows was almost completely gone, but I didn't dare light a candle and risk the lingering scent of smoke. I cast a quick glance around the bedroom—besides the narrow bed, there was a wooden trunk, a washstand, and a bureau. The only ornaments in the room were two elaborate prisms hanging in each of the windows. I dismissed the thought of rifling through the trunk and bureau—perhaps if I didn't find the key elsewhere, I'd search there, but I doubted it would be so furtively hidden. It wasn't a secret that Shaula had it, and her door was already guarded.

Nervous as a jackrabbit in the open, I went back into the parlor. The words of the Prophecy glared down from the wall tapestry, imposing and definite. An enormous, illuminated Book of the Prophecy sat on a thick wooden pedestal. The key wouldn't be in this space, not where guests might chance upon it. No, if anywhere, it would be in her study. I opened the door.

It was no larger than her bedroom, with the same prisms in the windows. Bookshelves lined the walls. A more worn Book of the Prophecy lay on top of a generous winged writing desk. The rolltop was closed, but not locked. Fingers shaking, I slid back the top. If I thought I might stumble across damning correspondence, I was disappointed. The work space was tidy, with only an askew penknife offering any hint of disarray. I peeked through the little paper drawers, picking through religious texts and letters to township acolytes as unobtrusively as I could. Quietly I set the top back down and turned to the deeper drawers along the sides of the desk.

Ink, blotters, paperweights, quills, parchment, notebooks waiting to be filled . . . I closed two, three drawers. I slid the fourth open with a sigh of relief—inside was a wooden document case labeled *Seventh King Celeno Tezozomoc*. I lifted it out, but my fingers paused on the lid. Underneath it was another case simply labeled *Gemma*.

I hesitated for the briefest second. Impulsively my hand shot out to unlatch the lid with my name on it. Inside were sheaves of papers, medical documents, records of my audit to assess my suitability for the monarchy, a copy of my thesis. Resting on the very top was a weather-stained vellum envelope, stamped with a foreign seal and bearing my full name and title in neat handwriting. A letter to me. Heart thumping, I pulled it out.

Shaula might come back and open this box tonight and find the envelope missing. She'd realize there had been an intruder in her room. She'd check through everything else and would find the key gone—by this point I recognized there would be no way I could replace it after I'd taken it away. My fingers tightened on the vellum. I didn't care. This was a letter to me, and I was going to take it. Before I could change my mind, I stuffed it down the front of my uniform and snapped the box lid shut.

Celeno's box contained his medical records and a smaller wooden box . . . which held the twin to the little brass key I knew so well. Quickly I pocketed the key, packaged everything away, and hurried from the room, laundry basket in tow.

Get into the palace. Get the key. Step one. Step two. Step three. Get into the physician's bag.

But first, step two-and-a-half.

Get out of the damned apartment.

I tiptoed to the main door and crouched down, setting my face to the crack under the door. Two shiny boots stood outside, facing down the hall.

I sat back on my heels, chewing my lip. I reached for the door handle and silently tested it—not locked. My eyes fell on my laundry basket.

"Time for you to do some work," I whispered. The fabric twitched.

Carefully I gathered up the cloth with the tarantula inside. I lowered her to the floor and worked her free. She sat by the crack, disoriented. Sending a quick prayer that this stupid plan might work, I gave the spider an almighty flick and sent her sailing out into the hallway beyond.

She recovered before the guard did. I watched the shiny boots leap to one side just as the tarantula righted herself and lifted her forelegs defensively in the air.

"Son of a—"

The tarantula, the beautiful little thing, hissed dramatically.

I heard the rattle of a sword hilt and saw a naked blade swipe toward it. The spider skittered backward, waving its claws.

The guard cursed and sheathed her sword. One of the shiny black boots disappeared above the crack in the door, and I was washed suddenly in a burst of regret.

No!

The boot came down with a *crunch*, splaying the legs out underneath it.

I gripped my basket. *Oh, little friend. I'm so sorry. I'd give you a medal of service, if I could.*

With a swipe of her boot, the guard kicked the body of the fallen tarantula toward the far doors leading to the Prism's courtyard. She followed it, kicking it again as she passed the acolyte hallway. I turned the handle on my aunt's apartment and slipped out into the hall. As the guard opened the exterior door, I turned the corner. I loitered, hidden, in the doorway of an acolyte's cell while I waited for the guard to pass back across the hallway. Just as she did, I heard the murmuring at the intersection of the acolytes returning from dinner. Sweating, almost dizzy with fear, I fled, restraining myself just short of running from the hall. One or two of the acolytes might have seen me, but with all luck they'd see an errant laundress rushing to complete her chores, not the traitorous queen sneaking out of her aunt's guarded apartment.

I didn't slow down until I'd put three corridors and a staircase between myself and the Prelate's apartment, and then I leaned on the wall, clutching my basket and trying to calm my heartbeat. The little brass key shifted in my pocket, and the vellum packet crackled in my uniform as I breathed deeply.

Step two-and-a-half, done.

Step three. The physician's bag.

In comparison, getting in and out of Rastaban's office was like a jaunt along the canyon rim. All I had to do was find a stray, unfamiliar palace guard, nod to my basket, and say, "bandages," and he unlocked the physician's door for me. The case was in a glass cabinet behind his desk. I took it out and turned my aunt's key in the lock, revealing a double row of poppy syrup, each vial labeled with the day of the week. My hands were steady but my stomach was in knots as I removed the one for that day, pulled out the cork, and drizzled the sticky solution into a potted aloe plant. When I'd wiped the last residue from inside, I pulled out the flask of honey from my mother's bees and poured it into the vial. The honey was slightly lighter in color than the poppy syrup, but it was hardly noticeable when I set the vial back with its fellows. Hopefully no one would have any cause to suspect it was anything other than that potent, sleep-inducing drug.

I left Rastaban's office.

Step one. Get into the palace.

Step two. Get the key.

Step three. Replace the poppy.

Step four . . .

Get into the king's chamber. Get in, and hide.

Hefting my basket, I turned for the familiar corridors that would take me to the place that until just a few weeks ago had been my safe haven and home.

Unfortunately, the halls were growing more crowded. Dinnertime for the court meant a transition period for the rest of the palace. I'd never thought much about it before, but now was the time that the palace was readied for the shift from day to night. Lamplighters were moving down the corridors, lighting the wicks in the red-shielded lanterns. Hearth maids were moving from room to room, toting buckets of burning coals. Caretakers were moving into the spaces occupied during the day, mopping the tiled floors and tidying the detritus left by both business and pleasure.

I climbed the staircase that would take me from the public halls into the more removed ones reserved for private concerts and events. There were guards posted at the top, but they didn't look twice at me. It made me a little nervous, actually, that any interloper dressed as a servant could move relatively easily through the halls—provided they could get inside. Again I blessed the Light that only Ancha and a few other folk knew anything about the termite baits, and none of them considered that a suitable route into Stairs-to-the-Stars.

I rounded the corner to find a caretaker mopping the landing to the staircase that led to the royal apartments.

"Hold tight a moment, else you'll leave prints," she said, dunking her mop in the bucket with a splash. I halted at the edge of the wet tiles. Behind me came the sound of footsteps, and another girl appeared—the hearth maid, going to light Celeno's fire. She stopped at the edge of the wet floor as well. I felt her look sideways at me, and hurriedly I busied myself with pointlessly arranging the bundle in my basket. I felt another twinge of sorrow for the tarantula.

The hearth maid was on my left side, and she didn't look away. I felt my face grow hot, trying not to make it obvious I was avoiding her gaze. I hoped I wasn't sweating off my freckles.

"New, are you?" she asked.

I gave as quick an acknowledgement as I dared. "Yes."

"Chara giving you a hard time?"

Yes or no? "Little bit."

She gave a sympathetic snort. "Try goldenseal."

I gave another quick glance. "Sorry?"

"Goldenseal, on that burn of yours. Lye can do that if it's too concentrated. They've got goldenseal salve in the staff supply room. Might help."

I ducked my head. "Thank you."

"I'm Mira," she said.

I stared at the mop as it sloshed in the bucket again.

"Ancha," I said, because it was the first name that jumped to mind.

"A word of caution," she said, clearly trying to be helpful. I peeked at her again. She gestured up the stairs on the far side of the landing. "I'm sure you're aware that things are a bit of a mess, what with the queen and all that?"

My cheeks blazed. "A bit."

"Get in and get out quick. That's you're best line of action. Their rooms are fancy, but don't linger or look around. Everyone's on edge since the queen got locked up."

I drew in a sharp breath and nodded, staring desperately up the staircase. *Please stop mopping, please . . .*

"When did you get here?" Mira asked. "I feel like I've seen you around. Were you in the kitchens before?"

"All right, skirt 'round this way." The woman with the mop gestured to the periphery of the landing, a hero. I jumped forward and tiptoed my way to the stairs, trying not to look like I was fleeing Mira. Fortunately, she spilled a spot of ash from her bucket as she crossed the floor, earning a verbal lashing from the caretaker. I hurried on, grateful for the escape.

My heart pounded as I climbed the stairs. *Get in and get out.* I should be so lucky. My plan relied on the idea that I could remain hidden in the royal apartments without being found out. It relied on the fact that even if Celeno wasn't dining with the court, he at least was in our private dining room and not sick in bed.

Which was a very, very big if.

I reached the landing, confronted immediately by a set of liveried guards. I gulped a breath and looked down. A moment of truth. I passed the royal guards every day—if anyone outside my old inner circle might recognize me, it would be them.

"Stop there."

I halted in my tracks, my head bowed. I arranged my basket so my stained arm was out in front.

"You're not authorized to be in this wing."

"Chara sent me," I said breathlessly.

"It's not time for the laundry."

"She got a message from the king's physician saying the king felt ill." I tipped my basket slightly. "He wanted fresh rags brought in case . . ."

"Hm." The guard clearly wasn't satisfied. "Chara should have sent the usual laundress."

Behind me, I heard Mira puffing up the stairs. "Don't give her a hard time, Pavo, she's new. Chara's probably running her all over creation for spilling lye."

The guard made another impatient noise and then jerked his head behind him. "Don't dawdle. And tell Chara next time to give us a note when she sends someone new."

I dipped a courtesy, thinking that Chara was going to get an undue earful from the palace guards. *"Yes-most-certainly-thank-you."* I moved past him.

"Oi," he called over his shoulder. I glanced back, panic flaring. Had he finally recognized me?

"There's goldenseal in the staff supply," he said.

I drew in a breath and dipped my head before hoisting my basket and rushing after Mira. I blinked—my eyes were stinging. Stress crying.

"They're all right, the guards," she said as we headed to the apartment double doors. "They have to be careful, you know. Once they know your face they won't give you any trouble."

She squinted at me again, her hand on the knob. "You *were* in the kitchens, weren't you?"

"The hearths," I confirmed.

She nodded, satisfied, and turned the handle. We passed into the antechamber. I was so used to the sound of rattling metal as the guards inside snapped to attention that I faltered briefly when it didn't come. The two merely glanced our way, leaning on one wall and holding a casual conversation. The nearest eyed my face before dropping his gaze to my arm, and his attention went back to his comrade.

"All right, Mira?" asked the second guard.

"'All right?' Glad to know romance isn't dead."

"My offer still stands, you know." The guard jerked his head inside with a rakish grin. "King's bed is free."

"I'm reporting you for unseemly behavior," she

said breathlessly, her brown cheeks a little redder. She turned the handle on the other side of the antechamber and passed into the front parlor. I followed, head down, flushed with embarrassment at the loose talk concerning my husband's bed.

"I know I said the guards are all right," Mira said as the door closed. "But some of them are imps."

I forced what I hoped was a chuckle. She headed to the fireplace and set down her ash bucket. Across the room, a man was washing the windows that looked out on the canyon, now hidden by darkness. A woman was sweeping up shriveled sage branches and replacing the vases with fresh, fragrant ones. With a surge of discomfort, I remembered that my face was displayed above the mantel, staring out from Celeno's and my wedding portrait. My gaze flew to the painting—and then my jaw dropped to see an embellished map of Alcoro instead.

They'd taken down our wedding portrait.

He'd taken down our wedding portrait.

"Bedroom's down that way," Mira said, nodding. "Wait till you see the embroidery in there."

I attempted an eager smile and failed, trying to wipe away the sudden feeling of betrayal—which was undeserved, because it was the other way around. I hoisted my basket and hurried down the private hallway that branched off the main parlor. The familiar scent washed over me, through me, an invisible wave. Our rooms were adorned with desert flowers in the summer, but I had always preferred the winter arrangements of sage . . . I inhaled deeply, my throat constricting with emotion. This hallway was home, once upon a time our only safe haven, the center of our intimate lives. The nearest were our study doors—first his, the Prophecy carved deep into the wood, and then mine. Out of curiosity, I tested the handle—locked. I was sure Shaula had had the whole place searched and then sealed off, hoping to make a decisive case of treason against me. My field sketchbooks, my textbooks, my research, all my correspondences—all being pored over and analyzed like an insect on a spreading board.

It could have been worse. I'd removed all my most private documents before leaving for Cyprien and hidden them deep in my wardrobe. I meant to retrieve them now, supplementing the vellum packet I'd taken from Shaula's desk. I moved on, past our breakfast room and private parlor, and came at last to our bedroom door. I turned the knob.

The evening caretakers had already been in to close the thick russet drapes and turn down the cream coverlet, both heavily embroidered in gold thread, as Mira had mentioned. My bedside table had been swept clean; Celeno's still bore the silver astrolabe—pushed to the back and collecting dust behind the washbowl that had been moved in the frequent event that he was sick in the night. I crossed the room, passing the cloth-covered telescope standing in the corner like a specter, to the nondescript panel in the wall. The paint and wainscoting were perfectly matched to disguise the seam, but when I pushed at the edge, it gave a little click and creaked inward. I peered into our escape route, an irregular tunnel in an elongated hexagonal shape, leading into the fathomless darkness. We'd never had to use it before, but twice our guards had orchestrated a practice escape, timing how long it took for us to reach the terminus outside the palace wall. That had been early in our reign, and Celeno and I had taken turns spooking the other and pausing for extended kisses—throwing off the guards' timekeeping and helping me tamp down the fear of the narrow, dark space.

I closed the door. There would be no such giggling and frippery this time to chase away my nerves, but there was nothing to be done about that. I turned away from the wall. My plan was to nestle myself inside my wardrobe much as I had in my aunt's alcove. I could see no reason why anybody would want to open it that evening, and the long overdresses inside would hide me well. But just as I started moving in that direction, a voice spoke behind me.

"I'm telling you, don't dawdle."

I whipped my head over my shoulder to see Mira bustling in with her ash bucket. She nodded to me. "You best get a move on—sometimes they finish up early."

I stood frozen for a moment as she knelt down by

the wide, tiled fireplace. Then, with no other option, I changed direction and went to Celeno's wardrobe. I opened it to the rows of starched boleros, their gems glittering in the light of the lamps. I pretended to rummage around in my basket, hoping Mira would finish her work and leave quickly. Hoping, too, that the guards at the door would lose track of who had come in and out. Was it likely, or even possible, that they'd make such a grievous blunder? I bit my lip at this oversight—I'd been repeating the gesture so often that evening I'd created a blister.

Behind me, Mira was chattering. ". . . nobody's sure what will become of the lady's maids, or the queen's valets and guards. My bunkmate wonders if she'll be reassigned, or let go entirely."

I gave a noncommittal answer and drew my fingers down the intricate embroidery of a bolero sleeve. It was the one with the golden fish on it. He'd worn it last Starfall. June. Just days before the bottom dropped out of everything. I had worn a sash with matching embroidery, and we'd laughed at the absurdity of wearing fish on such a hot, dry day. He'd sweated buckets and cast it off with relish once we finally retreated to the privacy of our star courtyard. As the night deepened and a breeze swept off the canyon rim, he'd picked it back up and tucked it around my shoulders.

The fire tongs rattled. "You know," Mira said, and her voice dropped to a conspiratorial whisper,

"I wouldn't go spreading this around, and I swear by the Light I'm no gossip, but Talitha in clerical told me there's even been talk of him executing her."

My fingers stilled as I pulled out a pair of embroidered gloves. "Executing the queen?"

"Of course the queen. It sounded like it was only a matter of paperwork, but everything's paperwork to clerical—more likely it's going before the council . . ."

My heart rattled in my chest, my mind racing back to Shaula's fragmented comments to her guard. She'd had the document in her hand. It had his signature. That was what she'd finally gotten him to sign.

The order for my execution.

I'd considered many ends, but I hadn't imagined it would go that far.

Stupid me. Stupid, sentimental, childish me.

"I'm done," I said loudly, despite having accomplished no visible task in the wardrobe. I stuffed the gloves back into their drawer and shoved it shut, pinching two of the fingers in the crack. Hastily I hoisted the basket back onto my hip.

"It's about time. Come on, let's see if . . . oh. Who're you?"

I hadn't heard the bedroom door open. I turned around, gripping my basket.

Two people stood in the doorway. The first was the rakish guard from the antechamber, no longer casual and boorish, but tense. He flexed his hands, as if preparing to reach for a weapon, his gaze drilling into mine.

"You there," he said sharply. "State your name and business."

Standing at his side, wearing a look of mild consternation, was the laundress.

CHAPTER 4

"Oh," Mira said again. She looked between us. "I don't understand."

The guard put his hand on the hilt of his sword. "Who are you?" he asked me.

I swallowed. "My name is Ancha. I'm running a special errand for Chara. I'm not usually on this shift."

"Chara's been out for a week because of her bunions," said the laundress. Her basket held freshly starched trousers, perfectly creased.

"Yes," I said quickly, as if this was obvious. "That's why she shifted me around. To cover for her."

The guard moved forward, his hand still on his sword. The laundress trailed behind. "Chara didn't alert the king's guard of the change."

"No, I expect she . . ."

"The king's guard are *always* supposed to know about staffing changes."

I fought the urge to back up against the wardrobe. He was staring me straight in the face. I squeezed my basket. "I'm sorry for the confusion, truly. I'll be off right away, and I'll tell her about the mix-up." Anything to get away—I'd just have to find another way to sneak into the royal apartment. Assuming they didn't triple the watch and set out guard dogs, as well.

But the guard wasn't convinced. "What's your normal station?"

"The hearths," I said. Mira was watching me curiously.

"Who's your superior?"

I couldn't remember who was in charge of the hearths. I couldn't even conjure the name of the head chef, my mind was so paralyzed with dread. I swallowed, aware that the brief moment that would have provided a reliable answer had sailed past. Not answering right away had sealed my fate.

Several things happened at once. The guard's blade slid from its sheath. Mira clapped her hand to her mouth. The laundress backed away. And the door behind the guard swung open.

I dropped my basket.

On the threshold stood Celeno, followed by the second guard from the antechamber, also gripping his sword. I followed Mira and the laundress into a deep courtesy, keeping my head bowed low. It would hardly matter—my wine stain, which had disguised me to everyone else, was now bare before the one person who knew it most intimately. Everything went deadly silent.

When the king spoke, his voice was quiet. "All of you, out."

"My king," said the first guard—still pointing his sword at me, I could only assume, as my eyes were on my toes. "This girl says she's a laundress but can give no account of what she's doing in the royal apartment."

"She's delivering clean linens, as you should have been able to observe, Nash. Put your sword away and let her finish her work. The rest of you, get out. And tell the others in the parlor to leave their work for tomorrow—I'm going to bed."

"Yes, my king." The guard sounded wholly reluctant, but I heard the slide of his sword back into its sheath. Mira's fire tools clanked as she rushed to follow the laundress out the door. When I peeked back up, Nash was still hovering on the threshold, scrutinizing me.

"My king," he said. "I should like to leave a guard with you."

"I should like you to leave a man to do as he wishes in the privacy of his own chamber," Celeno snapped.

Nash drew in a breath, as if finally understanding the suspicious nature of my presence. Face flaming, I looked back down at my boots. The door closed with a snap.

A moment of silence the length of the echoing canyon stretched between us. I stared at the basket at my feet, shame and defeat and anger all warring with each other in my chest.

"Did you think I wouldn't recognize you?"

I looked up slowly. His normally golden-brown skin was pale, and his eyes were shadowed by dark circles.

"I hoped everyone else wouldn't recognize me," I said.

"And did they?"

"Not that I'm aware."

"Then this is a palace of fools," he said. "You're unmistakable."

I flushed again, unable to interpret if he was chastising me or not. I certainly didn't think he meant it as a compliment, and anger won out briefly in my chest. I straightened slightly.

"Why did you cover for me?" I asked.

"I don't know," he said. "Shall I go get Nash?"

"I suppose so. Will you attend my hanging yourself, or skip it for something more pleasant?"

His lips tightened. Silence fell again, both of us staring at the other. A corner and one poster of the bed separated us, but it might as well have been the ocean.

Finally he let out a deep breath. "Rastaban will be

here in a few minutes. I don't know what you're doing here, Gemma, but in honor of the few happy memories we once shared, I'll give you the chance to get away. Take the escape tunnel. Get out of the palace, get out of Callais. If you do it now, I won't tell anyone you were here."

"Five years of marriage, and a dozen of friendship before that," I said. "And all it amounts to are a few happy memories?"

For the first time, he looked away, cutting his furrowed gaze to the corner.

"Which ones were the happy ones, Celeno?" I asked. "Was it flying kites over the canyon, or climbing the avocado trees? Was it picking apart the newest pamphlet from the University of Samna, or agonizing over our theses together? Was it sharing your hypotheses on meteor showers, or my discovery of cicada stridulation? Was it all the nights at the telescope? Exchanging gifts at Starfall? Dancing at our wed—"

"Stop it," he said sharply.

"I just want to know," I said, unable to stop myself, "so I know what you'll remember after they hang me—because I came here for you, and I'm not taking the tunnel without you."

"You betrayed me!" he exclaimed, cutting his infuriated gaze back to mine. "When confronted with choosing between me and our enemies, you picked Queen Mona and Queen Ellamae. How would you

feel, were it reversed? If I had flung my loyalty at a for-
eigner, instead of my wife and queen of my country?"

"That depends," I said. "In your hypothetical scenario, would I have just shot and killed an unarmed
civilian?"

His body seemed to spasm. "He was *not* unarmed—
he had incendiary grenades."

"They were in his pocket," I said. "He presented
no immediate threat."

"He was holding you captive!"

"And Queen Mona was negotiating for my re-
lease!" I took a step toward him. "You killed Lyle
Roubideaux to prove to her that you were capable of
doing so—that you wouldn't hesitate to kill Queen
Ellamae next. Did you hear me tell you I was unhurt?
Did you hear me tell you to talk to Mona?"

"So she could barter Alcoro to ashes!"

"So we could salvage something from the ashes
we've already burned!" I shot back. "If you had managed to bring Mona and Ellamae and Rou back here
to Stairs-to-the-Stars, we'd have had an allied East
rise up and march against us before their cell doors
were even closed."

He gave a short jerk of his arms, his palms skyward. "What would you have had me do? What do
you want from me now? Unlike you, *I* don't have the
luxury of suddenly changing sides."

The anger melted out of my body. He'd meant

the comment to be hurtful, but it didn't hit me with the barb he intended. I let out my breath. "No," I acknowledged. "You don't. What do I want from you now? I want you to let me help you, like I've always done. I want you to come with me, so we can set some of this right. I want you to refuse your poppy tincture tonight."

That last one threw him off-guard. "You what?"

"I want you to tell Rastaban you don't want the poppy tonight, and I want you to see what he says."

"I need it, Gemma," he said angrily. "I need it to sleep."

"I know," I said. "And you hate that you need it. So do me a favor. Or do yourself a favor, if you prefer. Conduct a little experiment tonight."

"Gemma . . ."

"Tell Rastaban you've decided to try to sleep without the poppy. Just for tonight, to see how it goes. Tell him you'll take it tomorrow if it doesn't work."

"To what utter purpose?"

"To see if he lets you."

"Of course he'll let me." The words hung there, thick with defensiveness. "But," he said quickly, as if hoping to cover them up, "I don't want to. I want to take it, because I want to get a decent night's sleep."

"That's fine. Take the tincture. Report me to the guards. Watch me hang tomorrow morning." I saw the light shift under the crack to the bedroom door, and I moved toward my wardrobe. "But whether Rastaban gives you the tincture or not, you won't be getting a good night's sleep tonight. I replaced today's dose with honey."

He stared at me in consternation. "You . . . did . . ."

Someone rapped on the door.

Celeno swung around. Hurriedly I hopped into my wardrobe, engulfed by the smell of starch and sage sachets. I caught one last glimpse of Celeno turning back in my direction before I swung the wardrobe door shut behind me. I could just barely see through the crack—he stood staring until the knock came again.

"My king?"

He shook himself. "Come in, Rastaban."

The physician entered with his case and gave a mild bow. "The Prelate tells me you're turning in early."

"I . . . yes." His gaze flicked to the wardrobe again. Behind Rastaban came my aunt, looking cool and unruffled and not at all like she'd discovered someone had been rifling through her office. After her came Celeno's valet, carrying a tray that he set down on the nightstand. He went to the king's wardrobe, pulled out the gloves I'd stuffed messily in their drawer, and replaced them neatly. He opened another drawer and removed Celeno's nightclothes.

Rastaban fished out the key around his neck and unlocked his case, seemingly unaware of Celeno's nervous fidgeting. Shaula took out a copy of the Book

of the Prophecy and turned a few pages. The valet
returned to his side and slid off his gloves.

"Actually," Celeno said quickly, "I think I'll stay up
for a while longer, and do some reading."

The physician pulled out the day's vial. I saw the
amber flash of honey. "On the contrary, my king, I
think an early night will do you good."

"No . . . I'd really rather sit up and read." The valet
slid Celeno's bolero off his shoulders.

"My king, your evening dose is measured specifically. You don't want to take it too late, or else you'll
miss your morning appointments."

"Well, then . . ." His voice was thick with reluc-
tance. "Then, Rastaban, I was thinking perhaps I'll
try not taking the dose tonight."

Rastaban poured the sticky contents of the vial
into the mug waiting on the nightstand. "That is not
wise, my king. I regret to inform you that you likely
won't be able to sleep at all."

Celeno waved away his valet and began unhooking the buttons on his shirt himself. "I'm aware of the
potential effects. I'd just prefer not to." Undeterred,
the valet moved silently to his feet, sliding off his tall,
polished boots.

The physician added a few pinches of herbs to
the metal strainer and poured a stream of hot water
over it. "My king, while I understand your reticence,
I must insist you take the tincture. Were it another

day, another week perhaps, when I could monitor your transition to another sleep aid, perhaps then we could talk."

"Your work is too important at the moment to tamper with your regimen," Shaula murmured, scanning a page. "Present circumstances demand your entire attention, and it would be irresponsible to simply take away the treatments that help you function."

"Fine, then," Celeno said. "Give me a half-dose. Let's start the transition now."

Rastaban stirred the mug. "Not tonight. If you like, the Prelate and I will discuss it with the council, and see if we can schedule a period to shift back to valerian."

"I don't want to go back to valerian," Celeno said impatiently, his shirt hanging open. "I'd like to try nothing at all."

Shaula selected a passage and marked her page. "Perhaps the spring, after current events have been sorted."

Rastaban held out the mug. Celeno's gaze fell on it. Desperately, it seemed, he looked to the case.

"You've used the wrong day," he said.

Rastaban checked his vials. "No, my king. Today is the eighteenth."

"I'm sure it's the seventeenth."

"No, my king. The seventeenth is empty—you took it yesterday."

I bit my lip at the frustration written on Celeno's face. "Then if you're determined to put me under, I'd like two doses. Give me tomorrow's as well."

Rastaban closed his case with a slow, deliberate movement. He studied Celeno. "How are you feeling this evening, my king?"

"I'm feeling fine!" Celeno snapped.

"Headache? Dizziness? Chills?"

"*No.*" Celeno jerked as his valet removed his unbuttoned shirt. The lamplight flickered over his bare skin.

"You were not this agitated at your Devotion a moment ago," Shaula said. "What has happened to have you in such a state?"

Celeno's gaze shot to my wardrobe, his mouth screwed up in anger. Rastaban didn't miss the look, but he misinterpreted it entirely.

"Ah." The physician turned back to his case. "I'm going to give you a measure of false dogwood, to ease your nerves . . ."

"Oh, by the Light." Celeno swiped the mug from his physician's hand and tossed it into his mouth. He swallowed and wiped his lips with the back of his hand.

"It tastes like honey," he said angrily, glaring in my direction. I held my breath. At least he'd taken it before Rastaban had added false dogwood—a harmless name given to an herb that was more commonly called *fishpoison.*

Rastaban gave a noncommittal grunt as he packed away his herbs. The valet stripped off Celeno's trousers and then fed his nightshirt over his head. As Rastaban took the king's pulse and checked his breathing, Shaula rested a hand on Celeno's shoulder.

"My king, now is a tumultuous time. Grief wreaks terrible havoc on body and mind—"

"I'm not grieving!"

"—and it's natural to be upset at the queen's betrayal," she continued. Celeno twitched against all the hands on him—hers on his shoulder, Rastaban's on his wrist and back, the valet's plucking and smoothing his nightshirt. "But remember that your success is the subject of prophecy, with or without the queen."

Rastaban released his wrist. "I've already added extra rounds of false dogwood and lavender to your daily regimen, and if you're feeling unstable in the evenings, I'll add a measure to your tincture."

"I'm not unstable!"

"You must trust your advisers," Shaula said, releasing his shoulder. "Do not tamper with your regimen now. Do not fend off our assistance. Gemma's betrayal has demanded more of you than ever. When the security of this country is assured and your responsibilities are less dire, we'll work on your transition. But not now."

"You mean not ever, if I must wait until Alcoro is secure," Celeno said bitterly.

The Prelate opened her book again. "You carry

doubt of the Prophecy in your words, my king. Do not travel down that road. Remember that your actions carry the will of the Light, and to ignore that is to work actively against the Prophecy." She found the passage she had marked. *"The Prophecy of the Prism gives an unprecedented mandate to the Seventh King, that his works and actions are divinely driven. Every action, no matter how small, is an advancement to the Prophecy, and as such those who assist him take part in the same mandate. An action done in the king's name is done in the Prophecy's name. A life taken or spared by his hand carries the will of the Light. Therefore let there be no room for doubt, for to doubt the king is to doubt the machinations of the Prophecy itself."*

My mother had remembered correctly—Shaula always did like reading her own religious theorizing best.

She closed the book. The valet turned down the covers on the bed, leaving the side that had once belonged to me tightly tucked. Rastaban gestured to the bed, and Celeno rather mechanically sat down. The physician thumbed his eyelids to check his pupils, and then patted him on the shoulder.

"Take some rest, my king. I'll return in the morning with your usual tincture."

He and the valet filed silently out of the room. Shaula was the last to leave, nodding to Celeno and then closing the door behind her with a distinct click.

He sat on the edge of his bed, pointedly staring

straight ahead, not turning to look at the wardrobe. I didn't move, waiting to be sure everyone had truly gone. A minute slowly slipped by.

Finally, I eased the door open and stepped out. Celeno still didn't look my way, his body stiffening slightly. His hands were clenched on his lap.

I circled around to stand in front of him.

"It all makes sense, you know," he said forcefully. "I know you probably feel like you've won, but what they've said makes perfect sense."

"I'm far from feeling like I've won," I said. "I notice you didn't tell them I was here."

His eyebrows snapped down. "If you're so keen to hang, why don't you go do it yourself?"

I turned and went to his wardrobe. I pulled out a hooded cloak and the boots he used to wear back when we took walks into the canyon. I set them down next to him.

"Come with me," I said.

"No," he replied. "Why should I?"

"Because I've learned about something that can help us both," I said.

"Is it a steep drop into the canyon?"

"It's another Prophecy," I said. "One that's nearly complete."

His eyes narrowed. "I don't believe you."

"It's not far from here, protected from the elements, not out in the open like the one in Callais."

"Who told you this?"

"A scholar," I said carefully. "I don't believe you've met."

He studied me. "You're a bad liar."

I flushed. "I'm not lying, Celeno."

"Then you're not telling me the whole truth. What is it you used to say when we were students? *What am I still missing?*"

"I can only give you so much information, because I haven't seen them myself," I said. "And I hesitate to speculate until I have."

"Where are they? How far away?"

I took a breath. "A few days."

"*Days?*"

"Probably longer."

"Gemma. They'll send out the army."

"Then we should start now," I said.

"And if I refuse?"

I turned back for my wardrobe and opened the drawer that held my star bands. "Then you spend a sleepless night lying here in bed, and a lifetime of being handled and medicated by your physician and the Prelate," I said.

"They'll let me transition off the poppy," he said angrily.

"As long as you're sure," I said, pulling out a few of the flat boxes containing my array of star bands. He frowned at my tone, but didn't respond. "In the meantime, I plan to go and find out exactly what the Prophecy says about you. And . . . we'll probably never see each other again."

"Would that be a loss for you?"

"Only the few happy memories," I said.

His lips twisted sharply, as if he'd swallowed something bitter. "What's in all of this for you?"

"Peace of mind." I selected the box that should have held the silver star band set with gray pearls and opened it to the sheaf of letters I'd stowed.

"That's it?" he asked.

I looked over my shoulder, the letters clutched in my hand. "Great Light, is that not enough? Would you prefer I say enduring fame in the Eastern World? Because there will probably be some of that."

He quirked an eyebrow, obviously unprepared for me to be joking. "How so?"

"Queen of the Seventh King, hanged for treason and abduction of the king?" I suggested, snapping the flat box shut and stuffing the papers in my shirtfront with the vellum packet.

"Yes, I suppose that will come with some longevity," he said flatly. "Tell me this—how do I know you're not going to spirit me away and deliver me to your newfound allies to the east?"

"Aside from the fact that literally no one would expect me to be able to accomplish such a thing?" I asked.

The corner of his mouth lifted in a non-smile. "Point scored."

I closed up my wardrobe and turned to face him fully. "Celeno, listen to me. You hate your title. You hate being the Seventh King. You hate what it requires of you. You've *always* hated it. And—I hate what it's done to you."

"It hasn't *done* anything to me."

"Yes, it has," I said softly.

His face screwed tight in a frown. "Then it's changed you, too, because the quiet, kindhearted biologist I married wouldn't ever have suggested we flee the palace in hopes of overturning the Prophecy."

The clever, excitable astronomer I married wouldn't have needed me to.

Wouldn't have traded fearmongering for his own sense.

Wouldn't have killed Lyle.

I reined in the tirade building inside me—it wouldn't do anything to get him through the door and into the tunnel. And shouting would bring the guards running.

"What choice did either of us have but to accept things as they were?" I asked, spreading my hands. "Now there's new data, new evidence. Celeno, how can we *not* chase after it? What if there's something else to your title, something we've missed all these years? Science moves and changes, history gets retold . . . why should this be any different?"

"A scholar through and through," he said flatly. "Though I believe your aunt would describe that as heresy."

"Yes, most likely. But in the end, she's just the Prelate, not the Prophecy itself." I gestured to the hidden panel in the wall. "The only thing I want is to go and see these things for myself, and for you to come with me. I'm not asking for your love, or even your trust." His face gave an odd sort of blanch, but I pressed on. "Think of it as a field study. How many scientists do we know who despise their research partners?"

He stared at me with an unsettled look, and he drew in a breath as if he might say something. But he didn't. He merely held it. His gaze flicked over me, from my servant's attire and bare arms to my dirt-covered boots.

"How did you get in the palace?" he asked.

"Through the crawl space under the laundry," I said. "Where the termite baits are."

"With all the tarantulas?"

"Tarantulas aren't dangerous," I said.

He let out his breath in what might have been a silent, mirthless laugh. He swiped up his stockings and boots and jerked them on his feet. He stood and swept the cloak around his shoulders.

"You know this changes nothing between us?" he asked.

"Nothing at all," I agreed.

"As long as you're aware." He gestured to the hidden panel. "Lead the way."

CHAPTER 5

The escape tunnel was narrow, musty, and pitch-black. *Another tiny space.* I drew in a breath, grateful at least that I could stand upright here. I tried to ignore the fact that getting through this tunnel was going to take far longer than crawling to the grate under the laundry.

Latching the door firmly behind us necessitated a lot of awkward elbows and knees. I pulled until I heard the *click*, and I brushed my hand over the smooth surface of the interior. The door wasn't meant to open from this side, in case an intruder somehow found their way in. Going forward was our only choice. Celeno's breath puffed short and shallow against my face.

"Assuming we get out of the palace," he said, skepticism heavy in his voice, "I suppose you have a plan for what happens next?"

I sidled past him with both hands brushing the walls. "We meet up with someone who can help us."

Hopefully.

"And you won't tell me who it is?"

"Not until I need to," I said.

"I take it I won't be thrilled by our benefactor's identity?"

"I doubt it." I took a few steps forward. "Come on."

We picked our way through the darkness, our steps short and shuffling. I nearly fell down the first set of stairs, my foot slipping right over the lip of the top step. They were rounded and uneven, and we hugged the wall as we inched down them.

"Should have brought a light," Celeno said.

"I'll remember one next time."

He huffed, unamused.

The stairs flattened out into a low-hanging corridor, the ceiling just brushing the top of my hair. Slightly stooped, ignoring the knot of dread threatening to unravel in the pit of my stomach, I continued on. We passed lumpy adobe walls that had been erected at the backs of rooms to create the passageway. One original wall even had tiles still laid into it; my fingers slipped over the mosaic pattern.

Our path led us mostly downward, out of the high reaches of the royal apartments. Despite this, I couldn't help but notice Celeno's breath growing faster and more ragged the farther we went.

"Do you have any water?" he asked as we stepped

over a threshold where the wall outside the corridor used to extend.

"Not on me. There will be some once we get out."

His breathing remained heavy and labored. A few minutes later I was just wondering if we should stop and rest, when despite my careful shuffle, I walked directly into a wall. I bounced backward into Celeno, who staggered. We landed in a pile on the floor.

"*Ow,*" he said.

"Sorry." I rubbed my forehead and crawled off him, reaching forward blindly. My fingers brushed another high threshold, as well as a low ceiling, leaving a gap perhaps three feet high.

"What's the matter?" he asked.

"It's just a small opening. I forgot it was here—there must be piping up above." I reached through the opening, expecting to feel the space open up again on the far side. It didn't. I frowned. "It goes a long way."

"Can we walk?"

"I think we'll have to crawl." Taking a breath, I stepped up onto the lip, my head thrust forward. He clambered up behind me—I moved forward to make room.

It was less of a crawl and more of a scoot, crouched with my knees at my stomach. I shuffled two, three steps, before reaching forward to find what must be the other side. My fingers slid only against adobe wall. I froze in my tracks—Celeno bumped into me from behind, unaware I'd stopped. The air was so close in here, so stale and old. I squeezed my eyes shut, my breath quickening. Heat flared in my blood, a wash of panic sweeping over me at the unexpectedly tiny space. I pressed my palms to the walls, my arms shaking.

"What's wrong?" he asked.

Unable to answer, I shook my head—which of course he couldn't see.

"Gemma?"

I cracked my lips and sucked in a breath. I shuffled one foot forward. "Nothing," I rasped. "Come on."

It was another five steps before the floor and ceiling evened out again. Clutching the opening, I set one foot down and stood on shaking legs. My stomach bubbled, sour.

I heard Celeno stand behind me. After a moment, his fingertips touched my elbow.

"Are you all right?"

"Fine," I said. I took a few steps, light-headed. "Come on. I think we're getting close."

I knew we were nearing the end of the tunnel when the floor went from wood and adobe to stone pavers. We were inside the exterior walls now, somewhere in the barrier that circled the moon gardens. The air got colder step by step, and the absolute darkness lightened to a washed-out gloom. A grated vent opened up next to our heads, letting in some feeble moonlight and a few wayward snowflakes. We passed another vent, and then a third—this one with the grate rusted out of it, the opening partially covered by leafless climbing vines. The strong stench of urine filled the air.

"Urrgh," Celeno said. "Guano."

I looked down at the glistening floor, and then up at the ceiling, barely a foot above our heads. In the dim light, I could just make out the shape of dozens and dozens of furry little bodies all packed tightly together. Bats.

"Good winter roost," I said.

"Let's hope they're nice and cozy."

I refrained from expounding on how they weren't likely to rouse from winter torpor, picking my way forward over the soiled floor. The tunnel began to slope downward slightly. We had to be nearing the end now. I walked with my hand outstretched. Finally, just when I was wondering how much more there could possibly be, my fingers touched wood. I let out a breath of relief.

"We're here," I said. I reached for the handle— another latch that could only open from one side. I lifted the chilly metal and pushed.

The door didn't budge.

I blinked in the darkness, and then leaned on my palm. Nothing happened.

"What's wrong?" Celeno whispered.

"It's stuck," I said. I put my shoulder against the door and shoved it. It didn't move.

"Let me," he said. I flattened myself against the wall as he edged past me, his back brushing my chest.

He set his shoulder against the wood and rammed it, once, twice. A sprinkle of dust fell from the ceiling.

"Is it iced over?" he wondered aloud, rattling the handle.

"It feels more like there's something in front of it," I said, sliding my fingers along the crack. "But that doesn't make sense—it's behind that hedge of willows. There's no reason to put anything here."

"Let's try it together."

With him holding the latch open, we both thrust our shoulders against the wood, our feet straining on the stone floor. The door didn't even wiggle. We tried pulling inward, to no avail. We searched for a bar or second lock, something that was inexplicably holding the door in place. Nothing.

We stood back, staring in silent consternation.

"Good thing we're not trying to outrun an assassin," Celeno said sardonically. "What do we do now?"

In the distance, a horn call shattered the night.

My heart jumped to my throat, and we locked eyes. It blasted four times and then repeated the pattern—an alarm call.

"Moon and stars," Celeno said. "How did they find out so quickly?"

A jumble of ideas jumped to my head—the guard from the antechamber had come back to check the bedroom, the laundress had asked about me, Shaula had noticed the letter and key missing from the drawer, the physician had come back to check on the king. It didn't matter, though—there was no mistaking the alarm. I grasped the handle and leaned on the door with all my might.

"It's no good, Gemma," he said. "They'll know this is the only place we can be. They're probably coming down from the bedroom entrance right now."

"No." I released my grip on the handle, my fingers stinging. "No. I'm not going to just sit and wait for them to scoop us up." I'd go right back to the Retreat, he'd go right back to his microcosm of medicine and religious theorizing. Outside, the repeating horn blasts were joined by a ringing bell. I wiped my nose, my eyes prickling from the stress, and turned back up the tunnel. "Come on."

"Where are you going? Even if the guards aren't already in the tunnel, you can't get back in the palace that way."

"We're not going back into the palace. We're getting out of here."

"How?" The word bounced as he picked up speed, hurrying to catch up with me. I ran back up the incline, my fingers brushing the walls, until my boots squelched on the floor. I looked up at the broken grate just above our heads.

Celeno groaned between breaths. "No, Gemma, seriously now . . ."

"I'll give you a boost," I said, lowering to one knee. "Then you help pull me out."

"It's barely wider than my shoulders! And what

about them?" He pointed up at the huddled mass of bats clinging to the ceiling.

"Even if they did wake up, what are they going to do to you?" I prompted. "They're insectivores, and tiny, and harmless." I patted my bent leg. "Come on, hurry."

He groaned again, but he set his boot, slimy with bat droppings, on my thigh. He hoisted himself toward the window.

"There're branches in the way," he said.

"Move them," I said as patiently as I could muster.

He tugged on a few of the vines, clearing out the grate opening. I heard a rustle from up above, but with Celeno blocking the light, I couldn't tell if we were disturbing the bats into flight.

He had his head and one shoulder out of the grate when he suddenly said, "Wait—shouldn't *I* be helping *you* out?"

I pushed up on his foot, levering him farther out of the grate. I heard the rattle of frozen vines as he clutched at them to keep from falling headfirst. He eased his waist out, and then his knees, using the lip of the grate to brace himself before pulling his boots out. He dropped out of sight.

I panted, looking up at the grate. Suddenly, without the noise of his boots scraping the adobe walls, I registered another sound echoing through the tunnel—the distant thump of boots, charging down from the palace.

I reached up to the grate. "Celeno," I called. "Give me your hand."

The leafless vines shook. "I can't reach the hole," he said. "The ground is a few inches lower out here."

I sucked in a sharp breath. A shout accompanied the oncoming boots.

"Gemma?" he called.

I backed up as much as the narrow tunnel would allow, pressing against the wall. Then, with only one good step to build momentum, I jumped for the grate, my arms straining to clutch the rounded lip.

Huffing, I eased my head through the hole. Celeno stood below, his arms upstretched, fingers a half a foot below me. I kicked at the wall with my boots—we had surely left streaks of guano leading up to our escape route, but it couldn't be helped now. Gritting my teeth, I managed to lever myself forward enough to balance my stomach on the lip. I freed one of my arms and reached down to grasp his.

"I'll catch you," he said.

I wasn't worried about him catching me—I was worried about us both crashing to the rocks below. The wall was on a little peninsula of stone, which sloped away gently at first and then dramatically, rolling toward the canyon rim. A bad slip would send us both tumbling over the edge.

He pulled, and I wiggled until my waist was free. Was I imagining the loud slap of boots on the ground? Expecting a hand around my ankle at any moment, I kicked again, and finally I shifted forward, sliding down toward him. He spread his stance wide in the gravel, throwing his arms around me before I could land face-first. Nothing about it was graceful or controlled, but at least we hadn't sailed into the canyon. Yet.

Wheezing on the winter air, we straightened ourselves.

"Okay?" he gasped.

"Yes. You?"

"I think so."

"Good. Come on, we have to get to the Stone Tree."

He crouched low and hurried along the wall after me. We were going to have to circle around the end of the tunnel to get to the track that would take us to the Stone Tree—but at least the guards inside wouldn't be able to get the door open. I could hear their footsteps, louder than I expected.

No, wait. It wasn't footsteps at all. What I'd taken for the sound of running soldiers now sounded more like a solid object repeatedly hitting wood. We were almost at the corner of the tunnel's end, and over the *chip chip* I was hearing came a murmuring of voices.

"Gemma," Celeno whispered with an edge of alarm.

Frantically I waved to the bank of willow scrub that normally hid the door from view. We slipped through to the other side. Shielded by the branches and the cover of night, we crept around the corner.

A group of five soldiers were at the tunnel's terminus. Four of them had their crossbows pointed at the door. The fifth was swinging a hatchet to break apart the door.

No—to break apart the wooden boards covering the door.

Silently I beckoned to Celeno, and we slunk past the scene, holding our breaths. When we'd put enough distance between us, we broke into a run.

We wound among the junipers and scrub oak along the canyon rim, scrambling through patches of scree. Horns were still blaring behind us. I prayed we wouldn't hear the sound of horses cantering or dogs barking—both signs the guards were starting to spread outward from the palace.

Celeno was breathing heavily again and soon slowed to a brisk walk. I dropped back to keep pace with him.

"They boarded up the exit," he said, panting. "Why?"

I glanced sideways at him. His brow was furrowed in the sliver of moonlight.

"I think it was to keep you in," I said.

His eyebrows knitted more, but he didn't say anything.

We kept away from the tracks leading into the city, picking our way along the rim, winding among the windswept juniper and sage that grew amid the snowy rocks. We darted cautiously across roads that wound down to the hobs in the cliffs below. The repeated horn blasts from the palace grew distant, and thankfully no alarm was raised in the city as we crept along the outskirts.

Finally, the little rise came into view, capped with a jagged column of stone. Alcoro's scientists had debated for generations about the process behind the stands of stone trees that were scattered through the arid Ferinno Desert to the west of us. Many posed different theories of how the wood had slowly become stone, while some argued that they had never been trees at all. I'd once attended a debate that had devolved into a shouting match and ended with one geologist pelting the other with fragments of the trees.

I didn't have an answer myself, and right now, all that mattered was getting to the only Stone Tree along the canyon rim. It was one of the biggest in the country, wide enough for five people to circle it with arms linked. I squinted at its base. Silhouetted against the sky was a person standing beside three stamping mules.

As soon as we were in range, my mother waved to us to hurry. We were hardly dawdling, but Celeno was still wheezing, his toes catching on the rocky ground. I urged him up the hill, nearly dragging him the last few yards to the foot of the towering, rock-solid trunk.

"Come on, quick now," my mother said. "I'd hoped they wouldn't raise the alarm this fast."

Celeno clutched his sides and squinted through the darkness, trying to make out her face. "Who are you?"

"We can do introductions later," she said. "You take the sorrel, and Gemma, you take the bay." She climbed onto Checkerspot, his back loaded with bulging saddlebags. Celeno looked like he wanted to challenge her, but I waved him toward the waiting mules. Irritated, he shut his mouth and climbed into the saddle. I followed suit, and soon we were both urging our mounts into a hasty trot after Checkerspot.

We rode for hours, splashing through creeks when we came to them, sometimes veering down washes only to double back. When we'd finally jumbled our path to my mother's satisfaction, she headed away from the canyon rim, leading us across the sage flats. In the distance, the Stellarange Mountains loomed crisp and indomitable, their jagged peaks blacking out the stars.

The shelter my mother and I had planned to reach for the night was tucked in the first foothills of the range, off a winding herders' track. We reached it an hour or so after midnight, and we dismounted our mules to lead them up the rocky incline to the door. It was a tiny hunting cabin, cloaked in snowdrifts. Leafless aspens stuck up around it like wiry hairs, and the hints of a little creek peeked through the snow, barely more than puddles of ice.

I watched Celeno slide unsteadily from his mount's

back, his legs wobbling when he touched the ground. I glanced over my shoulder at the snow behind us, cast into dim shadow by the half moon.

"We're leaving a trail," I said.

My mother looked back, too. "Can't be helped," she said. "My hope is that nobody has any reason to think we'll come this way."

There was no stable, only a little hitching post under a slanted roof. Once we'd seen to the mules, we collected the parcels from their backs and headed inside. Celeno hesitated on the doorstep, looking back out the way we had come. My mother noticed his pause as she lit the field lantern with a fire capsule.

"Thinking of backtracking, my king?" she asked, turning up the wick. "The mules have come a long way. I doubt you'd get farther than the caprocks."

He jerked around and closed the door behind him. "You mistake me—I'm merely pondering the somewhat ill-planned nature of this journey." The single room was tiny, and he stood in the middle of it, fists on his hips. He stared hard at her face, and then mine, and then hers again.

"So when will I have the courtesy of knowing who has orchestrated my kidnapping?" he asked.

"Your wife did," she said mildly, taking out a sack of corn biscuits. "Beyond springing her from the Retreat, I have mostly been her assistant."

"Who are you?" he demanded.

"You don't see the resemblance?"

He looked again to me, his frustration clearly written on his face.

"She's my mother," I said quietly. "Rana Maczatl."

His gaze jumped back to her. She nonchalantly held out the bag of corn biscuits to him—using her left hand, so that her prison tattoo showed on her wrist. He didn't take the bag. A look of brief surprise flickered over his face before being replaced by puzzlement.

"Oh," he said.

"Not as exciting as you'd hoped?" she asked.

"I admit . . ." He looked back to me. "I had expected someone more . . . I just mean, I don't particularly have anything against you."

"Well, that's gratifying," she said, taking a biscuit for herself.

He frowned. "I don't pretend to be pleased, of course, but it's better than finding out the queens of Lumen Lake and the Silverwood had organized my abduction."

"I told you," I said. "We're going to find a new Prophecy. I haven't had contact with Queen Mona or Queen Ellamae—or anyone, really—since Cyprien."

"Then why the heist?" he asked. "Why all the hurried and frankly reckless maneuvering to get me out of the palace—why not just make rubbings of this alleged Prophecy and bring it to the Prelate for consideration?"

My mother held up her index finger. "One, because I don't feel particularly inclined to hand myself back over to my sister again."

He gave a little start, as if just now realizing the full connection between Shaula and Rana. She continued, raising her second finger. "And two—when has that strategy ever worked before?"

"Perhaps if you dissenters didn't rush to cry that every scratch and divot are the work of the Prism himself," Celeno prompted.

I spread my hands, hoping to realign the conversation. "We need *you* to see them, Celeno," I said. "Our word won't matter at all to Shaula or the council. But yours carries authority, and you can take the time to decide what it means for Alcoro."

His frown deepened further. "And where are we going to accomplish such a thing?"

"Into the Stellarange," I said.

His eyebrows rose. "In the middle of December? With just a few cloaks and blankets?"

"We're not going up them," I said. "At least, not far. We're going inside them, into a cave system my mother's field team discovered."

"Inside a cave," he repeated. "To see a new Prophecy."

"Well, fragments of a Prophecy," my mother said. "It's not complete."

"It's *not complete*?" Celeno's jaw dropped.

"Of course it's not complete," she said, unpacking

the bedrolls from our packs. "The cave is full of running water. No glyphs would stay fully intact under those circumstances."

Furious, he rounded on me. "You told me it was complete!"

I bit my lip. "I said it was nearly complete."

He shook his head in disbelief. "You made it up," he accused. "You just told me that to get me out of the palace."

"I said it was *nearly* complete."

"Even if it's not complete," my mother said, flattening out her bedroll, "it raises significant concerns about the use of your title to justify Alcoro's political action."

He tossed up his hands. "So, in the end, this is just another ploy to delegitimize the Prophecy. Is that what I'm hearing? Is that really why we just threw Stairs-to-the-Stars into an uproar?"

"No," I said quickly. "No, Celeno. This is more important than that. This means finding a real, legitimate primary source, not relying on hearsay and speculation. This means changing how we make decisions. It could mean stopping an allied war before it begins. If this Prophecy changes what we know about your title, it could free us to pursue another route." The vellum packet crinkled in my shirt—I nearly pulled it out and offered it as proof. "That's something you've always said you wanted."

"Right now I want to get in my own bed and take

my evening tincture." He snatched up one of the bed-rolls and stomped to the corner of the room as if to put space between us, though it only gained him a few extra feet. Shaking it open, he laid it down next to the wall and wiggled down into it, his back to both of us.

I drew in a short breath at the ugly mood in the room. "Don't you want something to eat?" I asked.

He wrapped his cloak a little tighter around him-self. "No."

My mother rolled her eyes in his direction and held out the bag of corn biscuits to me. Dejectedly, I sat on my bedroll and shared a silent, stilted meal of biscuits and jerked venison with her. My mother bur-rowed down into her bedroll and fell asleep with the ease of someone used to sleeping in the field, but I sat cross-legged on mine, idly studying her map of the cave. When her breath had deepened, I quietly pulled the vellum packet out of my shirt. I turned it over to study the thick wax seal in the dim light coming from our red-shielded lantern. It was broken—Shaula had already opened it and read the contents. But despite the crack in the yellow wax, I could still make out the two stylized bolts of lightning around an angular *S*.

Samna.

Finally, the response from Samna.

As quietly as I could, I lifted the corner of the first page. It was dated four weeks previously, which meant Shaula had probably intercepted it around the same time that I'd been locked away in the Retreat.

> *Greetings to Queen Gemma Tezozomoc of Alcoro, may you stand tall in the Light,*
>
> *I have brought the matter before the board and am pleased to accept the terms of your proposal . . .*

I snapped the edge of the parchment back down, my breath quickening. I leaned my head against the wall, clutching the vellum to my chest. After months—no, years—of correspondence, after letters of introduction and speculation, setbacks and victories, my official proposal had gone before the board of directors for the University of Samna. They'd conferred! They'd accepted! How long had I dreamed of this? How many nights had I sat scribbling at my desk, while Celeno slept listlessly in the other room, drafting and revising and finalizing my letters? And now, here was the answer. They would send one of their own scholars to Alcoro, to open discussion about organizing our own similar institution of education.

An actual university.

Not a faraway dream, but right here in Alcoro. I thought of my mother's work, how a university would give it a place to thrive, along with all the other scholars whose work was passed over by the crown. Even Celeno's research on the movements of meteors had had to be abandoned upon his coronation, left with no way to grow or be handed over for others to continue. An *Alcoran university*. The jobs it could create, the revenue it would bring in . . . it could make Alcoro a hub of the Eastern World, not a border country grasping at its neighbors' wealth. Think, think, *think* of what it could do.

Celeno shifted on his bedroll, and I forced myself to calm down. Quietly, I opened the letter again and read the rest, scanning the time lines and discussion points the Samnese board had suggested. My excitement tempered somewhat.

It was a relief to have a response after months of waiting, but so much had changed since I sent my last letter on the week-long voyage across the sea. The attempt to reach out to Queen Mona had come and gone, followed by the subsequent disaster in Cyprien. The Samnese had made their agreements with the queen of Alcoro, and now I was little more than a fugitive, waiting to be tried and hanged as a traitor. On top of everything, now Shaula knew, too. My efforts to keep my correspondences secret from her had failed—at least in this instance.

I glanced over at Celeno, who was lying rigid and still, too much so for real sleep. I let my breath stream out and folded up the letter, tucking it back in my shirt with the others. I blew out the lantern light and slid down into my bedroll. The sky was clear that night, the moon a waxing sickle, giving just enough light to illuminate the cracks in the ceiling.

The petroglyphs. The Prophecy. The remaking of Celeno's title. That was all I could count on at this point. Whatever my plans had been before, I had lost the opportunity to carry them out myself. If Celeno saw the petroglyphs and managed to regain control of the country, I could pass on my correspondences to him. He could take the opportunity I'd created and bring it to fruition himself—while I disappeared.

Just like everything else.

I rolled over, as if trying to physically put my back to that little voice that had flared in my head. *It's for the good of Alcoro,* I thought angrily. If he could rebuild our country into something bright and hopeful, what did it matter whether I had a hand in it or not?

But can he really do it? asked the voice. *Will he really do it? He's angry at you. You've broken his trust. He's put his name on the order for your death. What if he takes your work and merely casts it aside, the folly of the failed queen?*

I bundled my blanket tight around my ears. I wouldn't tell him. I wouldn't tell anybody. I wouldn't tell them *anything,* lest it all somehow be twisted and misconstrued and preached away. I knew how this worked. I knew how easy it was to unravel an idea before it had fully spread its wings and taken flight. It had almost happened to my thesis, when the group of old-guard scientists nearly overturned all my work to reclassify the cicada. But I'd won then, by waiting and working and writing until there were no holes left in my argument, and I'd do the same now. I'd keep it all quiet until Celeno had wrestled his title back from the false ramifications of the Prophecy. And then I'd hand him my university—and run. He could bring it back as his own grand idea without any whisper of my involvement.

My stomach in sour knots, I closed my eyes and reached desperately for sleep, still aware that across the room, Celeno lay in a twin image of my own, curled up with his blanket holding back the world.

CHAPTER 6

When I woke to the sharp nudge of a boot toe
against my ribs, my mind immediately jumped to the
worst possible conclusion—we'd been found. The Alcoran army had followed us from the palace, climbed
the track to the hut, and surrounded us with loaded
crossbows. I sat up hurriedly, blinking up at the figure silhouetted against the midday sun.

"He's puking," my mother said.

I shook my head to clear it and got stiffly to my
feet—everything ached from all the out-of-the-
ordinary activity the previous day. "Celeno?"

"He's been tossing all morning," she said. "Just
a moment ago he threw off his blanket and barely
made it out the front door."

From the open door came the sounds of retching.
I quickly slipped back into my boots and went to the

threshold. Celeno was kneeling in the snowbank, still in his nightclothes from when we escaped the palace, trembling as he emptied his stomach into the pristine snow.

My own stomach squirmed. This was a scene that used to be a daily occurrence, one I had learned to anticipate and recognize before it happened. The number of times I had hurried out of the council room after him, or jumped from bed to accompany him to the washbowl . . . I scooped up a canteen and went to crouch beside him.

I touched his shoulder. He drew in a deep gasp and glanced at me, his arms clutching his middle. He apparently had been sweating—his hair hung in limp tendrils over his forehead, not stiff with leftover wax.

"Did you sleep at all?" I asked.

He shook his head and gave a dry heave, his body convulsing. I pressed the canteen into his hand.

"Drink," I said. "I'll get you a ginger pellet."

While he took short swallows of water, I went back in and rummaged in the pack with the medical kit, coming up with the pouch of dried ginger pressed into little pills. My mother watched as I plucked one out.

"Did he eat something off?" she asked.

I shook my head. "It's nerves. He's always had a bad stomach."

"Hm," my mother grunted.

I went back out with the ginger pellet and gave it to him between swallows. He set it in his mouth with shaking hands, and then accepted a change of traveling clothes from me—a thick, unadorned bolero over a plain shirt, sash, and trousers. Waving away my help, he slowly dragged them on and then returned his head to its former position hanging over the snow.

While he stayed crouched outside, my mother and I packed up our travel gear and brought it back out to the blanketed mules. Only when they were loaded and ready to go did I go to shake his shoulder.

"The mules are ready," I said. "Come on."

But instead of rising, he shook his head. "I can't."

"Why not? Your stomach?"

"It's not just that, I . . . my whole body feels . . . I can't stop shaking." He held out the canteen to illustrate.

I heard the creak of leather as my mother mounted Checkerspot. Not wanting to cause a delay, I put my hand under his arm. "Maybe you'll feel better after breakfast. You can eat while we're riding."

"I doubt I can keep anything down."

"Well, we have to move forward," I said. "We can't run the risk of lagging if someone picks up our trail. Come on. I'll ride behind you."

Somehow, despite his wheezing and wobbling, I managed to get him on his feet and into his mule's saddle. He sat hunched on its back, one hand on his stomach, the other clutching the reins and a fistful of mane. My mother watched with her lips twisted to one side.

"Go on," I said to her as I mounted the bay. "I'll sweep."

Our pace the rest of the day was slower than my mother and I had anticipated. Celeno seemed unable to keep his mule going at more than a plod, no matter how much my mother called to him. I rode just behind him, watching him hunch forward, head down, entirely unaware of the landscape we were passing through.

As much as I tried to keep an eye on him, I couldn't fully ignore our surroundings. The wide, plunging canyon of Callais was easily the most astounding natural feature in Alcoro, but we were slowly climbing into my favorite kind of landscape. The sagebrush flats disappeared, replaced by a steeper incline populated with cottonwood trees and, later, aspen groves. The aspens were beautiful in the snow, a perfect charcoal sketch, the black patches on their white bark stark against the frozen backdrop. The air carried the kind of quiet that only comes in winter, broken occasionally by the chipping of a few bald eagles and, somewhere, a late-season elk bugle. The higher we climbed, I knew, the land would turn to rugged slopes of alpine meadows, rushing creeks, and towering firs, all bedded under snow for the winter. A thread of quiet nostalgia distracted my thoughts all afternoon—my mother's and my twirly house had been tucked into such a place. Not so high that we forfeited a productive garden, but high enough that few days got too hot for comfort.

At the front of our line, her thoughts seemed to be similar to mine. "Remember the little lily field a few miles from the twirly house?" she called over her shoulder.

I smiled. "With the hanging lake and spruce-fir grove." My heart swelled as I recalled the piercing evergreen scent, and I realized with a start that I wouldn't be seeing those alpine meadows or smelling the conifer forests again. If my plan was really to bring Celeno to the petroglyphs and then flee—then these were my last days in my native country. I closed my eyes and tried to conjure images of Samnese beaches and tropical fruit trees. But despite the allure of warm white sand and salt water, the high, fresh field of lilies wouldn't budge from my mind.

Between us, Celeno coughed wetly several times and spat into the snow. I opened my eyes and focused my energy back on urging his mule to move faster.

The day was short, and because of our slow pace we didn't reach our destination until the light was nearly gone from the sky. Our mules' hooves caught on the rocky path as we directed them alongside the trapper's hut, the windows boarded up for the winter. It was even smaller than the hunting cabin the previous day, without even a roof over the hitching post. My mother directed Celeno to sit on the floor of the hut while we fed and blanketed the mules. The king sat with his knees drawn up to his chest and his forehead resting on his arms.

The hut was no warmer inside than outside, and small enough that the three of us and our saddlebags took up most of the space on the floor. My mother took out the food bags, handing me the bag of jerked meat. I extended it to Celeno, who turned his face away. My mother huffed, her breath clouding in the lantern light.

"There's no sense in a hunger strike," she said.

"I can't stomach it," he said.

"You need to eat something," I said. "Today was only a half day, but tomorrow's a full one."

"I *can't*, Gemma," he said with irritation.

"Here," I said, rummaging in the packs. "Take another ginger pellet, and have some of the pine nuts. Maybe those will sit better for you."

"Why don't you just leave me alone?" he said, his face turned away.

I paused with the ginger pellets clutched in my hands, stung. My mother snorted.

"Because she's trying to keep you from keeling over, you ungrateful child."

He turned his head slowly back to the two of us, his eyes locking with my mother's. "I would suggest sticking to *Your Majesty*, if you cannot manage the notion of *my king*."

She chewed a strip of jerky, regarding him. "It's not the title I've never been able to swallow. It's the means you use to uphold it."

He glared at her. "I suppose it was too much to

hope that five years in the Mesa prison might have reoriented you."

"It was ten years, my illustrious king."

My hurried mediation died on my tongue, and my gaze swung to her. "*Ten* years?"

She was still looking at him. "And you have a misguided view of the efficacy of your prison system if you think being a chattel in a long-dead mine softens one to the struggles of their monarchy."

"Shaula told me it was five," I said to her. "She gave me the release documents."

"Presumably, right before she explained that we could never see each other again," my mother said, wiping her hands on her trousers. She hooked a finger under her sleeve and pulled it back to reveal her prison tattoo. "The initial sentence was five years. The judge was reluctant to give more than that for my somewhat insubstantial charges. At some point, and with little warning to me, the term was doubled."

The M for Mesa was flanked by a row of ten small crosses—the vertical lines would have been tattooed at the beginning of her sentence, while the crossbars would have been added each year to show how much she had served. There were ten of them—the second group of five was darker and less blurry, as if they'd been done more recently.

"They must have found more evidence against you," Celeno said flatly.

She crooked a half-smile to him and slid her sleeve back down. "I can assure you that they used every scrap of evidence they could find to scrape together the initial sentence."

"But there *was* evidence," Celeno pressed. "You confessed to instigating and conducting treasonous activities."

"I'm flattered that you're so familiar with my political pursuits."

"You're my mother-in-law," he said hotly. "It was considered my duty to know."

"Well, whatever the motive, you're right," she said. "There was absolutely, decisively, one-hundred-percent evidence against me. I was a dissenter then, and I am now. I met with other dissenters every month to parse out and debate the discrepancies in the Prophecy, which, I might add, is the same thing my sister does with impunity. But five years is the sentence given to dissenters who have actually gone beyond just philosophizing, and ten years necessitates irrefutable harm against Alcoro or its citizens. And I can guarantee you there was no proof of my involvement in such activities."

"Are you suggesting they extended the prison sentence without proof?" Celeno asked. "I would like to think such corruption would be noticeable, at least given enough time."

She rummaged for the bag of corn biscuits. "Not if it's the Prelate orchestrating such events."

His brows snapped down. "That's a bold assumption to make."

"Is it?"

"Why would the Prelate manipulate the laws of justice in such a way against you?"

"I've always assumed it was to be sure my—frankly minimal—presence in her life was negated even further to counter any issues that might arise with her nomination to Prelate," she said, selecting a biscuit.

"You're saying she locked you up so she could rise to Prelate?"

My mother shrugged. "The previous Prelate was getting old by the time I was arrested. And he died around the same time my sentence was extended, along with all those acolytes during the fasting. I think with things in such disarray, she didn't want me ruining her chances."

I pursed my lips. I had forgotten about the three acolytes who had died in the transition period between Prelates, each overcome by one of the secret, potent tinctures they drank to purge themselves during the nomination of the next Prelate.

"Were you involved in Shaula's thesis?" I asked, finally breaking out of my thoughts.

They both looked at me, bemused at my change of subject.

"What thesis?" asked Celeno.

"Her thesis on millipedes," I said. "Done back before she joined the acolytes."

"I did her illustrations," my mother said. "My name is credited in the text."

"And do you have a copy?" I asked.

"No. I made two copies—one for her and one for the academic library."

"I imagine you had sketchbooks from that time, though," I said. "With rough sketches, trial-and-errors?"

"Naturally," she said. "That was a tricky technique, trying to convey the bioluminescence. That's when I started using wax to mask parts of the illustration. I've used it again on my sketches from the cave."

I gazed into the middle distance, my lips pressed together. "Hm."

Celeno shook his head at my drifting thoughts and turned stiffly back to my mother. "I still maintain that something must have been found against you to extend your sentence. Shaula wasn't even Prelate when you were imprisoned. How could an acolyte falsify such an action?"

"Don't ask me to fathom the machinations of your inner circle," she snapped. "Overestimating your dissenters and underestimating your closest advisors is a steadfast tradition of our beloved monarchy."

"I disagree," he said sharply. "Who makes the Ferinno Desert all but impassable to even the most heavily armed travelers?"

"Bandits and thieves," my mother said. "Not political malcontents. You forget that even among dissenters, there's a huge range of beliefs. Most disagree with the official interpretation of the Prophecy, but almost no one agrees on what the real interpretation is. Some demand an absolute literal transcription, that the Prism wasn't a person but an actual shard of broken light that carved the petroglyphs. Others think 'the Seventh King will rise' means that we lost track of kings somewhere and that a past one will rise from the grave. And many think the glyphs forming 'a thousand years' are more accurately interpreted as the length of a good growing season. To put it simply, you're protected, in large part, by the fractiousness of your own rebels."

"Well, we can only hope it stays that way," he said, clearly intending to end the conversation. His gaze passed over me as he unbuckled his bedroll from his pack. "Though I don't deny I've overlooked treachery in my own midst before."

My mother sent a poisonous look at the back of his head, but I barely saw it. I had too much to think about. My mind wheeled and turned long after the lantern had been puffed out and we'd lain down to sleep. I lay listening to Celeno's breathing grow more and more labored as the night deepened. When I finally slept, my dreams were thick and nonsensical—lilies growing on a white sand beach, a dark sky above spotted with pinpoints of crawling light.

"What do you remember of Shaula's thesis?"

My mother looked up from the pot she was stirring over the fire. We'd made slightly better time that day, thanks most likely to several strategic administrations of ginger and sweet birch to help Celeno along. He'd spent the day bent in his saddle, silent, while we climbed farther up the Stellarange. Our shelter for the night was a wide, natural overhang that clearly had been used by people for centuries—an old rock wall rose waist-high at the front of the cave, and the ceiling bore traces of a few petroglyphs, though they were too faint to make out.

We'd lit a fire, both to prepare a meal and supplement the heat we would lose to the open air that night. My mother poked at the venison and sweet potatoes that were bubbling in the pot. "Not much. I was working on drafting my own thesis at the time, and I only read enough of hers to do the illustrations. She was interested in the function of the bioluminescence—was it a predator deterrent, or a way to attract mates? I remember her painting the things black to hide the glow, and then putting them in a cage with rats to see if they got eaten any more readily."

"What was her consensus?"

"I don't remember. In fact, she might have even dropped her studies before she had anything definite."

"If she was so far into studying biology, why did

she make the jump into being an acolyte?" Celeno asked, eyes closed. He was sitting against the wall, bundled in a blanket with his arms across his chest.

"She always straddled the line," my mother said, poking at a sweet potato to determine its tenderness. "She and I often spent long hours debating the Prophecy—I thought she had a general dissatisfaction with its impact on our economy, like me, but turns out she had more of a religious obsession. By the time she was writing her thesis, she was already spending more hours reading the Prelates' theorizing than she was on her experiments."

"But she continued her experiments with the millipedes after she made the switch?" I asked.

"I don't think so," she said. "Not to my knowledge."

I pursed my lips. *Then why does she have a crate of the creatures in her closet?* I almost asked the question aloud, but I silenced myself. I needed more time to think about it, more time to study its many strange angles.

A scholar through and through, Celeno would have accused.

Yes, and if we're lucky, it's going to save us both.

My mother clanged her spoon on the pot. "Stew's ready. Get out the tin cups."

Celeno groaned, gripping his stomach, and turned his head away.

"Oh, you're eating tonight, Your Majesty," my mother said. "I'm not having any more listless mornings. We have one more full day of climbing before we reach base camp, and I'll be damned if I'm going to let you drop off the edge of the mountain. No, don't look to Gemma to rescue you." She held out her palm. "The cup. Now."

I slept fitfully on the cold floor of the cave. When the wind finally died down, the night filled instead with the rich, soulful howls of timber wolves. I shivered under my blanket, pulling my fur cap a little closer around my ears. There were no wolves near Callais. We had coyotes, the canyon often ringing with their yips and twirling howls—a joyful sound, I'd always thought, a family of parents and pups all chorusing together. The song of the wolves was different, deeper and sadder. I knew they were hunting nighttime animals creeping from their dens, but my thoughts strayed to the stone wall along the lip of the cave and just how secure it actually was.

Celeno didn't sleep well, either. I listened to him toss and turn, his breath ragged. He'd eaten a small cup of stew but had resisted any further ministrations from my mother. Short of shoving the food down his throat, she couldn't make him eat any more. I'd warmed some water for him so he didn't have to drink it ice cold and gave him another ginger pellet. I ignored my mother's narrowed eyes as I settled him into his bedroll with an extra blanket.

"You let him call you a traitor, and yet you fuss over him like he's a swaddled infant," she said in an accusing whisper after he seemed to have gone to sleep.

"I need him to be strong enough for the cave," I said. "We both do. He needs to be well enough to travel and think rationally about the Prophecy."

More importantly, he had to be well enough to go back and face the problems in Alcoro without me.

She snorted in dissatisfaction. "Tell me, has he ever gifted you the same kind of emotional labor?"

I met her gaze. "Once upon a time, it was the only thing I could count on."

She'd frowned but kept her silence as we settled in to our bedrolls.

I woke the following morning to her footsteps crunching over the snow. I sat up, my cheeks stinging from the cold.

"I smelled smoke," she said. Our campfire was banked and barely burning. "I just wanted to check."

"Did you see anything?"

"The firs are too thick to get much of a view. But I didn't hear voices or see any signs of a camp." She shrugged. "Maybe it's just a woodcutter's stove, or my own imagination. All the same, give our king a poke, will you?"

Celeno was on his side with his back facing me, and when I squeezed his shoulder, he let out a low moan. I turned him onto his back. He was sweaty again, his hair plastered to his forehead under his fur cap. He cracked his eyes open.

"Gemma?"

In the fog of sleep, he said my name thoughtlessly, without the layers of bitterness now attached to it. My heart squeezed to hear him say it so gently, as if it was just another morning in Stairs-to-the-Stars. The illusion lasted for the span of a breath, and then his brow furrowed.

"Gemma," he said darkly.

"It's time to get up," I said. "We need to go."

He tried to roll back over. "I barely slept."

"I know, but we think there are people somewhere down the trail. Best get moving quickly."

He doubled up, giving a sharp groan. "My stomach."

I heard my mother give an aggravated sigh behind me as she packed up our supplies.

"I'll get you a ginger," I said.

"It's not going to help."

Not wanting to delay and run the risk of discovery, I fetched him another pellet, which he took with continued complaints. My mother stomped around with more chagrin than necessary, making the mules cock their ears backward as she slung the loaded saddlebags over their backs. Finally, we mounted and proceeded uphill under a heavy gray sky.

We didn't make it far, barely a quarter mile from the cave, when the sound of retching filled the air. Celeno lurched over his mule's withers and vomited, causing the animal to sidestep at the sudden shift. I kicked my mount forward and reached out to grab his reins and a handful of his cloak. My mother turned around in her saddle.

"Sick again?" she asked.

I held him upright, sliding my hand under his sleeve. Despite the sweat still beading on his forehead, he was trembling violently.

"Are you cold?" I asked.

He bent over his saddle, drawing hoarse breaths. "I'm freezing."

"I'll get you one of the blankets," I said.

"We need to stop," he said, clutching his stomach, eyes squeezed shut.

"We can't, Celeno."

"I can't keep going."

I slid off my mule to get a blanket from my mother's saddlebags. "We'll go slowly. Do you want to try to eat something? More ginger?"

"I can't."

My mother pursed her lips as I approached Checkerspot to dig out one of the blankets, clearly unhappy with the feeble state of the king.

"Don't look at me like that," I said to her.

"Why not?" she asked.

I pulled out the blanket and made my way back to Celeno. "Because it makes you look like Shaula."

With the blanket wrapped around his shoulders, we started again, our mules toiling up the steep, zigzagging track. The land to our right dropped away, framing a rugged panorama of snowy peaks, but I found I couldn't admire the beauty of our route as I had the previous few days. My gaze was fixed on Celeno as he wavered first one way, then another, sometimes stooping over his saddle, once even leaning his forehead on the mule's neck. My mother grew farther and farther ahead despite constantly reining Checkerspot in.

When he vomited again, I didn't quite make it to his side in time. He half-slid, half-fell off his mule's back. He landed on his feet, but his knees buckled instantly, so he was practically kneeling under his mule's belly. I jumped off my mount and hurried to lead the animal away while he threw up clear fluid into the snow.

With a string of curses muddled by the distance between us, my mother turned Checkerspot around and rejoined us.

"What's the matter with him?" she asked. "Did you give him another ginger? Are you still sure this is all just nerves?"

Celeno answered before I did, his head still bowed. "It's not just my stomach! It's my head, my chest . . . my legs are cramping, my hands are shaking. We . . . we need to stop for a while."

"We've barely made it two miles!" my mother said.

"Then you go on ahead and leave me here to die!" he snapped back. He wiped the back of his mouth.

"Believe it or not, I'm not actually *trying* to make myself sick!"

"Let's rest a moment," I said to her. "Give him a chance to have some more water, and maybe some sweet birch." Perhaps an analgesic would help his other aches and pains.

My mother ground her teeth but led Checkerspot off the trail with the other mules. She dismounted and snatched up her canteen. "I'm going back down the trail to be sure nobody's riding up on our tails."

She disappeared through the firs. I settled Celeno down with a canteen and measured out some of the herbs in our medical kit.

"I can't do it, Gemma," he said when I brought him the medicine. "I'm too tired."

"Rest now," I said. "Close your eyes, and try to rest a little."

"We should never have come out here. We should never have done this."

"We can make it, Celeno. We have to—we have to know the truth." Samna, freedom, a new beginning—everything was riding on learning the truth.

He let his breath stream out, but just as he closed his eyes, they popped open again at the sound of hurried footsteps. My mother strode back into view—not running, but nearly so, her hands balled into fists. Her mouth was set in a stern line, and she looked between me and Celeno. Seeing him relatively incapacitated, she jerked her head at me.

"C'mere."

I rose and followed her through the firs as she marched downhill. We made it perhaps fifty yards from where we'd left Celeno and the mules, coming to the tight corner of a switchback, affording a view over the tops of the trees and into the valley we'd camped in the night before.

I drew in a sharp breath. Nearing our morning's campsite in the overhang, perhaps two miles below us, were five mounted soldiers, dressed in the russet and black of the palace.

A moment of heavy silence hung between us like a storm cloud.

"We can't outrun them at our pace," my mother finally said. "They'll catch us by lunchtime. The only advantage I can see is that they're on horses, not mules—they'll tire more quickly, and they'll be more finicky over the terrain. But it's a weak excuse for hope."

I watched the first of the neat line of soldiers turn the hairpin corner. "How far are we from the cave?"

"At his speed?" She jerked her head back up the path. "We should get there by afternoon, if he doesn't get any slower."

I thought carefully for a moment. My mother eyed me, as if expecting my answer.

"We'll go in on our own," I said.

"I thought you might say that," she said. "How long have you been considering it?"

"Since your house in Whiptail Hob," I admitted.

"I've seen you studying the map." She shifted. "Tell me—is it just for his sake, to do away with the notion that this is all just dissenter's rabble, or is there another reason?"

"It started out for his sake," I said. "But I'm becoming more convinced there's a bigger one, too. All this talk about your sentence, about Shaula, about the Prelacy . . . little pieces are starting to fit together in ways I didn't realize before. It could be all coincidental. But, the more I learn, the more I can't shake the feeling . . ." I let out my breath. "What's a millipede's defense mechanism?"

"Acid," my mother said.

"Cyanic acid," I said.

She frowned. "Cyanide." She said the word as if testing its plausibility.

"That's right." I looked back down at the soldiers as they turned the switchback. "It's going to sound far-fetched, but when I inquired after my lead councilor, I was told he was confined to his bed, close to death from a bout of stomach virus." I glanced sideways at her as she pursed her lips. "He often votes in my direction and can generally convince some of the others to, as well. Without his vote, I have no doubt that the council will call for my execution."

She nodded up the trail. "Doesn't the king have to approve your execution?"

"He already has," I said. "He signed the document a few days ago."

"*Bastard.*" The word broke from her, her mouth twisting in anger. "Why didn't you tell me?"

"Because I'm not going to stay, Mother," I said. "I'm going to get Celeno through the cave, and then I'm going to leave. I'm not coming back here."

She released her breath in a frozen cloud and stared down the mountain at the distant line of soldiers, her fists on her hips.

"I'll come with you," she said. "I'll wait for you outside the cave, and when you come out, I'll leave with you."

"No," I said. "I need you to do something else."

"What's that?"

"I need you to go back to Callais. Go to Izar, if you can secure an audience. If you can't, go to my old tutor, Ancha—she remembers you from lessons. Get a warrant to have Shaula's rooms searched. She's keeping a cage of millipedes in the alcove in her bedroom. I saw them when I was getting the key."

She turned slowly back to me. A few beats of silence passed.

"You think Shaula poisoned your councilor." Again she seemed to test the statement's validity.

"Not only him," I said, and then I stopped, reexamining my thoughts for the hundredth time. I glanced back up the trail.

My mother instantly read my mind. "You think she poisoned the *king*?"

"I don't know," I said quickly, turning back to her. "I don't know why she would. Except . . . well, it's certainly made running away a challenge, hasn't it? Only a few years ago, he and I used to spend whole days walking into the canyon and along the rim. We'd hike up the caprocks with all his astronomy gear. And now he can barely stay on the mule's back. Dealing with his title always made him nervous and ill, but this . . ."

She pursed her lips. "Far be it from me to try to clear my sister's name, but I thought he didn't take his tincture before you left? Or does she slip it to him some other way?"

"I don't know," I said. "I know it's questionable at best, but I can't shake the idea. But that's why I need you to go back." I gestured down toward the distant soldiers. "Shaula clearly isn't sitting idle, and if she's still in power when Celeno comes back, I suspect it won't matter what the petroglyphs say. And even if I'm wrong about his tincture, there's still my councilor, and that string of other poisonings around her nomination to the Prelacy—the previous Prelate, and those three acolytes. And now I learn that your sentence was extended without evidence and without anyone's knowledge—what if she was afraid you would come forward with information about her work? You were the only one who had the knowledge and courage to connect her to those events."

My mother stared at me, her face lined and hard.

"It is far-fetched," she said.

"I know." I swallowed. "Do you doubt it?"

"Not for a second," she said.

I sagged in relief. "Thank you." My throat tightened with the onset of stress crying. "I know I'm asking a lot from you, putting you back in Shaula's path, but if she has truly done these things—if they can be proven, and then if Celeno's title is made clear . . ."

"I don't care about Shaula." She looked up the trail again, her brows knitted. "But I don't like leaving you with him."

"He's not dangerous, Mother."

"I don't think he's going to attack you," she said flatly. "I think he's going to continue being an entitled ass, and that you won't do a thing to stop him. Gemma, honestly, addled by drugs or not, he signed your death warrant . . ."

"It's only until the Prophecy, Mother. It's only so he understands what his title means. Then I'll part ways. I'll go to the coast, and I'll go to Samna. You can join me there." The first tear seeped from my eye. "Think of all the insects we'll find. We can illustrate them for the university scholars."

She let out the last of her breath, and she reached out to wrap her arms around me. "Oh, Gemma." She squeezed me tightly, and I rested my forehead on her shoulder, my cheeks wet. The vellum packet containing my lost hopes for an Alcoran university crackled between us. "You can follow the map?"

"Yes," I said. "I know which blazes I need."

She sighed. "All right, then. Keep yourself safe. Wherever you end up, I'll find you." She kissed the top of my head, just under my star band. "The path splits in about a quarter mile. You two ride ahead. I'll try to cover your tracks and then lead the soldiers off. Don't tell the king until you're far enough away."

I nodded reluctantly. "All right. Be careful."

She huffed a silent laugh and released me. "No sense in being careful. Come on."

We headed back up the hill, where Celeno was still huddled under the fir tree. He cracked open his eyes.

"Everything all right?" he asked.

"Fine," I said, holding out my hand. "Come on. If we cover good ground, we can stop for lunch before noon."

"Try to keep up," my mother added. I winced. Perhaps it was for the best that we were separating—I wasn't sure we could have continued without one of them killing the other before the end.

While he mounted his mule, my mother and I exchanged a few items as surreptitiously as possible— the tin of fire capsules, the lantern, the map. Silently we negotiated switching places—me taking the lead, she taking the rear. Once everything was arranged, my mother nodded, and I guided my mule forward. Celeno followed silently behind.

We continued up the trail. I tried desperately to keep from glancing over my shoulder every half-second, sure we were about to be ridden down. After a quarter mile, we came to the split in the track, where a little side trail meandered off into the firs.

"Damn," my mother said loudly.

I swiveled my head. "What?"

"I think Checkerspot picked up a stone." She cursed again and swung to the ground. "Don't wait for me. I'll catch up." She bent over Checkerspot's foreleg and shifted him to lift his hoof. He heaved a sigh and patiently lifted his leg, unperturbed.

Stomach in knots, I turned back around and nudged my mule ahead. Celeno followed without a word. We continued in silence for ten minutes, fifteen. Distantly I heard a crash of timber, as if an old tree had fallen conveniently into the path.

"Should we wait for her?" Celeno asked.

"She said not to."

"Must have been a bad stone," he said flatly.

I swallowed and urged my mule a little faster.

We climbed the ridge, and despite my promise about lunch, noontime came and went. Celeno didn't comment—the few times I looked back, he was bent over again, his fingers tight on his reins. Buried in layers of anxiety, I continued, leading us on. The track narrowed; the firs grew so close they brushed our shoulders and dumped snow over our mules' haunches. Occasional breaks in the forest gave us views of the dramatic mountainscape, but we were still well below the tree line, and the vistas were quickly swallowed back up by snowy boughs.

In the early afternoon, as my mother had promised, the track crested a swell in the ridge and led into a small saddle between two peaks. At some point in history, a house-sized boulder had fallen from the cliffs above and made its resting place in the hollow. Propped against it was a two-sided lean-to, the rock making up its back wall. The front was open, revealing little more than a sleeping platform. A wooden crate served as both a worktable and a means to keep pests out of food supplies, and tucked in the corner was a stack of firewood. I led the way to the little holding pen of unworked logs and turned the mules into it.

As I hauled the saddlebags into the shelter of the lean-to, Celeno stood looking down the trail we'd just climbed. Carefully, I began to pack the items from the bags into the packs we would carry into the cave.

"Light's fading," I said, glancing up at the afternoon sky. "But given that we're going underground, I suppose it doesn't matter. I think we should get started right away . . ."

"I'm not stupid, Gemma."

I drew in a breath and looked up at his turned back. "I never said you were."

"Your mother went back," Celeno said, accusation heavy in his voice. "Didn't she?"

I looked down at the tin of fire capsules in my hands. "We were being pursued. She went to lead them away."

"Soldiers?"

"Yes. But she led them down a side trail. They're probably well away from us at this point."

"No sense in me riding back hoping for a rescue, you mean," he said.

Great Light, I hoped not. "No."

A few moments of silence passed. He drew his cloak a little more tightly around his shoulders.

"Lies, lies, lies," he said.

"Celeno . . ."

"Why won't you just tell me what the petroglyphs say?"

"I don't know! That's not a lie—neither my mother nor I know what they say." I tightened some of the buckles on my pack. "But even if I did, it would be irresponsible for me to tell you. What's the first principle we're taught in academic writing? In debate?" I watched as his mouth twisted bitterly. "Well?"

"Leading language," he conceded.

"Leading language," I agreed. "Leading language robs the scholar of the ability to come to their own conclusion. Our country has been ripped to tatters by folk trying to make the Prophecy mean one thing or another. We both have to approach this ready to accept what we see, not what we think we see."

"What's the point, Gemma?" He spread his arms. "A bunch of fragmented, faded glyphs in a remote mountain cave—you think it'll change anything? You think *my word* will change anything? You keep talking like they're a full Prophecy in pristine condition, but what if they're barely more than a few scratches? You're talking about a belief *literally* set in stone, what makes you think this will change—"

"Meteor showers, Celeno."

His words died in his throat. I hooked the field lantern to my pack and sat back on my heels.

"Our folk have studied the stars as long as we've been carving into the canyon walls," I said. "Our yearly calendar hinges around our biggest annual meteor shower—it's been the subject of both art and science for centuries. And for all that time, how did our astronomers explain the phenomenon of Starfall?"

He turned his head away, glaring into the distance.

"Atmospheric aberration," I supplied, if he wasn't going to talk to me. "Some kind of reaction that took place in our sky, like lightning, or rain. We thought we had the secrets of a meteor shower more or less figured out. And then a scholar came along who said, *wait, I think we've got this wrong.*"

His frown deepened, and he closed his eyes.

"What did your tutor say when you proposed

your thesis?" I asked. "Go on, what did she say when you suggested a cosmic source, instead of an atmospheric one?"

"That I was wasting my time."

"Yes. And despite that, you pursued it anyway. Years of work with the optical engineers to develop the right lens. Months of sleepless nights at your telescope." I could still feel the deep-set exhaustion as I slogged through my own lessons in the days after we both sat bent over his planisphere and squinting along his astrolabe, charting the exact angle and origin of the streaks of light flying through the sky. He'd been desperate to find an illustrator who would actually accompany him into the field, not just work from his notes, but I hadn't needed the double fee he'd offered to accept. His energy was infectious. I'd had a dutifully Alcoran reverence for the stars before, but his fascination quickly became my own, and I wanted answers to his questions as much as he. We'd hiked up a hundred different hilltops in the dead of night and shared every emotion between us. Frustration, when the night of peak meteor activity was obscured by clouds. Grief, when we sat silently in his star courtyard for the first time after his father's heart attack. Doubt, in our own eyes. Shock, when the evidence was undeniable. Joy, when his thesis was upheld.

"You changed the understanding of our most important national event—not just in Alcoro, but across the Eastern World," I said. "Lecture halls are filled now with astronomers detailing the cosmic origin of meteors—flying bodies from space, not in the clouds. You did that."

And I helped. After years of tiptoeing around my own losses, I helped him change astronomy books.

He looked away. "The origin of a celestial event is hardly the same as an entire belief system."

"I don't know, Celeno. Folk believed that what they knew was right. Now, I do wonder—would the consensus have been as quick to spread if it had come from a different scholar? One without a title and centuries of prophecy behind him?" I spread my hands. "I don't know. Other modern ideas have certainly taken longer to be accepted. But that doesn't worry me. You know why?"

"Gemma . . ."

"Because you're still the Seventh King," I said hotly. "Your words have a credibility no one else's have. That's something you've been running away from all your life. But Celeno, finally, right now, we have a chance to put that to actual use. We have a chance to find these petroglyphs, read them ourselves, and decide what they mean. And if the news comes from you, folk will believe it."

He had half-turned away from me, his arms crossed tightly over his chest. He stared down into the snow, a sharp crease in his brow.

"What are you not telling me?" he finally asked. "What?"

He shook his head. "You're still not telling me something."

My thoughts jumped to my worries about his tincture and the source of his persisting illness. But as I worked up the courage to tell him about Shaula, he turned his head to me.

"What's in it for you?"

My mind scrambled, switching tack like a sail in the wind. "You already asked me that question, back at Stairs-to-the-Stars."

"Yes, and you gave me an unsatisfying answer," he said. *"Peace of mind. Enduring fame.* What's your real motivation? What are you really hoping to get out of this?"

My mind flicked to Samna again, to the university. Building a new, quiet life in obscurity with my mother by my side—if we were lucky. It was a fantastical dream, one that relied on so many things to be fulfilled.

"I just want answers," I said. "I want a clear path for Alcoro—one that's based on fact, not speculation. Nothing else matters if that's not achieved." The university wouldn't matter if I left my country in ruins behind me.

He lifted an eyebrow. "I assumed you were expecting some kind of pardon at the end of all this."

I fixed the last clasp on his pack and pushed it toward him. "A pardon? No. I won't ask that of you. I have a hypothesis, and I want it answered."

He rolled his eyes toward the sky. "A scholar through and through."

I stood, slinging my own pack over my shoulders. "You know, at one time, I'd have said the same about you."

"It's been a long time since those days."

"Not that long, Celeno."

His lips twisted mirthlessly. "I suppose not." He sighed, stooped, and picked up the pack. He slung it over his shoulders. "All right then, in the name of science, let's go on."

CHAPTER 7

The air rushing out of the cave mouth felt like a spring breeze, though it couldn't have been more than fifty degrees. Celeno and I stood before it, studying the squat, lightless entrance. It was just a hair shorter than my head and hung with trailing moss, the snow around the opening melted by the cave's warm breath.

I had checked and rechecked our supplies and settled the mules in as well as I could in preparation for our absence. I'd reviewed the route on my mother's map, all the junctions to look out for, all the blazes that would bring us to our destination. But now, standing on the threshold, the nagging dread I'd been ignoring finally caught up with me.

Days. In this lightless, enclosed space.

Celeno was having second thoughts, too. "Gemma,

are you sure going in without your mother is a good idea?"

No, it was probably a terrible idea. I hefted my pack anyway. "It doesn't matter now—she's gone." I swallowed the lump in my throat and stepped forward. "Come on. The sooner we start, the sooner we come out."

I hope.

I ducked under the moss, the plants dripping water down my back as I moved forward. Fortunately, the space opened almost immediately, the ceiling arcing up and then down as the passage sloped away into the darkness. I heard the scrape of Celeno's pack on the rock as he straightened beside me.

I didn't see any sign of the *Arachnocampa luminosa*, but my eyes were still adjusting from the brightness of sun on snow outside. I took a few steps forward, placing my feet carefully on the damp rocks, trying to ignore the feeling of being swallowed by the mountain. We inched down the incline until finally reaching a bend that would take us out of sight of the entrance. I looked back once over my shoulder at the bright circle of light, familiar and reassuring.

"'Oh, that day would yet be quenched,'" Celeno recited drily, quoting from the traditional invocation in the twilight before Starfall. Normally it evoked an eager anticipation for the meteor shower yet to come. At the moment, it rang ominously. Heart pounding, I turned and continued around the bend.

My foot slipped on a loose rock, and I slowed, feeling my way down the slope with the toes of my boots. I was so focused on my feet and so intently trying to ignore the deepening darkness that I didn't think to look up until Celeno grabbed me by the elbow. I skidded on the slope, unsteady.

"By the Light," he exclaimed.

I looked up and sucked in my breath.

The glowworms. We had reached their beginning, and there truly had been no exaggerating them. They coated the tunnel ceiling as it arced downward, creating a long, straggling line of shining blue, like splashes of the galaxy painted overhead. Their deadly, silken strings hung down, diamonds on a wire, some drifting gently in the moving air as it rushed upwards toward the cave mouth.

"That's . . . not what I expected," he said. "These are what your mother studies?"

I nodded, mute. We stood silently for a moment, gazing down the broken rock tunnel. His fingers still clutched my sleeve—I could feel the tremor in them.

"It'd make a good painting," he said.

My stomach gave a tiny twist. I had just been thinking the same thing. It struck me that the best way to capture this sight would be to use similar methods that I used on his thesis. The night sky, glowworm colonies . . . little points of light against an encompassing darkness.

I shook myself and took a small step away. In response, he dropped my sleeve as if it had scalded him. I cleared my throat and pointed to the nearest larvae.

"The lures are sticky—try not to let them brush your hair."

He nodded, and by the light of the *Arachnocampa*, we continued.

The passage was not so much a trail as a rough opening cleaved through the earth—the ground was buckled and broken with old rockfall, and the walls were riddled with holes and rifts. Some of these were barely a hand's width across, while some were as wide as I was tall, and led away in different directions. But my mother hadn't been wrong about the way being marked. At every significant side passage, where there may be some confusion, white slashes were painted onto the cave wall, dimly reflecting the glowworms' light. These small signs of previous human presence eased the knot of apprehension in my stomach.

A little.

There was a stream, too, that flowed along the path, sometimes cutting from one side to the other, sometimes simply flowing straight down the middle. This worried me—as the light from the cave mouth grew fainter and fainter, I wasn't sure that we would be able to pick our way reliably among the rock and water. But before long, I realized we already were—a look over my shoulder yielded no additional light. The glowworms were the only illumination, and though both Celeno and I stumbled far more than once—he more than I—they cast enough light to distinguish looming shapes in the gloom.

Mostly.

There was a dull thud, and Celeno swore in pain. I turned to find him clutching his forehead above his eye and reaching out to prod a lumpy shape hanging down from the ceiling that I'd avoided by sheer luck.

"I thought it was moss or something," he said. "But it's stone."

I squinted up at the ceiling, where more hanging rocks made patches of darkness in the blue glow. I'd read about these . . . heard about them in geology lectures . . .

"*Speleothems,*" I finally remembered, running my fingers over the wet rock. "Cave formations—the running water deposits minerals in different ways."

"What's this one—a stalactite? Or stalagmite?"

"I don't remember." There was some clever turn of phrase my tutor had used to differentiate, but I couldn't recall what it was.

Celeno wiped his damp forehead, moving from the first speleothem to another patch of them near the passage wall—unlike the first, which was as fat as my leg, these were thin as reeds. "I wonder what makes them thick or thin—oh!"

He'd reached out to brush one of the skinny ones, and at the first delicate touch from his finger, it snapped off and landed on the floor of the passage, where it broke neatly in two. I stared at it at our toes, washed by a sudden feeling of remorse.

"Oh," he said again. "Does it . . . will it grow back?"

I looked up at the patch of fragile speleothems. A tiny bead of water gathered in the little crater left by the broken formation. As Celeno lifted his head, the droplet shivered and fell through the air, catching the faint blue light before it splashed onto his face.

"Eventually," I said as he wiped at the water. "But . . . maybe don't touch any more."

"No . . . no, I won't."

We continued. The passage leveled out, following the stream as it glimmered under the glowworms' light. After a while, the floor began to cant down toward it, making a slippery pitch that landed us both in the chilly water several times. Before long, I was soaked up to my knees.

We didn't speak. I tried to logically attribute it to the need to concentrate on finding our way in the gloom, but in reality, the deep loneliness of the cave seemed to quash the desire to talk. A few times, the stream flowed off into some hidden channel, leaving us without even the soft chatter of water. During these times, the silence seemed as solid a feature as the rock itself—a natural state of this place. Like the fragile speleothems, neither of us wanted to break it any more than necessary.

Mercifully, there were no cramped squeezes like there had been in the escape tunnel. I was able to keep a hold on my looming unease, taking marginal comfort in the high ceiling and wide walls. Still, I was shaky and tense, often finding myself holding my breath for no reason. At least the space smelled of wet stone—not stale air and dust, not dry wood, not the sweat drying on my skin . . .

There was a slow scrape and a splash. I jerked my gaze over my shoulder, jumpy. Celeno was on all fours in the stream. He coughed and got to his feet, shivering.

"Slipped," he said. "Kind of light-headed."

I tried to calculate the passage of time in my head, but it was impossible to know how far we'd come or what time it was outside. "Maybe you should eat something. If we find a good flat spot, we can stop. How's your stomach?"

"Bearable. Oh, look." He pointed above our heads. "Supper."

Several of the *Arachnocampa* lures started to swing wildly, the glittery strands wrapping around some doomed insect. As we watched, the larvae slid from its spittle hammock and began to draw up its thread.

Celeno cocked his head. "What do they eat? I mean, I see it's eating an insect, but it's winter, and we're deep underground. If they're trying to lure in flying bugs—and there's no others that I see—what do they eat?"

It was too dim to make out what insect had met its demise in the shining snare, but I didn't need to see it to identify it. "Each other," I said.

"Their own species?"

"The adults—once they pupate, they're just another flying gnat." I watched the insect twitch as the larvae drew it in. "Killed by their own kin."

He gazed up at the ceiling. "How morbidly ironic."

My laugh burst out of me—taking both of us completely by surprise. I choked it back, leaving the ragged end echoing off the stone. He stared at me as I pressed my fingers to my lips.

"What's so funny?"

My lips twitched behind my fingers. "Drowning cicadas."

His gaze dropped to the space between our feet, but not before I glimpsed his cheeks rounding into his own smile. I was filled suddenly with the memory of that day, lying in the shade of the cottonwoods on the canyon rim, the treetops thick with the drone of cicadas.

"I was trying to ask you to dance with me at Starfall . . ." he began, as if reluctant to dredge up the memory.

". . . and I didn't realize it," I said. "I was collecting data for my thesis . . ."

". . . and making me hold the vials while you shoved the poor wiggling things into the alcohol." He fought to get his smile under control before he looked back up. "It did affect the romance of the proposition."

It was my turn to look down. That afternoon was

the first time our friendship had inched toward something more intimate. We'd gone in increments—from mere acquaintances to students sharing a library table, and from there to assisting in each other's research. Friendship happened somewhere along the way, and then . . . that afternoon, filled with sun and awkward realizations and blushes and finally laughter, breaking the fumbling misunderstanding.

When I looked back up, his smile ghosted away, his gaze somewhere over my shoulder. "We didn't dance, though."

No, we didn't. Because that was the week his father died, and the country was plunged into mourning. Official Starfall celebrations were canceled, and the palace was draped in undyed linen. Instead of gowns and music and dancing until the meteor shower started, he and I lay silently on the gazing bench in his star patio, silent. He'd cried. I'd cried. We'd held hands, and when we both stopped crying, we had kissed for the first time.

The glowworm had reached its prey and was beginning to feast. Celeno let out a stilted sigh and wiped his brow—still sweaty, still with a shake to his fingers. I shuffled a bit, thrown by the unexpectedly intimate memories, and turned back around.

"I think there may be a wider chamber coming up," I said. "Maybe we can stop there for the night."

"*'Oh grant me not a starless night.'*" He gave a small,

joyless chuckle behind me. "And what a night it is, full of stars that devour their own kind. There's probably significance in there somewhere, don't you think?"

I was struck with an image of a sister imprisoning a sister, of a king executing a queen, of a country trapped by its own divine intent. A flash grenade on the riverbank.

"Or maybe they're just bugs," I said, turning away from the swinging lures.

Silently, he fell into step behind me, and we continued down the passage, leaving the cannibal larvae to its feast.

"Gemma."

"What?"

"What if it says a different king?"

I had just taken my star band off and looked up. We'd been silent for almost an hour, since pausing under the glowworms. We'd trudged on until the sloped ground rose into a kind of platform, curtained by speleothems, labeled *the Roost* on the map. It did feel like a little perch, well above the stream we'd been following. We'd set out our bedrolls with enough space for a bison to lie between us.

"What if they say the sixth king, or the tenth?" he continued, chewing on a corn biscuit. "What if they say the seventh *queen*?"

I turned my star band in my fingers, the three

gems catching the glowworms' light. "Maybe you shouldn't engage in speculation until you've seen them."

"Aren't *you* engaging in speculation?" he asked. "Surely you must be thinking about it. Go on—what do you think they might say?"

I threaded my fingers through my hair until I'd separated three distinct locks. "I don't know."

"Oh, come on. We used to live for scholarly debate."

"This has more impact than cicadas or meteors," I said. "And besides, I don't want to offer a suggestion and then have you cast it aside simply because it came from me. Leading language."

I started twining my hair into a braid—even trying to avoid the *Arachnocampa* lures, my hair had still gotten caught and tangled more than once. He was silent, chewing the biscuit. At least he was eating something. We'd taken the risk of lighting the lantern, and in the red-shielded glow, I could see the dark circles under his eyes and the sweat still glazing his forehead. I caught the scent of it, too, when he moved around, tangy and sharp.

"You seem to have no problem thinking I don't trust you anymore," he finally said. "You're not trying to deny anything or argue it away. You're just accepting it as fact."

"Maybe because I know there's no point in denying it," I said. "I acted against you."

"You threw a flash grenade."

"Yes."

"To let Queen Mona and Queen Ellamae and that Cypri rebel escape."

"Yes."

"He kicked me, you know," Celeno said. "In the head."

I did know. I'd watched the bruise form with my own horror.

He gazed at me a moment longer, chewing his biscuit. They were dry and crumbly, and he had to take a swallow of water before he could speak again.

"What are you not telling me?" he asked.

"A lot of things," I admitted, finishing the last few strands on my braid.

His brow creased in the ruddy light. "Why?"

"Because we have to see them first, Celeno." I tied off the end of my braid and let it fall down my back. "Nothing else matters until we see them ourselves."

He sighed in irritation. "Fine, then." He brushed off his hands and lay down, kicking off his boots. "Fine, we just won't talk about it until they're right there in front of us, and I hope that satisfies you. When will we reach them, tomorrow?"

"I'm not sure," I said. "We got a late start today, and we're moving slowly. It might take longer than we thought."

He huffed as he slid down into his bedroll. "For-give me if my wretched body isn't taking well to win-

CREATURES OF LIGHT 179

tertime mountaineering and corn tack. By the Light,
I want my evening tincture."

I let out a breath, feeling like a waterskin that's
been filled too full, ready to slop its contents at the
slightest nudge. I settled my star band back in my hair
and spread out my mother's map in my lap, looking
over our route. We'd made it partway down *Glowworm Avenue*. If my estimation was correct, we would
reach the *Ball of String* early the next day, a critical
confluence of several smaller passages that led in every direction, including up and down. It would be
imperative to follow the right one—the wrong passage would lead us into the tunnels my mother's team
hadn't yet mapped. No blazes, no trails.

No guarantee of an exit.

I pulled off my own boots and wriggled down
into my bedroll, the vellum packet shifting in my
shirt. I thought briefly of my mother—had she managed to lead the soldiers away? What if they'd caught
her? What if she couldn't make it back to Callais, or
couldn't convince anyone to listen to her?

I puffed out the lantern and settled on my back,
staring up at the patches of dim larvae colonies.
Their moon-blue light glistened off the lines of the
speleothems fringing the platform, catching in the
occasional drip from the pudgy ends of the stone formations.

"Tight," I said.

Celeno shifted and lifted his head. "What?"

"I just remembered," I said. "Stalac-*tites* cling *tight* to the ceiling. Stalagmites are on the ground."

He set his head back down and rolled over, putting his back to me. "Well. At least we have something figured out."

The Ball of String was aptly named, a massive dome-shaped hall riddled on all sides by passages, some large enough to send a cavalry through, others barely big enough to fit a jackrabbit. Several of the passages had blazes next to them, made up of specific shapes. I did a final double-check of the map.

"We want the single X," I said, looking for the right blaze across the hall.

"That passage there." He pointed. "Under the thing that looks like bacon."

The formation did look exactly like a piece of bacon, a giant ribbon of rock streaked red and white. It wasn't the only one—our little lantern gave glimpses of huge stone curtains sweeping from the ceiling. We craned our heads back as we passed underneath them, a hall of tapestries frozen in rock. I itched for my sketchbook.

The glowworms disappeared in the Ball of String and didn't reappear in the passage on the far side—we must have finally gone outside their habitat range, where even cannibalism couldn't sustain them. I lit the lantern again and held it out in front of us, trying to keep it from whacking against the slippery mounds of stone in our path, slowing and laboring our pace. Finally, after what felt like hours of clambering over and around lumpy stalagmites that rose like anthills from the floor, we stumbled into a much wider, straighter course. I blinked in the dim light— the floor shone like the surface of the moon in the lantern's reddish light, a perfect, flat trail meandering into the darkness. Even without looking at the map, I knew exactly where we were.

"Great shining Light," Celeno said in awe. "What is that?"

"The River of Milk," I breathed. "I didn't realize . . . I didn't think it would be so . . ."

"It's incredible," he said, crouching down beside it. "Like . . . snow. What is it, salt?"

"Calcite, my mother said." I crouched down, too. "Calcite deposits left behind by running water."

"Moon and stars." He peered into the distance, where the unmoving river ran straight and silent out of our lantern's reach. *"Reveal to me your light-led way."*

"You'll have quoted the entire invocation by the time we get out of here." I stood and edged toward the ledge that paralleled the River of Milk.

"It just seems so relevant." He paused. "Funny, that the Light should seem so present in such a dark place."

A few moments of silence passed. I set my feet carefully—the ledge wasn't entirely flat, and the wet rock was slippery. Though it was hardly a long fall into the dry creek bed next to us—only a few inches—I didn't want to land in the calcite. The surface was perfectly undisturbed, and the idea of marring it for all eternity rattled me.

"I wish we had known about this place before Cyprien," Celeno said.

I lifted my head. "To give us a route to Lumen Lake, you mean?"

"To what?" His pack scraped on the rock. "These go to Lumen Lake?"

"They might. My mother's team hadn't gotten there yet."

"You didn't tell me that," he said with a note of surprise.

"Oh—no, I suppose I didn't." I frowned, puzzled. "Wait, then why did you say you wish we'd known about them before Cyprien?"

He was quiet for several seconds. Then he gave a short, broken little laugh. "Well, because it would have been nice to explore them when you and I weren't at war with each other."

Heat rose under my collar. "Oh."

Yes, that would have been nice.

The silence became awkward, the air thick and stifling. The walls squeezed in dramatically, forcing me to walk in a half-crouch, tilted over to one side. The ceiling was also starting to lower, and the closer it got, the shorter my breath became.

"Why did you have to do it, Gemma?"

I banged my hand on a nub of rock as I steadied myself. Perhaps it was the pain, perhaps the anxiety of the constricting tunnel, perhaps just because I'd been carrying the question around with me for six weeks—the words just jumped out. "Why did you have to shoot Lyle Roubideaux?"

There was half a breath of shocked silence. "I've made my statement regarding that event. He was an armed rebel holding you hostage."

"We've *talked* about this," I said, ducking under an outcrop. "He was standing *behind* me, and the grenades were in his *pocket*."

"So you'll defend him before you even defend yourself—one of your abductors, the one who was going to use you to bleed Alcoro dry." I could almost hear him shaking his head. "What was he to you, that you're willing to put him above your own safety? Above *me*?"

"He wasn't anything to me!" I said sharply. "Not in the way you're implying. He was brilliant. He'd done incredible research. I liked hearing about his work. *You'd* have liked hearing about his work."

"I have heard about his work," he said with a touch of venom. "I've heard it's done wonders for our arsenal."

I stopped in my tracks. There was no space to turn around without my foot sliding into the calcite, so I simply clutched the rock walls, gritting my teeth.

"Say what you will about not being changed by the Prophecy," I said, "but there once was a time you never would have said that."

"Spare me the holier-than-thou attitude, Gemma. Forgive me if I haven't yet gotten over the memory of you bending over him, weeping, just moments before you betrayed your country. Betrayed *me*."

My eyes prickled as I forced myself to move forward again. "Maybe I just appreciated someone listening to me for a change."

"But they *weren't* listening to you! Those rebels, the Assembly of Six, Queen Mona—they would have leveraged you to take Cyprien from us!"

"We never *had* Cyprien!" I said. "We thought we had perfect control there, and we were wrong. They've been governing themselves since the annexation fifty-six years ago."

"All the more reason we needed that rebel as an informant, and the queens as assets! We could have stamped out the rebellion and the remnants of the Assembly, and secured our position in the waterways for good!"

This time I did whirl around, calcite be damned. My foot slid within an inch of the crisp white edge. Celeno skidded to keep from running into me, teetering into the sloping cave wall.

"And then what, Celeno?" I asked.

He struggled to right himself, sighing in irritation.

"And then a thousand possibilities that might have seen the Prophecy fulfilled, Gemma."

"What Prophecy?" I asked. "The one our folk have believed in for centuries? Or the one supposedly written on the cave wall?"

He pushed himself upright, his brow creased in the dim light. "You didn't know that at the time! You had no idea there was another Prophecy when you threw that grenade!"

I drew in a deep breath, my fists clenched. "Here's something I did know, after a week trapped on that little boat, listening to Queen Mona equivocate on Alcoro's actions, listening to Rou and Lyle discuss Cyprien's options: we can't take either of those countries a second time. Cyprien has shown us it's stronger than a single political system—it will outlast us whether we succeed or fail to uphold the Prophecy. And Queen Mona is in the process of allying the East in a way that hasn't been seen in centuries. Instead of gaining her friendship, we opened the door for her to rally everyone against us." I waved my hand. "Rou wouldn't have given you information—he'd have allowed himself to be killed first. And Queen Mona would have been useless as leverage."

Something in his eyes shifted. "I think you underestimate the effects a personal relationship has on political action."

He said it pointedly, each word weighted with

meaning—that he had mobilized Alcoro's entire presence in Cyprien to hunt for me, to bring me back safely from the hands of the River-folk. Because of that, we'd lost the harbor in Lilou, allowing our ships to abandon it to press inward, up the channels to Bellemere and Dismal Green. Because of me, we'd lost our most strategic holds on the country. Where we might have salvaged our control of the industry and infrastructure, instead we were battling open rebellion.

He wasn't wrong . . . except that none of that was my fault.

Or necessarily a bad thing.

A stilted silence passed between us, and then I turned back around, ducking under a protruding nub of rock. "I don't underestimate it at all. But I'm different from Mona, and Colm is different from you."

"Who?"

"Colm Alastaire, Mona's brother. She mentioned him in conversation." I scanned my memory to recall what the topic had been. "Star bands, I think. He was researching the history of star bands."

"So what?"

"So nothing. He's different from you, is all, and he was acting as regent in Mona's absence. There's no telling whether he'd have treated with us at all if we tried to use Mona as leverage. He was probably under orders not to."

"And Queen Ellamae?" he asked. "If we could have

broken the truce between Lumen Lake and the Silverwood, things might look very different for us."

"I don't know anything about King Valien or what
actions he would have taken," I said, "but I do know
that their truce was not casually won and wouldn't
have been easily undone."

His pack scraped the ceiling as he continued on
after me, so his following mutter was almost lost. "I
wouldn't have minded seeing her locked up in Callais, even if nothing came of it."

I braced my hands on the slanting wall, trying to
keep my breathing regular. "Why?"

"Great Light, she's the reason we're in any of this
mess in the first place. She led Queen Mona back to
the lake. She misled our soldiers to let the Lake-folk
stage their uprising." He sighed in aggravation. "If
only our informants could have been just a few days
quicker getting us the news of spotting her in Rush-
er's Junction, we might have made it to the lake before they did. *Ow.*" There was a thud as he knocked
his head on the ceiling. "How much farther does
this blazing hole go? Shouldn't we be close?"

"Yes," I said, my voice high from my own dread.
"Yes, we should be very close." *Please let us be close.*
The distance had looked like nothing on the map, just
a short walk down the River of Milk and into the side
passage to the petroglyphs. I hadn't reckoned on it
shrinking so dramatically. My whole body clenched

in on itself, my heart, lungs, head, and stomach all tangling and twisting together.

I had to keep talking. For my own sanity, I had to keep talking.

"Samna," I squeaked.

"What about Samna?"

It was the first thing that had popped into my mind, but I followed it. "The university. The winter pamphlet should be out."

There was a long pause. An errant drip of water splashed on my head and trickled down the back of my neck.

"Yes," he said. "It probably is out."

"You haven't read it yet?"

"Great Light no, Gemma."

I bit back my anticipated questions about the content of the pamphlet, the new academic articles and philosophical speculation by the university scholars. We used to dive into those pamphlets the moment they arrived on our shore, fantasizing for hours on end about making the trip across the sea ourselves.

"It came the day we got back to Callais," he said, his voice oddly strained. "I watched them take you away to the Retreat, and then I went into our rooms to find it lying on my desk. I don't think I've missed reading one since I was eight, but I couldn't bring myself to open it. Not then. Not after . . ."

A hundred things jumbled together in my head—the need to move quickly, the urgency of distracting myself from this tunnel, the rising panic of entrapment, the web of emotion stemming from thinking about those university pamphlets and how they had been a lifeline for the both of us. How he'd brought them to me on the nights I felt the most frightened and alone, sneaking out to the Prism's star courtyard to examine them by moonlight. How we'd pored over them together while sprawled along the canyon rim, our bodies carelessly draped across each other. How I'd read them aloud when he was sick in bed, his shadowed eyes closed as he listened.

"I thought someday we would go," he said quietly.

I didn't know how to reply—didn't know how to have this conversation that we used to have day after day, full of hope and eager anticipation, the possibility not yet extinguished. But my reply never came, because at the next forward shuffle, my hand slid into empty air. I stumbled a little in surprise—the passage had opened unexpectedly around a slight bulge of rock. I heard Celeno wobble behind me as he came to his own abrupt stop.

"What is it?" he asked.

"We're here," I said. "The side passage."

"Oh, good," he said. "Is it bigger?"

The tangles of dread in my body tightened into knots of pure terror. "No," I said. "It's not bigger."

"How can it be any smaller and still be a passage?"

"It's taller," I said, edging forward so he could see. "But it's narrower." So, so narrow—the walls swept in toward the ground, leaving only a narrow crevice to set feet in, but that was hardly the worst of it. From shoulder-height to the ground, the passable space was hardly wider than the twin span of my splayed fingers. The ceiling buckled and dipped just a half a foot above our heads. I thought back to my mother's description of her colleague who had mapped these tunnels—she'd equated him to a cockroach.

I hadn't fully grasped what such a title insinuated.

"We're going to have to take off our backpacks," Celeno said. "You're sure this is the right passage?"

"The double X," I said, pointing to the white paint on the wall. "It's the blaze to the petroglyphs."

"And then how far?"

"Not far, less than a hundred yards."

"Sure seems far when it's no wider than an open flue." He grimaced and slid his pack from his shoulders. "Let's get it over with, I guess."

How could he be so calm? How could he be so ready to put his body into this tiny space? I could barely keep control of my limbs—they alternated between hollow and shaky to heavy as a ship's anchor. Why hadn't my mother warned me about this passage?

"Come on," Celeno said, a little impatiently. "I want to see these things and get out of here."

Slowly I slid my arms out of my pack straps and lowered it to the ground. Taking a breath—my last deep one?—I turned my body sideways, clutching the lantern in my leading hand and my pack in the other, and shuffled a few steps into the tunnel.

The rock walls were damp and squeezed my breasts and stomach unforgivingly, and it occurred too late that I should have unbuttoned my bolero to avoid popping the clasps off. But Celeno was already moving next to me, and if I withdrew from this place, I wasn't sure I'd have the courage to try a second time. So I edged sideways, unable to see my feet or legs or anything beyond the red glint of wet rock just inches from my eyes.

There was no point in talking. Even if I had the breath to spare for it—the tight space was forcing me to take short sips of air—my brain was too blank to think. What had we been talking about before? The winter pamphlet . . . Lyle Roubideaux . . . star bands? I felt my own band slide a little as I ducked under a bulge of rock. Why had we been talking about star bands? *Had* we been talking about star bands?

Mona. We'd been talking about Mona.

No, we'd been talking about her brother, Colm. Dizzy and drifting, my mind latched onto that like a kind of buoy. Colm Alastaire, Mona's brother. One of two brothers. A scholar of cultural history. Doing research on the evolution of Alcoran ladies' traditional hair ornaments—among other topics. Reading the documents we'd left behind after he and his sister and an impossible host of others had driven Alcoro out of Lumen Lake.

History in Alcoro wasn't considered quite as prestigious a pursuit as the hard sciences and mathematics, practiced mostly by hobbyists and harmless eccentrics. The kind of religious bickering my mother used to engage in—*still does engage in*, I reminded myself— was the most common form of public history debate. But, as my mother could attest, delving too deep resulted in inquiries, fines, and, occasionally, jail time. Perhaps this was what had led to the general consensus that history was the realm of the Prelacy. Alcoro's history, after all, had always been coupled with the Prophecy. The words of the Prism were our country's past, present, and future—what else was there to study?

Certainly not the cultural practices of other countries.

My stomach, already a mess, squirmed further. A little itch tickled my brain, the same kind of spark that had flared back when I first started wondering if the cicada really was what scientists always said it was.

This is odd.

This is flawed.

What if . . . .

What if, hypothetically speaking, our relegation of history and culture as hobbyists' pursuits had somehow altered our international relations? What if—*hypothetically*—devoting ourselves to one singular History—the history made and forecast by the Prophecy—blinded us to those quietly carrying on around us, unconcerned with the interminable current of the Seventh King?

Moon and stars, I had only been trying to focus on something to take my mind off this horrendous squeeze, not found an entire thesis proposal. How had I gotten here?

Colm Alastaire.

A scholar of cultural history.

So what? *So nothing.*

My feet tripped underneath me, catching on a swell in the floor, but the passage was too tight for me to fall. I sagged, my knees cracking on the rock. The lantern banged against the wall, sending shadows tilting and spinning around us.

"You okay?" Celeno said behind me, his voice muffled.

"Fine," I said breathlessly, though I was far from it. "The floor rises a little."

"Can you get through?"

"Yes, it's . . . it's not bad." Swallowing, I twisted my foot at an awkward angle and slithered through the cramped space. My pack scraped along behind me. Sideways, sideways. I took another few steps, forced up on tiptoes by the narrow slice of passable ground.

Celeno puffed out a breath. "Good thing we haven't had more to eat than a few biscuits and jerky, or this would be *really hard*."

If it was a joke, I couldn't laugh. Devoid of my mental anchor from a moment before, I was too caught up in memories of closed doors, of tight walls, of bruised knees and elbows and the sense that nothing, ever, was going to change—there *was* no moving air, no sun, no open space. Only darkness and my own breath washing over my face . . .

With a shock like a plunge, I stumbled into empty space. I wobbled at the new freedom of movement, my body trying to reassess its surroundings. The ceiling remained the height it was—less than a foot above my head, but the walls swept away to form a small, irregular room, no bigger than the footprint of the bed we used to share.

"Woah!" Celeno staggered out of the squeeze after me. "Well, that's a relief. Are we here?"

I wiped a trembling hand over my brow. "I'm not sure." I lifted the lantern and shone it on the wall before us. It was ridged and striped with minerals, and it took me several seconds to realize there were no human-made carvings among the rippled stone. I turned to the next wall, and the next, running my hand over the wet rock, squinting at every divot and shadow, searching for the familiar lines and curves of the ancient script. But nothing jumped out—no fragment, no whisper.

"I don't understand," Celeno said, peering at a streak of orange mineral. "Where are they?"

I turned back to the wall opposite the little squeeze we'd just wedged ourselves through, my confusion rippling with the first drop of alarm. No, this couldn't be . . . my mother had said . . . I'd followed the blazes, we'd come all this way . . . *but, but, but . . .*

I tilted the lantern for better light, and that's when my gaze dropped down near our feet, to the black line I'd assumed was a shadow.

It wasn't a shadow. It was an opening under the rock, perhaps ten inches high.

Painted above it, bold and shimmery in the light, were two white *X*s.

"Oh, damn," Celeno said, following my gaze. "Do we have to go *under* that?"

No, no. No, that couldn't be right. I cast the lantern around the little chamber again, but the walls remained solid and immobile. There were no other passages or openings. Slowly I looked back at the little gap.

No. This *couldn't be right.* My mother would have told me. *Why hadn't my mother told me?* The lantern swung as my hand shook. The crevice remained unchanging in the dancing light, a solid yawn of darkness. I took an involuntary step backwards just as Celeno crouched down to peer into it.

"Hand me the light," he said, stretching out his hand. "I don't think it goes very far."

Numbly I passed it to him, and he held it to the opening.

"I think I can see where it rises," he said. "I'd say it's seven, eight feet, maybe a little more. We'll have to slide."

"I can't," I whispered.

"What?"

"I *can't*."

He looked up. "Why not?"

I squeezed my hands to my chest, my whole body bloodless. Eight feet or a mile, I could not cram myself into such a miniscule space. "I . . . I can't go in there."

"I think you can make it—somebody else already has, and unless they were tiny, I don't see why we can't."

My eyes were fixed on that dark void. "You're not afraid?"

"I mean, I'm not wild about the idea, but isn't this the whole point?" He squinted at me in the ruddy light. "Why, are *you* afraid?"

"Yes," I whispered.

"You crawled through a tarantula-infested cellar just a few days ago."

I would take the tarantulas over this—I would take *every* tarantula in Alcoro over this, and every rattlesnake and scorpion as well. I'd wade a hundred sewers and brave a thousand teeming middens over this lifeless, crushing sliver of dark.

"I can't do it, Celeno," I said again.

He sat back on his heels. "Well, then, what was the point of everything? Shall I just go through on my own? I thought you wanted to see them, too."

I did want to see them. I *needed* to see them.

We didn't have good transcription materials in our packs—only a single charcoal nib and enough parchment for one rubbing and one copy. This hadn't been meant to be a research trip. It had been meant to be a survey, to tell us if further examination needed to be done. What if Celeno didn't copy it just right? What if the wall was wet, like this one, and a rubbing couldn't be made? What if the parchment tore, or got soaked?

I needed to see them.

I let out my breath—not without first savoring the feeling of it in my lungs.

"All right," I said.

"All right?"

"All right, I'll go through," I said.

"Do you want me to go first?"

"No . . . I will." I stared at the shadows. "I will," I repeated, as if saying it again might make it easier.

"I mean, the petroglyphs *are* on the other side, aren't they?" he asked. "If we want to see them, we have to go forward?"

"Yes." I set my pack down by the opening—I would have to drag it next to me. "We can only go forward."

"All right, then," he said. "I'll follow."

I crouched down next to the crevice and peered into it. The light from the lantern, even shielded as it was, washed out the view of the far side, giving the impression of an endless chasm.

"Douse the light," I said, my voice steadier than I felt.

"What? Why—"

"We can't drag it through when it's lit. And besides . . ." I cupped my palms around my eyes, trying to shut out the burning wick. "I think there may be larvae on the far side."

He turned down the flame and plunged us into darkness. I blinked a few times. As my eyes adjusted, sure enough, glinting through the gloom was a faint blue glow, perhaps ten feet away. These glowworms. They were survivors, hidden deep in these barren holes, feasting on their kindred. Their light seemed to be magnified in the surrounding rock—was there more calcite here, reflecting the starry hammocks?

Oddly buoyed—in a grim, desperate sort of way—I lowered onto my seat and lay down onto my back. I almost rolled to my stomach, but I didn't like the idea of holding my head up off the floor. Without allowing myself any longer to think, I reached up and dragged myself under the ledge.

At first, it didn't seem nearly as tight as I'd thought. There was room enough for me to bend my knees and propel myself forward. I hauled the pack alongside me, using my free hand to find purchase in the low ceiling. One push, two, three, four—I was well under the ledge, with only my feet sticking out. I felt Celeno's hand rest on my boot.

"Everything okay?" he called.

I wiggled my foot in response, unwilling to break my concentration with words. I craned my head upwards, straining to see out the other side. There was that little ribbon of bioluminescence, dim and cool. I pushed again. My knees scraped the ceiling, chafing my already battered skin. I splayed them out slightly and moved a bit farther.

I couldn't see the ceiling up above me, so it came as a surprise when I craned my head again and my nose brushed cold stone. I drew in a sharp breath. Great Light, it was barely an inch above my face. My body flushed with a hot wave of fright. Trying desperately to ignore the countless tons of rock suspended above me, I pushed forward again. But the ceiling slanted downward, and my knees caught once more. I wriggled until my legs were straight, using my whole body to inch forward like an upside-down snake.

When the rock pressed my nose again, I stopped, my heart racing. I had no space to look for the opening. The panic I had somehow ignored before rose, sudden and strong, like storm rolling over the canyon rim. With the panic came a flush of memories— thick, sticky air, the smell of musty wood, a body I couldn't shift or move or even feel, my muscles seizing and cramping . . .

Slowly, I turned my head to the left and slid forward again. My right ear brushed rock. At first I tried to blink away the tears that sprung to my eyes, but after a moment I simply let them fall—I couldn't see anyway. I tried to relax my body, but the ceiling was crushing me now, front to back, squeezing me from temples to breasts to thighs. I was caught, moving in barest increments. The pack wedged in place, unable to squeeze through the scant inches of free space.

"Are you stuck?" Celeno asked.

I couldn't answer, couldn't shake my head, pressing against the wood—rock—praying someone would open the door . . .

And then, the realization.

We would have to go back.

Even if I got through this alive, we would have to turn around and go right back under.

Gone were the last threads of lucidity, replaced only by an ambient terror. It crippled my body, made it tighten and swell in the shrinking space. I writhed, kicking and choking, my muscles rigid and strangled. I couldn't draw breath, couldn't force air past the block in my throat . . .

Why hadn't my mother told me?

The answer rushed to me along with the dizzy memories. She hadn't told me, because she hadn't been this far, and she hadn't told me, because she hadn't thought it would matter this much.

This dread, this horror—this had all been born *after* she disappeared.

This had all been born *because* she disappeared.

"Gemma?" Celeno's voice bounced off the rocks. "I'm going to push you."

My voice broke from me. "No," I rasped, using my last slips of air. "No, don't—"

He put his feet against mine and shoved. My face scraped along the rock, peeling off a layer of skin on my cheek. I gasped, lost in a crush of panic, but he pushed once more, and to my surprise, breath rushed into my lungs, inflating them like crushed bellows. I sucked in another draught and cracked open my eyes. There, high above me, were tiny blue points of light, sparkling in jeweled strings. Even the walls seemed to gleam—not just the dull glint of water on rock, but a faceted, gem-like shine. Shaking, devoid of strength or thought, I dragged my hand out of the darkness and grasped the edge of the ledge. With a hollow-limbed pull, my chest broke free of the squeeze—indeed popping off a clasp on my bolero—and then I was through.

I lay panting on my back on the jagged stone, staring up at the glimmering ceiling and walls, my fist still clenched around my pack strap like a lifeline. I heard the scrape and puffing of Celeno following after me, the lantern rattling along with him.

"Damn," he grunted, his voice muffled. *"Damn."* A scuff, a slide. "Can you reach in and hook my pack? It's not wanting to come with me."

My body felt encased in sand, but slowly I rolled off my back and crawled to the opening. His head was about a foot below the ledge, waggling as he wedged his body through the gap. Numbly I slithered my leg back into the crevice and prodded with my toe for the pack.

"No, that's my cloak—there, you've got it. I'm letting go."

I hooked the strap with my boot and hauled it toward me. He placed both hands on the floor and pushed. The pack caught on a nub of rock, and I tugged at it. After a short resistance, it popped free, accompanied by the crack and shatter of glass.

"What was that?" Celeno puffed, his hair emerging from beneath the ledge.

"One of the shields," I said, dragging the pack the rest of the way out. "One of the lantern shields broke."

"Oh well." He grunted, and his forehead appeared, coated with sweat and grime. "By the *Light*."

I reached in and gripped him under his shoulders. Between the two of us, he slid free and sagged against me. We both lay for a moment, splayed on the stone.

After he'd caught his breath, he lifted his head. "Moon and stars, that was *awful*. Did we make it? Is this it?"

"I don't know," I said. I couldn't seem to raise my shoulders off the ground—what if we'd only gone partway, and there were still more horrors in front of us? I realized I was still crying—distantly so, the tears just seeping from my eyes like it was my natural state of being. Stress crying. Stress crying forever.

Perhaps Celeno noticed, because he looked down

at me where I lay staring at the starry ceiling with blurry eyes. "Are you okay?"

"I lost my head," I said softly. "I'm sorry."

"I can't say I'm looking forward to going back under," he said, and then paused. "But I forgot—you never liked small spaces, did you?"

"Not really," I whispered. It had never come up all that often. When did one go around squeezing through spaces too small to stand up in? Stairs-to-the-Stars was massive and airy, and any cramped quarters— carriages, ship cabins—had windows. Doors. Moving air.

A means to get out.

Again my memories swirled around me—that tiny cupboard in the twirly house, the one where we kept the basket of sweet potatoes, the ones we'd dug and washed so carefully the week before. Mother had pulled out the potatoes and thrown them haphazardly in the corner. *Hide,* she'd said. *Hide, and don't come out until I come get you.* It was a little space, barely big enough for a knobbly eight-year old to sit with her knees up at her chest, adobe wall on one side, the cupboard door on the other.

And I'd hidden. And I hadn't come out, because the door wouldn't open.

When it finally did, it wasn't Mother on the other side.

In the dim light, Celeno shifted. Hesitantly, it seemed, he laid his hand on my arm.

"Are you okay?" he asked again.

I shook myself, trying to banish the memories and panic and feeling of being crushed in the belly of the earth. "I will be, once this is over." I felt in the shadows for the lantern, wary of the broken glass. One side had been dented in the break—I hoped it hadn't affected the oil reservoir. Retrieving another fire capsule—we had seven left, I should be more judicious with them—I crunched one in the pliers.

The space around us blazed white, bright as a lightning strike. Celeno and I both yelped in unison, flinging our faces into our elbows.

"What happened?" he asked, his voice cracked. "Did the something ignite?"

There was no heat or crackle of flames beyond the little flare at the end of my pliers, and I hadn't even held it to the wick yet. Slowly, blinking tears out of my light-starved eyes, I lowered my arm.

"Oh!" I gasped.

Celeno looked up, his lashes wet, and squinted through the shine.

"Crystals," I said.

The chamber we had crawled into was long and narrow, the far end lost in shadow. Around us, growing like jeweled mushrooms from every wall and crevice, were clear, translucent crystals, some as big as my foot. They thrust in all directions, their perfect surfaces mirroring and diffusing the little flame in my pliers.

"By the Light," Celeno exclaimed, twisting his head this way and that. "Are they diamonds?"

The fire dimmed, having burned almost all of its paper, and quickly I held the last flickers to the lantern wick. The glow around us turned red, save for the side with the broken shield, shining a beam of white through the little hall. I turned the wick as low as it would go to avoid blinding us and set it near a cluster of egg-sized crystals. Gently, I prodded one. It was slightly warm to the touch, and almost silky, denting easily under my fingernail.

"Not diamonds," I said. "And not calcite, I think." I racked my brain for the handful of geology lessons I'd had, as well as the briefings I could remember from the few operational mines left in Alcoro. "Gypsum, maybe? I think it can create crystals like this, though I thought they had to develop in water. Perhaps this route used to be flooded."

"Are they valuable?" Celeno wiggled one spar the size of his thumb, and it broke off near the base. He held it in his palm, the light flashing off the cut surfaces.

"I don't know, maybe as a building material—don't break any more off, Celeno," I said as he reached for a bigger spar. "Don't—they're probably ancient. Thousands, maybe hundreds of thousands of years old. Please leave them."

He withdrew his fingers from a bloom of the moonwhite minerals. "I just thought, you know, wealth and prosperity, and all that. If we've been guided here by the Prophecy, who's to say it's not some kind of fulfillment?"

I was about to reply, when his shifting shadow drew my gaze up the wall behind him. My forming words fell apart into a sort of squeak. Drawing in a breath, I nodded to the wavering shadows. "Because we've been guided here by that instead."

He turned in place, following my gaze to the bare place in the rock where, whether by geology or supernatural intervention, the crystals failed to grow. Scratched into the wall, faded by the slow seep of water, the faint traces of petroglyphs flickered in the shadows.

We both stood at the same time, our boots sweeping scuff marks in the grit on the floor. I held the lantern high, directing the unshielded beam sideways across the marks to sharpen their appearance.

For an endless minute, we both simply stared. The silence crowded in around us, so intense I thought I could hear the pounding of his heart along with mine. I read the cyphers, and then read them again, and again. My gaze went from tracing a recognizable pattern to simply darting this way and that, as if searching for new meaning in serendipity.

E . . . RE . . . EATURES . . . F THE LIGHT, it began.

"No," Celeno said, as if in surprise. "No, these . . . Gemma, these are . . ."

Useless. Utterly, agonizingly useless.

E . . . RE . . . EATURES . . . F THE LIGHT
ND . . . OW . . . ERFEC . . .
D . . . EIG . . . SEVENTH KIN . . .
W . . .

"*Gemma*," Celeno said again, this time a little louder—was it panic, or anger? "Gemma, these aren't almost complete, or even a little bit complete. These say *nothing!*"

Numbly, I moved forward, as close as I could to the wall without clambering over the beds of crystals. I reached out and brushed the nearest cypher.

"All this way," Celeno continued behind me. "All this time, all the chaos we've caused back at home—Gemma, Alcoro's probably in crisis without me—all that for *this*?"

"There's something here," I said, my heart in my throat. "Something before the *seventh king*."

"Those cyphers could mean anything! I'm not entirely convinced that one on the left is more than a divot of missing rock!"

"It's real," I said, tracing it. "It's a *d* root, here's the stem, and the dot above . . ."

There was a shattering sound behind me, and a few fragments of crystals skittered my way. I jerked around to see Celeno standing over a broken pile of gypsum, scattered outward where he'd kicked a mound of the spars. He was staring down at the pieces, his face screwed up in frustration and pain.

Anger, then. Anger *and* panic.

"Celeno . . ." I said softly.

"I should never have come with you," he said, still gazing unseeing at the destroyed gypsum spars. "I should never have left Callais." He dragged both hands over his face and left them there. "And now we have to go *back* with nothing to show for it."

"It's . . . not nothing, Celeno—at least we've seen there are actual fragments," I said. "That's something. And we know there are more—if we can find them, compare them . . ."

"Aggregated field research isn't going to save us, *Gemma!*" he said sharply, his hands still over his face. He groaned through his fingers. "For some stupid reason I thought all this might change things, that it might give me something for the council, something to stop them arguing about your sentence . . ."

"But if we can—" I stopped halfway through my next plea. "To stop the council arguing? What's there left to argue about?"

He tossed his hands into the air, baring his pale, haggard face. "Oh, I don't know, only the warrant for your execution half of them have been hounding me with since Dismal Green."

"But," I said, my mind foggy with too many new variables. "But . . . you signed it already."

"Signed what?"

"The execution order!"

"I haven't signed it," he said, bewildered. "Axa and Telleceran have been after me for weeks, jumping out at me from every corner . . . that's half the reason I fled Callais with you."

I stared at him. "What?"

"You needled me about it, in the bedroom. Something about attending your hanging. I thought you knew they were trying to get me to sign it."

"I thought you *had* signed it," I said in disbelief. "Shaula had the document with your signature on it. She was sending it out to the generals for when they recaptured me."

"I never signed a death warrant. I've been slipping them for weeks, trying to figure something out, but I kept hitting dead ends. I thought maybe this would give me something to negotiate with."

The air resonated with silence. I faced him with lips parted and eyes wide, holding the lantern high as if it might make things clearer. He gazed back, his brow furrowed—I could actually see the thoughts turning over in his mind.

"Oh," he said, suddenly comprehending. "Wait a minute . . ."

"You didn't sign it," I repeated numbly.

"All this time—" he began.

"But she had the document . . ."

"You thought that I . . ."

"She said she finally had it."

"Gemma, did you really think . . ." He straightened. "Gemma . . . you didn't really think I would order your execution?"

"Well . . . yes, to be honest! I was already at the Retreat. It didn't seem a stretch . . ." I shook my head. "But do you know what this means? Shaula is *forging your signature*. She's not just acting in your name, she's *falsifying your own orders*. In matters of life and death!"

He broke his gaze away from mine, staring again at the broken gypsum on the floor, his eyes flicking unseeing over the ground.

"N . . . no," he began hesitantly. "Why would she? How could she?"

"Because you wouldn't do it yourself," I said. *He hadn't done it himself. He hadn't ordered my death.* "Because, in her mind, most likely, you were resisting the machinations of the Prophecy."

He twitched his head back up. "How does the execution of my wife have anything to do with the Prophecy? It *doesn't have anything to do with it*."

"To Shaula, everything has to do with the Prophecy." A thought occurred to me. "Did you order a military draft in Cyprien?"

He spread his hands, his voice tinged with rising alarm. "This doesn't make any sense—why would she do this?"

"*Celeno*. The military draft in Cyprien."

"What draft?" he asked. "The only draft I remember was the one the Council was debating before we made the decision to meet Queen Mona in Lilou. But you convinced them to stall it—and anyway, that was months ago."

I closed my eyes. "In Cyprien, one of the reasons Rou gave for the rebellion was the impending draft. The order had been put through to the governor before we arrived in Lilou. It was the first I'd heard of it—I assumed Shaula had convinced you to sign the decree without telling me."

"When have I *ever* done that?"

My eyes flew open. "Forever? My name never goes on official documents! Yours is the only one that matters! Your choices are the only ones that matter!"

"But I've never not *told* you . . ." My words registered. "You can't really think that?"

"Your actions have the Prophecy behind them," I said, trying to keep the bitterness from my voice. "Mine don't, Celeno. That's always been our truth."

"Gemma," he said incredulously. "I tell you *everything*. What would I be without you? Every decision I've ever made, you've helped me make it. That's how it was even back when we were students. I'd never sign something without asking you first. I never have."

None of this made any sense despite the pieces all lining up in a perfect row. I shook my head again. The lantern swung in my fist, making the crystals shudder and dance.

"You took down our wedding portrait," I finally said.

He paused again. "I couldn't look at it. I couldn't pass by it every day with you gone."

The silence pressed in around us, threaded with the scents of damp rock and mineral and sweat. My mind reeled with this new information—he hadn't ordered my death. Shaula had, and she'd done it without his knowledge. He'd been holding out—against the warrant, against the Cypri draft . . .

Against what else?

How many other things had he rejected and yet had slid through the Council anyway?

How many things had he approved that had been quietly overturned?

How long had this been going on?

How had I missed it?

My lips tightened. I hadn't missed it. I had always seen it, and accepted it as part of my role. I had always assumed that I simply wouldn't be part of everything. I'd always assumed I was an accessory to a monarchy that could just as soon operate without me.

Celeno let out another long, slow sigh, rubbing his face.

"We have to go back," he said again, his voice bleak. "*I* have to go back into that rat's nest, and figure something out. We're right back where we started."

Except we weren't right back where we'd started. We had made new discoveries. We had gathered more data. And we were halfway under the Stellarange Mountains, surrounded by glowing insect larvae and living crystals and fragments that somebody had carved here. Somebody—whether it was the Prism or one of his followers—had to trace a similar route that we had. Somebody had to squeeze their body under the same ledge we had. Unless the rock had moved and shifted that drastically in the last several hundred years.

Or, unless . . .

I looked down the narrow hall to where the room was swallowed up by darkness.

Unless there was another way in.

Another way *out*.

Celeno was still staring despondently at the bits of petroglyphs, his shoulders sagging. I noticed his hands trembling again—the muddy fabric of his cloak twitched with his movement.

"Let's get some rest," I said. "Have something to eat, and get some sleep. We can start again when we've had a chance to think a little more clearly."

He puffed out his breath, but without any further comment, he folded his legs and sank to the ground. The walls were too thorny with crystals to rest against, so he simply slumped down on his side, his head clutched in his arms.

He stayed that way as I moved about, parceling out some food and laying out our bedrolls. He moved only to take a few bites of jerky and a swallow of water, and then to wiggle into his bedroll. After that he rolled to his other side and pulled his cloak over his head, his breath labored and raspy.

But I didn't lie down. I sat on my bedroll, the crystals reflecting the barest light from the lantern, and spread out my mother's map. I stayed that way well into our supposed night, thinking, staring, calculating, guessing. I traced distances with my fingers. I gazed at the petroglyphs. I ran my fingers over the warm, malleable crystals, my mind full of the machinations and implications of gypsum and flowing rock, astronomy and cultural history, millipedes and glowworms, and people, people, *people.*

I looked at the nearest cluster of crystals. Despite what I'd said to Celeno, I reached for a fat, tapered one and broke it off. I gazed at it in my hand, the broken edge leaving a few specks of white powder on my skin.

Maybe we did have to go back.

But maybe we could go forward in the process.

CHAPTER 8

"Celeno, wake up."

He shifted under my gentle shake, his face slack with sleep. I hated to rouse him, but I'd given him as much time as I thought we could afford, and now I was anxious to get going. "Wake up."

He blinked blearily and coughed through his raspy throat. "Gemma? What time is it?"

"I have no idea. But you slept several hours, and now we need to go."

He sat up, groggy. "Did you sleep?"

"Some. But I also did some scouting. This isn't a hall." I pointed down into the shadows—even where the lantern beam faded away, crystals glinted in the light of the glowworms above. "The passage keeps going, and it's marked with blazes. I've done some figuring with the map, and it should bring us where we want to go."

He peered owlishly into the gloom. "Are you sure? I don't like the idea of going down an uncharted tunnel."

"I just told you, it has blazes. I went down it for about a half an hour, and there are Xs where the crystals don't grow. My mother's colleague must have mapped a little further."

"If there are blazes, why didn't we come in that way, instead of squeezing under that blasted ledge?"

"It's a roundabout route," I said. "It goes in a big arc—longer, but less tight." I glanced at the ink-dark slice we had squeezed under the day before, and I took a breath. "I . . . I can't go that way again, Celeno. I can't make myself go back in there. This way may be longer, but it looks bigger—bigger even than the passage along the River of Milk."

He sighed and raked his fingers through his grimy hair. "All right. I don't relish the idea of squeezing anymore, either. But, Gemma, if things feel off—if it seems like we're not going the right way, we need to turn around, okay? I'd still choose slithering under rocks over dying of starvation under the Stellarange."

"All right." I held out my hand to him. "Let's get going."

I bundled up his bedroll and fixed it to his pack, and then we set off. The way seemed especially bright now with the faceted gypsum crystals coating the walls, reflecting the beam from our broken lantern and the steady glow of the *Arachnocampa* above. The relative brightness helped me ignore my own nagging misgivings—they seemed to trail just over my shoulder, every now and then prodding me to rethink my decisions.

But I had already done a lot of thinking, trying to plot out the most realistic series of events that might transpire once we arrived back in Alcoro. Even the best-case scenario—one where my mother had managed to convince the Council to indict Shaula—still carried the persistent threat of war. Removing Shaula might stem the free-bleeding wound of corruption within Stairs-to-the-Stars, but it wouldn't undo the alliance of our neighboring countries, nor stop them from striking back at our forces already pressing further and further beyond our own borders. It wouldn't provide the pause we needed to examine the Prophecy without the entrenched opinions of stakeholders, politicians, and acolytes.

And that was the *best*-case scenario. It was far more likely that my mother was still struggling to obtain clearance to petition the Council—something that could take weeks even without an army on the move. If her claims sounded deranged enough—and the suggestion of a Prelate keeping a case of shining bug-things to poison her enemies certainly bordered on ludicrous—she may even be imprisoned before she could make contact with my old tutor.

Despite the significant possibility of this scenario,

I tried not to dwell on it—it made my stomach roil to the point of retching. If Shaula had already extended her sister's prison sentence once to negate her influence, what might she do if Rana popped up again with accusations of murder? My anxious mind started calculating the time frame for an expedited gallows sentence, but I forced myself to stop and focus on the route in front of us.

Fortunately, the way was wide and mostly clear—the main obstacles were places where the gypsum grew in swaths over the ground, forcing us to pick our way on tiptoe amid the blooms and spars. More than once we both slipped, earning us painful sharp-edges bruises, but the crystals were soft enough that they didn't slice our skin. In places where we had no choice but to step on them, we left a wake of crumbled shards behind like churned snow.

We didn't speak much during this point in our journey, and for this I was grateful. I was too tired to keep reopening the same hurts over and over with no remedy in sight. My secrets, too, were piling heavy on my shoulders. The vellum packet of letters in my shirt whispered and crinkled with my movements, reminding me that I still hadn't given Celeno all the truth. Too much talk might have worn out the last of my resolve. It was still too early, I told myself. Still too many unknowns, too many unanswered questions and persisting obstacles. Better to wait until I had as much information as I could gather, and then I would lay it all out, clearly, chronologically, as straightforward as an academic abstract. Surely things would fall appropriately into place—data, discussion, recommendations. Action. That was how it worked.

Please let it work.

I didn't know what Celeno was dwelling on—the petroglyphs, most likely, and the mess we faced back at home. He was quiet for hours, his breath ragged behind me, and quiet still after we stopped for the unchanging night. He only made one comment as I laid out a scant meal.

"We haven't reconnected with the passages we were in before."

"No," I said. "But we're heading in the right direction."

"I haven't seen any blazes."

"There haven't been any places for them," I said, nodding to the fine carpet of gypsum that covered even the floor—we were perched gingerly on our packs to keep our seats off the prickly ground. The night would be an uncomfortable one, for sure. "But the glowworms are here, which means we're at least not heading farther in. We'll reconnect sometime tomorrow."

Whether he believed me or was simply too tired to argue, he swallowed down just two bites of food, lay down on his bumpy bedroll, and turned his back to me. Still gnawed and nagged by anxiety and doubt, I did the same, staring up at the *Arachnocampa* colonies until they seemed to be burned into my mind's eye.

Sure enough, a few hours in to our march the next day—flanked at first by white Xs I made sure to point out to Celeno—we scraped out a side passage to find ourselves staring again at the crisp edge of the River of Milk. Its course was wider than before, with a comfortable ledge to walk along. The glowworms hung thick and luminous a few feet above our heads, writhing a bit in the beam of our lantern. I'd led us at a decent pace for much of the morning, so at this junction, I settled Celeno down against the wall and scouted a little ways down the passage.

"Good news," I said, panting as I hurried back to him twenty minutes later. "The blazes pick up again. We're heading in the right direction."

His eyes were closed, and the food I'd set out for him was untouched. "Good," he said, exhaustion heavy in his voice. "I was beginning to have my doubts. It seems odd to be going down, though, doesn't it? Shouldn't we be going up?"

I looked down the passage, lit beyond our lantern by the *Arachnocampa*. "Nothing in here makes sense. We may have been going steadily upward without realizing it, and now we have to make up that elevation."

He puffed out a breath. "Well, if there are blazes, it must be all right." He slit open an eye. "I'm sorry I doubted you."

Guilt quadrupled in my stomach. "It's okay," I said quietly. "I haven't exactly earned your trust."

He rubbed his forehead. "I don't pretend I fully understand where everything went wrong between us, but, Gemma, we've been partners for a long time. You earned my trust years ago."

I gnawed my lip. Maybe . . . maybe now would be the right time to tell him?

"Celeno," I began slowly. "I know things at home are a mess—"

His response was a thick, deep-chested sigh.

"—but," I continued, "what if there was another option we could pursue?"

"You mean the Prophecy?"

"No," I said. "I mean . . . what if we could solicit help from our neighbors? What if we could pull our armies back, withdraw from Cyprien—"

"Our stakeholders would *lose their minds*," Celeno interrupted with a hint of old frustration. "You know how many people have a hand in Cypri industry, as well as our military campaign."

"But," I pressed, "what if we could reroute that support, instead of cut it off entirely? What if we could put it to use elsewhere?"

"Where else?" he asked, spreading his hands. "There *is* nothing else. You know that. This is the problem we've always run up against, Gemma. Mining, agriculture, trade . . . nothing is robust enough to justify losing our hold on Cypri industry and shipping routes. And anyway, we're too far into this campaign now. We've made too many enemies outside our borders. No one will ally with us without pressure or incentive to do so. A treaty is out of the question."

I chewed on my lip some more, gazing unseeing at the crisp white calcite. It sparkled in the glowworms' light.

"What if it wasn't?" I asked.

He sighed again and closed his eyes. "What if, what if, what if. What if the Light suddenly turns the Stellarange to solid gold and floods the canyon with silver? I can't work with *what ifs*, Gemma. Who is going to ally with us? Lumen Lake? Queen Mona is more likely to hold my head under the water until all my breath is gone. The Silverwood? Queen Ellamae spent a week as our prisoner, hurling a different insult at me every half-hour. Winder? Paroa? Now bound up to Lumen Lake's flag. Cyprien? Actively rebelling against us. Samna is the only country I can think of that might not hold a personal grudge, and we have nothing to offer them. We *have* no allies, Gemma. We have to rely on our own resources."

"But Queen Mona has—"

"Queen Mona has the strongest personal vendetta against me of every ruling body in the Eastern World!" His eyes popped open again. "This is what I don't understand, Gemma—how can you continue to come back to her as a possible ally? Any kindness she showed you in Cyprien was designed to win you to her side, to separate you from me! I can't forget what happened when you had a choice to make in Dismal Green. Did she succeed, after all?"

I stood looking down at him, my fists balled at my sides. His chest heaved at the effort his sharp words cost him, the sweat on his forehead glinting. I struggled to regain control on my urge to spill every secret. I leaned back slightly, the vellum packet shifted against my bolero.

Still too early.

More work.

More time.

"No," I finally said. "She didn't. I still want what's best for you, and for Alcoro. That's all I've ever wanted."

He heaved yet another sigh and dropped his sweaty forehead into his hand. My resolve back, grimmer and sharper than before, I adjusted my pack.

"Come on," I said. "We should be getting close."

I held out my hand to him. He didn't take it, rising unsteadily to his feet and hauling his pack back over his shoulders.

We pressed on. A hundred yards down the passage we passed the first white blaze, and then the next several minutes later. I pointed them out to Celeno. He gave only wordless grunts in reply.

The gypsum crystals didn't grow here, and the way once again seemed darker despite the *Arachnocampa* overhead. These were growing thicker now, telling me that we were progressing more and more toward open air and my intended route. The path sloped steadily downward, and before long running water joined the dry River of Milk, at first running in its own channel next to the calcite deposits before eventually flowing into the powdery mineral. We hopped over rivulets that streaked the clean white with orange and red, and we slipped on slick rock as more and more water joined our route. Soon the precise edges of the calcite disappeared entirely, swallowed up by a broad, shallow subterranean creek.

The extent of our day must have been waning when the passage expanded, ballooning outward into the darkness. I could still see faint patches of blue light covering the ceiling, but they were far away, casting no extra light for us. The passageway beyond was indistinct as well—rather than solid walls on either side, the area was full of columns and stalagmites. I started chewing my lip again as we wove among the first few pillars. It felt very much like a maze, the walkable area twisting and turning and zigzagging back and forth. Some ways were flooded, going from solid ground to fathomless pools in a matter of steps. These were crystal clear and bitterly cold, with no bottoms that our lantern could illuminate. We edged along the ones that had passable ledges, praying we wouldn't slip into the invisible depths on either side.

More than once, I looked up from our desperate

circle of light to the *Arachnocampa* colonies far above our heads. The ceiling was so populated it gave the impression of a hazy blue sky overhead. More larvae meant more prey—more, perhaps, than just their own kin. How did they get in? Where were their secret cracks to the world outside the Stellarange?

We *had* to be close.

Didn't we?

The blister on my lip was back from biting it so often. I was squinting at an approaching column, trying to decide if we should go to the right or left, when my feet caught a lip of rock. I arced forward, the lantern swinging in my grip, and landed painfully on all fours in two feet of water. The lantern was instantly doused, plunging us into utter darkness.

"Gemma!"

I spluttered—my face had gone under, and I'd sucked in a startled gulp. Celeno groped for my shoulders and hauled me backward. The lantern scraped against the rock like a dead thing.

His hands gripped me as if I might dissolve into the dark. "Are you hurt?"

"No," I said. Just stinging palms and knees and the rising crest of panic. "I'm all right."

"Did the lantern break?"

"I don't know." Shaking from cold and fright, I slid my pack from my shoulders and rummaged for the fire capsule tin. With a crunch and a cloud of sulfur, the glass capsule lit. Celeno's face flashed in the gloom, tense. His brown eyes locked with mine before dropping to the lantern.

"Another shield broke," he said, pointing to the red glass.

"And the handle is bent." I felt around the base of the reservoir. "But I don't think it's leaking oil. Still . . ." I held the capsule to the wick—sure enough, it didn't light. "It's soaked."

There was a moment's hesitation while we processed this. "I guess we'll have to let it dry," Celeno said. "And hope the water didn't get inside."

The fire capsule went out, whisking us back into darkness and leaving a blurred spot on my vision. Slowly I lowered the pliers. I set them back in the tin and slid it into my pack. I sat with it in my lap for a moment. Silence crept in, like a stealthy animal that had been held off by our little circle of light. My knees throbbed where I'd landed on them.

"Where are we?" Celeno asked. My eyes hadn't yet adjusted to the near-darkness, so the most I could make out in the far-off light of the *Arachnocampa* was the barest shine on his hair. The rest I had to infer from his voice and shortness of his breath.

"Gemma?" he pressed.

"I'm not sure," I said.

A pause.

"Not sure, as in, not sure when we'll get back to the main passages, or not sure at all?"

Silence strangled me. I closed my eyes, pointlessly—as if the familiar dark of my eyelids was somehow more comforting than the skyless dark of the mountain's belly.

"Gemma, please. Where are we? When was the last blaze? Can we go back?"

I ran my filthy sleeve over my nose in preparation for the slow swell of stress crying.

"The last blaze was too long ago," I said. "We can't go back. We can only go forward."

"It's only been, what, two days since the petroglyphs? Maybe more? We can make it back there. I'll help you under the squeeze . . ."

I shook my head, invisible. Sniffing again, I opened my eyes and looked up again at the glowworm colonies—little constellations of living stars.

"Did you know," I said, "the Lumeni had a word for the different colors in the lake? *Waterhue.* As the light shifts and shadows, new colors melt in and out, ones we don't even have names for."

I could feel Celeno's palpable puzzlement.

"Okay," he said hesitantly.

"I read about it," I said.

"Okay," he said again.

"Sometimes I think that's really how the world works," I said, aware that I was spilling nonsense in the growing realization of my failures. "The Light illuminates things in ways we can't see or make sense of, and we build our truth based on what we perceive.

But everyone is different, from person to person and country to country. Why should we have a name for the changing colors in water? The Lumeni do, because it's their truth—it exists. But we don't. We don't need one. Instead we've put names to every celestial body in the sky. Instead we grasp for the Light in the cyphers that specifically name our country, our king. And we say any folk who don't do the same simply aren't enlightened, or privileged enough to do so. But . . . what if it's just waterhue? What if what we call *truth* is just our limited reality?"

"Are we lost?" Celeno prompted bluntly.

I shut myself up, biting off the rest of my building dissertation. My head felt wobbly and light with fatigue and anxiety, and my eyes burned with their usual film of tears.

"I'm not sure," I said. "Maybe. And if we are, it's my fault. I always forget that my decisions don't carry the same authority as yours."

He sighed, the sound thick with frustration. "That's a stupid rule, and I hope you know I've never believed it." His fingers fumbled along my arm until they found my hand. "Gemma, I have no idea what I'm doing. You should know that more than anyone. And Shaula can harp at me all she wants that my decisions are driven by the will of the Light, but it's never felt that way. I've always relied on you more. I've always needed your help. And I'm sorry it's gotten to where you don't trust your own choices. *I* do."

Oh, you shouldn't. You really, really shouldn't.

"When we get back, things will be different," he continued. "We're going to sort through this business of forgery, and we're going to have Shaula investigated. I'm willing to bet with a new Prelate, someone who's not so close to you, you'll feel better."

I sat up ramrod straight, focus suddenly flaring in my body.

"It'll all sort out after that," he said, unaware. "We'll be sure nobody challenges your authority, nobody suggests we can't rule together, as partners like before—"

"Hush, hush," I whispered sharply, squeezing his hand. "Quiet."

"I'm only trying—"

"Quiet!" I said again. "Listen."

He stilled. In the newfound silence, I strained my ears, desperate to find what I thought I heard before. At first, there was only the distant drip of water, the trickling of the mountain's veins. But then, there, in the vast space, another sound echoed, faint and indistinct, against the rock.

Voices.

There were voices.

In the space of a breath, we both scrambled to our feet, still clutching each other's hands. The sound died and then rose again, an intermittent swell. Many voices, twined together, as if in song. It came in waves, only reaching us when it hit the right notes.

I dropped Celeno's hand to dig for the crock of oil in my pack. Fingers shaking from anticipation, I pulled out the packet of papers from my tunic. I removed the vellum envelope holding them, twisted it into a rough wick, and dunked it in the oil.

"What is it?" Celeno whispered. "Is it a trick of the cave? How could there be voices? Did the soldiers follow us in? How did they get all this way without us realizing it?"

"I don't think it's the soldiers." There was a snap and a flare as I crunched a fire capsule. It burst through the darkness and greedily caught the oil-soaked envelope.

"Then who is it?" he asked. "Where did that paper come from?"

"Hurry," I said, shoving everything except the pliers and the burning wick back in my pack. "It won't last for very long."

"Where are we going?" He stumbled as I tugged his arm. "We're going *toward* the voices?"

"We're getting out of here," I said, an irrational hope surging in my chest.

"Out of where? Out of this chamber? Gemma, *wait*—"

"Quiet, Celeno, please!" I said, my voice cracking. "I'm trying to listen!"

Clutching the wick in the pliers, we wove through the columns, our hurried footsteps echoing off the rock. At every turn we stopped, straining our ears to hear the distant murmur. It was like chasing the wind, hoping to get close enough to grab a handful. Once or twice we lost the sound, trying to stifle our breath and beating hearts. But slowly it grew stronger. Soon it wasn't just coming in swells, but became a steady chorus. Before long, we could make out a melody.

Running water joined the voices—a river rushed out of the darkness to join us, purposeful in its path. The temperature dropped; the air began to move, making the flame on the dwindling parchment gutter. Still, the voices persisted. I could hear a repeated refrain, something sung over and over again, until I knew the rise and fall of the notes by heart.

The ground dropped. We rounded a bend and met with a wash of frigid air. The smoky flame clinging to the wick puffed out. But instead of closing us in darkness, it revealed an ambient glow, golden-white.

"Great blessed Light," Celeno said, his fist wrapped in my cloak. "Gemma . . . it's daylight."

We ran along the edge of the river. There were no columns or stalagmites anymore, unable to grow in the moving air. The cave that had been so quiet now rang with a cacophony of noises—rushing wind, chattering water, and the rise of singing above it all. As the light grew, I set my foot down and skidded, steadying myself on Celeno's arm. It was ice—there was ice riming the floor, first in small patches, and then in a continuous coat, until we were sliding rather than running toward the light. The wind whipping off the river started to sting, carrying snow and depositing it in drifts along the passageway.

Our pace slowed until we were crabbing along the riverbank, our hands clutching the frozen wall. The river became coated by a sheet of ice until we couldn't see flowing water any longer. Our breath swirled in front of our faces, our eyes tearing as they adjusted to the growing light.

When I turned the final corner, I had to skid to a stop and cover my eyes—it was like a mirror shining the strength of the sun. But when I lifted them again, blinking through the tears, I saw it wasn't even full daylight. A sliver of sky shone deep purple-blue, accompanied by a single star. Blocking the rest of the view was a wall of solid ice.

Celeno wheezed on the frozen air as he inched along behind me. "What is that?"

"It's a waterfall," I said, my feet crunching on the snow piled around its base. I reached out to brush the ice. "A frozen waterfall. And beyond it . . ." I pointed, and he squinted up at the single visible star—dawn or dusk, I couldn't tell, and at the moment, I didn't care. With the light stronger than it had been since we'd entered the cave, I could see the ashen color to his face, the limp tendrils of his hair where they'd soaked and dried with his sweat. He gazed at the single star with bewilderment.

"We found the stars again," I said, filled with a tense, almost giddy excitement.

His brow furrowed. "I don't understand. Where are we?"

I inched out over the thick ice covering the river, where there was a natural crack between the waterfall and the rock. A strong breeze whistled through it, the warmer cave air rushing outward into the cold. I put my eye against the crack.

A flat surface, shining blue-gray under the dim sky, broken in the distance by a shadowed landmass rising far out of my line of sight. The surface glimmered, moving.

"We're at Lumen Lake," I said.

"We're *where*?"

The wind shearing through the crevice died down for a moment, and in the relative quiet, I could hear the singing again. I craned my head, making out the shapes of boats rocking in the water. They were black against the surface, with no lanterns lit on any of them. They seemed to be bobbing in place, even facing the same way, as if waiting for something.

"Gemma!" Celeno's voice cracked with alarm. "Did you say we're at *Lumen Lake*?"

"Yes. Come on, if we break off some of this ice, we can fit through."

I sat down on the snow, too excited to register the cold, and began to kick the cascade of frozen water. My first few blows did nothing except send a painful jolt through my legs, but one hit near the edge and broke off a fragment the size of a dinner plate. I kicked it again, chipping off another shard.

"Gemma—*Gemma, wait.*"

But I wasn't going to wait. I'd done enough waiting. I kicked harder, the impact reverberating up my spine, channeling all my frustration—the silence I'd had to keep, the lies I'd had to tell, the trust I'd gained from no one, the time spent behind locked doors . . . a window-sized fragment broke off the waterfall, shattering on the rocks below. My eyes were tearing, but not from stress crying . . . the light was growing stronger, glancing off the frozen cascade, magnifying against the snow. A bigger portrait of the space beyond came into view—the tops of a mountain range thrust high into the pinking sky, looming over the lake.

"Gemma!" Celeno's hand closed tight on my shoulder. "Stop—great Light, think about what you're doing!"

I only realized what he meant as a splintering crash spliced the air. Ice shards flew, and I threw up my arms. The air brightened; the frozen cascades illuminated with golden-white light. With a lurch, I started to slip forward with the momentum of the ice, unable to find solid purchase.

My cloak tightened against my throat—Celeno must have grabbed it to stop my fall. But there was no way he could have held on to the slippery rocks himself, and in the next moment we were both sliding almost straight down. The world was growing impossibly bright, brighter than any normal daylight, too bright to see anything at all.

With a crunch that took my breath away, I landed in a pile of stinging snow. I slid down, my legs tangled in my cloak, my hands scraped raw on the grit. I came to rest where the snow met pebbled beach, the water lapping a short distance away. Between myself and the water, however, was a jumble of feet, all running in my direction. Black boots with silver buckles, leather boots with swinging fringe, a pair of heeled shoes with pearls on the toes, swept by an embroidered blue hem. This last pair came to a running stop just inches from my face.

"What in the blazing, blessed Light?"

Mona.

CHAPTER 9

I struggled to untangle myself from my cloak and sit up. Queen Mona Alastaire dropped into a crouch in front of me, the opulent embroidered hem of her royal blue gown trailing over the wet pebbles. Her face was split with consternation. I was too relieved to care about what I must look like—dirty and disheveled, with mud on my knees and snow in my hair, my eyes and nose streaming. The world was still intensely bright—too bright for dawn.

"Gemma!" Mona seemed unwilling to believe her eyes. "What in the world . . . how . . ."

"Move, move, earth and sky!" A second figure elbowed her aside, dropping to her knees on the rocks, unconcerned with marring her long green and silver tunic. Where Mona's skin was moon-pale and freckled, the newcomer's was burnished copper, darker than mine, her deep brown eyes sharp with alarm.

Ellamae.

She snatched up a handful of my sleeve and started squeezing my arms, up one side and down the other. "Thundering sky, you must have fallen thirty feet— what hurts?" She thumbed my eyelid. "Tilt your head—did you hit it on anything?"

"I'm all right," I said breathlessly. I struggled to break her grip. "Celeno—where's Celeno?"

Mona's face went white and still as marble. She stared at me a moment longer, and then lifted her gaze to the snow behind me.

It was then I registered the other noises, over-whelming my sensory-deprived brain. The crunching of boots on the pebbles, the rattling of gear and weaponry, the grinding of boat hulls on the beach, the myriad shouting of voices. I pulled away from Ellamae, who was kneading my scalp to check for swelling, and turned around.

I had to duck my head again—no wonder the world seemed so bright. Not only was the waterfall behind us massive, it had turned into a veritable pillar of mirrors, reflecting the early morning sunlight a thousand times over. I blinked against the wash of tears it brought. At its base, on top of the snow pile, Celeno was struggling to steady himself as two blue-liveried soldiers hauled him to his feet.

"You brought him *here*?" Mona whispered.

I whirled back around and grabbed her sleeve. "Give me time to explain," I said. "Let us get somewhere we can talk, and let me explain."

"Gemma," she said, and her voice was as stark as her face. "Do you understand . . ."

"You said you would respond to me," I said. "In Dismal Green, you said that if I wanted peace, it was in my power to make it happen, and if I reached out to you, you would respond." I tightened my grip. "Grant me at least that. Besides—I have news about Cyprien."

She stared a moment longer, her stormy blue eyes flashing with intensity. Then she sucked in a breath and rose to her feet. She held out her hand. Ellamae took me by my other arm, and together they pulled me upright.

Standing up, I was suddenly struck by the sheer number of people around us. Not just the people now surging every which way on the shore, but the people beyond, in the boats on the lake. Rowboats and sailboats, canoes, a few double-masted ketches. All were oriented around the little crescent of beach at the base of the waterfall. All had faces riveted in our direction.

Oh, by the Light. Could we have made more of a spectacle?

Face flushing, I dropped my gaze back to the folk on the beach. Ellamae had moved to my side, her fingers pressed over my wrist to take my pulse, and in

shuttering like hers often did, and he turned and strode down the pebbled beach. He lifted his arm and called out over the water to a rowboat bobbing not far away.

I hesitated, but then made myself turn back to Celeno. He'd finally found his feet at the base of the snow pile, but the soldiers didn't ease their grips. They hauled him forward, stopping a few feet in front of Mona. He was as ragged as me, miles away from the overpolished image his attendants had prepared for the negotiations in Lilou, but his jaw was set as he faced the queen. She looked him over coolly. I hurried to stand between them.

"Well," Mona said, as one might greet a dog that has made a mess in the house. Several yards behind her, Colm reached out to grasp the hull of an incoming rowboat. With a powerful heave, he pulled it halfway onto shore. "Celeno Tezozomoc, Seventh King of Alcoro, I did not expect we would be meeting again so soon, and certainly not on my own shores. I would be remiss if I didn't welcome you cordially to Lumen Lake."

He looked up at her, his face bloodless, took one sharp breath, and then crumpled to the ground.

The two soldiers flanking him lurched downward with his fall, just barely managing to keep his face from hitting the rocks. My stomach dropped, and I dove down to catch him.

"Oh, by the Light!" Ellamae's fringed leather boots

appeared at my shoulder. "Lean him back—get his feet up!" She rolled him so he was on his back, his head in my lap. She slapped away the soldiers who were still attempting to restrain his arms and waved toward the rowboat. "Val, help me get him into the boat."

Valien hurried to join us, winding his arms under Celeno's shoulders and hoisting him off the ground. Between the three of us, we carried him to the boat. I clambered in, cradling Celeno's head. Ellamae climbed in behind us, situating his feet up on the seat. After her came Mona, clearly displeased with the whole affair, and Valien and Rou. Arlen hopped into a second boat with a cadre of soldiers and skirted out into the lake. Colm leaned on our hull, giving us a shove out onto the water, and then jumped inside without getting his feet wet.

"Pull away," Mona called to the sailors at the oars, raising her voice over the wind. "And don't bother with the ship. Take us directly to Blackshell." She tucked the edges of her fur-lined cloak closer about her. "No sense in pretending to stand on ceremony."

With Celeno stretched out in the front half of the boat, the only free space was on the seat next to his feet. Colm stepped past Mona and the others to settle down on it. I dropped my gaze back to Celeno's slack face. Ellamae had moved up to his collar. She unfastened the sodden cloak around his shoulders and unbuttoned his top few buttons. Frowning at his clammy skin, she unhooked her own cloak, pine green and embroidered with laurel branches, and tucked it over him.

"Thank you," I said quietly. The wind carried my voice away, so I tried a little louder. "Thank you."

She grunted and held the back of her hand to his mouth. "He's a mess."

"We came a long way," I said.

"I meant it generally," she said dryly. "He's got the shakes, and his heart rate is through the proverbial roof. What's he on?"

"On?"

"What medicines is he taking?"

"I gave him some ginger a few days ago, for his stomach," I said.

"Indigestion? Or ulcers?"

My brain seemed to ratchet into place, as if finally reaching comprehension. Ulcers. Of course. He had always suffered from them when he was under stress. "It must have been ulcers."

"Try boneset next time, or comfrey. Ginger won't do a damn thing for ulcers." She lifted his eyelid and peered at his pupil. "Is he taking any narcotics?"

"Not in the past few days," I said. "He used to take a few tinctures throughout the day, and a sleeping draught at night."

She stared at me a moment and opened her mouth to continue, when a particularly violent gust of wind made the rowboat rock in the water. Her hands jumped to either side of the hull. A spray of freezing water swirled into the air, soaking my already dripping cloak and wet hair. I shivered and pulled Ellamae's cloak further up to Celeno's chin.

"Here."

I looked up to see Colm unhooking the pearl clasp at his throat. He held it out to me—it was midnight blue and embroidered with white thread.

I shook my head. "I'll get it dirty."

Ellamae plucked the cloak from his hand and passed it to me. "Take it. I'm not reviving anybody who comes down with the chills, and I'm willing to bet Colm has other pretty ones."

He nodded seriously. "I have at least two other pretty ones."

Reluctantly, I unbuttoned my own cloak and took his. It was double thick and quilted, and still warm from his body. Gratefully I eased into it, shivering.

Ellamae glanced over her shoulder, to where Mona, Rou, and Valien were engaged in a deep conversation. She leaned a little closer to me, trying to keep her voice low while still being heard over the wind.

"Did you get the letter?" she asked.

My heart jumped. From Ellamae? From the Silverwood? "What letter?"

Her brow furrowed. "Oh."

I looked past her to Colm, who was staring determinedly back the way we'd come, where the giant shining waterfall was losing some of its intensity. I started to call out, but the wind gusted once more. Ellamae grabbed for the hull again, squeezing her eyes shut. I closed my mouth and hunched forward over Celeno, giving up the idea of pursuing the conversation until we were off the lake.

Despite the wind, the three rowers made short work of bearing us across the mouth of the river that flowed into the southern waterways, and within a few minutes we were passing up the shore. To our right, the mainland rose in gentle snow-covered slopes until it began to buckle and soar into the great mountain range that made up the Silverwood. To our left, the misty lake spread out into the indiscernible distance, the horizon broken by towering islands. These rose high into the sky, much higher than I'd imagined, their peaks just emerging into the sun. Dotting the water were boats making their way homeward from the shining waterfall—I would have to ask exactly what solstice custom we'd interrupted, but I imagined that topic would be quite low in priority.

Quickly approaching along the main shore was Blackshell Palace, a tightly built construct of squat fieldstone towers with conical roofs. Much of it was built out into the lake, supported by stone piers and peppered with docks that extended out past the shallows. Staircases descended right into the water itself, some with platforms flanking them for swimmers and pearl divers in the warmer months. Dominating the nearest lakeside wing of the palace was a wide terrace running down toward the water, headed by a white stone statue. It was a woman, facing the lake, but we passed too far away for me to glimpse her face. She had a crown on her head—it must be a previous queen, then, or some character from legend.

We headed for a small dock. Despite the wind and snow, two crisp soldiers stood guard, eyeing us as we drew closer. Arlen's boat beat us to the moorings, so by the time we bumped against the dock, it was swarming with soldiers.

Celeno twitched as our hull scraped the wood, his eyelids fluttering. I leaned down over him.

"Celeno," I whispered.

He shook his head and opened his bleary eyes.

"Gemma? Wh'time s'it?"

I brushed aside his habitual question. "We're going to get inside, where we can rest and get warm. Do you think you can walk?"

"Somebody get a stretcher," I heard Ellamae call to the soldiers. "And get a bed ready in the healing wing."

Celeno's eyes widened and he pushed himself upright, the pine green cloak sliding down his chest. Without looking at him, Mona stepped smoothly onto the dock. Rou climbed out after her, followed by Valien. Ellamae stood with one boot in the boat and one on the dock, watching the soldiers scatter off to do her bidding. Celeno's breath began to quicken, and I bit my lip—it would have been better if he'd stayed

CREATURES OF LIGHT 247

unconscious if he was going to be carried into Queen Mona's palace.

Colm was the only one left in the boat. He stood up, bracing his feet against the rocking of the water.

He extended a hand to Celeno. "The healing wing isn't that far."

Celeno looked up at him. Maybe if his head was a little clearer, he'd have been able to make a guess at who Colm was, but there was no recognition in his eyes. He grasped Colm's offered forearm and got shakily to his feet. I stood as well and arranged Ellamae's cloak around his shoulders, fastening the silver pin at his throat.

Ellamae turned as they stepped up on the dock. "Hold on—we're getting a stretcher."

"I think we can make it in, Mae," Colm said, looping Celeno's arm over his shoulder.

Mona turned to face us for the first time. Arlen hovered at her elbow. "I want him brought to a cell, Colm," she said without looking at me.

Both Ellamae and I started protesting at the same time, but Mona flicked her hand angrily in the air. "I don't care, Mae—you have no obligation to treat him yourself, and a healer can tend to him just as well in the prison."

"No, they can't, Mona," she said. "He needs a fire and a bed, not a mat on some stone floor."

"I'll thank you that my prison has cots, unlike

yours," she said stiffly. "Regardless, I won't have him in the healing wing where there are a hundred ways to get out and access any number of weapons."

"He's exhausted, and sick," I said, trying to keep my voice low. "He's not going to attack anyone."

Her gaze fell on me. "You'll forgive me if I don't take that chance," she said coldly.

My frustration flickered and rose—I was too tired to fight it. "Mona, I didn't bring him all the way here just for you to—"

"I have a responsibility to consider my folk, as well as you," she interrupted crisply. "Every soldier on this dock, every attendant in this palace, spent three years in forced labor under Alcoro's flag. I'll help you as much as I can, Gemma, but I'm not inclined to ask them to relive colonization. I apologize for the poor diplomacy on my part, but I will not apologize for prioritizing my folk over your king."

Heat flared in my collar and cheeks, and I bit down on my lip to keep my emotions from spilling over at her. Celeno stared at the dock with eyes edged with outrage, his jaw working.

I wasn't going to let her put him in a cell . . . I wouldn't do it . . .

She stared me down with the unshakable look she'd given me all throughout Cyprien, the one that dared me or anyone else to challenge her. I bit harder on my lip, struggling to keep her unyielding eye contact.

Before either of us could speak again, Colm shifted under Celeno's arm. "Why don't we take him to a guest room, instead of the healing wing?" he suggested, his voice reflecting none of his sister's cool ferocity. "You can set guards at the door, and he can still be tended to. And we can all sit and discuss matters without having to gather in the prison, or get him out of bed."

Slowly, she turned her gaze on him, her demeanor unchanged. I relaxed a little out of its glare, but Colm didn't recoil or look away. He simply gazed back with no emotion written on his face.

After a long moment, she turned on her heel. "Fine. Though I want guards at the door to the patio, too." She spoke back over her shoulder. "And put him on the *opposite* end of the hall from Rou and the Wood-folk."

Celeno stared angrily at her retreating back. Ellamae heaved a sigh and waved to Colm. "All right, a guest room it is. Hey, you, with the hair." She pointed to a startled soldier with a vibrant red mop. "Bring me kettles to heat over the fire, and someone who's not an idiot with herbs."

As the soldier hurried off, Colm nudged Celeno forward. I took Celeno's free hand and squeezed it. As we made our way up the dock, he turned his head to me.

"We shouldn't be here," he whispered.

"It's all right," I lied, painfully aware that nothing was all right.

His brown eyes drilled into mine. "Did you know where you were going?"

Colm turned his chin slightly away, as if trying to grant us privacy despite having Celeno's arm looped around his shoulder. Swallowing, I reached into my bolero pocket and pulled out a spar of gypsum, its point now worn down to a nub. It was the crystal I'd broken off back in the room of petroglyphs. Celeno stared at it, uncomprehending.

"It's sort of like chalk," I said softly. "It leaves a mark."

He looked from my hand back up at my face, and I realized he still didn't understand—most likely because it didn't cross his mind that I would do something so dangerous, and so treacherous.

"I put the blazes on the wall," I explained. "After the petroglyphs. The ones we passed . . . I put them there, whenever I went to scout ahead."

His face blanched, flickering from confusion to shock.

"I had to," I said quickly. "We couldn't go back to Alcoro, the way things were. I had to get you here—"

He dropped my hand.

My steps slowed to a halt. He and Colm continued past me, flanked on all sides by Lumeni soldiers. They parted around me like a river, leaving me behind on the dock. Colm glanced back over his shoulder as they passed into the palace. Celeno didn't. I gripped the gypsum in my fist until it bit into my skin, my throat burning.

Oh, moon and stars, I'd done this all wrong.

Treason. Treason. *Treason.*

A hand slid into the crook of my arm. I turned to see Rou smiling wearily as he settled his elbow in mine.

"My granddad used to say that crawfish only clamp when there's nothing left for them to do."

"What's that supposed to mean?"

He shrugged. "Crawfish are weird, and so was my granddad." He patted my hand.

I smiled feebly and wiped my nose on my sleeve. He dug in his pocket—he was wearing a Cypri-style vest and ascot, but they looked like they were made of coarser Lumeni fabric, not the light embroidered silk I was used to seeing him in. Mona must have had them tailored from what cloth was on hand. He pulled out a handkerchief and handed it to me.

"Thank you." I blotted my face, trying unsuccessfully to hold back my tears. I drew in a ragged breath. "Rou . . ." I said softly. "I'm sorry about Lyle."

"I thought we were going to wait to do apologies."

"It couldn't wait. I'm so, so sorry."

He sighed, and with a soft nudge, we continued toward the palace door, arm in arm. "Me, too, Gemma. I wish we hadn't spent so much of our lives resenting each other. And I won't pretend seeing your king doesn't . . ." He drew in a short breath, his gaze on Celeno's back as we entered the corridor. "But when I see Lyle dying, I also see you giving him last rites. Don't think I'm not grateful for that."

It was literally the absolute least I could have done, and it had come on desperate impulse. "They burned his body." My voice was a whisper now. "I know it doesn't help, but . . ."

"It does help, Gemma. I'm glad for that." The Cypri burned their dead—though my folk had done it out of necessity's sake, as there had been no facilities for an entombing in our own fashion. Rou squeezed my hand as we rounded the corner of the guest wing. "And if we're doing the apologizing now, then I have my own to make. I'm sorry about that whole mess in Cyprien."

"Abducting me, you mean."

"Yes. The Assembly had to act as it saw fit, and I was obligated to carry out their plan, but I don't pretend it was the best strategy." We moved closer to one of the guest rooms, where Mona stood outside directing throngs of soldiers and attendants. "So many lives were impacted, in so many ways we didn't consider or anticipate. Mae was locked up in a ship's hold for a week. All the folk back home thought they'd lost their queens. You suffered for it. Mona suffered for it. And I'm sorry about that."

"At least you and Mona got to meet," I said.

"Ehh," he said, his gaze lingering on her as we drew nearer. "I don't know that she considers the whole thing worth it. She likes to recount to me the exact monetary value of the ship we sank."

I laughed through the tears burning my eyes, but I stifled it quickly, the sound incongruous among the stoic faces. Attendants hurried past us, carrying armfuls of firewood and linen. Soldiers milled about, organizing themselves in stations outside the door and at the ends of the hallways. The red-haired soldier appeared with a healer in tow, her herb case under her arm. Mona glanced at us approaching, her mouth drawn tight in a frown. I drew in a breath and lowered my voice, leaning a little closer to Rou.

"Don't make her angry at you just for my sake," I whispered.

He squeezed my hand again, smiling. "She's always angry at me for one thing or another, but normally it's because I complain about her food."

I shook my head. "Rou."

"Honestly, have you tasted a freshwater mussel? They're like shoe leather."

I struggled to keep back another laugh as we rounded the door to the guest room, which was fortunate—Celeno had just sat down on the bed and looked up as I stopped in the doorway. I dropped Rou's arm and tried to wipe away the last traces of my smile. I realized I was still clutching the offending shard of gypsum in my hand, and I hurriedly stuffed it back into my pocket. Celeno's face twitched, and he cut his gaze away to glare at the bed stand.

Colm was standing at the hearth, his back to me as he lifted firewood from the maid's satchel. Ellamae accosted the healer as soon as she entered the room, trying to wrestle the herb case out of her hands. Mona stood at the doorway, viewing the goings-on with displeasure. She shifted her gaze to me as I hovered in the hallway.

"The room adjoins," she said, pointing to the door in the wall. "I've sent someone to gather fresh clothes for you. Why don't you wash up a little, and then we'll all sit down and talk?"

"Thank you," I murmured. "Will you come with me? I want to tell you what I know about the events in Cyprien." It wasn't the right time to begin that conversation—Rou should be included, at the very least—but I wanted to get her away from the doorway, glaring at Celeno as if he was a cockroach. She gave a small nod, threw one more angry glance over her shoulder, and followed me into the next room over.

It was hung in shades of blue and white, with pearls glinting in the embroidery and wainscoting. The hearth maid was just finishing coaxing a blaze in a generous granite fireplace, the mantel carved with beavers and branches. With a rattle, the maid picked up her bucket and ducked out of the room, offering a courtesy to Mona as she passed.

I moved gratefully in front of the fire, sliding my chapped hands out from beneath Colm's cloak. Mona went to the glassed patio doors and drew back the curtain, revealing the frosty expanse of the lake. She craned her head to look through the window—probably checking to see if her guards were taking up their appropriate positions.

"So what is the state of Cyprien?" she asked, her face reflected in the glass.

"My folk have retaken four of the provinces," I said. "I'm not sure which ones, except Lilou is still being held by the Cypri—at least, it was when I left."

"My guess for the other is the Lower Draws," Mona murmured, referring to the southern stretch of deep, dark bayou we had traveled through just a few weeks ago. "Alcoro will have a hard time claiming that for themselves."

"I don't doubt that," I said. "But we have to consider the possibility that they will, or that they'll make the jump to Paroa even without all the provinces under our flag. We need to act as quickly as we can—it could mean the difference between a coastal invasion and an allied truce."

She let out a brief sigh, watching a soldier hurry past the window. "Gemma, I regret to inform you that a truce is already in place."

"I know that," I said quickly. "I know about the eastern alliance. I suppose . . . I was assuming . . . we might draft a new one to include Alcoro?"

My words lost their conviction by the end of the sentence. She was still staring out the window, and

I could see the furrowed frown in her reflection. I swallowed.

"I'm sorry for the nature of our arrival," I said. "Truly—if I had had a way to get word to you, if I could have managed it sooner . . ."

She sighed and leaned back from the glass, finally turning to face me. "I apologize, Gemma. I don't mean to insinuate that I'm not glad you made it safely . . ."

"But it was entirely unexpected," I said. "I know. I realize I'm asking a great deal of you, taking us in, upsetting all your plans, disrupting your solstice celebration . . ."

She waved a hand. "The Beacon lights up every morning, not just the days we gather around it. In a way, it's fortunate you arrived at that precise moment, or else you'd have been stranded at the base of the falls until someone happened upon you. But, Gemma . . ." Her gaze flicked to the door and back to me. "I admit, while I didn't expect you to show up at all, I certainly *never* would have expected you to bring him with you. Not after what he did in Cyprien. You do realize that even if we manage to achieve any kind of truce, he'll still have to answer to the Assembly of Six?"

I'd realized it but hadn't fully thought about it, and my just-warmed hands seemed to go cold again. "What will they rule?"

"I don't know, Gemma. Even without factoring all

the folk killed or imprisoned in his name, he personally murdered a Cypri citizen. In my country that's a gallows sentence."

Mine, too.

There was a short knock on the door and a maid poked her head in the room, her arms full of thick winter garments. A second maid stood behind her with a pitcher of steaming water. Mona waved them inside. The first laid out a stack of Lumeni-style clothes—long woolen skirts, buttoned blouses, shifts, and one-piece dresses that laced up the back, most in shades of blue and gray. The second maid filled the washbowl by the changing screen, set out a few pairs of stockings and boots, and together the two curtsied their way out of the room.

Mona shook out one of the skirts and held it to her own waist to estimate its length. "They'll have to be hemmed."

"It's fine," I said, unhooking Colm's cloak, shivering once I was out of its warmth. "There's no need."

She held it out to me, her gaze passing over my muddy, tattered bolero and trousers. "I find a well-fitting wardrobe does wonders to ease the mind." Her gaze fell on Colm's cloak draped over the settee. "Unlike some. I keep telling him that cloak is the wrong cut for him—it makes him look like a market tent."

It's warm, though. I took the skirt, blouse, and shift and proceeded to the changing screen. I stripped off my filthy clothes and sponged off—the water was hot and scented with mint, but it cooled quickly and left me covered with gooseflesh. I fumbled the new clothes with shaking hands—Lumen Lake was *cold*. Alcoro was no paradise in winter, but the sun shone more often than not, and the canyon floor was always warmer than the rim. Here, the great body of water seemed to lend everything a persistent dampness, and the sun was hidden by thick, steely clouds. I finished buttoning the blouse with clumsy fingers.

I was unaccustomed to my skirts cinching me low around my waist—Alcoran dresses were gathered by a wide sash under the bust, but the Lumeni skirt buttoned just above my hips. I wiggled a little, shifting the coarse woolen fabric, trying to get it to lie right. Doing this, I discovered one significant thing about the Lumeni skirt—it had pockets, deep ones. Carefully I gathered the bundle of papers I'd taken from my shirt, many of them damp and creased, and tucked them inside.

Just as I came around the corner of the screen, the door to my room swung open. In marched Ellamae, her cheeks flushed and her eyebrows knitted together. She stopped in the middle of the room, facing me with her fists on her hips. I fought against the urge to take a step back, away from her obvious anger.

"Poppy syrup?" she demanded. "Just to sleep?"

"What?" I asked.

"We *never* give poppy as a sleep aid," she said. "As

a sedative, maybe, but only in isolation, because it's so addictive. And fishpoison? For nerves? You know what my folk use that for? *Poisoning fish*." She shook her head. "No wonder he looks like a ghost resurrected, Gemma. He's having serious withdrawals."

Withdrawals.

From his physician's tinctures. *Of course.*

"I didn't realize," I said, not without guilt. "I was so focused on getting through the cave, and he's often sick when he's stressed. I just thought . . ."

"I'm amazed he made it anywhere at all," Ellamae said. "And it's no wonder he passed out by the waterfall. When was the last time he ate anything?"

I wracked my brain. "He ate a little here and there."

"But no real meals?"

"No."

"And the shaking?" she asked. "The sweats? Insomnia? What did you think that was?"

Cyanide poisoning?

Doubt at every decision I'd made since the Retreat clouded my head—I'd sent my mother back to expose Shaula's villainous string of murders . . . but had I been wrong? Was I so desperate to bring her down that I saw death in a crate of millipedes? My mother had put herself right back at the mercy of her sister . . . what if it was all for nothing?

You have always seemed to believe you could shape the world to meet your needs.

Ellamae was still staring at me, waiting for my mystery diagnosis. I drew in a breath, my flimsy confidence shrinking with every passing moment.

"I didn't think," I said. "I suppose I thought he had a fever, or that the trip was making his usual complaints worse. He's been ill for years, and I was so set on getting him here, I didn't think . . ."

A sick feeling twisted in my stomach, not exactly shame or remorse—merely a sharp bitterness at the mess things had become.

Ellamae sighed, running her fingers through her dark brown curls. "I sent to the kitchens for broth—hopefully he can keep that down. But he's a wreck, Gemma. How long has he been taking all that stuff?"

Forever, was my first thought, but that wasn't true.

"Six years," I said.

"Since he was crowned?" Mona asked acidly.

I looked at her, standing with her stiff certainty, and even though I'd sought her out, even though I desperately needed her help, I was suddenly done with her assuming the worst about my husband.

"Since his mother killed herself to let the reign of the Seventh King begin," I said evenly. "That was the day *before* he was crowned."

A somewhat awkward pause hung in the room. Mona was too good to break her perfect mask, but I thought I detected her lips tighten slightly. Ellamae heaved another sigh.

"What's his reaction to valerian?" she asked.

"It doesn't work," I said, moving past her for the adjoining door. "That's what he used to take before the poppy, but it stopped being effective."

"Wait, Gemma," Mona said. "We need to talk . . ."

"We can talk in here!" I said with much more assurance than I felt. Cheeks hot, I passed back into Celeno's room without turning to see if they'd followed me. My mind raced with a single thought.

This all could have been a very big mistake.

CHAPTER 10

Celeno looked up as I came in and then immediately looked away, his brow creased. Colm did the same thing, pulling his head out of the wardrobe, meeting my gaze, and then shoving it back in again, arranging a set of spare shirts on hangers.

"Leave that, Colm," Mona said, stalking past me for the door to the hall. "Let a servant do it." Colm continued as if he hadn't heard her, shaking out the last two shirts and threading them on hangers as she opened the door, unaware. "Rou, Valien—we'll be meeting in here. Arlen, are the guards all in place?"

"Yes," he said, hurrying to follow the others inside. "I've put in the order for a detail assignment."

"Good." She closed the door behind her and turned to the rest of us. "Sit," she said.

We sat. Rou and Valien took two of the armchairs.

Ellamae perched beside them on the bedside table, frowning at the contents of the healer's bag, which she'd clearly managed to commandeer. Arlen turned the hardback chair from the desk around. Colm took a position farthest away—leaning on the windowsill. I made a hasty decision and took a place at the end of Celeno's bed, just below his feet. He didn't give any response at all beyond shifting his gaze from the window to the comforter under his hands.

Mona didn't sit. She stood at the fireplace like it was a pulpit. "Well," she said. "It's probably unnecessary at this point, but let us make formal introductions. We have in our presence Gemma and Celeno Tezozomoc, queen and king of Alcoro." She nodded to us. "You've both met Ellamae Heartwood, queen of the Silverwood Mountains."

She said this stiffly, not addressing the fact that Celeno had known Ellamae longer than I, because she'd been locked and interrogated in the hold of his ship for a week while in Cyprien. Ellamae gave no response beyond crooking one of her thickly fringed boots over her knee, still absorbed with the herbs in the case.

Mona continued. "And her husband, Valien Heartwood, king of the Silverwood. By happy coincidence, they are here in Lumen Lake to observe the solstice Beacon lighting—though I admit, you will likely have to return again next year to have a more traditional experience."

Ellamae snorted, popping the cork off a bottle of herbs and sniffing it. Valien smiled at me, the silver embroidery on his deep green tunic winking in the firelight. "We have our own origin festival in a few weeks' time," he said. "If circumstances permit, you are welcome to join us."

"Thank you—we will," I said politely, privately thinking that an infinite number of cataclysmic things could happen within a few weeks' time.

Mona frowned, perhaps at Valien's casual declination to treat Celeno like a prisoner, and then waved a hand toward the other armchair. "You both know Rou, I suppose."

"Oh, don't introduce me like that," Rou implored.

"Fine," she said shortly. "King Celeno, Queen Gemma, I present to you Theophilius Roubideaux, unofficial ambassador to the Assembly of Six, diplomat, messenger, kidnapper, fire spinner, ex-steel worker and mail carrier, currently taking up a bed in my guest wing and generally complaining about anything that causes him the least discomfort." She lifted her chin. "Did I miss anything?"

"I can do a damn good headstand, too," he added.

Ellamae obliged him by laughing as she measured a pinch of herbs into a strainer. Mona's cheeks went pink, a reaction I remembered well from the punt in Cyprien as she strove to keep from breaking her mask with a smile. I wished she wouldn't hide her amusement—but maybe Rou knew how to interpret the look, too, because he warmed slightly as he gazed back.

"I'll try to complain less," he said humbly. "But only about things that can't be helped."

"The weather?" Mona prompted.

"I'll wear a few extra shirts."

"And the food?"

He winced. "Well . . ."

She closed her eyes briefly. There were a few more chuckles—though Celeno's frown only deepened. He picked at the embroidery on the hem of the coverlet.

"Last," Mona said with the air of someone trying to redirect conversation. "My brothers. Arlen Alastaire, who's acting liaison between myself and my generals." Arlen gave a wave that he quickly stifled and turned into a stoic nod—I got the impression he was trying hard to do a good job. I waved back.

"And Colm," Mona said. "My middle brother."

I waited for something else—a title, a modifier of some kind, but none came. He looked up from his place by the window. Despite his size, his shoulders were bent forward, giving him the impression of looking up at the world rather than down on it, like he'd grown accustomed to making himself go unnoticed. He hesitated a moment, as if weighing the right words.

"I'm glad for your safe arrival," he finally said, his words clipped with the same accent as his siblings'.

"Thank you," I said, aware of Mona's stare. "I am, too."

"All right," Mona said with a hint of relief. "Now. Tell us—what's this about a cave? How did you come to literally break into my country through the back of a waterfall?"

I took a breath, reached into my pocket, and after some blind fumbling among the sheaf of papers, drew out the map. I didn't turn to look at Celeno, but I could feel his gaze burning on the parchment.

"My mother is an entomologist in Alcoro," I said. "Her studies led her into the mountains, where she found a species of glowworm living in natural caves leading under the Stellarange. She formed a team with geologists, and together they mapped what you see here." I handed the map to Mona. Ellamae leaned over to look at it, stirring the contents of a mug. "With some time and effort, they form a route between Alcoro and Lumen Lake."

"*What?*" Mona's gaze jumped from the map to me. "How many folk know about this?"

"Very few," I said. "Probably no one outside my mother's team."

Ellamae frowned at the parchment. "Lumen Lake's not on the map."

"It was just a guess at the time," I said. "An educated one, but an unproven one—until now. My mother's team started encountering flooded passages and lakes, and some of the farthest ones had freshwater mussels in them. Based on geography, it only seemed logical that they'd reached the very western reaches of Lumen Lake. I just used their findings and added some of my own—mainly the reappearance of living creatures, and the changes in mineral growth in the cave system."

"And you just *hoped* we'd find a way out?" Celeno cut in.

I looked at him, his eyes shadowed in his pale face. His expression was different than it had been throughout our journey—not frustration, but resolute anger.

"I made the best decisions I could," I said, conscious of everyone's eyes on me. "We crossed a threshold in that . . . room." I couldn't bring myself to tell the others about the petroglyphs yet—that would only sidetrack the discussion we needed to have now. Time to discuss the Prophecy could only be won by halting the threat of war. "The biological environment, the mineral makeup—it was different in that passage. And knowing what we did about things happening back home . . . I had to try."

Valien took his knuckles away from his lips where they'd been resting. "He didn't know you were coming here?"

I tried to break my gaze away from Celeno's and found I couldn't. "I didn't tell him," I said softly.

"You *lied*," Celeno supplied. "You lied to me from the moment you appeared in my room. You've been lying for days—for weeks now. Or has it been longer?"

"No," I said, my face burning. "I . . . I tried not to lie to you, Celeno—really I did."

"You lied about the way being marked. You lied about where we were going."

I swallowed. "Yes, I did lie about that. I'm sorry."

"Did your mother know?" he asked. "Was she in on it, too?"

"No," I said. "I didn't tell her. She'd never have agreed to leave us if she thought we were going to the passages they'd barely explored. I needed her to go back, not come through with us."

He settled back against his pillow, the lines of his face tense and furious. "Well. At least I wasn't the only one, then."

"It seems Gemma made the best decisions with the options she had," Mona said coolly, and her subtle approval of me tricking my husband only made things worse. I dropped my gaze to the floor, wishing I could sink into it. "And it's bought us a significant opportunity—to all sit down and discuss, face-to-face, the present and futures of our countries." She glanced at Celeno. "That is, if we're all ready to attempt a civil discourse."

Before I could respond, he lifted his gaze to hers. "Don't antagonize me, Queen Mona—I'm tired of it. We tried civil discourse. I was not the reason it failed."

"You were the reason it was necessary," she said stiffly. "And if I recall, it quickly became uncivil."

"I was not the one to blow up a ship!" he said angrily.

"I was referring to you murdering a civilian," she shot back.

"Stop," I said, putting out a hand to both of them. "Please, stop. There were many mistakes, and Alcoro made most of them. I recognize that. But we were not the only country involved, and if this is going to work, we can't allow ourselves to devolve into arguing about blame and guilt." I looked at Celeno, his eyes glittering with anger. "You have to accept the catastrophe we caused here in Lumen Lake, and in Cyprien." I turned to Mona. "And *you* have to understand that there was more than just Celeno's hand at work, or mine. I'm not rejecting responsibility for it, but that movement was set in motion well before Celeno was king." I gestured between them. "We already have very little time to make decisions. Our folk won't be sitting idly in Alcoro—they'll be scouring the country for us, and continuing their campaign in Cyprien. Can we please, for the sake of our countries—for our *people*—try to stay rational?"

Mona drew in a sharp breath, but before she could reply, Celeno cut through the silence, his voice sharp.

"I'd like to speak to my wife," he said. "Alone."

Mona half-turned. "We've only just gotten started . . ."

"Alone," he repeated.

Ellamae uncrossed her legs with a sweep of her fringed boots and hopped off the bed stand. "It's probably best for you both to get some rest and eat something hot before we go any farther." She set down the mug she'd been stirring next to Celeno's shoulder. "Drink that."

"What is it?" he asked testily.

"Valerian and boneset," she said. "A little bit of sweet birch, and some sassafras for good measure."

"Valerian doesn't work," he said. "I told you I take poppy."

"And *I* told *you*, that's a ludicrous, reckless practice. It's one the reasons you're in the shape you're in—which is awful, in case you weren't sure. So drink up. I'll go figure out what's become of your broth." She clapped Mona on the back, who twitched forward, scandalized. "Come on, quit glaring. Don't we get breakfast on the solstice, or am I missing some Lumeni custom?"

Valien feigned a cough to hide his smile, rising to his feet and following his wife out of the room. Mona drew herself up, clearly brimming with frustration as the others rose from their seats. She seemed about to call after Ellamae, when Rou gently took her hand and pressed her fingers to his lips. She turned a steely eye on him. I had to give him credit—he dared a very small smile.

She let out her breath. "I'll throw you in the lake with the rest of them," she said.

"It'll make for gruesome pearl diving," he replied. He landed another kiss on her fingers before dropping her hand and following in her wake as she stalked to the door. He gave my elbow a little bump as he passed me.

Colm was the only one left. He uncurled his hands from his arms and stood from the windowsill.

"I read your thesis," he said.

Celeno looked over at him, brow creased.

"That telescope you developed," Colm said. "Did it correct for color aberration, or just spherical aberration?"

Celeno stared at him for a moment. Something stirred deep inside me—I remembered that telescope. He'd spent months with the engineers. The night they'd made the breakthrough, he didn't sleep a wink, homing in on what felt like every star in the sky, giddy with their new appearance through the more powerful lens. He'd only stopped to take a break as dawn neared and I had almost dropped off to sleep. I'd woken to find him on his knees in front of me, breathlessly asking me to marry him.

"It corrected for both," Celeno finally said. "It was achromatic."

"I thought so," Colm said. He nodded minutely at me. "That's what it looked like from the illustrations."

I'd done the illustrations.

We both stared at him as he passed the bed and made for the door. He set one hand on the knob.

"Wait," I said. "Colm—we should talk."

He nodded again. "We will. You talk first."

He stepped out into the hall and closed the door behind him.

Silence hung between us for a moment, and that warm memory of the night in Celeno's star patio slipped slowly back into the cold knot of dread in my stomach. With great effort I turned from the door back to him.

He was still staring after Colm.

"That's Mona's brother?" he asked.

"Yes," I said. "One of the two."

"He seems . . ." He shook his head. "A lot different from her."

"Yes," I said. "Why did you send them all away, Celeno?"

He shook himself, as if remembering that he'd done so. He turned back to me, his fists tightening on the coverlet. "You really have to ask? Gemma, *what are we doing in Lumen Lake?* Why did you bring us here?"

"We needed time, Celeno," I said. "Time to think about the Prophecy, and space to make decisions without the Prelate or the council or a slew of dissenters trying to drag us in all directions—which are both things we don't have back in Alcoro. Even if we can remove Shaula, it could be weeks, months more likely, before our forces can be withdrawn from Cyprien and their progress toward Paroa. And with this new alliance, even if we could rush the order to stand down, it might not happen before our neigh-

CREATURES OF LIGHT 273

boring countries march against us. We need to stall the fighting on both sides, and we never could have done that from Callais, or even Cyprien."

He put a hand to his eyes. "So your choice was *Lumen Lake*? The place we annexed, only to lose in a coup to a battalion of divers armed with woodworking tools? The place where *Queen Mona Alastaire*"—he waved agitatedly to the door—"would probably very much like to put my head on a pike on her tallest turret? This is hardly friendly territory!"

"Mona offered me sanctuary here while we were in Cyprien," I said, trying to keep my voice steady. "I couldn't take it until I knew I could bring you with me. But I didn't know how I would get us here until my mother mentioned the caves came all the way to the lake. Getting here was only a dream while I was in the Retreat. And then . . . suddenly I had a chance to make it a reality."

He was shaking his head, his forehead in his hand. "Right, a dream—a dream drenched in lies. You lied, lied, *lied* the whole time, while I risked everything to try to figure out how *not* to hang you."

I flushed with hurt and anger. "I took my own risks, too, Celeno. I'm sorry I thought you'd signed the death warrant, but I'd heard it from Shaula and had no reason to believe it wasn't true. You were angry enough at me that I thought it plausible. So I tried to act as best as I could, working in Alcoro's interest while knowing you wanted me dead."

He was silent for a long time, his forehead still in his hand. Finally, without looking up, he said, "The mules."

"The mules?"

"The ones we rode up the mountain—they're going to starve and die in that paddock. Did that cross your mind?"

"Yes," I said. "I left the gate partway open. My hope is that they make their way back down the mountain."

He blew out his breath, and then held out his hand. "Let me see the map."

Struggling against the burn of guilt I'd been carrying with me since the petroglyph room, I handed him my mother's map. He spread it over his lap, his gaze locking immediately on the petroglyph chamber.

"You drew in an additional passage," he said, eyeing my charcoal line where no path had been drawn before.

"In case you asked to see the map."

"I don't know why I didn't. I shouldn't have trusted you. But I suppose that didn't occur to me." He traced my betrayal with his finger. "You put the blazes on the walls."

My fingers tightened on my knees. "Yes."

He shook his head. "Gemma, we could have *died* down there—what if there hadn't been an exit?"

"I knew there must be," I said. "The *Arachnocampa* were back."

"Tiny bugs could crawl in anywhere!" he said. "A crack in a mountaintop could suffice!"

"They need the right elevation," I persisted. "And water that's not sterile, it only made sense—"

"*No*, Gemma, it made *no sense*. No amount of biological theorizing can force this to *make sense*." He flicked the map away from him, the creases back in his brow. "In the end, all you wanted was the same thing everyone else wants from me—the validation of my title. All you wanted was for me to scribble my signature on a few of Queen Mona's documents."

"That's not true."

"Tell me how it's different!" he said. "Tell me how it's different from a dissenter wanting the king's validation on a fake Prophecy, or how a councilor wants the king's approval on their particular agenda? *How is it different?*"

I took in a breath, stung. "I suppose I thought we were still working toward the same goals. Peace for Alcoro. Peace for ourselves. You . . . and me."

"You're just being vague, Gemma!" His hands rose partway to his face in frustration, his fingers gnarled on the air. "You're speaking in generalizations and abstractions. If I was critiquing your thesis, I'd think I was reading some fresh student's first attempt. Peace, diplomacy, civil discourse—give me something absolute!" He rubbed his face hard with both hands. "Shaula told me you couldn't be trusted anymore—I should have listened."

"How can you possibly say that?" I said, straightening angrily. "I think we've both found enough evidence that Shaula herself can't be trusted."

"But you didn't know that at the time!" His head shot up from his hand. "You *had no idea* she'd forged my signature. You had no idea she'd put out the order for your execution! You didn't know those things when you started! You're *still* lying to me, Gemma! *What am I missing?*"

I drew in a breath just as there was a knock on the door. Celeno let his head fall back against his pillow, his face a contortion of creases and furrows. "Come in!"

Ellamae pushed the door open with her hip, a laden food tray rattling in her hands. She crossed the room and set it down on the bedside table, and then frowned at the still-full mug cooling at his elbow. "I told you to drink that."

"I don't know what's in it," Celeno said, his eyes still tightly closed.

"I *told* you what's in it!" She yanked open the healer's bag and slammed down a little bottle of dark liquid, making his eyes pop open. "*Valerian*—to sleep." She withdrew a packet of crushed leaves. "*Boneset*—for your stomach." Next, a bottle of powdered bark. "*Sweet birch*—for your head. And *sassafras*"— a bottle of dried buds—"to make the daggum thing taste good. Look, they're all labeled. Just because *your* lot tried to poison *me* doesn't mean we all do it. Drink the damn tincture. And then drink *that*." She dropped a little pot of dark, fragrant broth next to the mug. "I know we're all supposed to hate each other, but I'm not wild about the idea of somebody dying if I can do something about it. Drink. And then rest. Then, if we all still hate each other, we can find a *civilized* way to kill each other." She shook her head in frustration. "Come on, Gemma, I've got a different vat of poison for you." She stormed to the adjoining door, carrying the food tray.

I hesitated at Celeno's bedside. He glowered at the cups on his side table.

"Please," I said softly. "Drink them."

With no reply from him, I crossed to the door and slipped back into my room.

Ellamae was unloading her tray onto my own bedside table—a bowl of soup, a half loaf of grainy bread, and a boiled egg. My stomach growled. But before I could reach the table, she turned to me.

"Gemma, listen. There's something I need to tell you."

I stopped short of the food. "What?"

"Your petroglyphs—the prophecy, or whatever. Colm thinks there are more, here in Lumen Lake."

"Down here? At the lake?"

"Well, not *down* here. Up on the Palisades, about halfway to the ridge. They're in a little overhang called Scribble Cave. That's what was in the letter we tried to send you—he didn't think a message could make it through Cyprien, so he decided to send it over the mountains and into Paroa. But I guess it never got to you."

"No." There was no telling where that letter was. My heart pounded. "How long would it take to get to them?"

"If you rode a horse to where the scout path splits from the main road, about three hours, one way."

"And you're *sure*," I said breathlessly. "*Sure* that they're the same? Have you compared them to a copy of the ones in Callais? Have you made transcriptions?"

Her dark brown gaze darted around the room. "To be honest, I wouldn't have known. Colm spotted it. We spent a night in that cave in May when we were crossing the mountains. After Mona took back the lake, he found your prophecy written in a bunch of your folk's writings and recognized some of it. I think he's acting so flighty and odd now because he doesn't want Mona to know."

"That's probably wise," I said.

She shook her head. "I'm not so sure. If it really is another prophecy, it changes everything your folk believe. She won't appreciate being kept in the dark on that. I don't know what Colm's so afraid of."

I could hazard a guess. "Can you take me to see them?" I asked. "As soon as possible?"

"It'll be hard to come up with an excuse Mona will believe, and it might take longer than usual with the ice on the Palisades." She blew out a breath. "But, yes,

I think the sooner you can see them, the better. Colm should come."

"And Celeno?"

"I'm not convinced he can make the trip."

"He made it this far," I said. "And I've already kept too much information from him. He should come."

She puffed out a breath. "If he drinks what I give him, he can come. But give him at least a day or two to rest."

A day or two felt like an eternity, but I doubted there would be any arguing with her. I nodded. "I'll try to get him to drink the tincture." Though at this point, he'd probably prefer to drink actual poison rather than give in to either Ellamae or me.

Which reminded me . . .

"Ellamae," I said. "Do you have any experience with cyanic acid?"

Her fingers paused on the last mug on the tray. "Uh . . ."

"I'm not insinuating anything," I said quickly. "I just didn't know—if you're familiar with herbs—if you'd ever treated anyone who'd accidentally ingested it."

"I can't see how they would," she said, setting the mug down. "It's not a common drug—I'm not even sure where it comes from, or how to distill it. Some seeds have it, don't they?"

"Some, but I'm thinking particularly of the kind released by millipedes."

"Millipedes?"

"Little arthropods, some of them luminesce . . ."

"I know what a millipede is," she said, affronted. "They're all over the slopes, even the glowy ones. I think they'd have joined fireflies as being sacred to us if they didn't set your skin burning. That stuff they leak out is cyanic acid?"

"Yes. Have you dealt with it?"

"I had a scout get some in her eye once, and she had the spins for a few days." She twirled her finger. "Dizzy, blurry sight, that kind of thing. She may have thrown up."

"What do you suppose would happen if a person ingested it?" I asked, trying not to sound too deranged.

"I dunno. A strong enough dose of anything can kill a person. But in smaller amounts . . ." She shrugged. "Your guess is as good as mine."

"All right. Thank you, anyway." I looked at the mug she'd set on the bedside table. "What did you give me?"

"Just chamomile," she said, tucking the tray under her arm. "After a tall pint of beer, I find it's the main thing I look forward to after a long slog in the woods."

I could have hugged her. Some of my nervous tension slipped away, and my eyes prickled. "Thank you."

"It's nothing."

"No—thank you. I know what it means for us to be here, with you all. You shouldn't have to help us . . ."

"You don't have to cry," she said, alarmed.

"Sorry." I dashed at my eyes. "I can't help it. But thank you all the same."

She headed for the door to the hall. "My husband would call it my chivalrous sense of duty, but Mona would probably say I'm just stubborn—though I think they're probably the same thing. Eat and rest. You're both going to need it if all our talks go like they did a few minutes ago."

She closed the door. I rubbed my face, over-whelmed, exhausted, famished. I pulled the desk chair close to the bedside table and ate everything. The soup was salty but brimming with carrots, potatoes, and chard, and I soaked up every droplet with the bread. I could have eaten a half-dozen boiled eggs but made myself savor the one before lingering over the mug of chamomile. It was piping hot and fragrant, and I bent over it like a miser over gold. My eyelids drooped as I drank, and I wondered if Ellamae hadn't slipped vale-rian in my mug, too. But no—this was the full-body exhaustion of endless travel, of heartache, of uncer-tainty. How many miles had we come? Had I done the right thing at all?

Would Celeno ever forgive me?

When I'd finally drained the mug, the bed called

temptingly. But I made myself stand and move carefully to the adjoining door. Turning the knob slowly, softly, I cracked it open.

Celeno was lying on his side in bed, his head bent over his arm. He didn't stir even when the hinges creaked as I opened the door a little wider. I tiptoed over the carpet and peeked into his mugs. The broth and the tincture were both gone. Sweat still shone on his forehead, but his breath was deep and slow with real sleep. I reached out a hand to brush his hair and then stopped. I didn't want to wake him. I withdrew my hand, tucked it to my chest, and hurried back to the door, closing it softly behind me.

Without changing into a dressing gown, or even taking off my stockings, I crawled onto the bed, wriggled down under the pile of quilts, and was almost instantly asleep.

CHAPTER 11

When I woke, the room was dark. A fire burned heartily in the grate, and a covered tray sat on my bedside table. Had I slept the whole day and into the night? I slipped out of bed, my body creaking and groaning in protest, and padded to the window.

The view out to the lake revealed snow-ribbed islands under gloomy sky. A few folk moved across the grounds, wrapped so tightly in cloaks and furred hats that they looked more like animals startled from hibernation. The horizon in the west shone a pale gray. So it wasn't fully night, then, but approaching evening—I'd slept most of the day. So much for starting diplomatic talks right away.

My gaze fell on the tray on my bedside table. My stomach growled, but before I reached for the cover, I pivoted and went across the room to Celeno's door.

Our morning conversation rang in my head, and it was with a wave of trepidation that I put my hand on the knob and turned it. What would I say if he was awake? What would *he* say? Should I tell him now about the petroglyphs up on the Palisades?

I should, shouldn't I?

I slipped into his room and instantly saw that he was still asleep, his face pressed deep into his pillow. I stopped a few feet away, a little too relieved to postpone another disastrous conversation. I listened to his breathing for a moment—regular and even but with a slight rasp to it—and then turned back for the adjoining door. I tiptoed across the floor, eased it shut behind me, and went straight to the tray on my bedside table.

The cover revealed more bread, salted fish with pickled onions, and a honeyed slice of pumpkin to provide some sweetness. I devoured it all, and then went to the washbowl. The water was cold, but I splashed my face and loosened my hair from the braid I'd been traveling in. It flowed over my shoulders, crimped into waves. I changed into a fresh skirt, adjusted my star band, and then made my way out the door.

I'd expected to have to wander the hallways, hoping to bump into an attendant who might show me to Mona's rooms, but as I stood outside my door, I heard familiar murmuring just down the hall. One of the doors to another guest room was cracked and spilling warm light. Without thinking, I headed toward it.

I realized my mistake at the same moment my knuckles struck wood. Hastily, I tried to step back, but my knock had already landed, and the hinges creaked a little wider. It was Rou's room, and Mona was there with him. In that half a breath, I saw them each as they tried so hard not to show themselves— she with her head resting wearily on his shoulder, he with his cheek pressed against hers, his eyebrows knitted together. Their fingers were linked on the settee, and his free hand twined in the short hair at the nape of her neck. As soon as my knock sounded, they straightened—she sliding automatically into that straight-backed posture, and he lounging against the arm of the settee, the picture of careless ease.

Dammit, dammit. Would I ever manage not to ruin a perfectly good thing?

"Gemma," Mona said. "Come in—I'm glad to see you're awake."

"I'm sorry," I whispered, nudging the door a little wider. "I didn't mean . . ."

"We accused Mae of drugging you both," Rou said, hitching up his warm grin where worry had been before. "To which she got a little cussy."

"No," I said. "I don't think she did—we were both just so exhausted."

"Come sit," Mona said, gesturing to the armchair. "There's tea—would you like some?"

I sank down into the chair, noting the tray was clearly set for two people. "Oh . . . I don't want . . ."

"I'll pass," Rou said. "Gemma—I can't tell you how happy I am you're here. These people *don't drink coffee.* No coffee, Gemma!"

"How glad I am for a political ally's objective observance of my country's preferences," Mona said sardonically, pouring dark brown tea into one of the mugs. "Else I might never know how backward our hospitality is. Honey or cream?"

"Both, please," I said.

"I might have to suggest political sanctions," Rou said. "Unless we can amend the trade compendiums."

"I can still throw you into the lake," Mona said, stirring my cup.

"Crying for a drop of coffee," he agreed.

Her lips tightened in that half-amused, half-exasperated expression as she handed me the cup.

"Thank you," I said, curling my fingers around the heat. "Where are the others?"

"Mae was ransacking the healing wing earlier," Mona said, pouring herself a cup. "I think she expects to find only leeches and whiskey, and keeps acting surprised when we actually have things in stock. *Honestly,*" she finished with a mutter.

"I vote she goes into the lake before me," Rou said.

"Don't think I'm not mulling it over." Mona stirred her tea. "She retreated with Valien a little while ago, and I haven't seen them since. Arlen is at the armory checking over the new shipment of Silvern bows they brought down with them."

She sipped her tea and blotted her lips.

"And Colm?" I asked.

"Oh," she said, as if he was an afterthought. "Who knows—the library, probably. Maybe the shipyard, hoisting rigging or hammering nails. I can never tell if he's in the mood to read philosophy or beat a ship's hull." She observed the inside of her teacup with interest. "I used to be able to tell."

"You were close?" I asked.

"We used to be all we had," she said to her tea. "Arlen's younger than us by enough that he was always a baby, but Colm and I are just a year apart. We were close even before . . ."

"My folk invaded Lumen." It was uncomfortable to use that word in place of *annexed*, but I supposed I should probably start.

She took a short breath and swirled her tea. "Even during our exile, he stuck by me, went along with everything I planned to keep us afloat, worked himself ragged to earn us money and keep his mind off the lake. But now he's drifting away from me. I don't know what he thinks anymore. I don't know why he does what he does. Sometimes I think he'd be happier back in exile, sitting at tavern firesides listening to merchant gossip and travelers' tales."

Rou stretched his arm along the back of the settee to brush the back of her neck. "I'm sure he's still trying to help."

"He counters everything I say," she said, looking

up from her tea. "He strikes everything down, turns it around. I'm not used to that from him. From Arlen, yes, and from my council, but not from him. We used to tack together—now we're sailing in two different directions."

"Maybe you're still trying to get to the same place, though," I suggested.

She gave a little flick of her head and went back to her tea. "I don't want to talk about Colm. Suffice to say, I don't know where he is or what he's up to. But while you're here, and while Celeno is still asleep . . ." She set her cup down on its saucer. "Gemma, Rou and I have been talking. About what could happen after all this, if we manage to stave off war."

I set my cup down, readying myself. "Yes?"

"Are you really, truly committed to liberating Cyprien?" Rou asked. "Withdrawing all Alcoran presence, restoring the Assembly of Six to full power, giving up our industry and trade routes?"

The thought made my head swim. I couldn't imagine Alcoro without Cyprien. "Yes," I said.

He puffed out his cheeks as he exhaled. "Then you know that Celeno will probably be tried as a war criminal?"

My blood ran cold. "A war criminal? But that . . . that's for . . ."

Crimes of war. I stopped short at the sight of their faces, both with a sudden film of wary pleasantry. I dropped my gaze to my teacup, my mind rushing.

Rou was kindhearted enough to speak the words I couldn't. "Countries invading other countries has happened before," he agreed. "But it can't be denied that Alcoro went a step farther, Gemma."

"Military-style execution of civilians, separating families, and general subjugation," Mona said stiffly. "Those things aren't part of the conventions of war."

The whole room seemed to close in on me, tightening my chest and stomach, pressing into my head. "What's the sentence?"

"Life in prison," Rou said. "Or, so I would expect. Cyprien has never had a law of execution. Our worst criminal offenders receive life in prison with no autonomy, sometimes in isolation."

"That's on top of the reparations that will need to be made," Mona added. "It's not going to be pretty, Gemma."

I'd hardly expected it to be pretty—but I hadn't considered the possibility of war crimes. I had a vision of Celeno in a Cypri cell, damp from the bayou, with no view of the sky. Growing old inside the same four walls.

I drew in a shaky breath. "I know I have no right to argue against it, but if you imprison Celeno, it may have worse consequences than you think. It won't unmake his title to Alcoro—they'll have almost no option other than to go to war."

"Against an allied East," Mona reminded me.

"I'm not saying it's a good idea," I said. "It will be

Alcoro's downfall—I realize that. But they won't have a choice. To all intents and purposes, the Prophecy hasn't been fulfilled, at least not the Prophecy that most folk believe in, and to remove the Seventh King before it's been realized . . . a majority of folk will say you're tampering with the divine."

Mona's jaw jumped as she clenched her teeth—she didn't believe in the Light, and she certainly didn't believe in the Prophecy, so I could imagine her outrage at being drawn into its storm. Perhaps to stave off a fruitless rant, Rou gestured to me. "And I suppose there's no good hoping you may still have some influence there?"

"I'm on trial," I said. "I'm no one in Alcoro anymore. They've set the warrant for my execution."

Rou's mouth twisted bitterly. "Wouldn't Celeno have to approve something like that?"

"I'm sure he already has," Mona said stiffly.

I bristled at her continued assumption of Celeno's behavior. "Actually—no, Mona, he hasn't."

Surprise flickered briefly on her face. "Then what's the impediment to your reclaiming the throne? If the warrant can be overturned, you can be reinstated, and we have the opportunity to solve things civilly."

"Well, it's—it's complicated," I said. "The warrant has been signed with Celeno's name, but . . . not by him."

"Not by him?"

"His signature was forged," I said, my face hot.

Could my country sound any more corrupt? "Neither of us knew it until recently."

"Forged by whom?" Rou asked. "Who could get away with something like that and not be found out?"

"One of our advisors," I said, trying to avoid stacking any more fuel on the fires of religious exploitation. "One of our inner circle . . . I know it sounds absurd, but it probably wasn't difficult for her to do it—and I have my suspicions that she's done it before . . ."

Mona nodded, as if in comprehension. "That religious advisor of yours. The Prelate."

My lips kept moving even as my words died. "Why . . . why would you . . ."

"I thought her presence in Cyprien was odd," Mona said. "I could think of no appropriate reason for you to include her in policy talks, but when she started nudging Celeno on our trade agreements, I knew she had a deeper role than I originally thought. I expect she's behind most of Alcoro's movements since her rise to power, is she not?"

"You saw her for barely five minutes," I said, stubbornly loath to admit how right she was. "And you hardly spoke to her at all."

"Perhaps—but I saw the way she handled you, and Celeno, and me," she said evenly. "I can recognize a fellow heartless politician." She waved a hand. "But I admit that's not my only evidence. In all the documents we have from Alcoro's occupation, and the treaties before it, hers is the only other name that appears next to Celeno's. All the writs and orders to your forces while you occupied the lake, all the missives between the monarchy and the captain—it's his *and* hers. I expect any documentation in Cyprien is the same. It couldn't have been a much bigger step for her to begin falsifying them completely."

That she could have gleaned so much about Shaula's actions from a few minutes of conversation and a handful of documents . . . how could she have hit directly upon a truth I'd been completely blind to?

Perhaps she understood my thoughts. "Sometimes it's harder to spot treachery when it comes from those closest to you," she said sagely. "We overlook those we think we can trust."

"Well . . ." I said, struggling to remember how we'd reached this topic. "Well . . . the order for my execution is in her hand, and to all relevant parties, it will appear to have been signed by the king. I can't go back to Alcoro while she's in power—and especially if Celeno's not with me."

"So we remove her from power," Mona said, as easily as if changing the date of a luncheon or boating trip. "She's committed treason. Her name is on the same documents we'd use to indict Celeno. We can remove her from power, along with Celeno, and open the door for you to step back in as queen."

For at least three inhales, I was reduced to simply gasping softly. I looked back and forth between Mona and Rou.

"No . . . no," I said thickly. "No, that won't work."

"Why not?" Mona asked.

"It . . . They'll still want to go to war," I said. "The Seventh King . . ."

"Gemma," Mona said, placing her teacup on its saucer. "You are—or will be—the queen of the country. Not a subordinate to the Seventh King, not a pawn of the Prelate—the sole ruling monarch. You will have the power to strike down the call for war. You will have the power to reroute the direction of your country. You will have the power to build Alcoro back up from what it's become."

"Not if Alcoro doesn't recognize me as a solitary authority," I said—why couldn't she understand this? "And they won't, without Celeno."

"Who will stand against you?" she prompted. "Your military? We'll have the combined forces of five countries to counter yours. Your civilians? We will control every trade route into and out of Alcoro. Your council? Your Prelate? When your country is under threat of losing all commerce, all cooperation with the rest of the East unless they accept you as their ruling monarch . . . Gemma, don't you see? We will *make* them recognize your authority."

"That doesn't make me a queen," I said before I could stop myself. "That makes me your puppet."

"An ally," Mona said evenly. "Perhaps conditionally so—I don't deny it. I regret to inform you that you'll be hard-pressed to reach a solution that allows

Alcoro full governmental control, when such freedom has come at significant cost to the rest of the East."

I spluttered a little, struggling for a cohesive thought. "You don't understand—you don't understand what replacing the Seventh King will mean to my folk. I didn't come all this way so you could . . ."

"Gemma," she said. "You asked me to help you. I am *trying* to help you, in the best way I know how. I may not understand the religious nuances of your country, but I *understand power*. My childhood was spent learning how to preserve and present authority. I have struck down forces both inside and outside my country that would have taken it from me—that *did* take it from me. A country is only ever as stable as its government. You want to understand how I took the lake back from you with no standing army? It was because folk knew to follow me. And we can make the same thing happen for you."

"You make the assumption that I'm the right person they should be following," I said, astonished that she could present such hubris as common sense. "That we're *both* the right people to follow."

"Nobody is the right person to rule," she said coldly. "I am no exception. The question is whether one wrong causes more harm than another. Having your husband and your Prelate in power makes you enemies to the rest of the world. Is that good for your folk? Removing them from the throne with no successor creates a vacuum, which breeds civil war. Is *that* good for your folk?"

"What's good is a monarchy they believe in," I said.

Rou cleared his throat. "If I may—and I realize I'm no king, but I do think I know about people, particularly those under bad leadership—Gemma, who's to say they *don't* believe in you? You've sat alongside Celeno for most of his reign. Folk are used to seeing you in a position of power, even if it's been overshadowed by the demands of the Prophecy. Even the Assembly, I imagine, would be quicker to recognize you over a stranger to the throne—known versus unknown."

"They wouldn't prefer we do away with the monarchy altogether?" I asked, a little vindictive at how gentle and reasonable he managed to sound. "Establish an elected government, like yours?"

"I won't pretend I don't find this all a bit cutthroat," he admitted. "Even the slander and muckraking of the campaign trail seems a good deal more genteel than forcing a country to accept a monarch's authority. But I'm trying to be realistic—Cyprien didn't transition from a monarchy to an Assembly. It's how we've always been. There's no telling what turning Alcoro into an elected government would take, or cost." He shrugged. "If we assume Alcoro's monarchy isn't going anywhere, and if the Prophecy's taking turns people don't expect, it's my opinion that your folk would be relieved to have a familiar face to lead them."

I didn't quite miss the warm look Mona gave him—she was too new to the sensation of being in love to fully mask a surge of affection. She turned expectantly back to me, probably waiting for me to sigh and sniffle and concede that they were both right—this really was the only way forward.

I did sniffle, but I didn't sigh. I fished for the handkerchief Rou had given me earlier and pressed it to my eyes. This was not at all how I'd hoped things might go. All the countless times I had pictured myself actively rebuilding Alcoro, it had always been bent over a sheet of parchment, pouring out dreams of a university, with visions of Celeno healthy and whole beside me and a nation reveling in the fulfillment of its beliefs. Not a solitary reign propped on the throne by a foreign power, with Celeno in a place I could never reach and my country in fractious shambles.

I had a glimpse of our monarchy gone from being pulled and pushed by the Prelacy to one in debt to its foreign neighbors, each with their own string of grievances against Alcoro. I would be able to do nothing without the blessing of Lumen Lake, and the Silverwood, and Cyprien, and Winder and Paroa. Would they allow an Alcoran university, or would that expense be too extravagant to undertake? Like everything else, I'd banked on the power of Celeno's title to ultimately make it a reality. Now, with only myself behind it and the country leashed to our neighbors . . .

Suddenly I didn't want to be in the room with either of them any longer. I lowered Rou's handkerchief and set my lukewarm tea on the table.

"I'm going back to bed," I said.

Disappointment flashed briefly across Mona's face, manifested as a tight purse of her lips. Rou, as always, was more transparent, his face etched with sympathy that was frustratingly genuine. I wondered if I'd ever reach a point in my life when people wouldn't pity me.

"I'm sorry, Gemma," he said.

"Me, too," I said, rising from the settee. They both rose with me. I busied myself with folding Rou's handkerchief.

"I'll wash this before I give it back," I said.

"Keep it," he said kindly. "Mona embroiders them like they're currency—I'm having to use them for napkins."

His humor rolled off me, only roiling my stomach further. The fish and onions from earlier squirmed a little. I slid his handkerchief in my pocket.

"I'll have them bring you breakfast in the morning," Mona said. "But ask if you need anything before that."

I murmured my thanks and went to the door, closing it with a snap behind me. I leaned against it briefly, overwhelmed by the ramifications of my choices stacking up on top of one another. In trying to find a solution, I'd made a mess. How could I make things right?

The Prophecy. Like before, the Prophecy was still the answer.

And now that I had gotten us here, the place I'd thought would be a safe haven for us, a place to think without the Prelate or the council or a crowd of dissenters—now I needed to speak to Colm.

Because I was only just now beginning to realize what I'd set in motion.

I'd hoped bringing Celeno here might mean the end of the war.

Now I realized it could mean the end of Alcoro.

The following morning, after I'd eaten breakfast, I tiptoed in and out of Celeno's room—he was asleep again, but a half-finished food tray on his bedside table told me he'd at least eaten a little the evening before. Back in my room, I dressed in a new Lumeni blouse and skirt, scooped up a woolen shawl to hold off the chill in the palace, and left to seek out the library.

I stopped a servant to get directions, and though his answer was terse, it sounded straightforward enough—Blackshell didn't seem to be a terribly large place. But I soon found that what it lacked in expanse it made up for in twists and turns. I rounded unexpected corners and wound up tight staircases, brushing my fingers on mother-of-pearl tiles and thick tapestries embroidered with swimming creatures, their pearl eyes glinting in the dim light. Between admiring the artistry and forgetting how many turns I had made, I soon found myself completely turned around. Hoping I was heading for the main wing of the palace, where I could reorient myself, I came instead to a short hall of portraits, with a view of the lake that told me I was nowhere close to where I wanted to be.

I stopped, trying to decide whether to continue on or backtrack, staring vaguely at the closest portrait. After a moment, my gaze focused, and I realized it was a royal portrait of a long-ago king and queen. I studied the painting style—narrow-eyed and small-mouthed, with tiny hands clutching bundles of rushes. Despite the old-fashioned technique, I recognized the dark golden hair the Alastaire siblings still shared today. I looked past it to the next painting. The style was much the same, but this king now had freckles, and the baby he held had round blue eyes. I was studying the third portrait, where I thought I detected the forerunner to Mona's crisp chin-tilt, when a figure turned the nearest corner, absorbed in a document. We both looked up and started a little—it was Valien. I hadn't heard his soft footsteps at all.

"Queen Gemma," he greeted. "How are you?"

"Lost," I said honestly.

"Ah." He nodded in understanding. "Me as well. I believe I've once again taken the long way to the Blackshell armory."

I smiled—he may have been joking to make me feel better, but I was grateful for it all the same. "I was hoping for the library."

"I believe it's one wing over," he said. "Along with the staircase I'm looking for. Shall we do some way-finding together?"

"Gladly." I fell into step next to him. We passed the next portrait, and I craned my head to observe the subjects—all six family members bore a remarkable array of freckles.

"We've got a hall like this," Valien said. "Though I tend to avoid passing through it—it always reminds me I should comb my hair." He flattened his thick black bangs over the silver circlet across his brow. "The common trait in my family seems to be egre-gious hair." He gestured to the nearest painting, where the style was becoming a little looser and more colorful. "Though we have a ring that goes from por-trait to portrait, too."

I had noticed the seal ring, made of mother-of-pearl and carved with rushes, traveling through each image, along with Mona's pearl necklace. I also no-ticed the ring he mentioned on his knuckle, a thick green stone set into wrought silver.

"Ours is a six-pointed star," I said, nodding to his hand. "What's yours?"

He held it out, the carved symbol winking. "A firefly. One of your little—what's the phrasing—creatures of light?"

"Yes, that's—oh!" The exclamation burst out of me, completely inappropriate for a seal ring. I pressed my fingers to my lips. "I'm sorry, I just . . . is your hand all right?"

"What? Oh." He turned his palm over, revealing a thick mess of old scar tissue that spiderwebbed between his fingers. "It's fine. Childhood injury. It hardly bothers me anymore, though Ellamae likes to remind me it makes me shoot cockeyed."

I gave a nervous laugh, embarrassed that I'd obligated him to show me. I instinctively twitched down the hem of my left sleeve.

If he was bothered, he didn't show it. He dropped his hand back to his side as we approached the final portrait and said, "Ah, the baby Alastaires. Mona still looks like she could take the throne at age six, doesn't she?"

I stopped in my tracks to examine the last portrait. The painting style had taken on a more realistic look, rather than the stiff, stylized portraits from previous generations. Arlen was only a baby in the queen's arms, and the king looked stooped and pale. But Mona and Colm stood in front, holding bulrushes in their fists and clasping each other's free hand. There were rushes on Mona's skirt, too, and set into the seal rings both she and Colm wore on their fingers, far too large for their little hands. I gazed at their solemn expressions—even in childhood, Mona's chin had a firm tilt to it, and Colm's had a tuck.

"She does look ready to rule the country," I agreed.

"I think my portrait at that age looked more like I wanted to bolt," he said, opening the door to the next hall and holding it for me. I moved past him and found myself on the landing of a stairwell. Outside, the sky above the lake was charcoal, the water foaming in little whitecaps as wind gusted across the surface. Snow was coming.

Valien pointed up the corridor leading perpendicular off the landing. "I believe that's the way to the library. And I believe this is my route to the armory."

"Thank you," I said. "I appreciate the wayfinding."

"If no one's seen you by lunchtime, I'll have them send out a search party," he said, descending the first few stairs. He looked back up at me, the gray light from the window glinting off the circlet under his hair. "And . . . Gemma, if you need anything, let one of us know."

I couldn't decide how to tell him that just having a normal conversation about seal rings and portraits was something I hadn't realized I'd needed.

"Thank you," I called again as he padded down the stairs, his soft-soled boots making almost no noise.

I turned up the adjoining corridor and came almost immediately to a set of double doors, open to reveal a wall of bookshelves. I blew out a breath of relief and crossed the threshold. The library was small and dark—and empty. There were four long tables, all of which were polished and unused except for the end of one, which bore a neat array of clutter—stacks of books aligned by title, sheaves of parchment organized into rows, spare quills and blotters at the ready. I glanced at the neat, cramped handwriting on the top page. Celeno's natural writing was a scrawl that became more slanted as he got excited, but years of penmanship had corralled it into a formal, if uneven, hand. In contrast, Colm's was unflourished and measured, with a sweep to his *s*'s that made them extend below the other letters with his *g*'s and *p*'s.

He was piecing together an account of an early Lumeni queen, it looked like—a fabled heroine who had united two warring islands and was gifted a crown that was supposed to outshine the stars. I admired his organization, cobbling together the account from several different sources—a history text, a lengthy ballad, a book of folk songs, a smattering of nigh-unreadable journals, and fanciful woodcuts of the alleged crown. I thought back to the white statue I'd seen at the end of the lakeside terrace—perhaps this was the queen depicted there.

I smiled appreciatively at his neat work, but it wasn't what I had come for. Slightly nettled at the time I'd wasted seeking this place out with nothing to show for it, I set the papers down and headed back to the library door. The sky was only getting darker through the thick glass windows, the first flurries of snow beginning to swirl, but I had one more lead to follow. I went down the staircase Valien had taken to get to the armory, realized it was the wrong one, backtracked, and somehow ended up in one of the squat turrets. Confused once more by Blackshell's layout, I tilted my face against the glass, trying to orient myself. I was almost directly above the great terrace three stories below, and if I craned my gaze to the right, I could see the toothy masts of the shipyard poking up past the palace wall. I went back down the staircase, hoping I would find a door leading out to the terrace.

What I found instead were Ellamae and Mona.

We collided around one of the tight corners, and Ellamae lashed out and grabbed my wrist before I could reel backwards.

"Ho!" she said. "Sometimes I let out a warning when I'm coming to a corner—Blackshell's twistier than a rabbit-packed warren."

"It's an old palace," Mona said a little defensively. "And at least it's not as drafty as Lampyrinae."

"At least I can find my way around Lampyrinae without a compass bearing," Ellamae said.

Mona rearranged the large pearl pendant around her neck, the one I'd seen in all the portraits. "Unless you're being chased by your own Guard."

Ellamae dropped my wrist. "Ex-*cuse you*. We *made it* to the damn Firefall."

I looked from one to the other, afraid I'd triggered some long-held animosity between them. But their postures were easy, with sparks of smiles in their eyes if not their lips. I shook myself, trying to fathom the friendship between these two outrageously different queens. I cast around for a way to reorient the conversation.

"I was trying to go out to the shipyard," I said. "Is the terrace the best way to go?"

Ellamae shivered. "Ugh, don't go wandering around the village right now—there's a howling good storm blowing in."

Mona's gaze jumped out the windows, her eyes not on the sky, but on the end of the terrace where the paving stones met the water. "And . . ." she began, sounding almost furtive. "The entrance hall would be better than the terrace. It'll put you on the main track."

Curiously, I followed her sudden glance, but I saw nothing at the end of the terrace besides the white statue and a few boats out in the water.

I nodded to the statue. "What figure is that?" I asked. "Is she from legend?"

She cut her gaze back to me. "Who? Why?"

I shrugged slightly, confused by her unease. "Sometimes there are similarities in the legends among countries. It would be interesting to see if we have a similar figure in our starlore."

She cleared her throat, and I noticed Ellamae, too, looked slightly uncomfortable.

"It's a purely Lumeni heroine," Ellamae said. "No question."

"I just wondered, because we have a princess with a crown of stars . . ."

"Her name's Ama, and she saved Lumen Lake," Mona said stiffly. "Come, let's get out of this hallway—it's too chilly for my liking. And I need to get your measurements, anyway."

Still a little puzzled by the odd timbre of the conversation, I followed her ushering to the next corner.

"My clothes don't need to be tailored," I said as we moved down the corridor. "They fit fine as they are."

"I have a gown I think will suit you well," she said. "It's too light for me—I look like a block of ice wearing it—but it should complement your complexion nicely."

"First rule of Lumeni politics," Ellamae said seriously, "is that wearing the wrong color will doom diplomacy before it begins."

Mona tutted impatiently. "Some of us take pleasure in such things. I notice you're wearing brown again."

"I brought this tunic just for you," Ellamae said, smoothing the short skirt over her breeches, a slightly different shade of brown than her top. Mona pursed her lips in annoyance.

"I appreciate your generosity," I said, "but do I need a gown?"

Ellamae gasped and clutched her chest in mock arrest, but Mona ignored her. "Normally on the solstice, after watching the Beacon light, we have a feast and a choral celebration in the music hall. Circumstances being what they were yesterday, I postponed it all to tonight. Do you think you'll feel up to it?"

"Oh," I said, flushing slightly at the thought of her rearranging the palace's celebrations around our arrival. "Yes, I would be honored."

She coughed slightly, and I could tell she was trying to decide how best to make her next statement. I hurried to do it for her. "Celeno, though, would probably rather stay in bed."

She relaxed. "All right. Well. I think the gown will look well on you. And if you'll accompany me to the tailor's studio, she can be sure it fits for tonight."

I cast another glance outside, desperately wanting to continue my hunt for Colm. But I couldn't turn down Mona's generosity, especially as I knew what it was costing her to treat Celeno as a guest and not a captive. And I had my suspicions that this was her way of making up for our tense discussion the night before. Reluctantly, I forced a grateful smile. "Thank you."

We progressed up a staircase, where I found myself back in the same hall as the library. We headed to the opposite end, passing a bank of windows. I glanced again at the darkening sky, casting everything in shades of bitter gray—until a flash of light caught my eye. I peered down at the shoreline below.

"Something's on fire," I said in alarm as I peered through the rippled glass. "Oh—no, I'm sorry. It's just Rou."

Mona checked in place and pivoted to look out the window.

"I mean, he's not on fire," I said quickly. "He's just doing that thing . . ."

She relaxed a little, her gaze fixed on him. "Spinning."

I'd only seen Rou spinning his two flaming wicks once in Cyprien, when I was housed in a room that faced the dock. It seemed like a downright reckless practice to me, whirling flames on the ends of chains like he was hoping for maximum ignition power. But then, neither the River-folk nor the Lake-folk had the same kinds of wildfires we did in Alcoro every summer. I tried to relax, but despite Rou being surrounded by water and rapidly falling snow, I found I couldn't.

"He'll catch his death," Ellamae said, looking casually out the window. "Can you imagine what a pain he'll be if he's sick in bed?"

Mona let out a little sigh. "No more than usual. He hates it here."

"Oh, no, he doesn't, Mona."

"He does." She straightened from the window. "I keep wondering when he's going to snap and run off down the river."

"Not any time soon, if we don't mop up things in

Cyprien," she said. "But I get the feeling even one of those fancy fire grenades wouldn't chase him from your side."

She took a breath. "He's an idiot."

"I never said otherwise."

I wondered if Ellamae's sarcasm wasn't making things worse. I remembered Mona's tearful collapse in Cyprien after she'd tried to put Rou in his place, and I put my hand on her arm.

"He's not going to leave out of the blue," I said. "He's too good-hearted for that. Besides, I get the sense he wants to stay with you for a long time."

"He's an *idiot*," she said again, with a slight crack in her voice. "What is there for him here? Can either of you honestly see him as a king?"

We were both quiet.

"No," she agreed. "Not because he wouldn't be good—he would be, even though he says otherwise. He is systematically garnering the adoration of everyone in my country just on the merits of his smile alone. Honestly, I've never met a person so insufferably likable." She shook her head down at him. "But he couldn't be king of Lumen Lake because *he would hate it.*"

I watched him whirl his flames in twin circles over his head. "Well . . ."

"He would," she insisted. "You heard him in his room last night. He passed it off as a joke, but there's always a grain of truth in them. He's committed to his own government, one run by his folk. Being shackled to a monarchy—and a foreign one at that—would drive him insane. And if I kept all the official responsibilities, and he was just a figurehead—he'd hate that more. Stuck here, away from Cyprien, unable to take part in the government he's fought so hard to liberate, always under my exacting eye . . . he'd resent me within the year."

"Have you asked him what he thinks?" I asked.

She was silent for a moment, watching him, a sort of distant sadness in her eyes.

"We go in circles," she said. "First he argues that he doesn't know how to be a king, that he doesn't think he'd be a good one, while I counter him. And then we switch sides, and I argue that I can't ask him to stay here and be something he doesn't want to be."

"And what does he say to that?" I asked.

"That he'd take it," she said. "That it would be worth it."

"Because he wants to be with you," I agreed.

"I can't trust that that will last," she said in a rush. She turned fully to me. "Has it lasted for you?"

I blinked at her blunt question. Ellamae gave a short laugh. "What a thing to say, Mona—why don't you just cut straight to the chase?"

"I'm serious, Mae." Mona shifted her gaze to her. "You're always going on about how you're not a good monarch, all evidence to the contrary. Do *you* like being queen?"

Ellamae thought for a moment, her lips scrunched to one side. "Yes," she finally said. "I mean, the etiquette and the expectations of the court can kiss my boots, but I like being queen. I like that I'm still a Woodwalker along with it. I like that I can finally fix the damage from Val's father."

Mona looked back to me. "Do *you* like being queen?"

I eyed her. "I'd have expected you to argue that liking it isn't the point."

"It's not," she said. "But you both had the choice of taking up the crown. I didn't. And now I'm suddenly facing the reality of asking another person to make that decision, and I'm wondering why on earth he'd want to."

"Part of it is marrying the person you love," I said.

"Part, but not all," she replied.

I studied the circle of fire down below. Rou had brought the wicks in closer to his body, spinning them front to back.

"I used to like being queen," I said. "Once upon a time, I really, truly used to. I liked making decisions, and having a hand in things—like you, Ellamae. But somewhere along the line, that got lost, and it became a dance around the Prophecy. I lost the ability to do things myself. Decisions that should have been straightforward became webs of religion and motive. Everything had to be done in Celeno's name, or else it was worthless." I looked back at them. "Now I don't think it's as simple as like or dislike. But it doesn't matter, because I'm not the queen anymore."

"Not yet, anyway," Mona said. "But I'm of the same mind—there's nothing simple about it. Queen is what I am. It's what I was raised to do, and it's not something I have the luxury of liking or disliking. I can't *not* be queen. And not just because I can't undo the title—I don't know anything else."

"Oh, sure you do," Ellamae said, seemingly wanting to lighten the mood. "You can dive and sail and write a mean treaty, and you know how to match your breeches and tunics."

Mona flicked her disapproving gaze once more over Ellamae's wardrobe.

"It's not that I *mind* dressing up," Ellamae said. "I just hate feeling like I can't react if something were to go wrong. Call it a product of exile, if you like."

"We're in one of the safest places in my country," Mona said, gesturing around. "What do you expect to have to react to?"

Ellamae tossed up her hands. "Rogue otters and renegade herons, or labyrinthine passages at the very least. Though I admit I mostly dress to piss you off now."

Mona rolled her eyes. "Well, at least some thought went into it." She sighed and waved a hand down the hall. "Come on, Gemma, let's get your measurements. Be careful, Mae, I might have them take yours."

"I'll fight you," Ellamae threatened.

Smiling again at their strange—but strong—relationship, I followed Mona, leaving our talk of kings and queens behind at the frosty window.

By the time the tailor had taken my measurements, fitted me for shoes, and discussed accessories with Mona—and after Ellamae had adopted a sparring crouch at the tailor's approach—it was lunchtime. I couldn't turn down their invitation to eat, my stomach growling again as if breakfast had never existed. When lunch was finished, Mona suggested having another round of diplomatic talks now that we'd all had a chance to rest. I managed to request an hour, explaining that I was still tired from the journey, and excused myself. I hurried through the Blackshell corridors until I finally found the entrance hall.

I was an idiot—the brewing storm had worsened since morning, and I was still only wearing the little knitted shawl. Not wanting to waste the time to return for a cloak, I trudged through the whistling wind with my head down and my arms pulled tight across my chest, looking up only to squint for the tops of the masts sticking up above the roofline.

My main concern, once I'd found the shipyard, was how I was going to find Colm amid the maze of dry docks and slipways. But I shouldn't have worried. As I approached the first ship, its sides cloaked in scaffolding, I caught snatches of song borne on the gusts of wind. Like the morning before—had it really only been a day since the cave?—I followed the voices. Shivering, I rounded the stern of a ship's skeleton and looked up.

Where all the other ships were empty, one was buzzing with activity. Folk clung to the yardarms, balancing on foot ropes and hoisting up the massive sails that were snapping in the wind. I stared up, my head spinning at the tilt of the three masts, but the shipwrights didn't seem fazed by it. They sang a song with a repeating refrain, with a dogged beat just the right tempo to pull in the rigging.

> *Buckles of brass and bearings of tin,*
> *Haul away, mates, each your line.*
> *It's weather ahead and the yards must come in.*
> *Heave away, mates, and haul down.*

I scanned the activity for Colm and found him on the deck, working a rope as thick as my wrist. His stance was spread wide, and he reached arm over arm in time with the others, his sleeves rolled to his elbows despite the snow.

> *A hot mug of this and a tall pint of that,*
> *Haul away, mates, each your line.*
> *Finish your work 'fore she blows herself flat.*
> *Heave away, mates, and haul down.*

I headed toward the ship, *Wild Indigo* painted on its side in bright yellow script, hoping to find an incongruous spot to wait where I wouldn't be picked out by curious workers. It took me a moment to realize I wasn't the only person approaching the dock—as the space narrowed, I came up on another figure, hurrying with his cloak hood thrown back. As I neared him, I recognized the strap across the back of his head.

Arlen.

I approached on his left side, unthinking, and rather than turning over his left shoulder, he pivoted around his right, fixing me with his uncovered eye.

"Oh," he said, surprised. "Queen Gemma."

"Hello," I said. "I'm sorry, I didn't mean to startle you."

"No, I just didn't expect—what are you doing here?"

"I was hoping to find Colm," I said.

"He's here?" He craned his head, but by this point, we were below sight of the deck, with only the rigging visible.

"On deck, on one of the lines," I said. "Why, what are you here for?"

It was only when he fidgeted uncomfortably that I realized it was a personal question. He looked up, his gaze searching and then locking on someone high up in the rigging.

"I figured they'd have to take the yards in, with

this wind coming in," he said. "They only just got the last one hung yesterday, so I thought . . ."

I tried to move the conversation in a different direction. "It seems awfully late in the season to be hanging sails?"

Unfortunately, it didn't ease his discomfort. "Ah, well, normally we'd stop before the winds change in November, but Mona wanted us to push through, in case . . ."

Oh, right. In the very real event of having to defend the lake from an Alcoran attack. I decided not to try to direct the conversation any more.

> *I've someone who's waiting with eye on the*
> *   storm.*
> *Haul away, mates, each your line.*
> *We'll weather far worse if we stand it alone.*
> *Heave away, mates, and haul down.*

Surreptitiously I followed Arlen's gaze up to one of the distant topsails, where three people balanced on the foot ropes—a young, scrawny boy, a burly man with a braided beard, and a woman with thick curly hair held out of her face by a red kerchief. Theirs was one of the last sails in place, the buckles tightened and the straps cinched. The final *haul down!* sounded, followed by a whistle, high and long. The curly-headed woman edged along the yardarm and swung one-handed onto the shrouds.

Arlen sucked in a breath. "I hate it when she does that."

The ship's sails secure, the wrights all began to filter off the boat and down to the dock. Some of them nodded to Arlen or touched their caps. A few gazes landed on me, jumping from my relatively darker complexion to the outlandish headband in my hair. They recognized the look of my folk, and most of them cut their eyes away, or furrowed their brows. I tried to shrink behind Arlen.

Colm appeared at the rail, swinging a cloak around his broad shoulders. He looked down and saw us, his gaze locking on mine for a long second before sliding to Arlen. He looked over his shoulder and gestured for the curly-haired woman to go in front of him. She descended the gangplank, pinning her own cloak, her cheeks reddened by the cold. Her eyes lit up when she saw Arlen waiting for her.

"Oh," she said, clearly pleased. "You didn't have to come!"

He shuffled a bit. "I just thought, ah . . . you forgot your hat. The other day."

He held out a knit cap.

"That's not my hat," she said. "That's your hat."

"Oh, is it?" He shoved it back in his cloak pocket without looking at it. "I guess I only . . . I was a little worried, with the wind."

She stood on her toes and kissed him warmly. Despite his embarrassment, it seemed, he threaded his arms under hers. Where her fingers clutched his collar, she wore a heavy seal ring made of mother-of-pearl, carved with the same crossed rushes I'd seen in the royal portraits. Arlen must have given his to her.

"Sorcha's the most sure-footed sail rat of the bunch," Colm said, joining us. "It'd take more than mere gale-force winds to shake her off the lines."

"That's what comes from being stuck up there nine hours a day for three years," she said, pulling away from Arlen. She turned square to me and looked me up and down without a hint of abashment. "Which I suppose I have you to thank for."

I blinked in astonishment. Arlen cleared his throat with force. "Ah, er, Sorcha . . ."

"No lectures, thanks," she said to him. "I was here. You weren't." She eyed my star band. "Your folk always used to have problems with their topsails snapping their lines. They thought they had a bad length of cord. You know what it really was?"

"What?" I asked, thinking I probably already knew.

"I filed halfway through the filaments every time we hung a new yard," she said. "They wasted more time on repairs for the *Mallow* than any other ship in the fleet."

"We're all working toward a truce now," Arlen said a little too loudly.

"I bet we are," she said. She flipped her cloak hood over her strawberry curls. "Meanwhile, in the real world, I'm famished for a bowl of bean soup."

She strode off toward the main road back to Black-shell. Arlen gave me an apologetic glance, his hands spread imploringly as he turned to follow.

"I'm sorry," Colm said behind me. "I won't do Sorcha the disservice of asking you not to take it to heart, but . . ."

"No, actually . . ." Her words hadn't stung me as much as I thought—and as I was sure she'd hoped they would. I turned to look up at him. "I'd be interested to hear what else she has to say. Do you think she'd talk to me?"

"Probably, but be careful what you wish for." He went to put up his hood and paused. "Where's your cloak?"

"I, well . . ." I could have kicked myself, realizing I was still bunched into a shivering ball against the wind. "Oh, no, Colm, please don't, really . . ."

But the clasp was already undone. He slid it from his shoulders and held it out to me. His own seal ring flashed under the cloudy sky, shadowing the two crossed rushes.

I shook my head, trying to keep my teeth from audibly chattering, feeling like the world's biggest fool. "Please don't."

"I'm roasting, honestly—that line was no shoe-string."

I bit my lip and unearthed one of my hands to lift it from him. It was less fine than the embroidered one from the day before, dark gray with no embellishments, but it was tightly woven and waterproof. Reddening a little, I pulled it around my shoulders—and tried not to sigh with contentment as it settled around me.

"Thank you," I said, tucking up the long hem so it wouldn't trail.

"We'll get you one of your own back at Blackshell," he said. He nodded after Arlen and Sorcha's retreating backs. "Let's get inside."

We set off through the snow. The last few shipwrights hurried along with us toward the main road. They all touched their caps or their chests as they passed Colm, like they had with Arlen. He nodded back, greeting many of them by name.

I searched for a topic safe to discuss among happenstance listeners. "Why do you come to the shipyard? Just something to do?"

"Something *useful* to do," he said. "Mona hopes to double our fleet by spring, so the call went out for all able bodies. Besides, it's gratifying to have a hand in building something tangible."

"What was that song everyone was singing?"

"A chanty, just one of many—most of them are like that, where one caller sings the verses and everyone else joins in on the repeats. It means they can be changed up with the job or weather and sung over and over again. You'd be hard-pressed to find a quiet deck these days."

"Because my folk outlawed singing," I said, deciding it was best to acknowledge it.

He tilted his head as we caught up to Arlen and Sorcha. "Yes, I suppose it is."

"This was all so much simpler in my head," I said. "Now I see there were a million things I didn't take into account."

"Everything is simpler before it happens," he agreed.

The last straggler veered off on a side road, giving us a brief moment out of earshot of anyone. I lowered my voice.

"Ellamae told me about the petroglyphs on the Palisades," I said.

He glanced sideways at me. "She did?"

"Yesterday," I said. "She thinks we should tell Mona."

"Mm." He looked ahead. "I wasn't even sure I should tell Ellamae. But there wasn't another way I could send that letter."

"I didn't get that letter."

He puffed out his cheeks, his breath swirling in a thick cloud. "It was a long shot, and probably of no consequence at this point. In fact, it may even be for the best."

"I don't know about that—but in related news, we found another set of petroglyphs," I said. "Celeno and I, on the way here. It was why we took the cave route in the first place. We had reports of another Prophecy."

He swiveled his head to me. "And?"

"And . . . they were nearly useless," I said. "They were so faded we could barely make out any new information. On their own, they wouldn't give us any way to change things in Alcoro."

"Aside from the fact that a genuine copy really existed, at one point."

"Yes, aside from that, I suppose. But it would be hard to drive cohesive change based on that alone. At any rate, I need to see the ones on the Palisades." I eyed Arlen and Sorcha up ahead—we had nearly caught up to them. "I asked Ellamae to take me up to see them, as soon as possible."

Colm looked up at the ominous sky. "It might have to wait if this weather gets worse."

"It can't wait, Colm," I said. "Not if we want to keep Alcoro from sending troops into Paroa—or destroying Cyprien in the attempt."

Sorcha glanced back over her shoulder, her arm threaded through Arlen's. I fell silent. We walked quietly behind the two, half-listening to the snatches of their conversation. The wall of Blackshell grew nearer.

"The reclassification of cicadas," Colm said.

I twitched my gaze to him at the jump in conversation.

"Were you ever able to see it through?" he asked.

"You mean from my thesis?" I asked.

"Yes. It ended with mere speculation—that cicadas should be assigned to a different order of insect than the grasshoppers and crickets. Were you ever able to get them reclassified?"

"Oh—yes. They're now considered a type of true bug," I said. "A hemipteran, not an orthopteran."

"And that's because of the nature of their song?"

"Well, no, not exactly. But that's what got me thinking about its classification. Grasshoppers and crickets stridulate their wings to produce their sound, but cicadas flex a tymbal in their abdomens to produce theirs. Different mechanism."

"I see," he said, nodding with satisfaction. "How clever of you."

I warmed with a sliver of pride—it *had* been a clever find, and I'd made a well-built argument. I'd been up against several loud voices who were convinced the cicada should remain a kind of locust—but in the end, they couldn't deny my evidence. I smiled as I remembered the joy of that victory—of seeing taxonomy change and new studies spring up, all thanks to my research.

I struggled to smother my smile. "It satisfied my committee, at least." I hitched up the hem of his cloak, which had started to slip. "I don't suppose you ever wrote a thesis?"

"We don't have the same education system you have," he said. "Children here get basic lessons from their parents, and then they attend school until they're fifteen. Mona and Arlen and I had tutors, but our folk have no academic journals or publications. We only have two book binders on all the twelve islands, and a handful of scribes."

"What would you have chosen to study, if you could?"

"Cultural history," he said instantly. "The story of people. Bias and belief, why we do what we do over and over again. How perceptions change and behaviors shift, and yet how culture perseveres through it all."

"That's incredible, Colm," I said, and I meant it. "You've obviously already done a lot of work. What resources have you been working from? I might know some of them."

"Mm, probably not," he said. "I've only read so much on the subject. The rest of my rattlebrained speculation comes from three years of travel." His voice carried no change that might remind me that I was the cause of his time away from home. "Listening to musicians and merchants all throughout Winder and Paroa, swapping origin stories with Mae, comparing ballads and nursery rhymes from place to place . . . it's all given me quite a bit of fuel. We've had a smattering of historians and philosophers in Lumen Lake over the years, but a lot of our history is just preserved orally—through songs, mostly, and story-telling. I've added to some of our literature, but only a little." He nodded to the gate guards as we passed through the Blackshell wall. "I always thought, in the back of my mind, that I'd go to Samna someday, and see the university."

I sighed in commiseration. "I always wanted to go, too. Celeno and I both did. We thought we'd have plenty of time."

But then his father died. His mother poisoned herself. He was crowned. We got married.

Lumen Lake.

"I've heard the island's water is so clear you can see ten fathoms below," he said as we approached the steps to the palace entrance. "And there are iguanas that lounge in the trees like roosting birds."

I smiled. "I've heard they grow five feet long and can dive like otters."

"Dive... in water?"

"In water."

He jerked his head to me. "They can never!"

I held up a hand in oath. "That's what I've read."

"They're lizards!"

"So's an alligator," I said with a laugh. "And a lot of snakes can swim."

He shook his head, his mouth bent in a resolute grin. "Lake-folk have been romanticizing just about every animal that can swim since we first learned to do it ourselves, and I've *never* heard of an iguana diving."

"You don't *have* iguanas!" I said, still laughing.

"We don't have alligators, either!" He caught the heavy door as it swung after Arlen and Sorcha and held it open for me. "I can say with almost absolute certainty that if an iguana could dive, it would be in the *Ballad of the Diving Menagerie,* which takes a trained choir six hours to sing, and I'll bet my illuminated copy it's not included."

I stopped in front of him in the doorway, my hands on my hips. "I will take that bet, and I hope you have a second copy of your book."

He looked down at me, a smile ghosting his lips—not in Mona's censored way, but as if it was a genuine expression, quiet but real. "And if I win?"

I thought for a moment. I hadn't brought anything with me that could be bartered away.

"I'll illustrate an iguana for you," I said. "Happily sitting in a tree, not diving."

"I'll take it."

"I think not," I replied.

He laughed, almost accidentally, it seemed—it bounded out of him, appearing to surprise him as much as it did me. He cut it off by dropping his gaze to the threshold under our feet. I was shorter than him by enough that I could still see his cheeks rounding as he tried to contain his smile.

After a moment, he looked up.

"You're different than I expected," he said.

"I'm sure I seem much bolder on paper," I said, thinking of my thesis.

He cocked his head. "I don't know if I'd say that."

"I *feel* much bolder on paper."

"As do I," he admitted.

"Sir," said a voice.

We both looked around—I realized we were still standing halfway in the open door to Blackshell. Snow flurried past us and over the tiles of the entrance hall.

An attendant hovered in the hall, shielding a guttering candle against the wind gusting through the door. "It's just . . . the heat."

"Of course—my apologies." Quickly, we both stepped over the threshold, and Colm pulled the door closed behind us. The entrance hall went dim—the attendant hurried on to keep lighting the lamps. Others passed here and there, some with shutter pulls to close errant windows, others with buckets of kindling to stock up for an unforgiving night.

Back inside and surrounded by people, I put a sudden check on my carefree repartee just a moment before—where had that come from? I looked up at Colm, whose smile crinkles were gone as his gaze flicked around the dim hall.

"Where can we talk?" I asked quietly. "Really talk?"

He nodded to the main stairwell. "The library."

"Right now?"

A pair of sharp-heeled footsteps echoed off the walls. Colm turned his head before I did—he must have recognized his sister's step.

"I wondered where you'd gone," Mona said, approaching us. "Celeno is awake, but he won't talk to me or Mae." She looked me over. "Is that another one of Colm's cloaks?"

I quickly unfastened it and slid it from my shoulders. "It was my own silly fault. I went out without one."

"I'll have someone fetch one that's your size—I didn't realize you meant to leave the palace." She glanced at Colm. "How goes the shipyard?"

"The yards on the *Indigo* are all stowed," he said. "If we can get another clear week, she should be ready to sail by January."

"Good. Don't forget about the solstice singing tonight." She gestured to me and turned, clearly expecting me to follow. I hesitated, looking back at Colm.

"After the feast and the singing," Colm said quietly. "We'll talk then."

I nodded and held out his cloak. He took it, and his fingers bumped mine.

"Your hands are cold," I said in surprise.

He swept his cloak around his shoulders. "Are they?"

By the time I'd wondered if he was teasing me— *was that a joke? Should I laugh? Did I misjudge?*—he'd given a short bow and turned to head up a different corridor.

Mona was disappearing around a corner. I shook myself and hurried after her, a little puzzled, a little jumpy, and—strangely—in significantly higher spirits than I had been that morning.

CHAPTER 12

The conversation between Celeno, Mona, Ellamae, Rou, and myself that afternoon achieved little beyond aggravating everyone. Valien, Arlen, and Colm weren't present—we'd decided on the smaller group to try to facilitate better discussion, but I soon realized the combination we'd chosen had all the even keel of a ship on fire. Mona and Celeno remained unable to give the other even the slightest leeway, which made Ellamae terse and lippy. Rou made one concerted effort to ease the mood, which backfired spectacularly—culminating in Celeno actually getting out of bed so he could stand eye to eye and return Mona's shouts. Once we'd finally gotten them to settle down, Rou mostly stayed quiet. All this left me in the awkward position of mediator, trying to navigate Mona's antagonism, Ellamae's impatience, Rou's silence, and Celeno's persisting anger at me and the world in general.

"I don't care if you're ready to hand them our country—I won't let them bleed Alcoro to nothing," he said vehemently as Ellamae stomped out after the others. She had left another mug of some herbal concoction on the bedside table, which he ignored.

I sighed for the thousandth time that hour. "I'm not trying to hand them the country, Celeno—please stop insinuating I am. I'm just trying to find ways we can all compromise."

"*They* aren't trying to compromise. They're trying to wring out everything we've worked for to benefit their own countries."

"Everything we've worked for has come at a lot of costs to them," I said tiredly. "I don't like admitting it any more than you, but that's what we're dealing with. The only alternative to taking responsibility is pursuing war—and I thought we were trying to avoid that."

"To be clear, I'm only getting my head around the idea that *was* the goal here—remember, I didn't have the truth of this journey until yesterday, and I'm still not so sure it's the full truth." I started to retort, angry, but he pushed on. "Regardless, I'm beginning to think war is the only realistic solution."

"It's not, Celeno. And if you would just try to cooperate a little, we can find an option that benefits all of us."

He made a sound of disbelief and ran his sleeve over his sweaty forehead. He looked less haggard after a full night's sleep and some decent food, but his skin was still sickly and his hands still trembled. He had the quilt pulled up under his chin to ward off the persistent cold seeping in from outside, where the winter snowstorm had only gotten fiercer—already the patio was covered in six inches of snow, and the lake was completely invisible. Mona had grudgingly allowed the soldiers stationed outside his windows to leave their posts. They'd come in blue-lipped and frosted white—the carpet was still drying where they'd trekked across the room to the hall.

Celeno sneezed and pulled the quilt tighter around him.

"How do you feel?" I asked.

"Terrible. I told her valerian didn't work."

"You slept," I pointed out.

"I slept, but I feel like I was rolled around a rock quarry while I did. I want my poppy tincture—there's a reason my physician gives it to me."

To hobble you, to control you, to keep you functioning like a clockwork toy. I bit back the urge to delve into that futile conversation—in his mood, he would only rebuff it out of anger, and I didn't have the patience to counter it. "Just keep taking what Ellamae put together for you. She said she added more sweet birch to help with the pain."

He turned his head away from the mug cooling

on the bedside table. "Alcoro has made the greatest medical achievements in the Eastern World," he said, "and she accuses us of being backward. Does the Silverwood even *have* analgesics, or are they still trying to pray sickness away?"

I bit back another sigh, annoyed by his offensive mood. He looked back at me as I pushed myself off the bed. "Where are you going?"

"I'm going to change for supper," I said. The meal couldn't come fast enough—not only was I famished again, but the quicker it was over, the quicker I could sit down with Colm and get the full story of the new petroglyphs. "I'm trying, Celeno—really I am. I'm trying to do what I can for Alcoro, and what I can for you. But it would be easier if you could try to reach out to Mona—she'll be more likely to negotiate your sentence afterward if you do."

"Negotiate my *what*?"

I stopped an arm's length from the door. Oh, excellent. Had I just said that out loud?

"What sentence?" he asked.

My remaining fortitude drained away, and suddenly I wanted nothing more than to crawl under the covers of my bed and stay there until the storm passed—the ones raging both inside and outside the palace. I rubbed my face.

"Gemma?"

It'd be nice not to tell him.

"More secrets, then?" he asked sharply.

I sighed again and turned partway back to him. "I spoke with her and Rou last night. They mentioned that we need to be prepared for . . . fallout from all this."

"Like what?"

"Sanctions, reparations."

"Isn't that what we just spent an hour arguing about?" he asked.

"Was it only an hour?"

"*Tell me.*" His eyes glittered angrily. "Stop lying to me."

"I'm not lying to you, Celeno. I'm just trying to figure out how to tell you this." I spread my hands. "Mona and Rou said the Assembly of Six will probably want to press charges. Against you. They're going to want to try you as a war criminal."

He stared back at me.

"For what?" he asked.

"For subjugating two countries," I said.

"We took Cyprien thirty years before I was born," he said.

I know. I know that it wasn't your fault, that you didn't ask for your title, that all these things have been done in your name.

I know that none of that mattered.

"What about you?" he asked in my silence. "Are they trying you?"

I struggled against the reflexive urge to bite my lip. "No, they . . . they want to put me back on the throne."

"Of Alcoro?" he asked bluntly.

"Of course Alcoro."

He stared at me. "So they hang me and prop you up on the throne alone?"

"It's a prison sentence," I said hurriedly—not that I expected it to help. "Cyprien doesn't have a law of execution, and Mona is deferring to the Assembly for the verdict."

"Prison for how long?"

"Life," I said, the word dry on my tongue.

He continued to stare. Then, with a quick, angry movement, he wrenched aside the embroidered coverlet.

"We're leaving," he said.

"What? No, we're not."

"Yes, we are. Unless Mona plans to keep me as a prisoner—which I will *happily* consider an act of war—we're done negotiating."

"Celeno, please, you're not well enough to travel . . ."

"It didn't stop you from hauling me over and under the length of Alcoro!" He planted his bare feet on the floor and stood, his eyes shadowed against the pallor of his face. He flung an agitated finger toward the closed door. "This is absurd—this is *wrong*. What about Cyprien violently abducting you and holding you captive? What about Queen Mona sinking our Lumeni fleet and murdering everyone onboard? What about King Valien and Queen Ellamae maneuvering a foreign power to supplant our own? *Why am I the war criminal?*"

His final words rang in the guest room, each one bouncing around like the ricochet of shrapnel. I realized my hands were twisted together at my chest, my lips curled shut. I didn't offer him any answers.

I couldn't, because I was still struggling with the same questions.

After a long silence, he turned away from me and stalked to the wardrobe. "Come on. Put on your travel clothes, so Mona can't accuse us of stealing."

"We can't leave right now, Celeno," I said.

He threw open the wardrobe door. *"Yes, we can!"*

"It's almost nightfall. It's snowing. Are we planning to walk down the river?" He didn't answer, jerking his travel-stained bolero and trousers off their hangers and throwing them over his shoulder. "Celeno, listen to me—at least give me tonight. Give me one more night. Let me go to the dinner, and then I'll come get you, and you can come with me to the library. Colm has information that could help us, that could change things—"

His shout was muffled inside the wardrobe. "Yes, let's let another *Alastaire* sibling make decisions for *our* country!"

My twisted hands tightened into fists, and I stepped closer to him. "He can help, Celeno—trust me."

He whipped around from the wardrobe, his clothes piled in his arms, his face creased in outrage.

"Trust. You?"

Those two words carried more weight and anger than an entire soliloquy could have, hitting me like shots from twin crossbows. I took a step back. We stood just a few feet apart, the air between us smoldering. His face twitched and jumped as he glared at me. I couldn't move, rooted.

Through the wall, I heard a voice in my room, and then a knock on the adjoining door. A maid peeked around the edge.

"My queen requested I help you dress for dinner," she said, oblivious to the tension between us.

Celeno's gaze bored into my own, waiting, watching for my reaction.

Slowly, I straightened. I didn't break his gaze.

"I'm going to dinner," I said as calmly as I could. "I'm going to try to smooth things over with everyone, and then I'm going to come get you, and we're going to go to the library to talk to Colm. You rest, and drink your tincture. I'll be back in a little while."

Using every ounce of strength left in me, I turned away from him and headed toward the adjoining door, where the maid was watching us with some curiosity. I passed her, shut the door, and slid the bolt into place. As soon as it locked, I crossed my room to the hall and poked my head out. Two burly guards stood in front of Celeno's door like ominous palace décor. They both glanced in my direction.

Good. He wouldn't be able to leave.

At least—not without a fight.

I stepped back into my room and turned around to face the maid. I was so jittery and distracted that it took me a moment to focus on the splash of glimmering silver-blue fabric hanging on the wardrobe.

"That can't be for me?" I said, stopping short at the sight.

"Yes, Lady Queen. The measurements should be right."

Dark colors and golden accents were considered the height of drama back at home—this gown would have stood out like a gem in a coal bucket, flickering and flashing in the firelight from the sheer number of tiny pearls sewn into the embroidery. Unaware or unperturbed by my dizzy apprehension, the maid shunted me to the changing screen. She reached for the buttons of my blouse.

"I can get out of my clothes," I said hastily. "And into the gown—you can fasten up the back."

"Be careful with the sleeves," she said. "The lace is delicate."

I'll say it was—the shoulders down to the wrists were fashioned out of exquisitely tatted blue lace, overlaid with iridescent seed pearls in swirling patterns. I eased my hands and arms through them, trying not to pull the fabric. I bit my lip as I studied my arms—I could just barely see my wine stain through the lace. Perhaps it would only be obvious to those who knew to look for it, but the thought unsettled me. I was already facing so many unknowns, I didn't want to have to worry about my marred skin. Experimentally, I pulled the neck of the gown closed behind my back—it, at least, was made of solid fabric and rose an inch or two above my collarbones. If I asked the maid to leave my hair down, it would hide any peek of my stain above the fabric.

She put my hair up.

After tightening the laces along the back, she sat me in front of the mirror and wound my hair into an elegant chignon, pinning it with pearl pins. She dotted rosewater behind my ears and threaded pearl teardrops through my lobes. As she was distracted with fetching my shoes, I turned my head this way and that, trying to memorize which positions were safe and which betrayed a slip of purple above my collar.

I had just gathered up the scalloped skirts—there were several layers, with the same pearled lace overlaid on the silk—when there was a knock on the adjoining door.

"Gemma?" Celeno called. "Are you still there?"

I hesitated, wondering what more he wanted to say to me, or what I would do if he demanded I leave the country with him. I certainly wasn't going to be doing anything more strenuous than raise a fork dressed like this. Arranging the gown, I unlocked the door and pulled it open. He stood clutching the coverlet around his shoulders. His face flickered briefly in surprise as he looked me up and down.

"Oh," he said, straightening. "You look . . . very nice."

He did not look nice. His hair was all mussed to one side, and his skin had started to break out from sweating so much.

"Thank you," I said without emotion. "Did you take Ellamae's tincture?"

"I will in a moment," he said. "It just occurred to me, though . . ."

"What?"

He took a breath. "I want you to take one of the guards with you."

"To dinner?"

"Yes. And anywhere else you go. I just . . . Gemma, anything could happen here. Now that I think about it, you shouldn't have gone out of the palace on your own." His gaze darted around my room, as if searching for assassins in the corners. "You've said yourself that we have to remember what these folk think of Alcoro, and all it would take is one angry villager, one angry servant . . ."

"We'll be in Mona's court dining room," I said. "I think it should be secure."

"Just take one with you," he said. "That's all I'm asking."

The words were out before I could stop them. "Why do you care all of a sudden what happens to me?"

They were cruel words, and I immediately regretted them, but I couldn't take them back. I forced myself instead to return his stare, his face frozen.

After a moment he broke his gaze away. "Never mind," he muttered. "It was just to give me some peace of mind."

I allowed myself a deep, internal sigh and a silent rebuke to my stupid, weak heart. "If you drink the tincture and rest, and if you agree to come with me after dinner, I'll bring one of the guards with me."

He pulled the coverlet a little tighter around his shoulders and gave a little sigh, turning back toward the bed. Taking that as a reluctant acquiescence, I closed the door and locked it again. I gazed silently at the wood for a moment, uneasy, before breaking myself away and heading to the door to the hall.

The two soldiers looked my way again as I stepped out. One was big and beefy and looked like he'd take a lot of pleasure in snapping a person in half. The other looked like she'd enjoy it just as much but might do it with less unnecessary pain. I nodded at her.

"I've been asked to bring you along with me," I said. "To guard my person in the palace."

"Our orders are to guard the Alcoran king," she replied.

"I will explain to Queen Mona why you're not at your post if the question arises," I said. "For now, please accompany me to the court dining hall."

If she disliked the request, she didn't show it. As she left Celeno's door, the other guard sidled until he was squarely in front of it, his meaty hand on the hilt of his sword.

Mona's dining hall was draped in white banners, with arrangements of beech branches along the walls, their golden leaves glowing in the firelight pouring from the double-wide hearth. A harpist sat in the corner, plucking out a delicate, unobtrusive melody on her strings.

Mona detached herself from a knot of courtiers and approached me. My trailing guard slipped among a few of the others posted along the edges of the room—they all shuffled slightly to make space.

"Welcome to the day after the solstice," Mona said.

"Thank you for moving everything on my account," I said. "And thank you for the gown—it's beautiful."

She held me at arm's length, looking satisfied. "That color suits you—I knew it would. It's nice not to have someone physically fight me off over an attractive garment."

I looked past her to Ellamae, engaged in a hearty debate with a Lumeni who was miming parries with an invisible sword. I thought she looked beautiful, wearing a stylishly cut tunic of rich green over silver breeches, her dark brown curls sweeping her back and her customary fringed boots beaded with mother-of-pearl. Valien seemed to think the same, because he kept smiling over the shoulder of the courtier he was chatting with.

"How's Celeno?" Mona asked ceremoniously.

"All right," I said, trying not to let the bad taste from our last interaction show. "He's resting."

"Good." I had the distinct sense that was all she planned to discuss of him tonight. She beckoned behind me. "Don't just hover in the corner, Colm."

I looked over my shoulder as Colm joined us, his cheeks a little flushed, perhaps from his earlier work in the wind. He was dressed in a similar royal blue as Mona, with an embroidered capelet that fell to his waist, fastened with a pearled pin.

"Colm informed me you watched the progress on the *Wild Indigo* this afternoon," Mona said, selecting three glasses of white wine from an offered tray and handing two of them to us.

"Just for a short while. I enjoyed the chanty they were singing," I said.

"Well, you'll hear more than that tonight. The royal choir prepares for the solstices all year long." Her gaze drifted past me, and her face reddened slightly. "Oh, Light. Excuse me—he's riling up my councilors."

She hurried to the far side of the dining table, where Rou was engaged in an energetic conversation with several Lumeni courtiers. They hardly seemed unhappy, though—they let loose a robust round of laughter just as Mona reached them.

Colm rotated his glass in his fingers.

"You look lovely," he said, and his cheeks flushed a little more.

I snapped my black thoughts away from Celeno, trying to force myself into a diplomatic mindset. It was difficult—I was out of practice. But our work depended on me maintaining my few tenuous alliances. "Thank you," I said. "Your sister has excellent taste."

"It's a strong point of hers." He looked down to study the capelet around his shoulders. "Though I admit I feel a bit like a flagpole wearing the fashion of the court."

"It's a handsome flag," I said. "In a high wind you'd be the pride of the turrets."

It was a poor excuse for witty banter, but he gave a good-natured laugh anyway. The sound shook away my last lingering threads of anger, and I smiled.

What a relief just to smile.

He cleared his throat, and his own smile broadened as he ducked his head.

"I, ah . . ." He shifted. "I went through the *Ballad of the Diving Menagerie*."

"The what?" My eyes widened as our earlier conversation in the palace doorway came rushing back to me. "The ballad! The diving iguanas! Yes, yes— and so?"

"I checked the appendices, and even cross-referenced the footnotes." He looked up, his eyes twinkling. "There is no mention of a diving iguana."

My mouth dropped. "You're not serious."

"Not a single line." He lifted his arm, where he'd had something clamped underneath the capelet, and withdrew an elegant leather-bound book, its edges worn with age, inlaid with golden rushes on the cover. He held it out to me.

"It's yours," he said.

"Wait," I said. "You just said . . ."

"They're not in the ballad. But I pulled our one book on Samnese natural history, and Maglean's *Biota Extant*." He opened the cover to a page of handwritten notes. "And as it turns out, they do, in fact, dive. The ballad is incomplete."

My laugh broke from me, and I clapped my fingers over my lips to muffle it. He laughed as well, and a nearby courtier looked over her shoulder in puzzlement. We both struggled not to break the pleasant murmur of the dining room.

Smiling, I took the book from him and thumbed through a few pages. It was clearly a relic, each page beautifully illuminated in an old Lumeni style, with intricate knotwork along the margins and boldly colored animals that grimaced and grinned. I admired a black and gold mink, brushing my fingers over its serpentine tail. My illustration style was too sketchy and loose to achieve such an effect—I itched to curl up somewhere quiet and pore over each page.

"It's a beautiful book," I said, looking up. "But I believe our bet was that the ballad would include iguanas, not that iguanas could dive." I handed it back to him. "I think *I'm* the one who owes *you* something."

He puzzled at the book. "That doesn't seem right, to win based on semantics and not accuracy."

I shrugged, still smiling. "We both agreed. After

the singing, I'll ink you an iguana. But I think I'll show it diving."

His smile twisted to one side, still genuine and bright. "You knew they could swim, ballad or no ballad. You knew the song was wrong." He pushed the book back into my hands. "I'll gratefully take a swimming iguana, but keep the book, as a reminder of my own silly fallacy."

"No, no—it's yours," I said, even as my fingers closed on the cover, my mind tracing the twining lines of the mink again.

"It is," he agreed. "And I want to give it to you. If anything, it will remind me to do better research before I make bets."

I couldn't help but smile, looking again at the rushes on the cover. "You're a better scholar than most of the academics packing our debate halls—able to accept a conflicting idea based on new evidence."

He shrugged. "It does no good to argue with truth. I still would very much like the iguana, though."

My burst of laughter was thankfully drowned by a rising glissando from the harpist, and we both struggled to quiet down as the ambient conversation in the room hushed. With a placid smile, Mona gathered up Rou's arm, forcibly guiding him mid-word away from the enchanted courtiers, and made her way to the head of the table. The court followed, taking their seats in some pre-organized arrangement. An attendant guided me to the end closest to Mona, seating me next to Rou and across from Ellamae and Valien. Colm took the chair on my other side, the corners of his mouth twitching as I surreptitiously set the book of the ballad under my chair. Mona lifted her wineglass and gave a short, cordial speech about allies and friends and the heralding of a new year, and then the meal began.

I could have cried—honestly, I was close—at the sight and scent of so much steaming food. Would I always be this hungry, or was it just a product of stress and uncertainty? I didn't know, and at the moment, I didn't care. I devoured the first course of fish stew and the plate of greens and dumplings that came afterward. I barely stopped to laugh at Rou's only partially concealed despair at the fried mussels, spearing as many on my fork as would fit at a time. By the time the meat pie was served, I had settled into a contented silence, happy to listen to the lighthearted conversations happening around me.

"You know, Gemma . . ."

I looked up at Ellamae, who was watching me with her cheek on her fist.

"You don't have to worry," she said. "I'm sure Mona plans to serve more food tomorrow."

I flushed, my mouth still full of venison and sweet potatoes. She grinned as the others around us laughed appreciably.

"Don't mind Mae," Colm said, lifting his wineglass. "I've seen her eat a bear's weight in wild strawberries. You'd think she was planning to dig a burrow and sleep for a few months."

"As I recall, we went on to liberate a country," Ellamae replied. "Besides, our only other meal had been prison food."

"Not quite true," Mona said. "We roasted fish on a stick up in Scribble Cave."

Ellamae chewed her venison thoughtfully. "You're right—we did. That was a damn smart idea, hiding out in Scribble Cave. You all might thank me for that sometime—getting us somewhere the Guard couldn't find us."

"I routed the Guard down the Palisade Road," Valien said. "Or else they'd have followed you."

Ellamae choked on her venison. "You did *not*."

"Camped them on the hardwood ridge," he said.

"Liar."

"With orders not to march until mid-morning, to give you time to get down to the lake," he finished.

"I will *tan* your sorry hide."

He lifted his glass to his smiling lips. "Not in front of Mona's court, I beg you."

While they exchanged a heated look that suggested something a bit more intimate than a flaying, Mona dotted her lips with her napkin. "You know, I've wondered about Scribble Cave."

Colm's fork and knife clattered unsteadily against his plate. I'd taken a swallow of wine and attempted not to cough on it.

"Those petroglyphs up there," she continued, seemingly unaware. "Such a strange place for them to be."

Ellamae broke her husband's smoldering gaze to jerk her head around to Mona. "Why do you say that?"

Mona shrugged delicately. "It's just so remote." She looked at me. "I wonder if you might like to see them, Gemma. Your comments about folklore earlier made me think about them. I'm sure the script is different, but some of the symbolism may be similar to yours."

My heart pounded, and my uncomfortably full stomach squirmed. Here we'd been wondering how to explain to Mona about the petroglyphs, and she was bringing them up herself! I jumped on the opportunity.

"I'd love to see them," I said. "It would be fascinating to compare them with our own."

She leaned slightly so a server could take her empty plate. "Perhaps when the weather breaks, Mae might take you up."

Ellamae cleared her throat somewhat loudly as a server placed a baked apple in front of her. "Sure thing."

I felt a slight nudge on my knee and tried to glance at Colm without turning my head. The corners of his lips were just barely turned up, his gaze on his own apple. My own relief rushed around inside me like a current—nobody would have to lie to Mona, or justify keeping information from her. We could go up, see the glyphs, and bring the news back that they were the same as Alcoro's. Our policy talks would fall into place, everything could be settled to everyone's satisfaction.

I could tell Celeno—tell him everything.

Smiling at my own dessert, I picked up my spoon. The apple was swimming in molasses and cream, and the first bite melted gloriously on my tongue.

"We need to get you folk a good pastry chef," Rou said through his own mouthful.

"I could tan *your* hide," Mona replied evenly.

"Please," he said. "Not in front of the court."

I giggled around my spoon, giddy with the turn of events and privately thinking that there was going to be a great deal of activity behind closed doors that night.

The concert hall adjoined the dining room. I tottered after the chattering court as they passed from one room to the other, the waist of my elegant Lumeni gown tighter than it had been a short while ago. The double doors to the corridor were open, with more folk coming in who hadn't been invited to supper. They filled in the rows of seats facing the stage, where a large choir was situating themselves.

I looked around, having lost Mona in the crowd, the book of the diving ballad clutched to my chest. I felt a touch at my elbow and turned to see Colm crooking his arm to me.

"I have made discreet inquiries," he said, "and I'm pleased to report that we'll hear an excerpt from the *Diving Menagerie* tonight, though I regret its inherent inaccuracy."

I slipped my arm through his. "I'm looking forward to it. Where do we sit?"

"Off to the side there, on the dais."

I followed his lead to a little raised box with cushioned seats. Mona was settling in next to Rou, trying not to smile too broadly at something he was saying. Arlen was behind her, with Sorcha at his side. Four more seats sat empty.

"Where are Ellamae and Valien?" I asked, craning my head. "I thought they got up from the table before we did."

Colm gave a short puff of laughter. "Sometimes they disappear."

"Making good on their threats from earlier, you mean?"

"Possibly," he said with half a smile. "They'll have Mona to answer to if they make a scene coming in—I hope they at least find someplace with a door to close."

I searched my memory of the palace. "The healing wing is one corridor over isn't it?"

He let out a soft groan. "And it's empty. Damn them."

I smiled as we climbed the dais, cheered by a full stomach, good company, and the unexpectedly encouraging turn the evening had taken. Mona glanced over at us, frowned at Ellamae and Valien's empty seats, and cast her gaze to the double doors out to the hall. The attendants were starting to move around the walls, turning the lamps down as the last few stragglers filtered through the doors. The choir was shifting in anticipation.

Somewhere down the hall, glass shattered.

Every head turned toward the double doors. Mona straightened, a glint in her eye. The guards who had been nearly invisible along the periphery of the room tensed in unison. I saw the one I'd brought from Celeno's room look from the doors up to me.

"What was that?" I murmured to Colm.

A figure appeared in the doorway, the fringe on his boots swinging as if he'd just pulled out of a run—Valien. He straightened slightly and moved casually into the room, offering a mild smile to the hundred-odd eyes all tracking his progress. He passed between the crowd and the choir, seemingly unperturbed by the attention riveted on him. Mona watched him approach, her posture rigid.

He stepped up onto the dais, and from this range, I could see the sharpness in his eyes behind his mask of pleasantry. "You should come with me."

"All of us?" Mona asked, matching his calm tone.

"At least you," he said. "And Gemma."

Mona rose gracefully from her chair. She turned partway to Arlen. "You stay."

He nodded. She turned back to the rapt audience and waved an airy hand.

"Please," she said. "Begin."

With that, she swept past me. Valien fell into step behind her, and I hurried to rise from my chair and follow. I glanced back once—Rou hesitated, and then rose too. I didn't see Colm make a decision before several guards detached themselves from the wall and followed in our wake. Mona led us around the back of the room and out the double doors. As soon as we were through, a wave of murmuring broke out behind us.

"What's going on?" Mona whispered to Valien.

He walked quickly down the dark hallway, his face grim. I picked up my skirts, trying to keep pace.

"Celeno," he said.

My insides froze as we turned the corner to the healing wing. Outside, the wind rattled the window-panes, tossing snow in drifts along the sills. It damp-ened all the light, making the hallway shadowed and cold, save for one open door lit with dim candle flame. Shadows played against the far wall. On the floor out-side the door lay several shards of glass, glinting.

Valien stepped over the glass and stood to the

side of the door. I steeled myself as I rounded the corner. Celeno was lying facedown on the tile, his head turned away from me. Ellamae knelt on his back, expertly pinning both arms behind him, holding him in place. Beyond them, a glass-front cabinet had tipped forward, littering the ground with broken fragments and the contents of the jars and canisters inside. The sharp bite of camphor oil lingered in the air.

"Celeno," I whispered into the stillness. I saw his back rise and fall with breath, but he didn't stir under Ellamae's grip.

"What happened?" Mona asked gravely.

"He broke into the supply room," Ellamae said. She nodded to the shelves around them, her face somber. "He's already given himself a round of poppy syrup."

"No." The word left my lips halfway to a moan. I put both hands to my face.

Valien very gently put his hand on my back. "We're not sure how much he managed to take."

"No," I said again, shaking my head. "No."

Ellamae tested her hold on his arms. "He fought me for a minute or two before getting woozy, but his pulse is way down now."

No.

My dearest Celeno—

It is clear to me now that your time is upon us. I am, and have always been, merely a placeholder. Do not grieve for me, my son—I am at peace with this truth. My greatest fear was to linger on, depriving our folk of the years the Prophecy has granted us.

I shook my head with force, as if trying to shake the current scene into oblivion, his mother's suicide note burning bright in my mind.

"Are you sure that was all he took?" Mona asked.

"No," Ellamae said. "I didn't see him with anything else, but a lot of bottles smashed when we hit the cupboard. He could have grabbed anything. He's going to need to be watched constantly until he wakes up."

You will do well, Celeno. Be blessed in the Light.
       Mother

"What happened to his guards?" Mona asked.

"The big hairy one ran by looking for him," Ellamae said. "I don't know what happened to the woman."

No, no, no, no, no, no.

Wiping my streaming eyes on my lace sleeves, I stepped over Celeno's legs and crouched so I could see his face, the glass fragments shifting under my shoes. His cheek and lip were bleeding freely, and his eyes were slitted.

"Celeno," I whispered. I brushed his sweaty forehead.

His eyes shifted behind his drooped lashes. "G'mma," he murmured. "Time is it?"

I looked up at Ellamae. "Let him go—please. Let him up."

She grimaced but loosened her grip on his arms. They slid down and landed limply on the glass-covered floor. I picked his hand up and held it close to my chest—it was cold and still.

Footsteps crunched on glass, and Colm drew up short at the corner, his gaze sweeping the scene. Seeing him only made all my simmering emotions flare—that swell of hope I'd felt just moments before, that unearned peace, now collapsed into nothing but nameless pain.

I forced my voice through my tears. "Help me get him up—help me get him back to bed."

Mona pressed her lips together. "I want him in a cell," she said.

I looked up at her imploringly. "Please, Mona."

"What happened to my guards?" she asked. "What did he do to them?"

"One of them came with me," I said. "I brought the woman with me to supper. Ellamae said she saw the other one."

"Why would you remove one of his guards?" she asked.

Because he wanted to keep me safe.

No.

Because he wanted one out of the way.

I closed my eyes. "Because I'm a fool," I whispered.

"I'll tell you what," Ellamae said. "I don't trust him being loose anymore, either, but I want him in a bed here in the healing wing." She nodded at the knot of guards who had followed us from the concert hall. "Somebody get an ankle cuff to fix to the bed. And find those two guards!" she called after them.

"You don't have to lock him up," I said.

Ellamae looked down at me, her face grim but not without sympathy. "It's for him as much as anyone, Gemma."

I bit my lips shut and looked back down. Celeno shifted and gave a soft groan. Sick with anger and guilt and grief, I struggled to pick his head up, off the slivers of glass. Colm stepped forward past Mona and Ellamae and grasped his shoulders, helping me roll him over without dragging him against the floor. He groaned again, rolling his head from side to side. A few droplets of blood landed on my skirt, staining the silvery blue fabric.

"Help me get him up," I whispered. Colm threaded his arms under Celeno's shoulders and hoisted him to his feet. His boots slid on the glass, and I put his arm over my shoulder. He leaned all his weight on me—I staggered to keep from tipping over. Colm took his other side. Mona watched with disapproval as we maneuvered him out of the ransacked supply room and into the healing wing across the hall.

We were halfway to a bed when Celeno gave a violent shudder and rolled unexpectedly off Colm's shoulder. I lunged to break his fall, landing hard on one knee. His fingers closed on my delicate lace sleeves. A long run instantly appeared up the right one, splitting the fine tatting. The left simply pulled apart at the shoulder seam. Seed pearls sprang loose from the embroidery and ticked away across the hardwood floor.

Celeno retched, his head bent forward, and Colm rushed to lift him off me. My left sleeve slid down from my shoulder, bunching at my elbow and revealing my dark, mottled skin. My face reddened—why not add this extra indignity? I stripped off the loose sleeve, and, gripping it in my fist, helped Colm move Celeno the last bit of distance to the bed.

Celeno rolled onto his side, gripping his stomach and letting out a groan. Ellamae marched in, winding a handkerchief around her palm—she'd been bloodied in the scuffle, too.

You're in one of the safest places in my country—what do you expect to have to react to?

A ruinous foreign king, and a queen too sentimental to make rational decisions.

Ellamae nodded at Colm. "Get some water. It'd be better if he gets this out of his system."

While he moved away, she fetched a basin from under the bed. When Colm returned with a pitcher and a full glass, she took it from him and hoisted

Celeno upright. Propping him against her shoulder, she tipped the water into his mouth, covered his chin with her palm, and pinched his nose shut.

He coughed violently, spraying water through her fingers. She kept her hands firmly in place until he'd swallowed at least some of the water, and then as he continued to gasp, she reached down and hefted the basin into his lap. Right on cue, he bent forward and emptied his stomach.

Mona came to my side, watching impassively.

"Gemma," she said. "I know I said I would help you, but you must realize how unstable—"

I turned to her, the ruined sleeve clutched in my fist. "My husband could *die* tonight."

Her mouth snapped shut, and she gave one of her usual tight-lipped frowns. Silently we watched as Ellamae forced more water into him and then laid him back against the pillow. A rattle behind us told us the guards had returned, one with an ankle cuff. He moved to fasten one end to the bed frame and the other around Celeno's ankle. While he did, the two guards who had been outside Celeno's door moved forward amid the handful of others. They stood crisply in front of their queen, their expressions clear that they expected the worst.

Mona looked them over.

"Names," she said.

"Britta Mornagh," said one.

"Conlan Sligh," said the other.

"What happened?" Mona asked.

"I was outside the king's door, my queen," said Conlan, looking straight ahead. "He came out and said someone was outside his window making threats. He said they had broken a glass pane."

"And?"

"A pane was broken, my queen."

"From the outside?"

"I didn't think to check. I went out on the patio."

"And he slipped out," Mona finished.

Conlan's face was burning red under his beard. "I'm sorry, my queen."

"And you?" Mona asked Britta.

"The Alcoran queen requested I attend her," she said. "I did not think I could refuse."

Mona gave a short nod.

"You are both dismissed from my service," she said. "Pack your belongings tonight and hand in your commissions tomorrow morning before breakfast."

I grabbed her wrist. "No, Mona, please . . ."

"That is all," she said.

The two guards gave deep bows. I didn't miss the twisted look on Britta's face as she rose and left the healing hall without a word, Conlan following silently after.

"Mona . . ." I said.

"The rest of you," she said to her guards, ignoring me and my grip on her wrist, "will take up position at every door and window to this hall and the wing beyond. You will let no one through unless they have my seal or a note bearing my signature, excluding the few folk already in this room. Anyone found disobeying my orders will be similarly released from their oath of service. Dismissed."

A murmuring salute rippled among them, and then they scattered to do her bidding. I ducked my head as several passed by, trying not to meet anyone's eyes.

The guard finished fastening the cuff around Celeno's ankle, having padded it first with a length of bandage. Ellamae tested it with two fingers to be sure it wasn't too tight and then got up from the bed, where he lay senseless. She brushed off her embroidered green tunic, now mussed and spotted with blood.

"I'm going to get changed, and to talk to one of the healers," she said. "Someone needs to stay with him and be sure he doesn't stop breathing."

"I will," I said.

"I'll fetch an attendant to do it," Mona said.

"No," I said. "I will." A hardback chair sat a few paces away, and I grabbed the back and pulled it along Celeno's bed, ignoring Mona's sigh.

"I'll send someone anyway," she said, and turned to leave the room. Ellamae followed with Valien.

Two arms wound around my shoulders and gave me a quick squeeze from behind. I glanced down at

Rou's steel ring, and my vision suddenly blurred. In another breath, he was gone.

I knew Colm was standing behind me, but I didn't turn to look. Looking would mean facing that short time just moments ago when I forgot myself, forgot my purpose, forgot that I was in too deep to draw hope and relief from an hour of laughter and enjoyable conversation. I realized I was still clutching the stupid sleeve in my fist, that my mottled purple arm was on view for any casual eye. I uncurled my fingers and let the embroidered lace fall to the ground. My skin prickled—I hadn't worn anything sleeveless since I was a girl, and I disliked the naked sensation now. I held back a shiver, focusing on Celeno's pale, slack face.

A hand softly rested on my shoulder, and I stiffened in surprise. It sat half off the torn edge of my sleeve, his palm warm on my skin. The shiver I'd suppressed released, my shoulders drooping. It had been so long since anyone had touched me there, on my stained arm. It felt alien.

It felt *wonderful*.

"Stop," I whispered.

His hand tensed, and then it disappeared, leaving a cold wash in its absence. There was a long moment of heavy silence, during which I didn't turn or open my eyes. I heard the soft flick of a pin being undone and the slide of fabric. I drew in a breath, steeling myself for the sensation that came next—the weight of warmed silk on my skin as the blue capelet settled over my shoulders.

And then, receding footsteps. A quiet turn of a knob, and a soft, slow latch.

I gripped the capelet in my fist, bent forward over the bed, and sobbed into my arms.

CHAPTER 13

Celeno slept all that night and most of the next day. I dozed fitfully in the hardback chair before finally conceding to curl up on the next bed over, lying bunched on top of the coverlet with my shoes still on. I woke any time someone came into the hall—Ellamae, various healers, guards hurrying to relieve their fellows from their posts. Valien came twice to kiss his wife's forehead and give me a pat on the shoulder. Mona and Rou arrived mid-morning—she with a fresh, simple day dress for me to change into, and he with a pilfered jam biscuit to supplement my breakfast tray. They stayed for only five minutes—Rou threw me an apologetic glance as he followed Mona out the door.

Twice Celeno's sheets were changed. Once the bandage was re-wrapped around his ankle. Three times I helped Ellamae force water and broth into his mouth.

"The good news is that his pulse and breathing are back to normal," she said near the end of the afternoon. "And his tremor's back—that means his body's fighting off the last of the poppy. I wouldn't be surprised if he woke up soon."

"Good," I said, quietly dreading the conversation that would necessarily follow.

"I'll probably put him on boneset again, and maybe a fortifying tonic." She looked up at me. "Has he ever been on johnwort before?"

"I don't think so." I wasn't familiar with the herb. "What's it for?"

"My folk use it to ease a person's spirits—mental pain, emotional pain, persisting grief, anxiety, that kind of thing."

I dropped my eyes back to his sleeping face. Already there was more color in it, though the circles under his eyes remained.

"It's not a fix," she continued. "It won't just make it go away, especially not without other support. But sometimes it helps. Colm says it helps him."

I looked back up at her. "Why would Colm need help?"

"Honestly, I'm surprised he doesn't need it more, being stuck back here in Blackshell," she said, inspecting a packet of yellow buds. "He's another who could be classified as a mess—all the losses here at the lake, and now being at odds with Mona. And I have my suspicions that their mother didn't exactly lay the greatest foundation for emotional wellbeing—but that's a whole other jar of junebugs. Suffice to say, he's got a lot on his shoulders. You could talk to him about johnwort—I think sometimes he takes fennel, too, that's a more common lake treatment—but you can also ask him about his other means of coping. I think he reads and writes a lot, and he dives—the Lake-folk often prescribe deepwater dives for persisting stress or low spirits. They say it rebalances the body's humors." She shrugged. "My folk have always believed in a day of retreat in as high an elevation as possible, along with the johnwort, but to each culture their own, I suppose." She rearranged a few bottles on the bedside table. "They've really never recommended anything for Celeno?"

"I don't know that anyone's brought it up in so many words."

"Not seemly for the Seventh King to struggle in such a way?" she asked matter-of-factly. "Sort of like how the queen shouldn't walk around showing her wine stain?"

I flushed. "I don't appreciate your insinuation."

"I'm not insinuating anything," she said. "I'm flat-out saying that your folk are so wrapped up in the idea of a divine king and queen that they've robbed you of the right to be human. It's a mark on your skin, Gemma. And if you don't like it and you feel better covering it up, that's fine. But if someone else, or some*thing* else is demanding it of you—that's *not* fine. Same as how it's not fine to let a person suffer for the sake of keeping up appearances."

I turned my head away. "Thank you for the lecture. Not all of us have the luxury of an idyllic monarchy."

"Are you *serious*?" There was real anger in her voice, and I jerked my head back to her in surprise. "That's a crap argument and flat-out wrong. I have a council who would very much like to have had me executed a few months ago, but I can't fire them and exile them to the bottom of the ocean, because checks and balances and all that. And I've hardly had the worst of it. Val grew up under the shadow of a disastrous king and a terrible father. He had to cover up a mark, too—burn scars from his father's temper. We became childhood friends because I was the best at treating his scrapes and bruises whenever Vandalen was feeling particularly vindictive. An idyllic monarchy, Gemma? You have no idea what you're talking about."

I vividly recalled the mess of scars on Valien's palm. *A childhood injury*, he'd said—not saying anything about the source of the injury. Suddenly, the idea that he avoided his family's portrait hall and felt like bolting during his own sitting made abrupt, painful sense.

"I'm sorry," I said. "I didn't realize."

She shook her head, her silver circlet glinting in her hair. "Here's one thing I've learned, over the

CREATURES OF LIGHT 367

course of struggling against an idiot king and then marrying his son. Some people just aren't meant to be monarchs. I might very well be one of them. It's the stupidity of this whole political system. Just because you pop out of a certain person—or marry another—doesn't mean you're automatically fit for anything. I'm not saying Celeno can't be a good king, or that needing medicines for the body *or* mind makes him a bad one—far from it. But he obviously hates it. He obviously doesn't feel capable at it. And at some point, we have to look past the crown and banner and think about *what's actually right.*"

Celeno shifted under his sheets, letting out a deep breath in his sleep. Ellamae and I both automatically reached for his hands—she pinched his wrist to feel his pulse. I threaded my fingers through his.

She sighed and released his wrist. "Sorry. I didn't mean to get philosophical on you. But I have strong opinions on bad kings and decisions that are made because of them. I lost five years of my life to one, and I still struggle to see what it's gotten me besides bitterness. I suppose it proved he couldn't drive Val and me apart—that's something. He knew if we managed to stick together, he wouldn't be able to stop us. Victory, I guess." She grimaced and pushed back her chair. "I'm going to find some food. Why don't you try to rest—he'll probably wake up soon."

She left the hall, leaving me silenced and staring in her wake.

If we managed.

To stick.

Together.

He wouldn't be able to stop us.

Without warning, Shaula's voice in the Retreat rushed back to me, a comment so unexceptional I hadn't even paused on it.

I thought you and he would be unstoppable.

My breath hitched in my chest. I looked down at Celeno, his brow twitching slightly in his sleep. How often I'd lain listening to his breathing in the dark, the trace of poppy syrup still lingering in the air.

But not always.

Before he started the poppy, those cold, dark hours of the night were our sanctuary, when we curled together in bed with none of the usual storm of the court and council to preoccupy us. Sometimes he had nightmares. Sometimes I did—closing walls, airless spaces, doors that wouldn't yield. After one of us would calm the other down, we'd lie a breath apart, trading murmurs about the things that used to energize us—the University of Samna, the latest scholarly speculation, the opportunities to grow our academic foundation in Alcoro. Those quiet moments had been snuffed out from the night he started taking an evening tincture to counteract his daily ones. And it had only snowballed from there—our easy breakfast discussions giving way to him, groggy and sticky-eyed, trying to burn away the remnants of the poppy with coffee and cacao pills. And then, the illness had crept in, consuming our precious free time, racking him with stomach pains and fevers and sweats the very moment we seemed to be making progress on something.

I thought you and he would be unstoppable.

I'd assumed my aunt's words had been to shame me for losing the king's trust and partnership. But no—that's not what she'd been saying. It had been an explanation, a rationale.

A reason.

Can't plan for revolution when one of you can barely get out of bed.

Can't overturn a regime when only one of you can act—and it's not even the right one.

All my earlier suspicions about Shaula's actions, and then my doubts of my suspicions, came rushing back to me. It had been easy, almost relieving, to dismiss the thought of her slipping cyanide into Celeno's tincture, because what on earth was the point? Why purposefully make him sick? Why would she, obsessed as she was with the very notion of the Seventh King, want to weaken him?

Could it honestly have been to drive the two of us apart?

I shoved my chair back and stood, staring down silently at Celeno, suddenly overwhelmed by the impossibility of our lives. Our marriage, our reign. It had all started so strong, so full of promise and potential. Could it really have been forcibly pried apart, manipulated into the smoking ruin it was now?

Some people aren't meant to be monarchs.

That could easily be said of both of us.

He hated it.

I hated what it had done—to both of us.

I thought you and he would be unstoppable.

The door to the hall opened with a creak. I looked up as Colm stepped through. My stomach made a little swoop, and that wasn't fair—that *really wasn't fair* that I should have such a reaction at such a time. My guilt and confusion doubled. His hand on my shoulder played in my memory, as if his fingers were against my skin again. I shivered, trying to shake the sensation. Not here, not right now, not when things were the worst they'd ever been.

Not at all.

Not. At. All.

He came to Celeno's bedside, a few books under his arm. He had his chin tucked forward again, as if looking up rather than down from his height.

"How are you?" he asked.

"All right," I said.

"Have you eaten?"

"Yes."

"Have you slept?"

I glanced at the next bed over, the coverlet slightly rumpled. "A little."

He took the books out from under his arm. "Why

don't you go rest for a while? I can sit with him. I'll let you know if he wakes up."

I hesitated, looking down at Celeno's closed eyes. My gaze traveled to the books Colm was setting down on the bedside table.

Compendium of Lumeni Astronomy

Dubhlac's Night Phenomena

The Goose's Pearls and Other Star Stories

My eyes prickled, and suddenly I realized why I hadn't wanted to leave before. If Celeno had woken to an unfamiliar healer, he might be confused. If he'd woken to Ellamae, she'd be brisk and blunt in her usual way. I didn't dare think what it would be like to wake up to Mona.

But Colm . . . Colm would be all right.

I dashed at my eyes. "Thank you."

"You're welcome."

We still needed to talk, he and I. But I didn't want to do it across Celeno's sickbed. Silently I left the room, my dismal spirits tangled with the buoying feeling of leaving a heavy weight behind.

The halls of Blackshell were quiet as I went back to my guest room. It had been tidied in my absence, with the bedcovers turned down and my borrowed clothes hung up in the wardrobe. My gaze fell on the bedside table, where the *Ballad of the Diving Menagerie* lay on the corner. I picked it up and thumbed through it again, the intricate knotwork and entwining animals as convoluted and tortuous as my own thoughts. I closed my eyes briefly, drawing in a slow breath, and then went to the wardrobe. I rummaged for the skirt I had worn the first day, pulling out the packet of papers I had brought with me from Alcoro. I sat down on the bed and rifled through them, little lifelines, sparks of hope I'd mismanaged and misjudged. My mother's map. The letter from Samna. Pages and pages of cramped, even writing.

Clutching them all to my chest, I lay back on my pillow, and without really meaning to, I fell almost instantly into sleep.

"**L**ady Queen."

I woke with a start, disoriented. It was dark, and someone stood in front of me with a candle. It took me a long moment to remember I was not at Stairs-to-the-Stars or the Retreat, or even the cave under the mountains. I sat up, and the Blackshell attendant stepped back.

"The king is awake," she said.

"Oh . . . oh." I rubbed my eye. "What time is it?"

"Just after dawn, Lady Queen."

Moon and stars, I'd slept the whole night—I'd *left Colm* the whole night. I stumbled out of bed. The letters I'd gone to sleep holding were rumpled and scattered; hurriedly I swept them into a pile and stuffed them into my pocket. I started for the door, checked on the threshold, and hurried back for a cloak.

I followed the attendant back across Blackshell to the healing wing. I was surprised to find that the palace was not in a silent pre-morning stupor. We passed several attendants hurrying up and down a grand flight of stairs that I assumed must lead to Mona's chambers. The entrance hall echoed with the clattering of hooves on cobblestones in the courtyard outside. I scurried to keep up and stay out of the way of the folk rushing to and fro.

It was just starting to lighten, with darkness still clinging to the corners and rafters. But Celeno's bed was lit with a steadily burning lamp, illuminating the two figures sitting upright in its glow.

Colm didn't look as if he'd passed an uncomfortable night in the hardback chair. He was leaning forward over his knees, peering at a book open on the coverlet. Celeno was sitting up, bolstered by several pillows to accommodate the length of the cuff attaching his ankle to the bedframe. He flipped several pages in the book.

"That one, there," he said. "We call it Blue Eye."

"To us it's Garm-Sue," Colm said. "A corruption, I think, from archaic Northern. You say it has rings?"

"Sort of—an annular disk. It looks like rings in the scope because of the variations in density, but they're all part of the same band. I'd only just started to document it in the spring . . ."

He looked up as my footsteps registered, and his voice died. I stopped a few paces away.

"Gemma," he said.

"How do you feel?" I asked.

He closed the book on Lumeni astronomy. He looked at the blank back cover. Opened his mouth. Closed it again.

"I don't know," he said.

I looked at Colm. "I'm sorry . . . I didn't mean—"

"It's fine," he said. "He woke up about an hour ago. We got to talking, and I forgot to send someone to get you." He tapped the book cover. "Our understanding of the near cosmos is all wrong."

"Just out of date," Celeno said. "That's all."

I moved forward. Colm hurriedly gathered up his books and began to rise from his chair.

"Wait," I said. "Stay. We need to tell him."

He hesitated, his gaze locked on mine, and I knew this was going to be as painful for him as it would be for me. Slowly, he sank back down into his seat.

"Where do we start?" he asked.

"From the beginning," I said.

Celeno looked between us. Colm nodded. I took a breath, reached into my pocket, and drew out the bundle of parchment.

I didn't get a chance to begin. Just as I worked up my courage, the double doors to the healing hall swung open. We all looked to the threshold, where Mona stood, if possible, more rigid than I'd ever seen her. She seemed to be carved out of stone, a twin to the statue of the queen out on the terrace, her face thrown into sharp relief by the lamps. Flanking her was a squadron of guards in full armor, the light glinting on their weaponry.

Ellamae must have been somewhere behind the group—I saw her trying to push a guard out of the way.

"Mona," she said loudly. "*Mona.*"

Mona's fiery gaze settled—not on me, not on Celeno. On Colm.

"Guards," she said, and her voice was stone as well. "Arrest Colm Alastaire for treason to the crown."

CHAPTER 14

"**W**hat?" The word rushed out of me, breathless.

"*Mona*," Ellamae shouted, trying to drive her elbow into the ribs of the guard blocking her way. "Hold on a minute . . ."

"For betraying Lumeni secrets and aiding a foreign enemy," Mona continued, like a character in a play with lines that had to be read, "with full knowledge of the cost to our allies, I sentence you to immediate imprisonment and a trial by council."

Oh, blessed Light—she'd found out. I jumped to my feet as the guards streamed into the room. The papers in my hands scattered over Celeno's bedcovers. Behind Mona, Ellamae finally got through the dispersing knot of guards and snatched Mona's arm. Arlen stood to one side, his face paper-white and stunned.

"I don't understand," Celeno said.

Colm's face was weary and lined. Keeping his movements slow and steady, he rose from his chair, gazing at his sister with nothing but regret. She, in turn, looked back with anguish etched across her face, her mask rather startlingly gone.

"A letter was intercepted in Winder and brought to me an hour ago," she said. "From you to Queen Gemma, detailing the movement of Lumeni troops and betraying allied strategy." Her lips were white. "Do you deny it?"

"No," he said, his voice gravelly. He held out his wrists to the closest guard, who fumbled for a set of irons. He didn't take his eyes from Mona.

"I'm sorry," he said to her.

Footsteps pounded up the hallway, and around the corner whirled Rou, his nightshirt loose over a pair of hastily drawn-on trousers. Valien followed, hair mussed.

Rou looked between Mona and Colm, his eyes wide. "Valien said . . . What's going on?"

"What's going on?" echoed Celeno. The chain on his ankle cuff clinked.

"Mona," I said, jumping forward several steps, as if I might put myself between her and Colm. "Wait, please—there's been a mistake . . ."

"My mistake was trusting you," she said, "and not following my instincts on what was happening around me. It will take me a while longer to determine the correct sentence for a ward of state." She let out a short, uncharacteristic laugh. "One crisis at a time." She waved at her guards. "Take him away, please."

Ellamae shook her elbow, practically hollering in her ear. "Mona!"

Mona jerked her arm out of Ellamae's grasp. "Don't think you're not next! You knew, as well! And you?" She rounded on Valien. "Did you know?" Without waiting for an answer, she whirled to Rou. "Did you?"

He flattened himself against the wall, his eyes wide as the guards and Colm moved past him. "Know what?"

"He didn't, Mona," Colm said softly as he passed her, his wrists fixed behind his back. "And Mae and Valien didn't know—not really." He nodded slowly as he approached Arlen. "I'm sorry, Arlen."

Arlen looked positively bloodless. "S'okay," he said automatically, his voice high.

With a last glance over his shoulder at me, Colm followed the nudge from his own guards and disappeared around the corner.

No—no, I was not going to have this. I started forward.

"You stay right where you are," Mona said, and I lurched to a halt. "Every single one of you." She shook out a letter in her hand with a snap and held it before her eyes. My whole body seemed to squeeze in on itself—the lost letter Colm had tried to send over the mountains.

"*Gemma*," she began, and then looked up at me. "That's a curious thing, is it not? Not *Official greetings to Queen Gemma Tezozomoc of Alcoro*, or even *Dear Queen Gemma*. Just *Gemma*." She gave the letter a flick again and cleared her throat. I was intensely aware of Celeno's short, rapid breathing behind me.

Not now, not like this.

"*Gemma*," she began again.

"*I have not heard back from you, but I choose foolishly to believe it's because no message can make it through Cyprien. I am taking a different approach. I've run the risk of telling Mae about my thoughts on the petroglyphs in Scribble Cave. As far as she knows, this is the first time you and I are corresponding. It was the only way I could ensure a reliable messenger without my sister knowing.*"

Ellamae, who had fastened her hand on Mona's sleeve again, dropped it suddenly, her eyebrows raised. I lifted both my palms and pressed them to my cheeks, wet with hot tears.

Mona's eyes continued to burn down the parchment. "*Mona is actively moving against Alcoro. By now she has secured the alliance of both Winder and Paroa and has bound us all in a military agreement. She means to move against the Alcoran forces in Cyprien. I have considered telling her a dozen times about the cyphers and our correspondence, but I always stop myself. She'll only think of them as a liability, something that will encourage Alcoro to lay claim to the lake with even more temerity than before.*

I'll reiterate that Lumen Lake is a sanctuary for you. If you send me a route in your next letter, whether through Cyprien or around the coast, I will endeavor to coordinate our forces to allow your safe passage.

I'll say it again—I'm sorry, Gemma. Nothing went as planned, and I take full responsibility for it. I can only continue to pray for your safety.

And—should you happen to receive my previous letter, please consider disregarding it. I wrote it in haste and anguish, and I didn't fully weigh my thoughts. Please excuse my ill-chosen words. I hope it is not the reason I've not heard back from you.

Respectfully yours,
Colm."

The room rang with silence. My gaze was riveted to the floor, my cheeks flowing with tears behind my hands.

"What was that?" Celeno asked behind me. "What the blazing sun was *that*?"

Drawing in a deep, shuddering breath, I took my hands away from my face. I turned to him, realizing in that moment that it was over now, this thing I'd tried and failed to save. The creeping and secrets and false starts had all been for nothing—I hadn't just broken his trust, I'd burned it and sown it over with salt. Slowly, like moving through water, I went back to his bedside. He physically leaned away from me, the cuff on his ankle shifting under the sheet until it was taut. Numbly I gathered up the letters and placed, them, one by one, in order on the coverlet—page after page of neat, tight handwriting, the *s*'s swooping in little flourishes.

I stepped back. Haltingly, Celeno leaned forward, and when he did, the others pressed in, too—Mona and Ellamae, Valien, Rou, with Arlen slowly taking a final position, walking with the haze of a sleepwalker. I stood behind them, my fists clenched together under my chin, eyes shut as I mentally read along with them.

July 1

Greetings to Queen Gemma Tezozomoc of Alcoro,
　　My name is Colm Alastaire, and I am the brother of Queen Mona of Lumen Lake. I will not do you the disservice of trying to talk around the issue at hand. It has been just over a month since the events here in Lumen Lake, and I recognize the tenuous position of our countries, and indeed the rest of the Eastern World. While my sister is convinced that a conglomeration of military might is our best line of defense, I am aware of the implications of the Alcoran Prophecy and recognize that an impediment to its progress will not be tolerated by your folk. In the interest of preserving peace in my country as well as

yours, I feel the need to present a finding that I believe
will interest you.

I have been studying the texts left behind by your
folk, including the copies of the Prophecy present in
Callais. I was surprised to find, therefore, that the
cyphers present in Alcoro bear startling similarity to
a set not far from Blackshell Palace. In the Palisades
escarpment that separates Lumen Lake from the
ridgeline of the Silverwood Mountains, there is a small
cave used as a satellite camp by the Silvern scouts.
Carved into the back wall is a set of petroglyphs that
are almost identical to the ones in Callais. I have
included them in full to the best of my ability below,
along with the two identical pictorial symbols. We do
not study archaic Eastern here at the lake, and there
are only a few fragments that I can use to translate
them, so I regret that I may have made errors in
forming the new cyphers. But I at least can tell there is
more to this set than what is present in the fragmented
version in Callais.

I have told no one about this connection. While
my sister and the chief Woodwalker in the Silverwood
are aware of the cyphers, I do not think they recognize
the similarities between the set and the ones of the
Prophecy. I submit them to you for consideration and
welcome a discourse on your preferred line of action.

I regret that I do not have the authority to extend
a reliable invitation for you to come witness them
yourself. As you might expect, the queen is not

currently amenable to the idea of diplomacy with the nation of Alcoro. But if you find these marks to be significant to you, I will try to suggest the idea of peaceful talks.

There may be a question as to why I have sent this letter to you, rather than to the Seventh King. To this I point to a letter of correspondence between yourself and the captain's wife, the single piece of writing by your hand I have found in the many letters between the monarchy and the colonist army. You conclude the letter by asking her, "I have heard the lake is so large that one cannot see the far reaches, and that the surface may at once reflect every color of the rainbow. Until I have the fortune to see our annexation myself, please indulge me by revealing if my poetic vision of this place is correct or wholly exaggerated."

Lady Queen, I write this letter to you as the sun sinks over the distant mountains, which indeed are so far away that they provide only a hazy line between earth and sky. The nearest water reflects the deepening blues and violets of creeping twilight, while farther out the surface shines with the pinks and yellows of sunset. The closest island is casting a shadow of green so deep it is almost black upon the water. And this is not even considering all the in-between colors, which we call waterhue—those shades that mix and melt together to create the spectrum that has no name. Your image of the lake is no exaggeration. The folk of this country are no less complex or worthy of admiration.

We are a people united by the waters of our home and the guiding strength of our monarchy.

I reiterate that I send these with the hope they may clarify the machinations of the Alcoran Prophecy and thus help secure peace for my country and safety for my folk.

> *Respectfully yours,*
> *Colm Alastaire*

August 5

Greetings to Queen Gemma Tezozomoc of Alcoro,

I thank you for your prompt reply and am glad to hear the cyphers I sent are of such interest to you. I shall answer your questions as well as I can.

First, yes, what I have included is the entirety of the carving. If there was more at another time, there are no traces left. I apologize for the illegibility of the second line. I will attempt to return to the site to make another copy, but it may be difficult to do without drawing questions from my sister.

Second, I have made inquiries to knowledgeable sources in the Silverwood and am quite certain it is not a product of their culture or a forgery based on the set in Callais. The Wood-folk stopped using archaic Eastern around the same time my folk did, and I doubt the idea of them spending the time and effort to copy something they could not translate into a remote cave wall.

I thank you for your kind words. While I do not speak for my country or my sister, I, personally, accept your apology. I do not pretend the loss to myself was insignificant, and like my sister, I cannot pretend that it was an act of unfortunate misunderstanding. But I possess a keen interest to push forward, and I am of the belief that the only way to do that is to recognize humanity where it exists.

On perhaps a related note, in the materials left by your folk, there are copies of academic texts, including your thesis. I have seen your maiden surname cited as the illustrator on several other texts, including the king's. I'm curious—are you aware of the work out of the University of Samna on periodic cicada broods? While in Sunmarten last year, I attended a lecture by a visiting scholar and found the subject fascinating.

> *Respectfully yours,*
> *Colm Alastaire*

September 2

Dear Queen Gemma,

Yes, the lecturer in Sunmarten was Kalikwe Waitu, and yes, she was every bit as eccentric as her literary style suggests. I am glad you are familiar with her work—my sister was horrified in equal parts by the subject of the lecture and my willingness to spend my month's savings to attend.

Given that some of my transcription was unreadable, I agree that meeting in person would be in everyone's interest to allow you the opportunity to see them yourself. I will begin to get a feel for my sister's inclination to the idea. It may be best to suggest a place as neutral as possible, such as Matariki. I will offer to go in her place, but if I know her, she will not be open to the idea and will prefer to meet with you yourself. If that's the case, she will want me to stay behind to act as regent. In all honesty, though, she is not familiar with the petroglyphs on the Palisades—I doubt she has given any thought to them since we returned to the lake. If you were to ask anyone, I would suggest Ellamae Hawkmoth, the Woodwalker I mentioned in my first letter. I will attempt to bring up the topic with her, but it will be difficult as she is preparing for her wedding next month.

I understand the need to keep silent on the petroglyphs if things in Alcoro are as tenuous as you say. My sister will likely be much more open to discussing trade than the idea of being host to an item of religious Alcoran significance. If trade is a beneficial avenue for you to pursue on your end, I say pursue it. The important thing is facilitating a meeting face-to-face, during which either you and I may talk together, or you can talk to Ellamae. The implications are too broad to convey by letter to all the parties affected.

Respectfully yours,
Colm

October 8

Dear Queen Gemma,

    I'm afraid this letter may be too late, but I would emphatically recommend not suggesting Lilou as the meeting place. Mona is not pleased with the Alcoran presence in Cyprien and is not likely to view it as neutral ground. Please consider Matariki, even with the dock tax.

    I have made excuses to my sister and plan to stay in Lumen Lake during Ellamae's wedding—in this way I hope I'll be the first point of contact for your ambassador, rather than my sister. But you must know that the Silverwood scouts now watch the southern waterways for us, and in all likelihood my sister will call for a show of arms against approaching ships. If this is the case, I'll have no option but to fall into rank. I will do my best to diffuse the jump to violence.

    Again, I pray this letter isn't too late, but for ultimate success, I suggest: send one ship, preferably a small one that is not outfitted for war. Fly a white flag from the mast. If you're met with resistance from the Silverwood slopes, make berth in the river and explain the diplomatic intent of the mission. This will help prevent panic from both the lake and the mountains. And suggest somewhere other than Lilou to conduct the meeting. I'll do everything in my power to talk my sister into going—or better yet, sending me in her

388 EMILY B. MARTIN

place, though I'll be hard-pressed to come up with an excuse she'll believe.

Here's hoping, Gemma. If we get this right, it could mean everything, for your country and mine.

Respectfully yours,

Colm

It was agony waiting for them all to finish. I stood in the lightening shadows, watching their faces change. Some of them went back a few times, jumping back to reread earlier passages. Celeno was the last to finish, having read each letter twice. He looked up with the others, regarding me as if trying to recognize a stranger.

"That's all it was," I said in half a whisper. "Those four letters. I got the first a few weeks after our forces arrived back in Alcoro once we lost the lake. After that, I started researching other possible traces of Prophecies. I found records of others in Alcoro, and another one here in Lumen. They were all fragments, but they all matched up with the set Colm sent me from the Palisades."

"And?" Celeno said. "What does that one say?"

"I'm not sure," I said, still quiet. I handed him the last sheet of paper, written with the meticulous hand of someone who can't read what they're copying. Colm had done a decent job—better than my mother's colleague had done, anyway. But the transcription still wasn't entirely readable, with a few misshapen cyphers devoid of meaning, and some others too ambiguous to determine their translation. But there could be no doubt that there was more to the set than were present in Callais. Celeno's gaze traveled down the parchment, taking in the new legible fragments.

"What do they say?" Ellamae prompted.

"The parts that are readable say *we are creatures of the Light, and we know it imperfectly*," I said. "Not *we know it is perfect*, like the fragment in Callais. There's no doubt about that in the transcription."

"The second line is worthless," Celeno said, his gaze fixed on it.

"Some of the cyphers are wrong," I agreed, trying not to sound small and defensive. "But he copied at least four or five new words that aren't in our translation—including some kind of qualifier to *the seventh king of the canyons*. That alone is the most significant thing about this set. There's something that precedes your title."

"We knew that much from the ones under the Stellarange."

"Which makes these all the more valid," I said. "They support each other."

He frowned and jumped down to the third line. "*Peace shall come from peace*. What's this next word—wealth?"

"*Wealth shall come from wealth*," I said. "The latter

half isn't formed quite right, but I'm almost certain that's what it says. Not *peace shall come from wealth.* Peace from peace, wealth from wealth."

"What does that even mean?"

"I have an idea," I said, my thoughts flickering back to the university. "We've gone all these years, all these generations thinking it meant material wealth, physical wealth—turquoise or steel or pearls. But . . . what if it meant a different kind of wealth? One we already have, one we've become accustomed to as part of Alcoran culture?"

Mona frowned. "Trade?"

"Game," suggested Ellamae.

"No." I fixed Celeno with an almost entreating look. "*Knowledge.* Scholarship. Science and literature, astronomy, mathematics . . . we have the minds, Celeno, we have the work. If we could just organize it, structure it . . ."

He let out a disdainful scoff, a sharp, ugly sound that knocked the breath out of me. He tossed Colm's letter back on the coverlet with the others. "I thought there might be something like that underlying all this. Our *theses* will save us, Gemma? Our pamphlets and bickering philosophers?" He waved at the patchwork of parchment littering the bed. "Just when were you going to tell me about all this? You knew, all this time, that these glyphs existed . . . in the cave, back in Alcoro . . ."

"You knew in Cyprien," Mona said to me with sudden recognition. "On the ship in Lilou, all through the bayou . . . you knew all that time they were here in Lumen Lake."

"I didn't know for sure what they said," I said, desperately trying to make them understand. "I still don't know. I thought it would be a straightforward thing—to request a diplomatic visit to Lumen Lake. Maybe not simple, or easy, but I didn't think . . . I didn't think I would have to keep it quiet this long. I thought it was just until Lilou, and then . . ."

The Cypri had attacked our ship, Lyle had been murdered, and all my begging for freedom had been utterly useless.

I dashed at my eyes. Rou was staring at the bed, unseeing, his fists clenched at his sides. Ellamae and Valien exchanged looks of trepidation. Mona drew herself up like a thunderhead building on the horizon.

"I tried to give you the chance to come to Lumen Lake in Cyprien," she said. "Why didn't you take it?"

"Because I needed Celeno to see them, too," I said softly. "Nobody would have believed me if only I brought the news back. And . . . in Dismal Green . . ." I turned back to Celeno, who was still staring at the ceiling, his face ablaze with anger. "Don't you see, if you'd taken Mona and Ellamae and Rou back to Alcoro . . . there never would have been the chance. Our countries would have torn each other apart—by the time we could interpret this Prophecy, it could be too late. That's all Colm wanted—he just wanted us to see them. He wasn't trying to betray you, Mona."

"Well, he managed it anyway," she said sharply. "None of this changes the fact that he was passing secure information outside of the country. What if his letter had fallen into your folk's hands in Matariki, or in Cyprien? That's treason, pure and simple."

"He's your brother," I whispered. "He loves you. He's loyal to you."

"If you were so concerned about loyalty," she said, "you could have told me in Cyprien. You could have told any of us." She nodded at the bed. "You could have told your husband, the person it affected most."

That was the biggest blow, and I felt it like a physical slap. Mona hated Celeno on every level it was possible to hate a person. And yet, in this, she chose to defend him. I'd driven her to take his side.

My whole body trembled. "I made mistakes. I know I did." I spread my hands. "But how could I introduce something that changed everything so drastically if I wasn't sure of the truth? How could I push for something that would change the foundation of our country if I didn't know for certain what they said?"

"*A scholar through and through,*" Celeno said flatly. He finally dropped his fierce gaze from the ceiling down to me. "You idolize research to a fault. Relying only on primary sources, keeping everything hushed up until a hypothesis is upheld—maybe that works in a scientific study, but it doesn't work like that in the real world."

I let my balled fists drop to my sides, and I looked at each one of them in turn. Celeno and Mona, ironically, both wore the same look of angry betrayal. Ellamae and Valien were grave and focused. Rou drooped, tired and sad. Arlen—poor Arlen—still looked pale and frightened.

"I'm sorry," I said. "I tried to make the right choices, but clearly it all went wrong." I nodded to Mona. "But don't punish Colm for it. His information didn't fall into the wrong hands, and he was only trying to find a path to peace."

"By keeping secrets, and misleading me," she said. "After everything, he chose you over me."

"He didn't chose me, or Alcoro. He was only—"

"He did," she said firmly. "And it utterly baffles me, and I refuse to let it go. Because when it comes right down to it, Gemma—I notice he's conveniently left this out of his letters—when it comes down to it, you killed his wife."

CHAPTER 15

The storm had left the terrace outside Blackshell covered with a crisp blanket of snow eight inches deep. The pale blue sky was streaked with milky clouds that reflected in the lake, but I barely registered the sight. I gazed up instead at the stone statue, carved in the image of a woman with a kind, gentle smile and thick waves of hair. On her head, fixed into the stone, was a crown identical to Mona's, set with real pearls.

"Her name was Ama," Mona said behind me. "They got married the year before your folk invaded. When your ships attacked, and Arlen, Colm, and I fled the palace, she took my crown and went back. She's the one you executed instead of me."

My whole body was numb as I stared up at the Lumeni heroine I'd casually wondered about. I dropped my gaze to her feet, where there were dozens of tokens scattered around the pedestal—a little wooden fish, a pearl brooch, a child's shoe. Below these was a list of names five columns long—the names of the dead.

"It happened right here," she said. She pointed out into the lake. "We were treading water out by the deepwater docks. We watched."

I closed my eyes. All this time, all those letters, each one becoming more fuel to fan that spark of hope . . . somehow I had managed to consider myself absolved from the events in Lumen Lake. It had been a policy mistake, but it was over and done now, and we could set things right. Folk had been lost on both sides. The popular report was that the only Lumenis killed during annexation had been those who had chosen to fight. Never mind the report of councilors being executed for refusing to work with our installed government. Never mind the realization, upon the resurfacing of Queen Mona, that we had somehow killed the wrong queen.

I rubbed both my hands over my face. With a great deal of effort, I turned to face her. She stood at the edge of the water, a cloak wrapped tightly around her shoulders.

"It divided us," she said matter-of-factly. "I didn't really realize it at the time, but losing Ama drove Colm and me in two different directions. For me, it was a constant, burning reminder of the sacrifice she had made to give Lumen Lake a chance—it meant I *had* to get back. I had no other choice. She had bought me that opportunity, and to pass it up would be to let her die for nothing."

She looked up at the statue behind me. "But for Colm, she and the lake both became ghosts. He never wanted to talk about coming back. Oh, he went along with everything I said and planned, but the thought terrified him. I thought he would settle back into it, that he would somehow find his feet again. But he hasn't, and now I realize he never planned to. He's had his eyes set down the river since we arrived back on the shore."

"But he's stayed," I said. "He's stayed because he's loyal to you."

"He's stayed because he has no other choice," she said. "He's stayed because he's too afraid to leave."

"That's not true," I said quietly.

"How would you know?"

I had no answer for her. My lips moved soundlessly, full of wordless protestations. She gazed at me impassively.

"You don't know," she said. "You don't know him. And you can pretend to understand what happened here, Gemma—you can pretend to understand the crimes of war, the loss of culture and economy, the *personal* loss to families and individuals and me and *my brother*—but you *don't know*."

Wrapping her cloak a little tighter, she turned and began retracing the two lines of footsteps in the snow.

"May I go see him?" I called after her, knowing the answer.

"No."

I held back the *please* that rose in my throat, watching her trudge back to the palace, leaving me alone by the silent statue of Ama Alastaire.

"**A**rlen."

I'd caught him at a corner, and he stumbled over his feet as he reeled backward. "Gemma!"

He still had that bloodless look to him, his movements furtive and quick, like a creature who knows it's under the eye of a hawk. I added another layer to my guilt—his brother and sister were perhaps the only two rocks in his life, and I'd torn them apart. I felt guiltier, though, for exploiting his shock for my own ends.

But not guilty enough not to do it anyway.

"I need to see your brother," I said. "But they won't let me in without permission."

"What does Mona say?" he asked automatically.

"She's busy," I lied. "Please—won't you give me a note, or a token?"

He wavered at the corner.

"N . . . no," he said, as if trying out the word. It hung in the air between us. He stepped backward. "No. I'm sorry, but—no."

He made a wide berth around me and continued

hurriedly down the hall. I could have called after him, tried to tug at his heart, asked him to do it for his brother's sake—but I didn't have the courage.

And besides, I was a little proud of him.

"Good for you," I murmured, my eyes tearing.

My boots flapped loosely around my ankles, making my footsteps echo off the stone walls. They were wet from the trek in the deep snow to the prison, and the guards at the door had stripped the bootlaces off after a thorough search of my person. They'd been reluctant to let me in, but they couldn't doubt the seal carved into the mother-of-pearl ring I clutched in my frozen fist. They let me pass.

The cells were built of burly fieldstone blocks, with bars blocking the sides buffering the narrow corridor. Oily lanterns guttered, and the place was as cold as the cave had been despite a fire smoldering in a central hearth. But what was more startling was the low ceiling—Colm had surely had to keep his head ducked as he was brought through. Between that and the narrow corridor, and my own inner feeling of entrapment, my body was tight with suppressed claustrophobia. I passed a long row of empty cells until I came to the one at the end. Taking a breath, I stepped into view.

Colm was sitting on the cot along the back wall,

his long legs stretched out in front of him and his hands in his lap. He looked up.

"Gemma," he said. My name released in a cloud of breath in front of his face. "How did you get in?"

I held out the mother-of-pearl ring. He squinted at it in the dim light.

"That's Arlen's."

"No," I said. "It's Sorcha's. I saw her wearing it in the shipyard. Arlen must have given it to her as a token of his affection."

He looked up at me. "How did you convince her to give it to you?"

"I offered to put her in charge of the board overseeing Alcoran reparations," I said. "She made me sign three separate statements saying I would." Carefully I tucked the ring back in my pocket. "She's a smart one."

He gazed up at me, his eyes flicking over my face. "Did you show them the letters?"

"Yes," I said. "And then Mona told me about Ama."

In a slow motion, he turned his head and rested it back against the stone wall, letting out a long breath.

We both spoke at the same time, and we spoke the same words.

"I'm sorry."

"I . . ." he began.

I shook my head. "I didn't . . ."

A short pause followed.

"Let me go first," he said.

"No, let me," I said. "Don't apologize to me for not saying anything about Ama. It wasn't something I had a right to know."

"Then you don't get to apologize for her death."

"I do, and I will." I curled my fingers around the cold metal bars. "I'm sorry, Colm, in every possible respect. But it doesn't matter, because no apology will ever, ever be enough. So here's what else I'll apologize for—I'm sorry for not giving adequate thought to my own role in the invasion of Lumen Lake. I'm sorry for relying on your goodwill to solve the problems caused by my country. And I'm sorry for ruining things so badly—for taking the opportunity you opened and turning it right back in to more suffering."

"By the Light, Gemma." He swung his legs off the cot and crossed the cell in two strides. "Do you think I don't take equal blame? I made plenty of mistakes, too. If my transcription had been better, if I had thought to make rubbings, we might not be in this mess. I thought I was keeping the petroglyphs from Mona in the interest of national security, but if we're being honest, it's because I was afraid. I knew I was betraying her, and I was afraid to tell her."

I blew out my breath and leaned against the edge of the cell door, struggling against his corroboration of his sister's accusations. *Afraid.*

I closed my eyes, the cold stone biting through my cloak.

"I wonder," I said, "if there is no such thing as bravery—if it's just fear coming from a different direction."

"You were brave to come here."

"No, I was just afraid. Like you. And I'm still afraid." I rubbed my eyes. "I've always been afraid."

He curled his fingers around the metal bars. "But . . . the thing is, at least you moved forward anyway. I don't think bravery is the absence of fear. Bravery is being afraid and taking action anyway. You've done that."

"Your letters made me less afraid," I said. "They made me feel like I could make decisions again, like maybe the Prophecy doesn't give divinity to his actions and nothing to mine." I closed my eyes. "But that must not be true, because every decision I've made has only made things worse."

Colm didn't answer, and when I opened my eyes, he was staring into the middle distance. I looked around in the corridor for a bench or stool but found none, so I crossed my legs and sank to the floor. He did the same on the other side of the bars.

I leaned my head back against the stone. "Your cells are very small," I said softly.

He looked wearily around. "Yes, they are, aren't they?"

"I hate small spaces," I said.

He turned to me again. I ran the back of my sleeve over my nose.

"My mother was arrested for treason when I was eight," I said. "Did I tell you that?"

"No."

"Well, she was. She was part of a group of political dissenters who would meet and discuss the Prophecy. One of them was caught setting fire to a banner of the petroglyphs, and he panicked and ratted out the whole group. The soldiers questioned them one by one and found most of them guilty only of verbal dissension. They got fines and a warning. My mother got word they were coming for her—she assumed, since she hadn't been involved in anything beyond just talk, that her sentence would be similar. But she didn't want them to see me—I'd been around for a lot of their meetings. What if they questioned me? What if they took me away? So she opened up a cupboard and told me to hide and not come out until she told me it was safe.

"So I got inside," I said. Slowly I dragged my feet up so my knees touched my chest. "I sat like this. I heard the soldiers come. I heard them question her, though I couldn't make out their words. Then it all turned in to shouting. I heard them struggle. Something broke. And then it went quiet. It went quiet for a long time."

I rubbed my knees, my calves. "My legs cramped and went numb, but I couldn't straighten them. The air got hot and thick. I waited and waited for my mother's voice, telling me I could come out. But it never came, and finally I couldn't take sitting like that any longer. I reached up to push the door open."

I remembered that feeling, that anticipation of relief from my building pain, thinking I'd endured all I could endure—only to find it had just begun.

"The door wouldn't open," I said. "The latch on the outside had fallen down. I pushed and pushed, but it wouldn't budge. I pounded on the wood, I shouted, but no one came."

The day had grown longer—first the cupboard grew stifling hot, so that I pressed my mouth against the crack in the door, trying to reach fresh air, and then it grew cold and dark. The blood pooled in my legs—when I squeezed my feet, I couldn't feel them. I grew desperately thirsty. I wet myself.

"I was there for fifteen hours," I said.

"How did you get out?" asked Colm.

"My aunt, my mother's sister, came looking for me. She knew I should be there, despite the soldiers saying they hadn't seen me. When I heard her come in, I used my last bit of energy to knock and call again. She unlatched the door."

Sometimes I wondered if that first glimpse hadn't colored her opinion of me for the rest of my life. I'd fallen out of the cupboard, crying, at first unable to uncurl myself, and then unable to stand for another hour. I stank of sweat and urine. I was incoherent and inconsolable. She had gotten me a cup of water and a

404 EMILY B. MARTIN

corn cake and waited while I worked on them, sobbing the whole time. Until finally, she'd had enough.

Stop it, Gemma, she said. *Great Light, you're out now. Stop.*

"What happened?" Colm asked. "Did she take care of you?"

I thought for a moment. "She took charge of me. I don't know that I'd call it care."

Stop crying. Sit still. Be quiet. Pull your sleeves down. Do nothing to throw shadow on the Prelate or the Seventh King.

"There was one quality, I think, that she valued in me," I said. "And that was my tendency to do as I was told. More than anything, I think that was why she was so set on crowning me queen. Because she knew I wouldn't get in Celeno's way. She made sure I understood that his success was my entire purpose, and then she stepped back and let the rest fall into place." I ran the heel of my hand under my eyes. "And I know it's wrong, but I can't stop feeling that way— that everything I do must be for his benefit. But now I've lost him, and I've set everyone else against me, and I have no idea what to do next."

Inside the prison, it was quiet. I rested my chin on my knees.

"What do you want to do next?" Colm asked.

Mona's voice echoed in my head. "What I want doesn't matter."

"It might not change anything," he admitted. "But

if you could do anything at all, what would you do? Would you go to Samna?"

I gazed down the hall, my arms wrapped around my legs. White beaches. Warm sun. Iguanas that dove like otters, and scholars who consumed and produced knowledge like it was the very air they breathed.

"If I could do anything at all?" I asked.

"Yes."

"I'd stay," I said. "I'd go back to Alcoro, and I'd see her settled. I'd take a breath in my own country, at peace with itself—Prophecy or no. That's still what I want. Samna was a beautiful distraction, but I don't know that I could actually get on the boat and sail away. I want my own life in my own country, not a salvaged life in another."

He gave a little sigh and rubbed his hand over his beard. I looked at him through the bars—we were sitting almost shoulder to shoulder on either side of the cell door.

"A little far-fetched, I know," I said.

"It shouldn't have to be." He sighed again. "Has Mona given any indication that she's taking action against you?"

"Not yet," I said.

"Then will you do me a favor?" he asked.

"What?"

"Go to my room. It's the second one in the royal wing. The letters you wrote me are in the trunk under the window, folded inside a copy of *Our Common*

Origin. Take them to Mona—it might convince her that you've only been trying to help."

"All right," I said. "If you think they'll help."

"I do. But then . . . there's something else. Something I've been meaning to do for a long time, but haven't built the courage. At this point I don't know that I will."

"What's that?"

He took a breath. "On the bedside table, there's a little box. Wooden, with a fish on it. Inside is a ring." He held up his pinkie. "It's small, with five pink pearls set into it. It's Ama's. I carried it around with me all throughout our exile, and I put it away once I got back. I kept thinking I would dedicate it, but any time I went to open the box, I stopped. Will you take it out for me, and put it on her statue?"

I ducked my head. "I don't think I'm the right person," I said.

"Please," he said. "I can't do it myself. And at this point, under these circumstances—" He waved at the cell around him. "I've done her memory enough dishonor."

"She died to save the lake from Alcoro," I whispered. "You've been working for the same thing."

"And I've managed to rip apart the monarchy she was trying to save," he said. "Please, Gemma."

I sniffed. "All right. Yes, if that's what you want."

"It is."

Silence settled down on us again. The cold seeped in from all sides—the floor, the wall, the row of bars. I thumbed the tears from my eyes. I didn't want to leave. Despite the bare loneliness of the prison, I didn't want to go back to Blackshell, back into the heart of the mess I'd made. I put my head on my knees again.

"Gemma," Colm said.

"What?"

"May I touch you?" His voice was soft. "I should have asked when I did it before."

My eyes prickled, and I felt a new surge of guilt, though I wasn't sure what for. I searched the emotion for its root and returned with no justification other than I knew it was what I should feel. It was right, for me to shy and bow away from such a question. This sound logic wasn't strong enough, though, to overcome the sudden, encompassing desire to simply be touched by someone who didn't—miraculously—despise me.

I laid my hand down on the stone floor between two of the cell bars.

"Yes," I whispered.

His fingers slid forward, and his big hand closed around mine. He had callouses on the ridges of his palm, and one at the end of his middle finger—callouses both from working and writing. His hands were cold, like mine, but the feeling of skin against skin sent a thrum through me that eased the knot in the pit of my stomach. I bit my lip, struggling to keep my tears in. It didn't work. The stone walls magnified my first gasp.

Colm's fingers tightened over mine. I tried to wipe at my eyes with my other sleeve.

"Sorry," I whispered.

He shifted, and his free hand snaked partway through the bars. It didn't fit past his wrist, but it was far enough to reach my knees. He pulled gently, drawing me closer, right up against the metal. The bars were freezing cold, but they were overwhelmed by the heat from his body. He pressed forward until our bodies touched in the spaces between, and he leaned his forehead against mine.

"You cry as much as you need to," he murmured.

We stayed that way, pressed against the bars of his cell, for a long time—long enough that I forgot about the cold floor and biting metal. His thumb occasionally traced the back of my hand, but more often it was still. The silence between us was a comfort—it carried no secrets in it, no animosity or frustration. It was just peace.

After a length of time, the door at the far end of the corridor groaned on its hinges. We both shook ourselves, leaning back from each other. A set of boots tromped down the passage, and his fingers slipped out of mine. An unfamiliar soldier strode into view.

"The queen is requesting you return to the palace," he said.

Mona would be furious. I held in the sigh I wanted to heave, and I got stiffly to my feet. Inches away, Colm did the same. In the presence of the guard, faced with the reality of having to go back into that swirling fog where everyone was angry at me, I suddenly felt timid again. I bunched my cloak in my fists, hesitantly meeting Colm's eyes.

"I'm sorry," I said. "I'll try to talk to your sister."

"It's all right," he said. "Be gentle with yourself, Gemma."

He unfurled his fingers between the bars, and despite the guard, I rested my hand briefly in his. It was cold.

With a rush of inspiration, I drew my hand away and fumbled at my throat. I unpinned my cloak, making sure the guard saw me put the pin in my pocket, and stuffed the fabric through to him.

It would be too small, and hardly sufficient to keep away the persistent chill. But he gathered it wordlessly in his hands and drew it close to his chest, as if I'd given him something precious.

"Thank you," he said.

The guard cleared his throat, gesturing for me to follow him back up the corridor. I hurried in his wake.

Outside, a sharp, stealthy wind blew off the lake. I bowed against it as it sliced through my clothes, my arms wrapped tightly across my chest. We passed back along the outer edge of town to where the high stone wall loomed around Blackshell. I followed the guard through the gate and almost took a step back— the grounds beyond were a cacophony of clattering hooves and running boots. I dodged out of the way of a stable hand hurriedly leading a chestnut horse away, draped in forest green livery.

"What's going on?" I asked the guard as we neared the palace doors.

He didn't answer.

The entrance hall was no less busy. Folk rushed to and fro with an air of agitation—almost panic. I picked up my pace. It was just reaching noon—I hadn't been gone *that* long. What had happened in the short period of time to throw things into such disarray?

We made for the grand sweeping staircase that led up to the floor above, and I realized the guard was taking me to Mona's rooms. I started to flick through possible approaches to facing Mona's inevitable anger. Should I stand defiantly before her? Attempt to reason with her? Ask meekly for forgiveness?

Should I simply turn around and see myself into a prison cell?

The landing above was flanked by intricately embroidered tapestries and capped by an arching timber-framed ceiling, but my gaze was drawn to the doors along the left side. We passed the first, and then the second, carved with the country's crossed rushes. I studied it until I couldn't do so without craning my head. Colm's room.

His wife's little ring.

I continued after the guard, trying to resist the urge to open the door right then, until we arrived at the end of the hall. One of the double doors was propped open, and three guards stood in the anteroom beyond. We passed by them—me avoiding their glares—and into the next room.

My first impression of Mona's parlor was that it suited her perfectly. Elegant blue and white hangings covered the walls, flanked by silk-covered chairs. A painting of the Beacon, shining in the morning sun, sat over the crackling fireplace. And then there were the pearls—pearls everywhere, big robins-egg pearls studding the doorknobs, miniscule ones sewn into pillows, gray ones tiling the mantelpiece, white ones roping along the draperies. The whole room glimmered.

To the left was a closed door, presumably to a bedroom. The guard led me to the opposite wall, where another door stood open, revealing a long polished worktable and a stately writing desk. Both were currently scattered with stacks of paper and maps. I leaned out of the way as yet another person rushed past, realizing at the last second that it was Arlen. I drew in a breath, hastily preparing myself for his anger, as well, but he barely looked at me, despite me being on his right side. He shuffled the packet of parchment under his arm and practically ran across the parlor into the anteroom beyond.

Filled with swirling trepidation, I followed the guard's gesture into the study.

Mona and Rou were standing at opposite ends of the long table, and for once I didn't seem to have interrupted an intimate moment between them. Their faces were both tense, their postures rigid as they faced each other. I sidled inside, and they broke their sparking gazes from each other to me.

"Gemma," Mona stated.

I glanced over my shoulder as the guard closed the door behind me, giving me the distinct feeling of being trapped like a rabbit in a cage.

"What's going on?" I asked them. "If this is about . . ."

"Whose side are you on?" she asked sharply. "Tell me quickly—I have decisions to make."

"Wh . . . what?"

"Your folk are coming," Mona said. "Six triple-masts are sailing up the waterways, flying Alcoran colors, armed with ballistae and some kind of mounted trebuchets. A contingent of Mae's scouts showed up an hour ago with the news."

My mouth opened and closed like a fish's.

"Oh," I said.

"How many soldiers on each of those ships, would you estimate?" she asked.

I looked between the two of them, my breath quickening as I processed this news.

"I . . . don't know," I said. "It would depend . . . on how many they could have mustered in such a short period of time, and how many are still in Cyprien." The council must have acted immediately upon Celeno's disappearance for ships to be here this quickly. Shaula must have made executive decisions . . . my heart pounded. What did that mean for my mother? Had she made it back to Callais at all?

Rou dragged his hand over his face and behind his neck, without any trace of levity. "I need to get back to Cyprien."

"There's no point in that," Mona said with emphasis, and I got the sense this was the subject of the tense discussion I'd walked in on. "If the Wood Guard saw the ships when they say they did, they're well past Cyprien."

"The Alcorans may have staged more ships in Lilou," he said. "They may be waiting on more to sail around the coast. We need to communicate with the Assembly, Mona."

"We'll get word to them when we can," she said. "Right now, we need whatever information Gemma can give us before trying to communicate."

Rou turned to me, his voice heavy. "Are your folk moving a force overland in addition to up the river?"

"I don't know," I said.

"Are they planning to fight through the Cypri lines or circumvent them?"

I flushed hot. "I don't know."

He nodded, expecting my answers, and started to gather his papers. Mona's parchment ruffled at the sudden shake in her hands—I had never once seen her hands shake before.

"There's no sense in going down the river if Alcoran ships are sailing up it!" she said.

He straightened his stack and tucked it under his arm. "I can set out when it's dark and hope to slip by them."

"I'm not sending you back to Cyprien!"

Rou's chest heaved with a deep sigh, and I could see how much effort it was costing him to stand against her. "I'm not asking you to send me back, Lady Queen. Yours isn't the only country in harm's way."

Under her silent stare, he headed for the door. I bit my lip as he moved past me, gazing straight ahead until I heard the soft click of the latch.

Mona's eyes were on fire as she stared at the door over my shoulder, to the point that she looked slightly wild. A terrible moment of silence slid by, and then she slapped the papers in her hand onto the table. She rested both her fists on the wood, head down, as if physically corralling her surging emotions. When she spoke, her voice was low and curt.

"Your folk will be here in less than a day," she said. "I need whatever information you can give me."

I wavered. "Celeno would be a better—"

"Celeno is gone," she said, looking up.

My heart froze. Gone? Gone? What did that even mean?

"Gone where?" I asked numbly.

"Up the Palisades," she said. "He left not five minutes after you did this morning. Mae and Valien went with him. They're taking him to Scribble Cave."

"Both of them?"

"I don't think either of them wanted the other alone with him," she said. "They took a handful of guards, too."

"And . . . you let them?" I flicked my head. "It's just . . . I thought you wanted him in a cell . . . I thought Ellamae wanted him in bed . . ."

"I've come to understand that what you lot do is well beyond my control," she said flatly. "And Mae . . . it was her idea. She unlocked the ankle cuff. She had the messenger wait to tell me until they had been gone for an hour. And now your folk are coming and *I need to know if you're going to help me or not.*"

The sudden anguish in her voice made everything lock into place. I straightened slightly, comprehension dawning. She'd been betrayed, one by one, by the people she thought she could count on, leaving her with only her youngest brother struggling to pick up the slack. Colm had shattered the trust between them and was left sitting in a cell, waiting to be tried for treason against her. Ellamae had freed Celeno from her iron grip and left—*left*, to bring him to see the cyphers she hated so much. Valien would always be loyal first to his wife and second to his allies. And now Rou, choosing his own country over her.

Leaving her with one final option.

Me.

Under her piercing stare, I moved forward to look at the maps scattered on the tabletop. I studied the detailed illustration of the shore along Blackshell.

I pointed to a little peninsula jutting out from the island near the river's mouth.

"That was a strategic staging place for us last time," I said. "The flagship was meant to berth there to keep visibility with the rest of the fleet."

She gave a short, clipped nod and circled the peninsula on the map. She straightened, affording me a view of her red-rimmed eyes as she fought to keep her emotions dammed back. Her jaw was set in a hard line.

She gestured at the map.

"What next?"

CHAPTER 16

We worked until well after dark, talking until our voices were cracked and raspy. I answered questions from her council and generals. I walked Arlen through the layout of the invasion plan three years previously. We calculated exactly when the first ship might make its appearance, based on wind conditions and ship load and the configuration of her rigging.

We also marked the exact spot along the river mouth where Celeno and I could most feasibly wave down the flagship and halt the attack before it began. This was my most desperate hope, because every other option carried the sharp, broken feeling of finally, fully betraying my country. Because the Lumeni weren't just going to defend themselves. They meant to fight back. They meant to take the lives of my folk who were sailing to take theirs. And I was helping them do it.

Treason, treason, treason.

Mona cut us all off before the night got too late, knowing the ships would be on the doorstep come morning. She sent us all away with a steel-edged glint in her eye—I doubted she would sleep tonight. I wondered if she would go find Rou. He'd been in a few of the sessions, taking careful note of the strategizing taking place so he could bring the news back to the Assembly. But he and Mona hadn't spoken, and I wondered if he planned to slip down the river in the dark early morning before the ships had arrived, or after they were moored at the entrance to the lake.

Outside Mona's room, I loitered briefly in the hallway. As the last few people filtered away down the hall and her double doors latched shut behind me, I crept out of the shadows and went to the door carved with rushes. I put my hand on the knob, half expecting it to be locked. It gave under my push, and the door edged open. Drawing in a breath, I slipped into Colm's room.

There was a pilot lamp burning next to the door, its flame low and blue. I turned up the wick and let the light wash over the room. Colm had a foyer, smaller than Mona's parlor—barely big enough for a tea table and two armchairs clustered around the hearth. But there were bookcases, and a wide window bench under the darkened panes. There were two other doors set into the far wall—studies or breakfast rooms or something else . . . one had probably been Ama's. Swallowing the lump in my throat, I crossed to the door in the opposite wall and turned the knob.

It was dark and quiet, hung with the subtle scent of ink and beeswax. I lit a few of the candles and set my lamp down, gazing around. There was a canopied bed, the curtains drawn back, and a fireplace with an oddly low mantel. The room was tidy, with just enough oddments out of place for it to look lived in—a book askew on the bedside table, its pages marked with ribbons, a set of boots cockeyed on the floor, a solitary glove resting on the trunk under the window. I went to the trunk first, moving the glove and setting the lamp down on the floor. There was a wooden frame tucked behind the trunk that I had to shift to make room for the lamp. I opened the trunk and peered inside. I picked carefully through packed summer clothes until my fingers brushed the copy of *Our Common Origin*. I pulled it out and opened the spine to find pages of my handwriting, neatly creased. I removed them, replaced the book, and closed the lid. I set the glove back on top—perhaps running the empty fingers through mine briefly before feeling foolish and setting it back down.

Drawing up my courage, I went to the bedside table. Behind the book and the candelabra was the little wooden box, its mother-of-pearl fish winking. I opened the lid, tipped it to its side, and caught the ring in my palm.

It was small, but no smaller than my own finger, with a graceful bloom of pink pearls on top. I ran my thumb around the circle, the metal barely worn.

"I'm sorry," I whispered to it. I looked up around the room, a room which had once housed a happy couple but was now full of ghosts. "I'm sorry," I said again. My gaze lit on the mantel, and I realized what was so odd about it. It wasn't the mantel itself that was strange—it was the blank wall above it. The open space stretched conspicuously to the ceiling, topped with a thick nail in the plaster, as if it used to house a large painting.

I had a jarring image of the mantel in my own parlor back at Stairs-to-the-Stars, the wedding portrait replaced by a map of Alcoro. Slowly I turned back to the trunk under the window, where the wooden frame peeked out from behind it. My feet moved forward of their own accord, and I stood in front of the trunk again. I pushed it aside until I could slide the frame out and turn it around.

Ama had a heart-shaped face and twinkling brown eyes, her lips curved upward in a smile that suggested it was her easiest expression. Her wedding dress was the same pink as her ring, and her chestnut hair was twined with roses and ribbons. I clutched the little ring in my fist. She was lovely, confident like Mona, but without her cold edges and hard outer shell.

CREATURES OF LIGHT 421

But it was Colm who drew my eye. When had this painting been made? Mona said they'd been married a year before my folk invaded, which would put it at just over four years old.

It may as well have been forty.

The artist portrayed Colm's face with a buoyancy to it, an unabashed light that was extinguished now. His smile was bright and fully reached his eyes, not shuttered or sheltered. He held his bride's hand with both of his, looking guileless and boyish, even more so than Arlen, even though he must be around the same age as when this portrait was made. I found myself reaching to brush the pigments of his face and altered my course at the last second, landing instead on the deep gold of his hair. Ochre, I thought, picturing the painter choosing the colors to mix on their palette. Deepened with a little sienna and brightened here and there with cornsilk. My cheeks heated slightly— Colm's image laughed merrily at my embarrassment.

He wouldn't laugh that way now. He'd smile, close-lipped, and even though it would be a genuine expression, it would carry gravity in it.

Was his face a mask, like Mona's?

Or was that eager happiness simply gone?

I was snooping, I knew it. This portrait had been taken down and hidden behind the trunk for the same reasons Celeno had taken ours down, and I had no right to examine it now. I looked back at Ama once more. She smiled at me as if she had every confidence in my ability to face the heinous thing that had been done to her by my own inaction.

"I'm going to try to set it right," I whispered. "I don't know that I can, but I'm going to try."

They both continued to smile.

Carefully I turned the portrait around and slid it back behind the trunk, shifting everything into its former place. I stood back, casting one last look around the room. My gaze lit again on the blank wall, and then moved past it to the bookcase in the corner.

There was a stack of blank parchment on one of the shelves, along with ink and quills. I set the sheaf of my letters and Ama's ring down on the foot of the bed, and then went to the shelf. I shook one of the bottles of ink and popped the cork off, dipping a trimmed quill.

I worked carefully, thinking before each stroke, envisioning its look on the page. The nib scritch-scratched over the parchment. I left things loose and a little messy, embracing the quill's finicky nature. It was better to be a little sketchy, I thought. It helped disguise the fact that I had never drawn an iguana before.

I gave its back and tail a serpentine curve to it, its clawed legs drawn loose against its body like I recalled from the few illustrations I'd seen. I drew spines and detailed its blunt face, adding the suggestion of scales and defining everything with my mother's directional hatching. A few bubbles and quick strokes hinted at the surf around it.

I leaned back and examined the sketch. It wasn't

anything that would receive acclaim in a biology pamphlet, but it was decent enough. I tapped the end of the quill against my lips. I wished I'd read more of *The Diving Menagerie* to know how the verses were structured. After a moment of pondering, a thought occurred, and I bent over to scribble in the margin.

I've heard of a lizard that dives in the sea.
Haul away, mates, each your line.
It does it despite what we think it should be.
Heave away, mates, and haul down.

Blushing at the childish work, I corked the ink bottle and stowed everything back on the shelf. Carefully, I rested the sketch on the mantel. It looked small and silly in that big open place, and I wondered if Colm would even be allowed back in his room, or if a servant would sweep the parchment up and pack it away somewhere. I turned, leaving the swimming iguana on its perch, and gathered up the ring and my letters. Tucking them in my pocket, I cast one last look around the room, cold and quiet, and then headed back to the foyer door.

I listened at the crack for a moment or two, not wanting to explain to any guards what I was doing. When I was sure the way was clear, I eased the door open and slipped out.

There were guards on the landing, but they were facing away from me. I tried to set my footfalls a little louder so they would hear me coming. One turned his head and regarded me with eyebrows raised.

"What are you doing here?" he asked.

"I was helping Queen Mona," I said. "But I'm done now—I'm going back to the guest wing. Would you prefer I was accompanied by someone?"

The guard hesitated. "No," he said. "The queen has not given orders to escort you, and any part of the palace you shouldn't enter will be guarded. But I'm not letting you back into this wing unless I have word from my queen."

"I understand. Thank you." I passed them and headed down the steps, sharing a similar conversation with the guards at the base of the staircase. I first headed to the healing wing, but finding it dark and empty, I continued back to the guest wing. It was dark as well, with no guards outside Celeno's door. Hesitantly, I pushed it open and went inside.

The windowpane Celeno had broken to distract his guard had been tacked over with a wooden board, and a tendril of cold air seeped around it. I stirred up the fire in the hearth to try to coax a little heat into the room, and then I carefully laid out my letters on the bed. My gaze scanned each one, remembering each emotion at the time of writing them. The first was written with barely contained shock, still reeling from the loss of Lumen Lake and unwilling to believe this incredible piece of news that had arrived unexpectedly on my desk. My second was more coherent, rife with fervent speculation. And the third . . . the third was the longest, full of hope and plans and promises—all diplomatic in nature but tinged by a kind of passionate optimism not present in the others.

I laid the fourth one out, a short, tense note explaining that his last letter had indeed been too late, and that we had already sent our ambassador on her way to Lumen Lake. I smoothed the last page on the coverlet. When Celeno came back—when they all came back—I'd walk him through each one, laying to rest any last questions about my mistakes. I didn't care what the outcome was. I had no illusions about forgiveness or trust rebuilt. I just wanted him, finally, to have the whole picture.

At first I paced to stay awake, chased from one end of the room to the other by my anxious thoughts. When my toes started catching on the rug and my eyes blurred with exhaustion, I finally took a seat, perching stiff-backed on the edge of the armchair. I forced my brain to think of something academic and landed on my thesis—despite it being ages ago, I could still recount the basics of my abstract and methods. When I reached my results section, I realized my head was resting against the wing of the chair. And then, my discussion section seemed to blur oddly with iguanas and call-and-response work chanties.

I've someone who's waiting with eye on the storm.

Haul away, mates, each your line.

We'll weather far worse if we stand it alone.

Heave away, mates, and haul down.

When my eyes opened again, the edges of the window curtains were tinged with gray light, and Celeno sat cross-legged on his bed, his gaze on the sheaf of my letters in his hand.

I straightened too quickly, and my neck seared in protest. I sucked in a breath, and he looked up.

"Good morning," he said.

I tried to roll the kinks out of my shoulders as I staggered out of the armchair. "When did you get back?"

"About fifteen minutes ago. I think Ellamae wanted to cuff me to the bedframe again, but in light of the approaching ships, she rushed off." He waggled his boots back and forth. "It's nice to have some freedom of movement."

I stood a few paces away, studying him. He was dressed in the clothes he'd worn through the cave, but they'd been washed and pressed. After several days of damp Lumeni nightshirts, seeing him back in a black bolero and a dark red waist sash was strangely relieving. He looked more like himself than he had in weeks, and it wasn't just the wardrobe. There was a flush of color in his cheeks, perhaps from the hours spent in the winter air, and his hair tumbled loosely around his ears.

"You're looking at me like I'm a specimen under a glass," he said.

I shook myself, flustered by my sudden awakening and his drastic change. "I didn't expect . . . you look well."

"I feel terrible," he said casually, rifling a few of my letters. "I puked three times, twice up and once down. My head feels like it's roosting pigeons, and I think I could probably sleep for a month." He squinted at something on the page. "But for some reason, none of it is actually bothering me at the moment." He looked up, and his eyes were clear. "I saw the petroglyphs, Gemma."

I wavered slightly, and he set down the letters. He patted the mattress next to him.

"Come sit with me," he said.

I hesitated, haunted by our last conversation, but then walked around the other side of the bed and crawled up next to him, leaving a foot of space between us. Together we stared at the fire, which had burned low, leaving only glowing fragments of wood in the hearth.

He reached into his bolero pocket and withdrew a creased piece of parchment. I saw the edge of a cypher written in charcoal in one of the folds, but he didn't open it just yet. He turned it slowly in his fingers. The anticipation in my head was shot through with weariness—I couldn't even muster impatience. I was just tired.

"*We are creatures of the Light,*" he said, "*and we know it imperfectly.* That part Colm had right."

"And the next line?" I asked. The one that had words before his title, the one that we'd been unable to decipher.

The one that had dragged me over, under, and through three countries, chasing its ephemeral possibilities.

"The next line," he said, each word measured, as if he was still digesting it. "The next line says, *During the reign of the seventh king of the canyons, one will rise to bring the wealth and prosperity of a thousand years.*"

I turned my head to face him. He gazed at the fire, his eyes bright. "During the reign?" I repeated.

He slid his finger into the crease of the parchment and unfolded it. His writing was less even than Colm's was, but the cyphers were all formed boldly and with surety, each one clear in its meaning.

Sure enough, the second line began distinctly with those words. *During the reign of the seventh king.*

I took the paper gingerly from him. "That makes it sound . . . like . . ."

"A time frame," he said. "Not a title. A mark on a calendar."

The fire popped. A log slid slightly in the grate.

"Which means . . ." he began.

"You're not the fulfillment of the Prophecy," I said.

"No," he agreed. "Someone else is. And sometime during my reign, they'll do something great."

I leaned my head back against the headboard, my mind picking apart each new word. *During. The. Reign. One. Will. Rise.*

He pointed to the next three lines on the page. "Did you see the final name?"

I had, but I could only process so much at once. I read the new lines again, lingering on the final word, the one too faint to be legible in Callais.

Peace will come from peace. Wealth will come from wealth.

I am a Prism, made to scatter light.

Syrma

Below it was the human figure, arms and legs bent at right angles off the body. Above its head were three dots, the ubiquitous mark in Alcoro to denote a woman, the foundation of the three-gemmed star bands every girl wore from infancy.

"Syrma," he said. "The Prism was a woman."

Whether the Prism was a man or woman or neither didn't matter. What mattered was that she had traveled, leaving her words scattered throughout the Eastern World. What mattered was that her words were different from what we had believed for centuries.

"They match up with the fragments we saw in the cave," he said. "There was a *d* root before my title, remember, and the remains of a few other cyphers. *During the reign.*" He said it slowly, as if still coming to terms with its implications. "Yesterday you said you researched the traces of other Prophecies. Do the others match up?"

"The bits I've pieced together—yes," I said. I was tired, *so tired.* "None of them were as complete as this one, but they all support these new lines."

"Then we were wrong," he said. "Our translation

is wrong. The Prelate was wrong. Even if Lumen Lake is the key to fulfilling the Prophecy, pursuing it in my name means that it was wrong."

He was gazing at me. I couldn't turn my head.

"You don't look relieved," he said.

Carefully I folded the paper, hiding the new cyphers. "I've been through too much in the last six months to trust in relief."

"We're going to have to go back to Alcoro," he said. "We're going to have to set things right. But I think it will be easier now." He tapped the folded parchment. "These make it easier. Once we get down to the river, and stop our folk from sailing in to the lake, we can bring some of them up to see them. After that, everything will be easier . . ."

He trailed off, still looking at me, watching for a reaction. I found I still couldn't turn to face him. In the hearth, an errant spark found an uncharred fragment of wood and sent up a little flare.

There was no divine force guiding his hand, giving him authority.

My choices were just as valid as his.

That should have made me happy, or at least satisfied. But all it did was take away the rationale I'd come to rely on—that all my work failed because it didn't have the Prophecy behind it. Now his didn't, either. And the only person I could blame for my own failures was myself.

Maybe I'd suspected it all along.

He shifted a little.

"Gemma . . ." he said hesitantly. "About the healing wing. I wasn't trying . . . to do the same thing as my mother. I just wanted the pain to stop for a little while. I didn't mean for it to go that far."

"I'm sorry that's what it took," I said. "I'm sorry I couldn't help you more."

"You've always helped. I know I haven't always been grateful, but you've always helped me. And I know . . ." His gaze dropped to the letters in his lap. "I know that's what you were trying to do here." He rifled a few of them. "Are these all of them?"

"Yes," I said.

"And when we got here . . . that was the first time you and Colm met in person?"

"Yes."

"So there was nothing . . ."

I was silent, and for some reason my heart was sadder than when we'd begun.

"Yes," I said. "There was something between us. I didn't realize it until the past day or so. But the thing is . . ." I ran the back of my hand across my eyes. "He listens. From the first letter, he listened. He answered my questions and expanded on my thoughts. We were in sync right away. And so . . . instead of coming to you, instead of trusting you with this thing, I went to him instead."

The fire popped slightly, spitting a few sparks.

"But these are all the letters?" he asked again.

"Yes."

"Do you love him?" he asked.

"No," I said. "I don't know him well enough to love him. But I do trust him. And for that, I feel like I've let you down."

He shifted. "You're allowed to trust other people."

"At your expense?" I asked.

He drew in a breath and smoothed the letters out in his lap. "You know what Ellamae did on my ship while we hunted you down in Cyprien?"

"She broke her lock a few times, didn't she?"

"Well yes, but aside from that," he said. "She was questioned over and over, sometimes by the Prelate, sometimes by the ambassador. But twice, I questioned her, alone. And somehow, by the time both sessions were through, she was questioning *me*. Asking me why this and how that—when did we start tracking the Prophecy, how did we know exactly what it meant, why did I drink that foul-smelling tincture all the time. And . . . she listened, too. Oh, she was brisk about it, don't get me wrong—you know how she is. I'm sure her kindest opinion of me is that I'm a reckless idiot." He ran his fingers through his hair. "But at least she listened."

I nodded, staring at the fire. "Folk don't often listen to us."

"No," he said thoughtfully. "They obey, but they don't listen." He turned his head to me. "And, it seems, somewhere along the line, we stopped listening to each other, too. We grew apart. Didn't we?"

"Folk pried us apart," I said.

I could feel his gaze locked on my face.

"What do you mean?" he asked.

"We were dangerous together," I said. "We made big things happen when we combined our efforts. The origin of meteors, the reclassification of the cicada—those were warning flags. Together, we were able to change science. We could have changed the country." *Unstoppable.* "And that was dangerous. The Prelates have always had a vision for the Prophecy. It needed to be upheld. And so we needed to be separated."

He was silent. I didn't turn to meet his eyes.

"I . . . don't believe that. I *can't* believe that." His voice changed—he repeated his words, but they took on a new meaning, one of dawning comprehension. "I . . . I can't *believe it.*"

"I can," I said.

"It's . . . sinister—laughably so." The creeping shock in his voice conveyed no mirth whatsoever. "It's fairy-tale-villain stuff."

"It's what the Prophecy necessitated," I said. "I'm sure Shaula believed she was helping to guide you back to your true purpose, away from my bad influence. She doesn't think she's evil—nobody does. She believes she's helping you do what you aren't strong enough to do on your own."

His silence was longer this time, his gaze drifting over to the fireplace. "She's wrong," he said finally. "That's what you've always done."

I pressed my lips together. My throat started to tighten. Stress crying.

He shifted sharply, turning back to me. "I'm sorry, Gemma. I do wish things had gone differently here— that you had been ready to trust me with Colm's first letter. But I know why you didn't. And I'm sorry for pushing us to that point. You've been there for me since the beginning. You were there when my father died, when my mother died. You were there when we took the lake and when we lost it. Despite everything, *through* everything, you were there for me."

His voice kicked a little, suddenly infused with a ghost of his old excitement. "And now . . . Gemma, now it doesn't have to be like that. I'm not in charge anymore. I don't have to be. The stupid Prophecy, the petroglyphs, Shaula—it's all different now. I'm still king—I'm just not a special one. And that means I can just as easily transfer my power to you. *Gemma* . . ." It was as if all the ramifications of the past five years were sweeping up to him at once, and I actually leaned away slightly as his words tumbled out. "*You* can lead Alcoro—let *me* help *you*. We can be strong together again—we can go back to how we were be-fore."

I was holding my tears back, making the world blurry. I couldn't make myself speak the words aloud,

I couldn't make myself remind him that there was no going back, there was no chance at being together again. That even if we'd come to an understanding of his title, Mona and her allies still would require atonement for the things we'd wrought in our wake. For him—prison, alone. For me—the throne, alone. Those days along the canyon, those nights murmuring in bed of all the things we could accomplish—so many dreams, so many ideas, ready to be watered and grown and spread through the country—those things were gone now.

There was a nudge at my hand, his fingers brushing mine. I knew he wanted me to turn my hand over, to accept his, but I found I couldn't. He laid his palm gently over the back of it instead. I couldn't make my mind focus on just one thing—it swirled from thought to thought as quickly as they came. The new lines of the Prophecy, Lumeni work chanties, cicada resonance, a kiss under the stars, two hands linked on a cold stone floor . . .

Somewhere outside, the distant sound of thunder split the air.

I froze, trying to believe what I'd just heard. As the report died away, I whipped my head around. My widened eyes locked with Celeno's.

"Oh Light," he breathed. "They're here."

"I thought we had more time," I said, knowing that voicing that thought meant nothing. "I thought we had . . ."

The next boom echoed across the lake, accompanied by the sound of grinding rock. Somewhere out on the palace grounds, a trumpet blasted an alarm call, shrill and fast.

I scrambled off the bed and dashed across the room to the patio door. I flung it open to the bite of frigid air and ran out to the rail. The morning sky was streaked with pale pink and gold, a perfect sunrise. The Beacon was shining with the strength of the sun. But marring the air by the river's mouth was a thick plume of black smoke. The first in the line of ships was making a hard tack to starboard—bearing not for the little peninsula on Perch Island, but up the shoreline.

For Blackshell.

"They're coming here first," I said aloud. "Oh, Light." A glut of fire spewed into the air, the sound reaching me half a heartbeat later. I streaked back to the patio door. "They're releasing incendiaries on the shore!"

Celeno was hopping on one foot, trying to draw on his calf-high boot. "Go find Mona! Go find Ellamae—have them meet me in the front hall!"

"Where are you going?"

He stamped his foot to shove his boot the rest of the way on. "To stop them, of course."

"I thought we'd be hailing them at the mouth of the river!" I said. I ducked instinctively as the next blast rent the air—much closer, it seemed, than the previous one. "I didn't plan on approaching them while they're actively firing!"

He swung his traveling cloak around his shoulders. "We can stop them before they make it here. We can stop them before they get out to the islands." Seeing my incredulous look, he smiled—by the Light, I hadn't seen him smile in months. It flooded through me, the ringing shock of recognizing a long-lost friend.

"I may not be the fulfillment of the Prophecy," he said. "But I'm still the seventh king of Alcoro. That counts for something, doesn't it?"

He dashed to the door, flung it open, and ran into the hall beyond. My feet started moving a half-second later. I charged out after him, only to jump out of my skin when a door banged open behind me. Rou came stumbling out of his room, wrenching his arms through the sleeves of his vest, his face wide.

"Rou . . ."

"Did you see?" he said hoarsely. "They're lobbing Lyle's grenades. Those things won't douse with water—it'll only make them spread. The Lumeni soldiers have to know or they'll burn the place to the ground—where's Mona?"

Without waiting for a reply, he streaked after Celeno, his boots slapping the hardwood floor. Hitching up my skirt, I took off after them both, following the hem of Celeno's cloak as it whipped around the corner of the guest wing.

The palace was in chaos. Armed soldiers ran in

one direction, night-clad servants fled in the other, towing children, shoving those who had just been roused from sleep. Folk called out; horns blared. The entrance hall was a crush of people all fleeing through the open doors, the gusting wind dousing the lanterns and making the embroidered hangings weave and snap.

Across the melee, I saw Celeno's cloak again, toiling through the current of panicked Lake-folk. But they were all trying to get to the same place, scores of folk all pressing through the double doors, and he was caught in the teeming crowd. I struggled toward him, trying not to quail under the sound of the latest grenade blast, so close it shook masonry dust over the terrified crowd below.

To my right, a figure appeared on the wide sweeping stairway—Mona, dressed in a long tunic and trousers, surrounded by a swirling knot of guards that bristled with naked swords and swerving shields. She swept her gaze once over the bedlam before her, missing me in the crowd, before her eyes flew to the distant window over the doors to the grounds. I knew instantly what had pulled her attention. She was looking out over the snowy lawns and gardens, past the perimeter wall and the village beyond, out to the prison. She wouldn't be able to see it from here. Her fists were clenched by her sides.

I knew because my thoughts were there, too.

I put my head down and pushed forward until I

was within reach of Celeno. I lunged through the crowd, snatched a handful of his cloak, and hauled him backward with as much strength as I could muster. He staggered under my pull, his panicked gaze locking with mine.

"Gemma!" he exclaimed. "I can't get through this damned crowd!"

"We can't just run out into the streets!" I pulled him up the first few steps of the staircase, one flight below Mona, who was occupied with her knot of guards. "Not without some kind of plan. We need to think . . ."

"There's no *time*, Gemma . . ."

"Mona! *Mona!*"

Ellamae's shout cut through the ambient screaming, and we turned to see her darting through the throng. She had a painted flatbow in one hand and a fistful of arrows in the other, and the silver pins gleamed against the dark green of her Woodwalker uniform.

"Pull your folk back!" she called, joining us on the steps as Mona hurriedly descended. "Alcoro is setting up to blow the perimeter wall!"

Mona's eyes flashed. "What?"

"They sent a contingent of foot soldiers up to blow the gate—I'm sure they mean to trap folk here in Blackshell while their ships fire from the water . . ."

Celeno grabbed Ellamae's wrist. "They're *here*, on the ground?"

"There's a phalanx forming outside the wall—it doesn't look deep, but it's enough to repel civilians. We need to send a contingent out to . . . *oh no you don't.*"

She seized Celeno's sleeve as he started to move past her. "No sir, I did not spend a week nannying you so could run out and get shot by friendly fire."

He pushed her hand off his arm. "If I can just get in front of our folk, I can stop this—I can stand our folk down."

"There's no way you can get to the gate and up on the wall without running into crossfire—they're already lobbing flash grenades willy-nilly over the ramparts. Arlen's setting up his javelins by the courtyard—you'll be caught in the middle even before they break through."

"Get us to the terrace," I said suddenly. I looked up at Mona. "We can't get through the wall—and stopping the ground attack won't stop the ships. The flagship is heading straight for Blackshell—if we can get to the terrace, we may be able to hail it before they start a siege. They can signal a ceasefire for the foot soldiers."

"The terrace—yes!" Celeno swept his gaze over the packed entrance hall. "Which is the quickest way?"

"You'll be running right into range of their trebuchets!" Ellamae protested. "The ships—"

"Get me something white," I said. "Something we can signal a parley with."

I looked expectantly at Mona, waiting for her reply. Her gaze flicked from me to Celeno, and finally to Ellamae, who let out a growl of frustration.

"It's a terrible plan," Ellamae said, shaking her head.

"What else can we do?" I asked her.

She tossed up her free hand. "I don't know. If we wait any longer, we'll all be trapped within firing range of the ships."

Mona's face was pale and tight. "Arlen's in the courtyard?"

"Yes."

"Where's Valien?"

"On the grounds somewhere—he has a contingent of swords," Ellamae replied.

"Bows?"

"No bows."

"Where's Rou?"

We all shared a breathless silence.

"I last saw him in the guest wing," I said. "He was running to warn the soldiers about Lyle's grenades."

Her face gave the slightest spasm, the barest twitch of anguish, but she didn't hesitate any longer. She turned to one of her guards. "Go to the courtyard and tell Arlen we're attempting a parley on the terrace." As the soldier ran off, she beckoned to us. "This way—the fastest path from here will be off my patio."

We followed her up the staircase and along the landing, the din from the entrance hall growing distant be-

hind us. Our pounding footsteps were drowned out by
another grenade blast—this one had a different sound,
less resonant and much, much closer. The initial report
was followed by the tumbling crash of rubble.

"They've blown the wall," Ellamae said grimly,
pulling an arrow from her hip quiver.

Mona's voice was strained as a wound spring.
"Let's hope Arlen can hold them."

My chest tightened. *Let's hope we can cease fire before
Arlen has to hold them.*

We flew down the corridor to her double doors
and piled into the parlor beyond. The glassed doors to
her patio showed a blue sky choked with ash, and the
first glimpse of the flagship's bowsprit as she neared
firing range.

Celeno raced to the doors, but Mona called after
him. "Wait!"

She rushed to cut him off and grabbed a handful
of the elegant white drapery hanging over the doors.
I moved forward to help, winding the expensive silk
in my fists—it was meticulously stitched with repeating silver bulrushes. Celeno released the handle and
added his own strength, and together we pulled with
all our might. The seam fixing it to the curtain rod
strained and stretched—a few pearls popped loose
and leaped from their embroidery. At the next thunder of grenade fire, Ellamae clamped her arrow in her
teeth, drew a knife from her belt, and with a jump,

slashed the elegant fabric near the seam. The drapery ripped loose in a ragged line. Pearls rained down on us like a cloudburst.

"Go," I said breathlessly to Celeno, bundling the white fabric in my arms. "Go, go!"

He didn't need any persuading. He wrenched open the doors, and together we dashed out onto the patio and down the staircase beyond, our boots skidding on patches of ice.

"Stay, Mona!"

I glanced over my shoulder. Ellamae was leaping down the steps after us, setting her arrow to her string. She jerked her head at Mona, who halted on the top step, still surrounded by her orbit of armed guards.

"You stay!" she said again. "You'll be safer up here."

"Mae, I should be there when—"

"Join us when we start negotiating!" Ellamae called back. "Once we manage the ceasefire, then come down to the terrace—that's when we'll need you most!"

Mona clearly didn't like it, but she didn't follow us down the staircase. With a wave, she motioned two of her retinue to follow us—they obediently hurried down the steps, atlatls in hand. This done, she lifted her gaze out over the lake, her face pale and grim. Breathless, I turned back around, focusing on placing my feet on the icy staircase.

The lakeshore was a nightmare. From Blackshell

down to the river, orange flames leaped freely from roof to roof, heedless of the snow. The ships were launching the incendiaries with deck-mounted trebuchets, allowing them to stay well out of reach of any bowfire from the shore. The flagship—the *Splendor Firmament*, the warhorse of our fleet—was making a hard tack toward the deepwater docks that led off the terrace—perhaps planning to berth and unleash more soldiers while continuing its projectile assault. I clutched the white flag to my chest, my lungs burning on my breath.

So close. So close. So close to flagging them down, to halting the trebuchets, to ending this building catastrophe.

We reached the final step of the staircase and veered left on the tiled walkway that wound along the water's edge. It was narrow, bordered by the lake on one side and a waist-high retaining wall on the other, and it was rimed with ice, making each wild footstep treacherous. I set my boots as carefully as I could while keeping pace with Celeno, unable to rely on my occupied arms for balance. From the far reaches of the palace grounds, I heard the first sickening echoes of metal on metal—the two battalions of foot soldiers had met. Had Arlen's javelin line failed? Had Valien led some kind of charge? Where was Rou? Was Colm safe in the prison? Would Mona be safe up on her patio?

The possibilities for death were endless.

My boots pounded the walkway, beating a repeating refrain in my head—*the ship, the ship, the ship*. The *Splendor Firmament* had reached the deepwater docks and dropped anchor with a grinding clank. The deck bristled with swords and crossbows; the great trebuchet counterweights were slowly being hauled down into position.

We rounded a final corner to see the great terrace sloping away from us, the sparkling snow on its surface incongruously pristine. I sucked in a sharp breath of relief. All that separated us from the open space was a row of archways, probably home to flowering vines during the summer—now they were bare and bleak. Through the last archway, I could see the distant statue of Ama Alastaire, standing like a lone sentinel, daring her enemy to mar the water with another drop of blood.

Celeno was several feet ahead of me and had just run under the first arch when the space between us was punctured by a flying object.

"Down—*get down!*" Ellamae snatched the back of my blouse and brought me skidding to a halt as another crossbow quarrel whistled through the air—if I'd continued running it would have struck a clean shot. She shoved me below the line of the retaining wall—my boots slid in the snow, my arms tangled in the white banner.

Piled at the corner where the Blackshell walls met the terrace were six soldiers in russet and black, their crossbow sights trained our way. Celeno didn't stop, running at breakneck speed through the line of archways. He was windmilling his arms and shouting at the distant ship. I watched as a russet-clad soldier jammed another quarrel into their crossbow and brought it up to sight.

"They don't recognize him—stop!" My voice rose in a shriek. "Stop—Celeno—*stop!*"

But he passed under the final arch and burst out into the open. Ellamae leaned around the side of the arch and drew her bowstring back to her cheek. One of Mona's guards did the same with his atlatl, cocking a wicked-looking javelin back over his shoulder.

"No—no, wait!" I struggled to my knees, freeing one hand from the banner.

It was no use. With a twang, Ellamae's arrow sprang from her string.

Thump.

The foremost soldier went down.

"Stop! Stop!" I lunged for her tunic as she pulled another arrow from her hip quiver.

"Get off!" she snarled. "Unless you want him spitted by your own folk!"

"Let me get by—let me go after him!" I hefted the banner, watching as Celeno sprinted farther and farther away from me, alone, still waving, still shouting. "If I can just get to him—"

The precious second of idleness cost us. A crossbow snapped, and the Lumeni soldier beside me staggered backward, tagged with a quarrel in his chest. His boot slipped out over open water, and with a mighty splash he tumbled off the walkway into the lake. I stared at the rippling waves in shock. The water wasn't deep here—once it stilled we could see him lying immobile just under the surface, eyes open, the end of the quarrel sticking up like a bare flagpole.

I gasped and ducked my head as another quarrel whistled overhead. Ellamae swore and dropped to her knee below the wall.

"Gemma—they *don't recognize you!*" She flinched, her hands around her ears as a third quarrel skipped off the archway. "I know it's hard, but if you don't let me take them out . . ."

There was a shout and a clang. Together we lifted our heads over the wall just enough to see a pale sword cleave an arc through the five remaining Alcoran soldiers. Another fell, giving us a glimpse of green and silver—Valien. He ducked a blow from one of my folk and used their momentum to propel them face-first into the stone corner of Blackshell Palace. But it was the last clean hit he landed—the three others pounced on him en masse, the winter sky flashing off their bare blades.

Ellamae swore like a career sailor and leaped heedlessly onto the retaining wall, wrenching her bowstring back to her ear—leaving the narrow walk before us clear. As her arrow flew, and before the other Lumeni soldier could shout or snatch my shirt,

I scrambled to my feet and sprinted past them, making for the end of the stone arches.

Celeno was in the middle of the terrace, still shouting fruitlessly at the distant ship. I raced to catch up, letting Mona's white drapery unfurl in my arms. I lofted it over my head, letting it stream behind me like a sail. A hundred terrifying sounds muddled my head—the crashing of swords on shields, the blast of incendiary grenades, the screams riding the breeze, the roar of my own blood in my ears. But one new sound cut through the others—one that froze my bones. The release of a winch, the *whrzzz* of freely spinning gears. I caught a glimpse through the final arch of the *Splendor Firmament,* where three of the trebuchets had loosed their counterweights. I watched in horror as the massive arms arced through the air, graceful in their paths. The slings convulsed forward—*one, two, three*—and I opened my mouth to shout just as I reached the final archway.

My words were swallowed by the blasts.

The world went white and silent—like a bolt of lightning shot straight between my ears. I was in the air—my feet had lost contact with the ground. I twisted, reduced to basic impulse, until I hit something solid on my right side. The breath drove out of my lungs, and I rolled, chafed raw by snow and grit. Unthinking, I curled up, clutching the back of my head and neck, shielding my face from falling debris.

I choked, my throat thick with dust and smoke. The flash of heat gave way profoundly to icy cold as the initial explosion dissipated. My head throbbed, my blood was thick and fiery. I smelled copper on top of the acrid smoke and wondered vaguely which painful place on my body was bleeding.

Despite this jarring symphony of sensations, the world was still silent. I shook my head, dizzy, leaving streaks on my vision, and tried to lift my shoulders off the ground.

I'd been saved by the archway—it stood incongruously amid the pile of rubble on all sides. The terrace was no longer flat and pristine, but buckled and streaked black with smoke. Dazed, I staggered upright, clutching the stone pillar for support, trying to organize the blur of shapes and shades around me into a recognizable picture.

The first sound reached me, distant and muzzy. I turned back over my shoulder. The second Lumeni soldier was facedown in the water, flanked by pieces of a broken archway. Valien had leaped the remains of the retaining wall and was plowing through debris like it was underbrush, half his face red with blood. Not far behind me was a slip of forest green under the rubble. I saw his lips forming her name, but I could only register the blurred suggestion of each syllable. *Ell-ah-may.*

He lunged downward and heaved her upright, her

dark brown hair and copper skin coated white with masonry dust. The dust on her face cracked and split as she grimaced, and as he freed one of her arms, she waved it under her own power. Alive, then. Alive and shouting at him about something. Waving her hand forward. His head lifted and he locked sights on me where I slumped, clutching the archway for support. And then he looked past me.

The muffled cloth in my ears was being replaced by ringing, high and sustained, bringing with it the continued shouting and horn blasts from around the palace. I turned back to the terrace and took one step away from the arch, wobbling. I took another step, letting go of the pillar, still clutching the white banner, now streaked with soot and blood that could only have come from me.

The muddy shouting grew more distinct, and I realized it was because Valien was gaining on me, struggling over the demolished walkway. He was calling my name. I moved faster, slipping over a chunk of a paver that had buckled in two. The terrace was smoking—patches here and there still spit fire as Lyle's incendiary grenades gobbled up their fuel reservoirs. Down by the lakeside, there was no more white statue—Ama Alastaire lay in pieces in the water.

"Gemma! Gemma, stop!"

I broke into a run, wild and loose-limbed, picking out the flicker of red sash, black fabric amid black stones.

Valien's voice grew clearer, sharper.

"No, Gemma, get back! Don't look, go back—*Gemma, don't look!*"

CHAPTER 17

There was a lot of screaming.
I think it was me.

CHAPTER 18

I strode up the gangplank to the bobbing *Splendor Firmament*, heedless to the row of crossbow quarrels pointed at me from above. My right ear still rang—I couldn't hear anything on that side, splitting my world into two halves. I carried the white banner of parley in my fist, the stained fabric still shedding the occasional pearl, leaving a shiny, straggling trail behind me. A knot of Alcoran soldiers stood clustered at the rail, uneasy with the sudden pause in the assault. I snapped at them once, and they scattered, giving me space to pass through them.

Shaula was storming down from the quarterdeck, her black fur-lined cloak billowing out behind her. The commodore, ship's captain, and an abundance of officers were with her, but they were of no importance to me. I headed straight for them—sailors and deckhands scurried out of my way like roaches from lantern light.

"What is this?" boomed the commodore, his helmet gleaming in the morning sunlight. "What are you doing—"

"Be quiet," I said sharply to him. "Don't speak again."

His words turned to a rasp in the back of his throat, his jaw hanging open.

I gestured to the mainmast. "Signal the rest of the fleet to cease fire and make berth in the river."

"The commodore will do no such thing."

I turned my gaze to Shaula, who was regarding me with her usual stern look, the same sort of disapproval as when I'd rolled out of my mother's potato cupboard, sobbing.

"If you had any sense," I said to her, "you would kneel."

She didn't move, and neither did any of the officers. "Gemma," she said with the voice she'd used to scold me as a child. "You are a traitor to your country at least five times over at this point. I'm afraid you have no authority in current company."

"Who ordered this assault?" I asked. "No siege or movement of state military can take place without royal decree."

"I gave the decree," she said. "You forget, as always, that the Prelate has the ability to act for the monarchy when circumstances require it. It's the most basic form of balance between the monarchy and the council."

"I didn't forget," I said. "I wanted you to remind my officers." I pointed at the deck. "Kneel."

She still didn't move, her face twisting from disdain to anger. "Enough of this, Gemma. Where is the king? Answer that question, and we shall consider ceasing fire until he is returned."

"You have killed your king," I said.

A ripple ran through those gathered onboard, a collective intake of breath, of sideways glances. The knot of officers shifted, the sunlight glancing off the golden emblems of the Seventh King on their boleros. Shaula narrowed her eyes.

"You stoop to great lows to find ways to circumvent—"

"He was killed in the incendiary blast to the Blackshell terrace," I said. "He was approaching to hail the ship and halt the attack when the trebuchets released. If it wasn't the percussion that killed him, it was the impact from debris."

One young officer was twisting her cloak in her fists. The captain was muttering rapidly to the pale-faced commodore. Whispers flurried behind me, lost to the ringing in my right ear.

"I beg your pardon," the commodore said briskly. "But the Prelate guided the ships to Lumen Lake upon a revelation from the Light. There was no indication the king and queen were here. How could she know where to find you if we were not meant to be here?"

"Miraculous things happen around the Prelate, don't they?" I murmured, my gaze locked with Shaula's. "So many miraculous things that one may even start to believe some of them were divinely driven. Where is my letter?"

She lifted her chin, and with expertly practiced disdain, she said, "What letter?"

"You destroyed it, didn't you?" I asked. "The letter to me."

She sniffed in a non-answer. "I don't know what you're talking about."

"A loss, then." I shrugged. "At least no one can use it against me."

The bait fell true. Because Shaula would never, ever pass up an opportunity to declare my shortcomings to me.

"You would deserve it," she said poisonously. "It clearly was not the first. Exchanging love letters with a lakeman, an enemy to our country. Unfaithful, ungrateful little queen—you were never fit to stand beside the Seventh King."

I saw several brows furrow, and the young officer, with less of a leash on her tongue, puzzled out loud, "So . . . there *was* a letter?"

"Quiet, Lieutenant," said the commodore. His gaze flicked between Shaula and me. "But . . . there was a letter?"

Shaula frowned, but she was poised enough to recover quickly. "The Light reveals itself in many ways, and it is not the Prelate's obligation to disclose any of them. But you continue to distract us from our more pressing matter. We took care to plot where the king was likely to be held. We noted where each of the prisons were on the shore and on each island, and we organized our strategy accordingly—"

"Did the king ever divorce me?" I interrupted. "Did he ever sign the annulment papers?"

Shaula sputtered, perplexed.

"Did the council ever complete the arraignment?" I continued.

"The order stands for your execution," she said. "Signed by the king after you escaped imprisonment."

"No," I said. "It was signed by you, but it wasn't a signature authorized by the king, and that makes it invalid. And when the king is incapacitated, the authority comes to the queen, not the Prelate. Am I not still your queen?" I asked. I washed my gaze over the knot of officers. "Am I *not still your queen*?"

"Yes," cheeped the young officer.

"Oh, Light," murmured the commodore.

Shaula twitched a hand, as if hoping to puncture the swelling panic. "This proceeding cannot possibly take place without—"

"*GET. ON. YOUR. KNEES.*"

She gave a start at the lash of my voice, at the step I took toward her. Behind her, with the creak of leather

458 EMILY B. MARTIN

boots and starched uniform trousers, the young officer dropped to kneel on the deck. The others followed suit. A flicker of action in my peripheral vision told me the sailors and deckhands who had been standing slack-jawed a second ago were sinking to the deck.

Slowly, arranging her thick black skirt around her, Shaula lowered herself down. She furrowed her brow, staring straight ahead, appearing to think very hard.

"Commodore," I said.

"Yes, my queen."

"Signal the rest of the fleet to cease fire and make berth in the river."

"Yes, my queen."

As the commodore hurried back to the quarterdeck, Shaula looked up at me. Even with her eyes two feet below mine, she still managed to convey an air of authority.

"You cannot remove me," she said. "You cannot try me like a civilian. The title of Prelate ensures—"

"I don't want anything to do with you," I said. "I am handing you over to Queen Mona Alastaire to be tried for war crimes against Lumen Lake. You forget, as always, that when the Prelate assumes the voice of the monarchy they assume the retributions as well. It's the most basic form of balance against a corrupt prelacy."

I turned my back on her and waved to the line of soldiers who were kneeling by the rail. "Four of you, come with me. The rest of you, stow your weapons.

A contingent of Lumeni soldiers will be aboard momentarily to arrest the Prelate. Make no attempt to interact with them. Your only job is to keep the Prelate in her current location until she is in Lumeni custody. The *Splendor Firmament* will then make berth in the river, where you will wait for further instruction."

There was a flutter of gloved hands as they silently saluted me. I looked back over my shoulder. The commodore was up on the quarterdeck speaking to the signaler clutching the semaphore flags. My gaze dropped to the cluster of kneeling officers flanking Shaula and locked on the young one. She was looking at me, but seemed to regret it.

"Lieutenant?" I asked.

"Second lieutenant," she replied.

"*Lieutenant*. Come with me."

The newly promoted officer hurried to rise, and I turned and made my way across the deck to the gangplank. At the mainmast, the pulley rattled as the signal flag was lofted into the air.

"Gemma!"

Shaula's voice was direct and disbelieving. A few soldiers rose from their knees as I passed, perhaps to flank her side as she got to her feet.

"Gemma!" she demanded again.

I kept walking without looking back. I kept walking until I had crossed over the rail, descended the gangplank, and reached the far end of the deepwater docks, her voice eventually lost to the hush of wind and the ringing in my ear.

Mona stood at the end of the dock, her arms wrapped tightly across her chest, looking back at the smoking ruins around Blackshell. The three trebuchets had blasted apart the corner of the palace that abutted the terrace, and odd bits of interior décor—a twisted lamp, a scorched curtain, half a wingback chair—littered the broken flagstones. Ellamae was next to her, half-sitting on a mooring post, beating the dust out of her uniform. Her right leg stuck out awkwardly, wrapped in a hasty splint Valien had lashed together from fragments of roof timbers and strips of his cloak. Another strip wound around his forehead, though the blood on his face had yet to be cleaned off. He didn't seem to register his own injury, though—he hovered at Ellamae's shoulder, his fingers occasionally landing in various places on her body as if to check to be sure she was really alive.

Mona turned to face me and the group trailing me as we approached. "Did she . . ."

I nodded. "Send them in."

She waved to the cluster of Lumeni soldiers behind her, and they made their way past us for the *Splendor Firmament*. I looked to Ellamae.

"Is there a stretcher?"

She nodded.

"Good." I beckoned to the group of Alcoran soldiers and the lieutenant, and then proceeded off the dock and back toward the palace.

The grounds seemed oddly hushed after the chaos just shortly before. In fact, the parts of the palace that hadn't been impacted looked positively peaceful, the layer of crisp snow sparkling in the morning sun.

The terrace was quiet as well, but it was not peaceful. A harried guard of six Lumeni soldiers stood tensely around the cloaked body on the ground. Two were shifting a stretcher close to the edge of the cloak.

"Away, all of you," I said. They looked up, and without waiting for a nod from Mona, who trailed behind, they scattered backward.

I knelt down on the broken stone pavers, far more slowly than I had not long before—there were still skid marks in the soot and snow from where I'd lunged to the ground. The blood in the cracks of the pavers hadn't dried, thanks to the cold, adding new stains to the ones already streaking my skirt. I looked up at the young officer.

"Lieutenant—?"

"Itzpin, my queen."

"Lieutenant Itzpin, you understand you'll be asked to testify?"

Her lips were bloodless but set. "I understand, my queen."

With fingers strangely still and calm, I pinched the edge of the cloak and pulled it back so only she could see.

She maintained admirable control, unlike I had. I watched as she struggled to memorize the sight, using her face as an anchor to keep from looking down. I didn't need to see again. I wouldn't ever unsee it— the blood coating both sides of his neck where his eardrums had ruptured, the loose angle of his jaw, broken. Despite this, his eyes were closed in an ordinary way, and his hair lay in curls over his forehead. I thought of that instead—as if it were early morning, and I'd woken up to find him in the last threads of an easy sleep.

Gemma, came his usual murmur. *What time is it?*

Always checking, always wondering how much time we had—just us—before the day truly began.

I gestured to his wrist, lying near the lieutenant's boots. She crouched down and pinched it in her fingers. After a long moment, she lifted her hand to his blood-soaked neck but stopped herself and reached for the vein in his thigh instead. Finding no pulse in either place, she leaned back.

"Verdict?"

"Deceased," she said. And then, more softly, "Oh, blessed Light." She removed her plumed helmet.

I lowered the cloak and nodded to the soldiers. "Move him onto the stretcher. Lieutenant Itzpin, see that he's brought to the healing wing and guarded until I return. This Lumeni soldier will show you the way." I pointed to the red-haired soldier from my first day at the lake—he startled, jittery.

I stood back as this was accomplished, watching them carefully heave the king's covered body onto the stretcher and pick it up between them. They followed the lieutenant, her helmet tucked under her arm, as she walked after the redheaded soldier.

The silence behind me was profound. I turned to the others. Ellamae leaned heavily on Valien's shoulder, her splinted leg propped up on a broken paver. Mona stood woodenly by. They were regarding me with the alert caution of something that might erupt at any moment.

I suddenly registered the missing faces.

"Where's Arlen?" I asked.

"Taking a contingent to the river," Mona said.

"And Rou?"

Something behind her eyes flickered. "No one's seen him."

"Was he near the terrace?"

"I don't know."

I looked at Ellamae. "Were any of your scouts killed?"

"Two," she said gingerly. "No injuries among the rest."

"They can form a search for him?"

She nodded but didn't move. Neither did Valien. Neither did Mona.

"Go on," I said. "He could be hurt—what are you waiting for?"

"Gemma," Mona said, her voice barely more than a whisper. Her hands twitched toward me. "I'm sorry."

No, I didn't want to do this now—I didn't want them to suddenly conjure pity. Ellamae nudged her husband in the ribs, and he helped her hop forward, reaching for me. She meant to embrace me—Ellamae, who'd wrestled Celeno to the ground three days previously, wanted to wrap me up in a hug.

I stepped back, out of her reach, and her fingers closed on thin air. She wobbled on her one good leg, and Valien grasped her elbow to steady her. I looked back to Mona, standing, for once without her shoulders thrown back.

"You have some closure, at least," I said.

Her mask fractured—I could practically see the fault lines as it splintered and fell away. I watched as she struggled to find something to say, but she didn't get the chance. A voice called from up near the palace.

"Queen Mona! He's here—we've found him."

We all turned—Ellamae clutching Valien's sleeve—to see a few soldiers waving from the very edge of the rubble. Dashing the back of her hand across her eyes, Mona hurried toward them. I followed, with Ellamae and Valien progressing slowly behind. We reached the group just as they heaved a timber beam to one side and hoisted a dust-covered Rou from the pile of bricks.

He coughed forcefully, sending a cloud of dust floating away. His eyes slit open, and he cocked his head as Mona crouched down next to him.

"Rou," she said.

He closed his eyes and let his head rest back against the ruined palace wall. "Think I've figured this whole thing out."

"Are you hurt?"

"So you're the head, see," he continued, tapping his dusty curls.

Mona looked between Ellamae and me, worry creasing her brow at his nonsensical statement. But he pressed on.

"You're in charge of everything—you drive everything." He fluttered a hand, his voice raspy. "Mae's the hands. She gets things done. She acts." He cracked open an eye to find me. "And you're the heart, Gemma. *Thump thump.* Head and hands couldn't operate without the heart."

"Rou," Mona said sternly. "Did you knock your head?"

He rolled his face to her. "Know what that makes me? *An ass.*" He let out a laugh that turned into a cough, masonry dust clouding into the air.

"Rou," Ellamae said. "Celeno is dead."

Rou swallowed his cough mid-gasp. Both his eyes snapped open and fixed on me, his levity instantly replaced by horror. After a moment of shocked silence, he struggled on the pile of bricks.

"Get me up—get me out of this damned hole." He slid a bit on the rubble, clutching Mona's sleeve.

"You're not hurt?" Mona asked. "Not at all?"

"The beam made a pocket. Nothing actually hit me—I just couldn't get out." He struggled to his feet. "Oh, Light, Gemma—"

"Don't," I said. I leaned away from his outstretched hand, and he paused with it in the air. I stepped backward, slipping slightly on the broken rock. I looked to each one of them in turn. "Don't do this right now—any of you. Don't think I don't understand what this means." Their attention was riveted on me. I gestured at the lake. "Things are fixed now, aren't they? Things are solved. You . . . all of you . . . it only makes your lives easier. It only brings you justice. Don't lecture me," I said, pointing at Ellamae, who had taken a preparatory inhale. I moved my finger to Mona. "Don't dissertate at me. Whatever you have to say, I don't want it."

They were all silent, each staring at me with their own version of shock. It manifested in different ways—Ellamae's brow was furrowed, Valien's was raised. Rou's dusty face was creased with distress. And Mona simply looked stunned.

The silence stretched out. No one seemed to know what to say. Finally, Ellamae shifted. "Then . . . what *can* we do for you, Gemma?"

I drew in a short breath. I hadn't expected that question. "Gather everyone together—anyone who's needed to make important decisions. The council. Arlen. Sorcha—I promised her she would be involved. I'll bring one or two of my own folk. And . . ." I turned to Mona. "Get Colm."

She took a little sip of air, and then gave a single nod. "It may take a little time to bring everyone together."

"It's fine," I said, taking a few careful steps through the wall. "I'm going to need it."

I wrung out the cloth, the fragrant steam rising from the washbowl. Carefully, I lifted the edge of the sheet that had replaced the cloak as a shroud and dabbed at the dried blood on Celeno's cheek. I'd already washed his other side, getting his ear as clean as I could. By the time I was done, the water in the bowl had been pink and copper-sharp. I discarded it and filled it with fresh water and herbs.

I hadn't been in the room when the guards brought Shaula through to witness his body. It had happened in the few minutes before I showed up, and by the time I arrived in the healing hall, she had been taken away to the prison. Part of me knew it was right for her to see him bloodied and disheveled, but I wished I'd had the chance to wash him before she'd come.

He wouldn't have liked her seeing him this way.

I moved carefully, trying not to bump his jaw, which was still covered with the sheet. Lieutenant

Itzpin was at the end of the bed, slowly easing the tall boots off his feet.

I laved his exposed forehead. "You seem to have something to say, Lieutenant."

She gave a little start. Her eyes darted to our four guards, who made a perimeter about ten paces away, facing outward at full ceremonial attention, swords drawn. They hadn't moved a twitch since I'd come in to the healing hall.

"It's just . . . I don't understand," she said quietly. "How could this have happened?"

"A poorly planned attempt at a siege, without proper consideration to conventions of wartime," I said.

She flushed as she eased off his other boot. "No, I mean . . . the Prophecy of the Prism. How could this have happened before it was fulfilled?"

"How do you think it happened?"

She bit her lip. "It . . . could mean . . . that the Prophecy was wrong?"

"That's one explanation," I said calmly, dampening Celeno's curls with the wet cloth and threading them through my fingers. "Can you think of another?"

She set down his boots. She studied the tips, reaching out a finger to brush at the coating of dust. Searching in the lining pocket of her bolero, she drew out a handkerchief and began to clean off his boots.

"Maybe . . ." she said. "The Prophecy *has* been fulfilled, and we just don't know how yet?"

"Another valid thought," I said. "I can see how

you rose to lieutenant so young. So, Lieutenant Itzpin of the Royal Alcoran Navy—which answer do you think it is?"

She moved to the buckles of the boots, polishing them without really seeing them. After a long silence, she looked up at me.

"I don't know," she said.

I looked down at Celeno's half-covered face, as clean as I could get it. I brushed a few of his curls over his forehead.

"I don't know, either," I said.

The murmuring in Mona's council room stopped when I walked in, dressed in a fresh skirt and blouse without bloodstains on it. The commodore followed over my shoulder, the closest approximation I had to a royal official. He wavered, not entirely without apprehension. Perhaps I should have brought the lieutenant.

Everyone had had the chance to clean up—Rou was no longer coated with dust, and Ellamae had a real splint on her leg, propped up on a second chair. Arlen sat white-faced next to Sorcha, who studied me with an eagle eye as I entered.

In fact, the only one not looking at me was Colm.

He sat at the end of the long table, his elbows on the wood and his fingers clasped in front of his lips. His eyes were closed. His brow was knotted upwards—not a look of anger, but of anguish. A Lumeni guard stood over his shoulder, a reminder that he was still under a prison sentence. At least his wrists weren't cuffed.

He was still wearing my cloak.

Mona pushed her chair back and stood, which necessitated that everyone else stand, too. Chair legs scraped and jostled. Ellamae, of course, didn't stand. Colm did with everyone else, but he kept his head bent down, bracing both hands on the table.

Strangely calm, I went to the empty seat in the middle of those gathered. The commodore followed, and everyone sat when I sat. Mona poured a cup of tea from the tray on the table, added cream and honey, and passed it to me. The steam curled toward my nose, herby and hot.

By the Light, I wanted a cup of coffee.

"Well," Mona began, less sure than I'd ever heard her before. "Councilors, allies, we're gathered to discuss . . . the imminent future of our countries. But before we begin . . . let us observe a moment of silence for Celeno Tezozomoc, the seventh king of Alcoro, who was killed this morning in an incendiary attack."

The slight ambient shuffling went absolutely still. Ellamae and Valien both leaned together and turned their hands over, their palms facing the ceiling. Rou closed his eyes, his knuckles against his lips. Mona folded her hands on the table in front of her.

I waited patiently for them to finish, observing the swirl in my teacup where the cream hadn't fully mixed yet.

"May he be blessed in the Light," Mona said. The others murmured back this common phrase. I lifted my teacup, letting it scald my lips. It was all a façade—Mona didn't believe in the Light.

She cleared her throat. "Now . . . er, Queen Gemma, did you have . . . a particular subject you hoped to address first?"

I set my teacup down. "Yes, several. First, am I right in assuming I am still considered the reigning monarch of Alcoro by all those present, despite previous miscommunication?"

"Yes," Mona said. Ellamae and Valien nodded together, along with Rou. I glanced at my commodore.

"Yes, my queen," he said.

"Good. As such, I want each of you to understand that there have been at least two instances of invalid Alcoran documents forged with the king's name. Any orders you have—any correspondence you may receive—" I turned from the commodore to the Lumeni councilors. "I need to verify its authenticity before it is acted upon."

There was a murmur of agreement around the table.

"Next," I continued. "I need messages sent to Lilou requesting representatives of the Assembly of Six join us here. We can't fully begin talk of reparations without them. In the meantime, I'm going to need documents of damages suffered here in Lumen Lake and the related cost of reimbursement."

They were all silent and staring—I wish they'd look at something else. Their hands, the wall, each other—instead, they were all riveted on me like I was a planet to be orbited.

"Finally," I said. "Before official talk of reparations begins, I need to make you all aware of the action I have planned once I am back home in Alcoro, so you can take it into account."

"What action is that?" asked Mona.

Colm's eyes opened, and he turned them on me, creased.

"I'm going to found a university," I said. "Like the one in Samna."

There was a polite silence around the table. My commodore looked puzzled, as if trying to remember if he'd heard of this plan or not.

"I see," Mona said. "Have you, er, detailed your plan at all?"

"I have a letter of collaboration from the Samnese board," I said. "Giving suggestions for its foundation. Once I have the seed money in place, they've agreed to send a representative to assist with the implementation."

"I hope you're not asking *us* for seed money," Sorcha said. Arlen's face burned red, and Mona cleared her throat, most likely to reprimand her, but I shook my head.

"No," I said. "I'm not asking anyone for money. I have the seed money—or, at least, I will once I recover the funds allocated to the governing of Cyprien. I'm not asking anyone here for anything. I'm going to found a university in Alcoro. Whether or not you take an interest in it is up to you."

Ellamae shifted her splinted leg a bit. "And who are you planning to accept at your university?"

"Anyone," I said. "Anyone throughout the Eastern World who wants to attend."

"Do you . . ." Mona began. "I just mean . . . do you have teachers? I know you have scholars, but are there enough to teach in this type of setting?"

"I have three so far," I said.

She thinned her lips, as if forcing patience.

"Myself," I said. "And my mother. Natural sciences."

"That's two."

"And Colm."

She shifted her gaze down the table. He was watching me, as he had been, with a mixture of grief and hope. His eyes cut straight into me.

"Cultural history," I said. His beard by the corner of his lips twitched.

One of Mona's councilors fidgeted in his seat. "Colm Alastaire must still stand trial for treason, of which prison is the most typical sentence."

I looked from the councilor back to Mona. "Even after everything—even now?"

"Nothing has changed," she said softly.

It seemed like such a strange statement to make when things had so utterly, irrevocably changed.

Rou coughed slightly. "What if we focus on first things first, and draft the letter to the Assembly? Then I can go south first thing tomorrow, and we can sort out the rest after we're all back together."

"Yes," Mona said with an air of relief. "I'll send a contingent of our folk with you to escort the Alcoran ships back out to sea. Arlen can go with you." She glanced at me, still edged with wary hesitation. "Er . . . was that all, Gemma?"

Was that all? Yes, that was all. A university, a war, a monarchy torn in half. Life, death, and every state of being in between.

"At the moment," I said stiffly.

She nodded and waved her hand at the others seated around the table.

"Councilors, you may go—I'll have a draft of the letter for you to review before the evening is out."

As they all shuffled and stood, the Lumeni soldier leaned down and tapped Colm on the shoulder. Without a word, he stood, and I realized that he was going back across the grounds and into the cold little cell.

Mona cleared her throat. "Officer. Take him instead to his room and set a guard. We'll move to stationary arrest for the time being. No visitors."

The soldier nodded. "Yes, my queen."

Colm didn't say anything to her or to me as he followed the councilors out the door.

I hesitated for several seconds as Mona arranged an inkwell and parchment in front of her. Then, just before the door to the room closed, I pushed back my chair. She and the others looked up at me, but I turned before they could speak. I caught the almost-closed door and hurried out into the hall.

"Colm," I said.

He and the soldier both turned next to the sill of a thick-paned window. The creases in his face came back as I approached. His hair lit up in the sunlight, that same golden ochre in his wedding portrait. How could it be sunny right now? How could the skies be so clean and bright?

"Gemma," he said, his voice gravelly. "Gemma, I can't begin to tell you how sorry . . ."

I dug deep in my pocket and held out the little ring. His gaze fell on it, the pink pearls glinting softly.

"I didn't get a chance to put it on the statue," I said around the block in my throat. "And now the statue is destroyed. It was broken apart in the blast . . ."

His big hand closed over mine briefly, just long enough to give gentle pressure before taking back the ring. "It's all right. Really, Gemma—I shouldn't have burdened you with it in the first place."

"She was very beautiful," I said. "And she looked happy next to you."

He didn't ask where I had seen her face, and he didn't smile. He looked, if possible, more anguished than before. He reached out, almost impulsively, and gripped my hand again.

"You know what the thing is about that kind of

happiness?" he said, his voice strained. "It doesn't go away. It's what you remember."

A world of time and space passed between us in that fraction of a moment. His eyes flicked back and forth between mine, desperate in their need to convey his comprehension.

Not pity.

Empathy. He'd faced this beast himself.

The soldier nudged his elbow, and he drew a breath, leaned back, and dropped my hand. After a final pause, he turned, tucking the ring deep into his pocket.

"I'm sorry, Colm," I said. "I'll try . . ."

He shook his head. "Don't worry about me, Gemma. Really—please don't worry."

He followed the soldier's ushering down the hall, his hair lighting up in each window they passed.

I sucked in a deep, shaky breath.

"I need someone to worry about," I said after him, but he was gone.

CHAPTER 19

I didn't go back into the council room. I wandered instead. The light turned deep and ruddy in the windows, reminding me that the day of Celeno's death hadn't even come to its close yet. And like a child, like a girl with a mind full of shadows, I was terrified of nightfall. Night was the hardest—I remembered it looming over me in the acolyte's cell as I practically smothered myself with my pillow to keep from crying too loudly. I remembered it deep in the inner sanctum of our rooms, tinged with worry and dread. I remembered it creeping in through the padlocked windows in Cyprien, reminders that time was irrevocably slipping away.

Night was the time of memories and ghosts.

I went to the library but I didn't sit or read. I simply paced up and down the aisles. I wandered out through the darkening halls, running my fingers over the glimmering pearl wainscoting. I padded through the empty music room, the arched ceiling echoing with silence. I tiptoed back down the portrait hall, avoiding the eyes of the generations of the monarchy as they followed me from end to end. I climbed the spiral stair up to the turrets, my rushing thoughts chasing me in my wake.

The last colors of sunset were fading outside the turret windows. I moved closer to the glass, and then halted, nearly flinging myself backward onto the staircase—*there was a face in the window, and it was Shaula's*. I gripped the railing, my body trembling, until my surging mind righted itself. There was a face in the window, and it was my own, reflected by the dim light of a pilot lamp. The thick glass was distorting it, making it twisted and grim. Or maybe this was simply how I looked now—maybe grief had done the same thing to me outside as it had done inside. I reached up to touch my face and watched Shaula's hand mirror mine to brush her cheek.

With a violent shudder, I snatched at the pilot lamp and snuffed out its wick. The tower room was plunged into darkness. Shaula's face disappeared. But she didn't go away—it only felt like she was behind me, or standing in the shadows, waiting to lay out my failures to me.

Queen Mona would execute her. She'd try her for the same things she'd itched to try Celeno for, and she'd hang her without a moment's hesitation. I covered my face with my hands. What if this was yet another mistake, the worst one yet? What right did I have to send her to her death, to atone for my own actions? She'd taken me in. She'd kept me from dying in a cupboard.

She'd killed four people, and dismantled so many more.

She'd killed the king.

She'd *killed the king*.

I drew in a ragged breath.

Or . . . had that been me?

Slowly, numbly, I lowered my hands. Outside, the upper reaches of the sky were speckled with stars, wobbling in the thick glass. Shivering, I stepped forward and looked out over the dusk-swallowed lake.

I would use a lot of black, I thought, to paint this scene. I didn't often like to use black—few things in nature were truly black, more often gray, or brown, or a deep shade of some existing color. But the sun was below the distant range, and the islands were a true black in silhouette, with no hint of color or distinguishing landmarks.

My gaze dropped to the surface of the lake, mirroring the last gasp of twilight. My peripheral vision had simply said *blue*. Shades of blue throughout, perhaps with some hazy purples. But as I studied the glassy surface, I realized my eyes had simplified things. It was the definition of waterhue—the ribbons of indigo and plum melting into sheets of silver-blue and violet.

Unfathomable green brushed against periwinkle, and brief ripples of some in-between color were birthed and reclaimed in the gently shifting surface.

I watched the water move and change for an unmeasurable length of time, until it was too dark for my eyes to distinguish color any longer. I kept waiting for tears. They never seemed to come. I looked up at the stars through the rippled glass. Nothing.

What was wrong with me?

You're the heart, Gemma. Thump thump.

You know what the thing about that kind of happiness is? It doesn't go away. It's what you remember.

But Celeno hadn't been happy. Celeno had been so unhappy it had robbed him of health and sanity. The eager, energetic scholar I married had slowly been eaten by his title—his title which turned out to be wrong. And in the end, I had only made it worse. I had been the one thing he thought he could trust in. And I'd taken even that away.

So why couldn't I cry?

I stayed in the turret until my teeth began to audibly chatter, and then I wound my way back into the halls below. I glimpsed palace guards and attendants here and there, all standing at seemingly incongruous corners and doorways, but none of them spoke to me. I continued on to the guest hall.

It was late—I'd expected to find it dark and quiet, but light spilled from one of the open doors. I slowed my steps as I approached—it was Ellamae and Valien's room, but it wasn't just their voices I heard hushed inside.

"—haven't even seen her cry, have you?"

"She's still in shock, we're going to have to give her time."

"It's just unusual . . . she always seems to cry so easily . . ."

"Don't talk about me," I said from the shadows.

The voices stopped. A chair creaked, and Mona appeared at the door, the light behind her making her shadow long and thin.

"Gemma," she said. "Will you come sit with us, please?"

"I don't want to."

"I know, but we have a few things we want to tell you. And we have supper. Come sit by the fire—the turret must have been freezing."

I recalled all the out-of-place guards and servants. "You were having me watched," I said accusingly.

She nodded calmly and took my hand anyway, leading me into the room. It was indeed warm, seeping into my chilled fingers and toes. I curled them in relief.

Ellamae sat in one of the armchairs in front of the fireplace with her leg propped on a footstool and a crutch leaning on her chair. Valien was next to her. Arlen was leaning against the mantel. His patch was off, revealing the lines of scar tissue over his left eye. Rou scooted over on the settee, patting the cushion next to him. In their midst was a table bearing covered dishes all curling with steam.

"Tea?" Mona asked, sitting back down on my other side.

"No, thank you."

She lifted the cover on one of the bowls. "Soup? It's nothing heavy—just good broth and some vegetables."

"We're all going to fuss until you're holding something hot," Ellamae added.

I didn't doubt that. "Soup, then."

Mona ladled a cup and handed it to me. I wrapped my fingers around it—it did smell nice. Parsley and thyme and just a touch of garlic.

"We drafted the message to the Assembly," Mona said. "There are six letters written out, but they're not sealed yet—would you like to see them?"

"No," I said, swirling my spoon in the broth. "I'm sure they're fine."

"Rou and Arlen will leave tomorrow morning, then," Mona said. "My flagship will escort your fleet down the river and berth in Lilou."

I nodded and sipped a little soup despite myself. It washed over my tongue with a comforting amount of heat.

A stilted silence followed. Mona rearranged her fingers in her lap. Rou ran his hand over his face. When it was clear neither of them were going to say anything, Ellamae shifted in her chair.

"Gemma, I know this is hard to think about," she said, "but if your ships are leaving, something should be decided about Celeno's body."

"You are welcome to inter him here," Mona rushed to say. "But I don't know . . ."

"He wouldn't have wanted that," I said.

Another awkward pause. I sipped some more soup. There were little pearl onions in the broth—tiny and sweet.

"It's just . . ." Ellamae began again. "Your folk entomb, don't they?"

All those pockets in the cliffside, filled with shrouded figures, the desert mallow wreaths withering under the sun, the juniper smoke lost to the wind. Twice he and I had stood side by side below the royal tombs, dressed in undyed linen, listening to the endless prayer of the dead. Both instances were surreal—the first time we were still stricken with shock at his father's sudden heart attack. The second was swallowed by the looming preparations for his coronation mere hours after his mother's body was laid to rest. Instead of juniper smoke and silence, the streets were filled with crushed sage and music, a cacophony of jubilation for the coronation of the Seventh King.

He'd been sick all week.

"I don't know that we have the right embalming materials for you," Mona said hesitantly. "My folk do water burials. And if the body isn't prepared properly, and has to endure a week or more at sea . . ."

"When the River-folk light their pyres," I said to Rou without turning toward him, "what do you do with the ashes afterward?"

His thumbs traced the rim of his teacup. "Some people keep them in family mausoleums." He was on my right side, and his voice was muffled in my ear, still ringing from the blast. Reluctantly I turned my head slightly to hear him better. "But most folk will scatter them in the rivers."

I nodded. "I think something like that would be best. It would make everything easier for everyone."

They were all silent. Ellamae raked her fingers through her curls. Valien rubbed a callus on his bow-string finger.

"Gemma . . ." Mona began.

"It shouldn't be about what's easiest," Ellamae said.

"Why not?" I snapped. "It solves the problem of him lying in the healing hall under a sheet."

Ellamae sat forward, the footstool shifting under her leg. She stretched out her fingers, but she couldn't lean past her knee. "I'm too far away, dammit—Val, take her hand."

Valien leaned over and closed his fingers gently over mine. I looked up at him in surprise, and then to Ellamae.

"Gemma," she said, her dark brown eyes fixed on mine. "We know these circumstances are making everything that much harder. You're not at home. He was unhappy here. Lumen Lake has bad memories for both of you. He was killed by his own fire. And all of us here have struggled against Alcoro and Celeno specifically in some way. But, Gemma—you're still our friend. Politics and wartime aside, we care about you. We understand that Celeno was more than what we knew. We know you both were important to each other. His death isn't a relief to us, and making sure he's taken care of isn't an inconvenience. He was your husband. He was king of your country. And he was a person—one you knew better than anyone. He deserves to be properly honored."

My hands shook around my soup bowl, my tears springing almost instantaneously. I drew in a sharp breath, and then I was done for—I set my bowl down with a clatter and leaned forward, sobbing into my arms. A flock of hands descended on me, warm on my back and my shoulders and my knees. At least two handkerchiefs were pressed into my palms.

"It's m-my fault," I said. "All of it—everything that happened, everything that went wrong—it's all my fault."

"Dammit, dammit," Ellamae said again. "Here, Val, help me up." I heard the footstool scrape and several thumps as she hopped across the floor. She shoved the food tray aside and sat down on the tea table, her leg stuck out to the side. Her hands came to rest on my elbows.

"It's not your fault, Gemma," she said.

"If I had been with him . . . if I had just c-caught up to him with the flag, they might n-not have fired . . ."

"Or they might have killed you both," she insisted. "Gemma, it was *not your fault*. Death can't be broken down into blame."

"Ama," I gasped. "Ama's d-death can. Ama's death was our fault, as well."

The hand on my knee squeezed. "Was it?" Mona said quietly. "I thought so for a long time. But if that was the case, why has Colm always blamed himself? He let go of her hand to run. He left her behind without checking." She brushed my hair. "Why have *I* always blamed *myself*? I am the queen of this country, and I fled when she didn't. A civilian showed courage that hadn't even crossed my mind. She died in my place."

"But we killed her."

"Your executioner killed her, under orders," she said. "Orders given by a commanding officer, under oath to the crown."

"Don't you see, it all comes back to . . ."

"Attempting to carry out a sacred belief," Mona continued. "Attempting to make decisions set in motion by the generations before you. Gemma, my heart isn't big enough to forgive or forget Ama's death. But I don't blame you or Celeno for it anymore. I blame a world that distorts a leader until death seems like a justified action."

I persisted. "Lyle," I said. "You can't possibly pretend Lyle's death wasn't—"

"Gemma." Rou's hand on my shoulder gave a little shake. "You can't take the blame for Lyle's death, and you can't take the blame for Celeno using the crossbow. A person is responsible for their own actions. Celeno was sick, inside and out, and panicked over losing you. I'm like Mona—I'm not quite decent enough to work up to forgiveness yet. But I can say with absolute certainty that none of this has been your fault alone, queen or no."

Mona sighed next to me. "Maybe none of us should be monarchs at all—maybe there should be no kings or queens. It makes us *all* sick."

I stayed bent over. My tears slowed but didn't stop. My muffled ear throbbed. Their words seemed to melt off me, not sticking, not quite bouncing off. I couldn't make sense out of any of it, blame and guilt and grief. Their hands all stayed where they were, little isolated pockets of warmth amid the cold still locked in my body.

"I never forgave him," I said into my arms. "He apologized just a few minutes before it started, and I didn't take it."

I thought they might try to soothe it away, murmur that he knew I had forgiven him—*had I?*—argue that I didn't need to—*did I?*

They didn't. There was a long silence.

"I'm sorry," Mona said, her hand still on my knee. "That's painful."

"We know it is," Ellamae said. "It's horrible to feel like things have been left unsaid." She rubbed my arms. "It's all right to wish things had been different, but don't let it turn into blame."

The swirling storm inside me settled somewhat. It *was* painful. I did wish things were different. But . . . I was grateful they hadn't tried to whisper it away. My fingers tightened slightly on one of the handkerchiefs in my hand, and I lifted my head to wipe my eyes and nose.

I drew in a thick breath and looked up for the first time, meeting Mona's gaze. "Mona . . . about Colm. Please, you can't lock him away. He made a mistake—we both made a lot of mistakes—but he's loyal to you."

She looked at her hand on my knee. "It's already gone before my council. There can be no denying one of his letters led enemy ships to attack the lake. The trial has to go forward."

"But—"

"*But,*" she said over me, squeezing my knee. "But I have the authority to suggest exile."

My chest tightened. "Exile?"

Her eyes were the saddest I'd ever seen them. "You were right the other day—I haven't given him the credit he deserves. He's stayed here because of me, and I don't know that he could make the choice to leave himself. He'd feel like he was turning his back on me. But I could make that decision for him."

"But . . . he couldn't ever come back?"

"I can suggest a term," she said. "A number of years until the sentence terminates. It shouldn't be hard to pitch to the council—they like him more than they like me."

My heart beat loose and wobbly in my chest. "Mona . . . that would be . . ."

"We need to be careful, though, Gemma. We need to make sure everything proceeds by the book— nothing that would give the appearance of favoritism." She squeezed my knee again. "Please don't go sneaking to find him again."

"I won't."

"I'm sorry about that," said a voice behind me, and I realized that the hand on my back was Arlen's—he had come around to stand behind the settee. "Sorcha . . ."

"Great Light, marry her," Mona said, twisting around to look at him. "She's got more backbone than my whole council put together."

There was a quiet ripple of laughter among us. I wiped my eyes again with the damp handkerchief.

"He'll still feel bad about leaving you," I said. "Both of you."

Mona sighed again. "Yes. He will. And I'll feel worse. But it will let him do this thing with you— found this university. I can't think of anything he would rather put his energy into. It's the kind of thing he's always dreamed of."

"And we think it's a good idea, Gemma," Ellamae said. "We know you've given it deep thought, and we know you can do it. We'll help in whatever ways we can."

I let my breath stream out, folding the handkerchief—it was embroidered with rushes. "Thank you. I know I didn't adequately describe it to you earlier. It's not just a dalliance. I've been working on it for a long time. It just got swallowed up by everything else. But I believe it can really, truly make things better—and not just for Alcoro. And . . . I *do* have more than two other people interested."

Ellamae smiled and hefted herself off the tea table. "We know." She hopped back to her armchair.

"I admit, I'm intrigued," Valien said, leaning back in his chair. The other hands on me slid away as everyone settled back into their seats. "What gave you the idea?"

"I've always wanted to see the one in Samna," I said. "But it wasn't until we lost Lumen Lake that I started realizing what building one ourselves could do for Alcoro. So much of our academic work is never given the chance to grow, or it's left unfunded because it's not useful to the crown. So many scholars have had to set aside their work because there's no place for it to thrive."

"Like you," Rou said.

"Well, like me. And like Celeno." I closed my eyes. "And folk from other countries. I think your brother would have appreciated the idea."

"I'm willing to bet he'd have even cracked a smile," Rou agreed.

The corners of my lips flickered but didn't rise. Lyle. He'd have been such an asset to an Alcoran university.

He and Celeno both.

"What subjects will you offer?" Valien asked.

"Natural sciences," I said, thinking back to the suggestions by the Samnese board. "Chemistry, mathematics. History, philosophy. Literature and the arts, eventually." I smoothed the handkerchief. "Astronomy . . . I thought Celeno would develop astronomy. He'd have liked that." I looked up at them. "And . . . regarding the pyre . . . I think he would have liked that, too. At least . . . I think he'd understand. It will be hard to explain back home, because there's already a tomb for the Seventh King, but at least his ashes can still be interred there."

Rou's shoulder was warm against mine. "If you think that's best, we can make it happen."

Mona nodded. "We'll plan something appropriate. Just tell us what you need."

"Do you have juniper?" I asked.

"The Silverwood's got juniper," Ellamae said. "Earth and sky, have we got juniper."

I smiled and wiped my eyes a final time. I drew

in a shaky breath and looked at the tea table, where everything was in disarray from being shoved aside.

"Did my soup make it?" I asked quietly.

Mona smiled and topped off the bowl. She set it back in my hands, and I sipped it again, quietly relishing the warmth and flavor.

A comfortable silence crept in. The fire snapped in the hearth. Mona swirled her tea. Ellamae adjusted one of the straps on her splint. Arlen took up his place at the mantel again, staring at the fire.

"Wait," he said suddenly. We looked up at him. "If Colm is exiled, can he not come to the wedding?"

Mona pursed her lips and set her teacup down. "We can make a condition about the river. It would be nicely symbolic, anyway, to hold the ceremony on the river, halfway between both countries."

The silence that followed seemed to ring, like the aftermath of a bell. Ellamae's mouth fell open as she stared at her. Rou's eyes widened, his gaze fixed on the tea tray. I shifted to look at her, smiling at her slip. Mona looked around at us, blank-faced, until comprehension hit her.

"Oh Light," she gasped into the silence. "Oh great Light, I meant . . . oh Light, you were talking about *your* wedding . . ."

Ellamae threw back her head and howled with laughter. Mona clapped both hands to her face, pink as dawn. Rou cleared his throat, running a finger under his collar.

"No, this isn't . . ." she sputtered. "I didn't mean to . . ."

Ellamae was still howling, slapping her good knee. Valien had buried his smile behind his fist. Arlen was just staring slack-jawed at his sister.

"*Rivers to the sea.*" Face blazing, she smoothed her hands over her skirt and turned to look past me at Rou on the other end of the settee. "Rou . . . shut up, Mae, honestly . . . Rou, will you marry me?"

"You hadn't even *asked* him yet?" Ellamae gasped, clutching her side.

"We've talked about it," Mona snapped.

"We've talked about it a lot," Rou agreed. "Hours and hours."

"Yes."

"And I thought we'd both decided that I can't be a king."

Ellamae swallowed her laugh mid-gasp. My spoon clinked against the soup bowl in the sudden silence.

Oh, this was very awkward.

Rou drew in a short breath. "I don't know how, Mona. And I don't know that I want to. I don't think I could be the king you'd deserve."

My cheeks flushed, and I started thinking of all the ways we could excuse ourselves en masse from the room. But instead of wilting with dismay, Mona nodded.

"I don't need a king," she said. "I don't want a king. But . . . I could use an ambassador. Someone folk like, someone folk trust. Someone kinder than me. And someone who can put this alliance before . . . personal things."

I forcibly bit back a smile, suddenly realizing what Rou had done to secure his favor in Mona's eyes. Just a day earlier, when everything was on the line, he'd chosen his country over her. She'd watched him do it, felt him place her second. She was the only person I could think of to whom that would pass as the greatest test of character. To anyone else it would have been callous and low, but to her it was the highest form of integrity.

"Is that . . . can we do that?" Rou asked incredulously.

"I've been going through our legal texts," Mona said. "I've yet to come across anything in writing that says a monarch's spouse must be crowned. A coronation is separate from a marriage. There's nothing that states otherwise. And if there is, I'll rewrite it. Will you be my ambassador?"

We all swiveled to look at Rou as if we were watching a game of pole ball. He spread his hands in his lap. "I'll be anything you want, my queen. But we don't have to get married just for that."

Ellamae's grin could have lit a wet wick. Arlen grabbed an idle teacup and tipped the contents into his mouth—I was fairly sure it was empty. I arranged my skirt and stood.

"I think I'll stand over *here*," I said lightly, proceeding to the fire, letting the heat add to the warmth blooming in my chest.

Mona pointlessly rearranged her teacup and saucer on the table. Ellamae picked up her crutch and jabbed her in the hip.

"Go on," she said.

Mona drew in a sharp breath and looked back to Rou, who couldn't seem to decide what to do with his hands.

"And I love you, of course," Mona said.

Rou's grin flared even brighter than Ellamae's. "Well, that changes things. Yes, I would like to marry you very much."

"Finally," Ellamae said. "Go on, kiss."

"I'm not sure I want to give you the satisfaction," Mona said, her face still glowing pink. Despite this, her fingers linked with his on the cushion between them.

Ellamae gave an almighty stretch and yawn. "Right, then, I think I'm ready to go to bed. All of you, get out."

Arlen didn't need any persuasion. "Blazing Light," he muttered, shaking his head and fleeing to the door.

Mona and Rou stood—Rou couldn't seem to contain his grin. Mona couldn't seem to stop blushing. Despite this, she nodded at me, clearly trying to maintain a solemn composure for my sake.

"Gemma . . . please tell us what you need. Whenever you need it. We're here for you, all right?"

"And us, too," Ellamae said.

A smile, though small, came surprisingly easily. "Thank you."

I followed Mona and Rou out into the hall, hanging back a little so they wouldn't feel obligated to let me walk with them. I shouldn't have worried—they made their way down the hall with a single-mindedness, pressed close together. Still smiling softly, I slipped back into my room. The fire was lit. The bed was turned down. The adjoining door was closed.

The night wasn't any easier, but at least there were fewer ghosts.

CHAPTER 20

The prison was no less cramped and cold than before, but this time I was let in without any scrutiny or royal seal. Shaula was in a cell halfway down the corridor, closest to the central hearth. She sat on the edge of her cot, stiff and sharp as ever, bundled in her thick cloak. She eyed me coolly as I stopped on the other side of the bars.

"So you condescended to see me before they tie the noose," she said evenly.

I swallowed, still not immune to her disapproval. "The trial will begin shortly. This will be our last chance to speak together."

"What could you possibly have to say to me?"

"You saw the king?" I asked. "You saw what you have done?"

"I saw his body," she replied. "And I shall remind

you that it was by your choices and your actions that he was brought here. Whatever misdeeds you hold against me, you share them in equal part."

"I would agree with you if it was only the king's death I hold against you," I said. "And I do hold it against you, Shaula—if it had not been during the attack, it would have been from illness or overdose. How long did you lace his tincture with the same poison you used on the others?"

"Poison." It was a statement, not a question.

"That's right. Izar, the three acolytes, and your predecessor, Mirach. You gave them cyanic acid harvested from your little creatures of light."

Her face didn't change, didn't even twitch. "So Rana told you at last."

"No," I said. "I guessed. You just confirmed it."

The skin around her lips and eyes tensed slightly, the lantern light thrown just barely into sharper relief.

"I should have given it to *you*," she said, "and been done with it."

"But you didn't," I said. "Because in the end, you still saw some use in me. I could be his mouthpiece. I could be his stand-in when he was too ill to govern himself—keeping suspicions from ever getting too strong that the Prelate was acting outside her station."

"It's so easy for you to think me a villain, isn't it?" she asked, a new glint in her eye. "The wicked Prelate, misusing the Prophecy for her own gain. You fail to remember that the Prophecy is my domain, and the king's work is the Prophecy. My role and his were one and the same."

"No, they were not!" I retorted. "No, they *were not*. You were his advisor, not the driver of his every action! Not the governor of his personal life! *How often did you tamper with his medicine?*"

"Only when he required it," she said without a shred of contrition. "Only when he was allowing himself to be led by you, or his books, and not by the words of the Prism."

"And the forged documents?" I asked, curling my fingers around one of the cell bars, the cold metal biting my fingers. "The falsified orders, the decrees in his name—how long has that been going on? Did it start with the extension of my mother's prison sentence, or even before that?"

She gave a small, almost sad shake of her head. "Everything I have done, I have done by the revelation of the Light for the advancement of the Prophecy. Your own sacrilege blinds you to that perfect truth, and for that I pity you. I pity the emptiness left by such lack of faith, and I pray for your ultimate repentance."

We stared through the bars at each other, and I realized, unnerved, that she did not—would not—feel any remorse for what she had done. That she truly believed she had been in the right. The deaths and illnesses and treason were all simply stepping-stones to the Prophecy, and that made them incontestable. Necessary. Destined, even.

To herself, she was absolved.

She was gazing at me, too—I was unable to fathom what was going through her mind. I let go of the cell bar. "Where is my mother?" I asked.

Her lips pursed very slightly. "Not in prison, to my extreme displeasure."

"She wasn't captured by the soldiers?" I asked. "She never made it back to Callais?"

"I would not know," she said. "We left Port Juaro the morning after we found the king missing."

"Which means you had my letter well before that moment," I said.

"It was waiting in your study upon our return from Cyprien," she said. "I confiscated it along with everything else, of course."

"And yet you preached to our officers that you were divinely guided to this place," I said.

She made the subtlest of shrugs. "The Light reveals itself in many ways."

"No," I said, a little unsteadily. "You can't just take happenstance events and claim they were orchestrated by the Light." I shook my head. "You've accused me of trying to shape the world to meet my needs. But if I do, Shaula, it's because I learned it from you." I straightened a little. "And we're both going to pay for it—you by facing Queen Mona's gallows, and I by going back into the ruins of Alcoro and trying to salvage something of it."

Her gaze had grown sharper the longer I spoke,

until her eyes were narrow and creased. She tilted her head slightly as she regarded me.

"I've turned you into a queen," she said.

"I became queen well enough on my own."

"No," she said. "I mean now you've finally settled under that crown—ready to send a person to her death for what you yourself believe is right. That's something even Celeno didn't achieve." Her lips thinned in a bitter smile. "Long live the queen."

My stomach soured and clenched, and I took a step back. I tried to refocus my mind on the calm, confident manner I'd sworn I would face her with. I thought of Mona, of Ellamae, of how they'd stare her down and make her recant, make her sorry for her words, her actions, the wounds she had torn in the world and in me.

But I couldn't do it.

I turned and fled.

I sobbed throughout the entire trial.

Mona was staunch and terrifying, laying out every act done in both Celeno's and Shaula's name from the moment our ships reached the lake four years ago. She read out the names of those killed in the attack, and then the others killed in rebellions throughout the years of annexation. She detailed the military-style execution of an innocent, Ama Alastaire. She listed off cultural grievances and economic setbacks from the three years of occupation. Disruption to the Silverwood by a return trip through the mountains.

When she shifted over to the actions against Cyprien, I made the mistake of looking up from the handkerchief I'd been folding and refolding in my lap. My stomach turned over. Shaula was gazing straight at me, the lines in her face set and cool. I quickly dropped my eyes, but I couldn't unfeel her stare, and the few times I peeked up again, she hadn't moved. She was spending the entire reading of charges looking directly at me.

I had made a decision that morning in a spurt of defiance—I was wearing a scooped blouse that swept over my collarbones, leaving my neck bare. I'd thought of it as a sign of victory, but here, now I hated it. Real or imagined, I could feel every eye in the room on my stain—hers more than anyone's. I wanted to tear my hair out of its bun and swath it over my shoulders. I wanted a cloak or a massive scarf to wrap around my neck.

I would never be like Queen Mona, able to rise from a pile of ashes stronger and more powerful than before. I would never be like Queen Ellamae, whose steps never faltered, who walked with the confidence of knowing exactly where she belonged and what she was meant to do. I would always have one foot in the past.

The charges were finished. The sentencing was done. The rope was ready. I had told myself that morning that I was going to watch, I was going to meet her gaze, the person who'd undone so many lives. But I didn't. I balled the handkerchief over my face and cried all the harder. Ellamae was on my right side, and Valien on my left. Sorcha was there, too. I was too far gone to feel all three of their hands touching me throughout the creaking of wood, the shifting of fabric, and the sudden swing of metal hinges.

Whether it was a product of grief or stress or the days of hard travel catching up to me, that afternoon my traitorous body rebelled and saw me burrowed in bed, shivering with fever. Ellamae came in and out, replenishing the broth and sweet birch and mullein on my bedside. A few unfamiliar healers filled in the gaps, bringing wet cloths that were stinging cold straight from the lake. I drifted in hazy sleep, dreaming vivid dreams of childhood and beyond. My mother's twirly house, rosy and bright. The darkness of the potato cupboard, my legs seizing up in response. A swath of stars, the warmth of Celeno's body pressing against me. The broken pavers of the terrace, he limp and distorted in front of me.

It was two days, or some approximation, before my fever broke. I surfaced amid the tang of sweat, my body aching but my mind clear of the clouds. The room was silent besides the soft crackling of wood in the hearth. My right ear was sore, still ringing from the blast on the terrace. Shifting under the sheets, I cracked open sticky eyes to find Colm at my bedside.

He looked up as I turned my head, closed his book, and smiled at me.

"Hi," he said. "How do you feel?"

"Terrible," I said honestly, my throat dry. "But better."

He set his book on the bedside table and poured me a cup of water. I took it gratefully and sipped a little.

"What are you doing here?" I asked.

"The trial concluded a few hours ago," he said. He spread his palms. "I've been charged with relaying secure information and sentenced to exile."

I slowly lowered the cup of water. "For how long?"

"Eight years."

My newly cleared head spun, and I sucked in a deep breath. "Colm." I closed my eyes. "I'm sorry."

"Gemma."

I opened my eyes.

"I couldn't have left otherwise," he said. "I couldn't have made that choice on my own. Now I have no choice, and that's easier."

I wanted to argue, insist that he see the same courage I saw, but I understood what he meant. I sighed.

"I'm the same way," I said. "It's easier to have others make the decisions. I'd rather be the quiet one who sits in the corner and watches—that's what I'm best at."

"Gemma," he said seriously. "I don't know if you've realized—but it's really not."

I looked down at my cup. "I couldn't stand up against what was happening in Alcoro. I couldn't rise up like Mona or take a stand like Ellamae. I couldn't throw everything on the line, like Rou."

"The world can only handle so many Monas and Maes and Rous," he said with a warm edge to his voice. "We're quiet workers, you and I. We're happiest on the edges. That's okay. It doesn't make your accomplishments any less great than theirs—yours were just achieved with less . . ." He flashed his fingers in the air in an imitation of fireworks. "You still took a stand. You still fought for your country. You still chased after the truth. And you, ultimately, brought this thing to its close."

"With their help. With your help."

"Nothing is ever done without help," he said.

That was true. I looked back up at him. "Will you help me now?"

He smiled. "I'd be honored."

"I'm a stress crier," I warned him.

He nodded. "I argue with myself when I'm writing. Out loud."

I hiccupped a laugh. He smiled, and his gaze traveled to the book he'd set down on the bedside table—the copy of *The Diving Menagerie*.

"Thank you, by the way," he said. "For the iguana."

"You're welcome." That little sketch seemed years ago. "It was . . . just silly."

"It made me smile," he said.

I gave a nod of acknowledgement. "Then maybe it's not so silly."

His smile grew, and he looked down at his hands. His hair fell down over his forehead, a little wind-swept. I wanted to brush it, either smooth it back into place or muss it further—I wasn't sure.

His smile shrank a little as he studied his hands. "I dropped Ama's ring into the lake."

The warm, wobbly bloom in my chest suddenly went cold. "What? When?"

"Just before coming here," he said, looking up at me. "Right after the sentencing. I sailed out into the deeps, where we sink our dead. It's much too deep to dive." He flattened his hand, palm up on his knee. "I held it under the surface and just tipped my hand."

I thought of him kneeling at the bobbing hull of the sailboat in the cold wind, watching the little ring flicker away into the depths. He was looking at his palm, as if he couldn't believe he'd really done it.

"I cried," he said.

I reached out and unfurled my fingers to him. Without hesitating, he placed his hand in mine, and then slid his second underneath. He let out his breath and bent his head forward, his eyes squeezing shut.

"I'm sorry about Celeno," he said, his voice deep and quiet. "I'm so sorry."

My throat worked. "I miss him."

His big hands pressed mine, warming my fingers. "You're going to miss him for a long time."

I let out my breath. We shared a silence together—a thick silence, but not an awkward one. My eyes stung behind my lashes—I let the tears fall without trying to keep them back. His hands remained wrapped around mine, comforting in their simplicity and the full depth of his understanding. That he intimately knew what I was feeling, that he had suffered and struggled with the same horrific loss and still come through with the ability to forgive and to love—nothing could have consoled me more.

When my tears had slowed, I blotted the remnants from my cheeks with the edge of my sleeve.

"What did the letter say?" I asked, opening my eyes. "The second to last one—the one I never got?"

"Oh." He rubbed the back of his neck. "It was . . . mostly asking you to come to the lake, for your own safety."

"I don't believe that's all it said."

"No." He cleared his throat. "I wrote it just after Mae and Mona came back from Cyprien, and I wasn't . . . terribly sensible. I thought I'd killed you, Gemma. And I realized I hadn't just wanted you to come to see the petroglyphs, but I wanted to meet you, too." He shook his head. "I overstepped my bounds . . ."

"What words did you use?" I asked.

He colored slightly. "Something stupid and asinine, I believe . . . *I've come to care greatly for you just from our short correspondence and pray for your safety both for our countries' sakes and mine . . ."* He shook his head. "Don't laugh at me."

I took my free hand away from my lips. "I'm sorry. But they're nice words."

"I was in the wrong—I wrote too freely." His gaze dropped to our enjoined hands. "And now I feel horrible—I feel sick, like I had been hoping . . . like I'm glad that he's . . ."

I squeezed his hand. "I know that's not the truth, Colm. You were kinder to him than anyone else, and I'm grateful for that. And . . . I'm glad I didn't get that particular letter, in a way. I wish it hadn't fallen into Shaula's hands, but . . . it would have changed things for me. I'm glad I didn't know how you felt, or it would have been difficult for me not to answer back in a similar way."

The corners of his mouth flickered as if he were fighting back an impulsive smile. He brushed his thumbs over my palm, studying the curl of my fingers, the dark tan of my skin against his paler color. It was my left hand, and the sleeve of my nightshirt was loose. He ran his fingers up my wrist, brushing them gently over the beginning of my wine stain. I closed my eyes, my heart fluttering.

He looked up suddenly.

"May I kiss you?" he asked. The words came quickly, like they'd tripped out before he could think about them.

My pause made him flush, bringing a pink tinge to

his cheeks and ears, smothering a few of his freckles. I smiled slightly—it made the gold of his hair shine just a little more.

"No," he acknowledged. "I'm sorry."

I settled my head back against my pillow. I shifted my hand so my fingers linked through his.

"Not yet," I said.

"Can I open them now?" I asked.

"No, no, keep them closed—just sniff."

"Am I going to regret this?"

"I sincerely doubt it."

I inhaled through my nose and was flooded with the most glorious scent of roasted coffee beans. My knees almost buckled in response. I peeled my hands away from my eyes to find Rou grinning with the bag held out before him.

"I brought back two eight-pound bags," he said. "So we should be good for a few days, right?"

"Oh," I sighed, taking the bag from his hands and cradling it. "Thank you."

"You're welcome. I have a multi-step plan to get Mona drinking it—then she's sure to include it in her trade manifestos."

My smile widened and then slipped as two people entered the room behind him, talking quietly together. One was a woman with umber skin and black hair held away from her face by a hammered gold band. The other was a tall man with earthy brown skin closer to Rou's color and hair in long twists down his back, the black streaked here and there with steely gray. They both stopped speaking as their gazes fell on me.

I drew in a breath, aware I was still cradling the bag of coffee. "Senators," I greeted.

"Lady Queen," replied the woman evenly. She held out her hands, and suddenly recalling that the Cypri shook two-handed, I thrust the coffee bag back to Rou and placed my hands in hers.

"Senator Eulalie Ancelet, the Lower Draws, and First on the Assembly," Rou said. "And Senator Arnau Fontenot, Alosia. Senators Dupont and Garoux stayed behind, and we couldn't make contact with the other two in time."

I shook Senator Fontenot's hands. "So the reign of the Seventh King has ended," he said.

"Yes," I said, trying not to make my voice sound small.

"May he be blessed in the Light," he said a little dryly.

"Thank you." I looked between them. "The state of Cyprien?"

Senator Ancelet smoothed some of the fringe on her elegant green traveling dress.

"We'll rebuild," she said finally. She looked up at me with a spark in her eye. "But we do have stipulations."

"Of course," I said.

"We would like to begin negotiating as soon as possible."

"Yes," I said. "I believe Queen Mona had plans for our first session this evening." I took a breath and glanced first at Rou, and then over their shoulders, as if she might walk in at any moment. "Before we join the rest, however, I have something to ask you—something I would appreciate your guidance with."

Both senators raised their eyebrows. Rou tilted his head, curious.

"I would be very grateful," I said, my stomach knotted but my hands steady, "if you would assist me in planning a transition in Alcoro to replace the monarchy with an elected government. Something similar to the one in Cyprien."

They all three stared at me—Senator Ancelet actually leaned back, as if to scrutinize me more completely.

"That means you would not be queen," she said. "Or hold a title at all, potentially."

"Yes. I am very much aware."

The silence persisted.

I fought against twisting my hands. "I understand if you don't wish to be a part of it, and I can try to do it on my own, but I thought you would be able to—"

Rou's grin broke across his face. He dropped the coffee bag with a thump on a side table, took a step toward me, clasped my face in both hands, and kissed me smack on the forehead.

I gazed up at the rock wall, the cold air stinging my cheeks. Scribble Cave could almost have been a hob in the canyon, with a slightly curved rock ceiling that sloped to meet the floor. A windswept copse of trees even stood guard near the edge, like in Whiptail Hob. The major exceptions were the frozen waterfall that curtained one end, and the petroglyphs carved into the wall—not faint and scattered, like those over my mother's house, but bold and precise.

We are creatures of the Light, and we know it imperfectly.
During the reign of the seventh king of the canyons,
one will rise to bring
the wealth and prosperity of a thousand years.
Wealth shall come from wealth.
Peace shall come from peace.
I am a prism, made to scatter light.
Syrma

My gaze traveled over them again and again. They were tall and narrow, like the ones in Callais, and worn with age despite being well preserved by the overhang and relatively harder rock that made up the Palisades. It must have hurt, I thought, for the Prism to carve these here. It must have taken forever. I looked down at her signature again, next to the figure crowned with the three stars over her head. Had she really been driven by the Light to secret these words in pockets across the Eastern World? Did she have her own private agenda? Had she simply been insane, as Mona probably thought?

Did she know what her words would wreak? Did she stop once to think about the dissolving of human lives into mere marks in stone, or did she carve without pausing to wonder about the cost of fulfillment?

I moved forward and placed my hand on the frigid rock—something that was strictly not allowed on the weathered cyphers in Callais lest they wear even more. For months I had fought to find a way to be right here, doing exactly what I was doing now—reading these marks that changed so much. From Alcoro to Cyprien to the caves to Lumen Lake, this had been my one goal. But now I was here, and things had already changed. The whole world had changed, shifted so dramatically it seemed to tilt as I walked, as if I was a ship that had broken a few of her moorings.

It could also simply have been my ear. It had grown less sensitive, but sounds on my right side were still fuzzy and faint. I seemed to be constantly turning in circles in conversation, trying to face the person speaking. I'd cried about this once—of course I did—but in the past few weeks, I noticed it made me listen harder, focus more. It made me lift my gaze and make eye contact. Which was good.

But also exhausting.

Colm was standing off to the side, near the frozen waterfall, looking out at the lake. I turned to him

514 EMILY B. MARTIN

now. Our talk in the last few weeks had been easy. I'd
cried a lot. We'd talked about the university, hashing
out timelines and preliminary budgets. But more often we were silent, usually sitting with a few feet of
space between us, I with a cup of coffee and he with
tea, appreciating the need not to talk or look or listen.

He heard me turn and nodded at the petroglyphs. "So?"

"They're just as Celeno said," I said. "If they're not
written by the same hand, then they must be an almost perfect copy. Either the Prism traveled here to
Lumen Lake, or a follower of hers did." I set down
the case I'd brought and opened it to a pack of blank
parchment and charcoal sticks. I planned to make
four copies of rubbings, along with at least as many
sketches. Colm helped me set up the materials, labeling the pages for rubbings while I shook the bottles of
ink. I smoothed a brush, thinking back to my mother's letter that had arrived a few days previously.

She'd been in equal parts stunned and horrified
by the mere fact that I was in Lumen Lake, on top
of the events that had happened here. The page was
spotted with little ink dots, as if she'd paused with
her nib on the page before writing each sentence.
She had offered condolences that had a sense of shock
to them. News had reached Alcoro before our ships
had arrived back in Port Juaro, and already I could
tell that rumors were spreading. I'd written back hurriedly, asking her to please set the most important

facts straight before too much damage was done. But I knew there was only so much I could do.

She at least had managed to avoid capture by the soldiers in the mountains and seek out her old colleague Ancha, and together they had secured a warrant to have Shaula's rooms searched. They'd found the millipedes and the cyanide she'd harvested from them, contained in neat little vials inside a box of decorative prisms. Councilor Izar, when presented with these findings and the purported cause of his own brush with death, had put out the warrant for her arrest, which slid through the council's vote, five to two. But Shaula had already been dead by that time, and I was going to have a lot of questions to answer when I finally arrived back on our shores.

My mother had written her letter from prison. She was back inside a cell, under arrest for kidnapping the king and queen. But, she wrote, things were in such disarray that there was no trial or gallows sentence in place yet. Besides, she said, Councilor Izar had put a freeze on any action at the royal level until I had returned to set things straight. He was fending off petitions and had quelled rioting in the streets by proclaiming that the queen had struck down the alliance building against Alcoro and instead united the East to a common cause.

I'd groaned and clutched my head as I read these words. Oh, there would be so much to do when I got home.

I looked up, studying the petroglyphs, mentally sketching out my first brush strokes. Colm finished labeling the parchment in his neat hand, and he looked up at them, too.

He cleared his throat, glanced at me, and shifted slightly so he was closer to my left side.

"During the reign," he quoted, a little hesitant. "One will rise."

I uncorked a bottle of ink. "That's what it says."

He smoothed his parchment. "I suppose you've thought about . . ."

I stared at my page, trying vainly to picture my first marks.

"His reign is technically over," he continued. "Which means, theoretically, that whoever is supposed to fulfill the Prophecy has already risen." He cut his gaze sideways to me again.

I drew in a breath and looked up from my page.

"Colm, I've had a lifetime of speculation about the machinations of the Prophecy. I'm done trying to find significance in every minute detail to prove its words at work. I'm just going to keep doing the best I can. If it's the Prophecy pushing me along, so be it. But I'm through with using it alone to measure my own worth and success."

"No, I'm not suggesting you should," he said. "And I don't think the Prophecy is pushing you along." He paused, turning a piece of charcoal in his fingers. "But

I do think the university is going to be an incredible thing, Gemma."

A little smile flickered at the corners of my lips. I dipped my brush and made my first stroke.

The hull of the *Wild Indigo* rocked slightly at the deep-water docks. In the five weeks since I'd found Colm working on it, she'd been fully finished and readied to sail. Her maiden voyage would be down the river and out to sea, around the coast of Cyprien and into the dock at Port Juaro in Alcoro.

Colm squinted up at the mast, where Lumen Lake's banner snapped in the breeze.

"She's a fine little boat," he said with a hint of pride.

I smiled. He shifted, and the chains on his wrists clinked. My gaze dropped to the set of irons—they were merely symbolic, but I hated looking at them all the same. He didn't seem to mind, gazing out at the winter-bright lake with visible ease, not at all like he was getting his last look for the next eight years.

I had a small trunk nearby that held little more than a few changes of clothes and reams of documents— mostly copies of the sanctions that had been drawn up against Alcoro and the plans detailing the withdrawal from Cyprien and the transitioning of our monarchy. I now faced the daunting task of bringing all these things back to Alcoro and setting them into motion, but the fact that our three neighboring countries all had identical signed documents made it easier to envision. Senator Ancelet had even promised to send an Assembly representative sometime in the spring to help firsthand with the installation of an elected government.

She and Senator Fontenot were making their goodbyes as well—they were joining us on the trip back down the river. As they saw their things boarded, the others made their way down the long dock. Ellamae and Valien had rejoined us—they had traveled back up to the Silverwood four weeks ago to mitigate their long absence. Ellamae had come back shortly afterward, bearing a cartload of juniper boughs, fragrant and ready for burning. She also brought a small, handsome box of solid Silvern chestnut, which had been inlaid with mother-of-pearl stars by the Lumeni smiths. That box rested on top of my trunk.

Celeno's funeral had been quiet and small, not the hours-long affair usually given to Alcoran kings and queens. There'd been no lengthy Devotion or week of hushed, smoke-filled streets. It was just Mona, Rou, Ellamae, Arlen, Colm, and me gathered around the pyre. The senators had chosen not to come. Sorcha hadn't come. Valien was still in the mountains. None of my folk were left at the lake. So the six of us merely stood, watching the flames overtake the shroud, the scent of juniper thick in the air.

Now they joined Colm and me at the end of the dock. Ellamae was still using a crutch to get around, but at least she could put weight on her leg again. She handed her crutch off to Valien and wrapped Colm in a tight hug. I heard his spine pop.

"You know what's nice about Alcoro?" she asked, crushing his arms to his sides.

"What's that?" His words were short and a little breathless.

"There's no poison ivy there," she said. "But there are rattlesnakes. Don't get bitten."

He smiled at some inside joke and let out his breath as she released him. His wrists still locked in place, he accepted a clasp of his arm from Valien and hugs from Arlen and Sorcha. They'd been married two days earlier, not wanting to wait until Colm could come back to be present. It had been a joy-filled day, with a stunning display of Lumeni singing and lanterns lit across the water all night. I'd attended the ceremony but had discreetly slipped away at the beginning of the celebration. I was still getting dark looks from the Lake-folk, and I didn't want to take away from the festivities. I sat contentedly by the fire in my room, listening to the singing rising off the lake and reading *The Diving Menagerie*.

Now I was ready, more than ever, to get back home. But our goodbyes weren't quite done.

Mona took a breath. She'd been quiet for most of

the past day. Now she stood in front of Colm, straight and tall but a little pale. He gazed down at her with a small smile.

"Mona," he said. "I'll miss you."

"Yes," she said, struggling a little. "We . . ." She gestured between herself and Rou. "We're getting married in the river."

"Not *in* the river," Rou said seriously. "I haven't got the lung capacity."

She pressed on, a little frazzled, as if she hadn't heard him. "It'll be during summer at the earliest—possibly later . . . I'll send you the date when we've set it, so you can make arrangements . . ."

Colm leaned down and kissed her forehead. "I won't miss it, not at all."

She released her breath and gestured sharply to one of the soldiers standing by. "Unlock these irons—this is ridiculous."

The soldier obediently moved forward and removed the irons on Colm's wrists. As soon as they slid off, he opened his arms and gathered his sister against him. She pressed her face into his shoulder. Some muffled words slipped out against his shirt.

"It's all right," he said. "It's all right—I'm happy, Mona. I'll miss you. But I'm happy. And you'll be happy, too."

She pulled back and waved at her face, splotched pink. She turned to me.

"Don't let him . . . I don't know, write himself

into oblivion. Sometimes you have to remind him to eat."

I smiled and took her hand. "We'll both look out for each other."

She dotted her face with a handkerchief. "You'll come to the wedding, too?"

"If you want me to."

"Yes." She straightened a little, her voice a little steadier. "Yes, and we'll have plenty to talk about by that point." Her gaze traveled to the ship, and she paused.

"Gemma," she said. "Are you sure about all this? I know you can build your university, it's just—to dismantle your monarchy?"

I smiled. She'd been largely silent on the matter since I'd introduced the idea—I got the sense she was processing exactly what it would take for she herself to consider making such a decision.

"I'm not meant to be a queen, Mona," I said. "I never was. I don't like it. But I do want to help rebuild Alcoro—and I hope I've found the way to do it."

"I'll say." Ellamae clapped me on the shoulder. "Maybe we should give it a shot in the Silverwood."

Valien paled behind her.

Ellamae hugged me with the same force she'd shown Colm. "Take care of yourself, Gemma. We'll see you soon."

I returned her hug, and then exchanged one with Rou and the others in turn. Finally, with a look at Colm, he and I both turned toward the gangplank.

A deckhand was about to take my trunk onboard, and I swiftly retrieved the chestnut box with Celeno's ashes inside and held it in my arms. The Lumeni soldiers who had come along as part of Colm's exile sentence lined the end of the dock to where the gangplank began. They shifted a little—many were obviously struggling to keep their faces expressionless. Colm picked up his bag, and I heard him quietly sigh.

We had almost reached the first of the soldiers when Mona's voice blurted impulsively behind us.

"*Attention.*"

The soldiers reflexively straightened, their chins lifted and their shoulders back.

"Present arms," she ordered, her voice a little cracked.

In a single movement, their fingertips hinged sharply to their temples. I clutched Celeno's ashes to my chest. Colm ducked his head, ran a knuckle under his eye, and then returned the salute as we both passed among the honor guard to the ship.

On the deck, the wind blew cold but steady from the north. Commands were given to cast off and lower sail. One of the sailors took up position at the capstan and belted out the beginning of a *heave away* chanty. As voices across the ship joined his, I crossed the deck for the little berth that belonged to me under the quarterdeck. Inside, I crouched down and settled the chestnut box securely next to my trunk.

There would be grief and mourning in Alcoro, there would be weeks of smoke and undyed linen. Someone—one of the acolytes—would give lengthy last rites as his ashes were interred in the sacred cliff-side. I would cry until I was exhausted. But I looked forward to what would come after—a rest. Finally, a quiet, a calm, under a kindling evening sky. A rest for him, and for me.

We couldn't go back.

We could only go forward.

But maybe forward would be all right.

I placed my hands on the pearly stars on the lid of the box.

"I'll see you at home," I whispered.

I went back out into the wind and the singing and the bright morning sun. Colm stood at the port rail with the two senators, looking back out at Blackshell and waving to the others down below. I passed him and went to the bow. The Beacon was shining against the western cliffs. Already some of its cascades had started to thaw, and a frozen sheet had reformed over the part I'd broken away on our way out of the cave.

I turned my gaze down the river, where the sun streamed up from the coast. It would be lighting the rim of the canyon, turning it yellow and gold and amber under the dusting of snow. I closed my eyes and breathed in, almost able to smell the sage and juniper on the wind. The ship rocked with its first forward momentum, and I gripped the hull.

I'm a creature of the Light, I thought. *And I know it imperfectly.*

It was a relief. And it was heartening. I tucked a few strands of my hair behind my star band and loosened my cloak a little, letting the wind blow against my bare neck. Swaying with the movement of the deck and the beat of the chanty, I opened my eyes and watched as the bow pointed down the river to the sea.

ACKNOWLEDGMENTS

And here we are—the end of the trilogy. So many people deserve endless gratitude for the progress and completion of this series, so let's get started:

Thank you to my agent, Valerie Noble, of Donaghy Literary Group, for being the first to take a risk on these characters, and for seeing the trilogy to its close. Thank you to my editor, David Pomerico, for your tireless work on refining and strengthening the manuscript. I am especially grateful to both of you for seeing the potential in this story even when it didn't come through the first (or second . . . or third . . .) time.

Thanks to my publicist, Michelle Podberezniak, my copy editor Libby Sternberg, Jena Karmali, and all the Harper Voyager team for your dedication and hard work.

To fellow ranger and ex-Carlsbad guide Ben Hoppe,

and the other adventurers—Patrick Holladay, Amanda Chivers, Gil Molina, Ila Hatter, and Caitlin Clark—who shared their cave experiences and helped make Gemma's journey through the mountains more vibrant. Thanks also to the rangers of Wind Cave and Jewel Cave for bringing those places alive for me.

I'd be remiss if I didn't thank the rangers, staff, and volunteers of Oconaluftee Visitor Center, Great Smoky Mountains NP, summer season 2017, for being unwitting victims of my three-month deadline extension. Thanks for bearing with my frazzled distraction and for shouting after me when I forgot my flat hat or radio. At least the rewrites kept me away from the elk.

To librarians everywhere, but particularly those in the Anderson County library system—thank you for being powerful champions of books and readers. Y'all are truly magic.

Thanks, as always, to Caitlin Bellinger—for everything. I can't put into words how much you mean to me. Thanks also to Anne Marie and the Martin clan for your continued support.

To my family, thank you, especially to my parents—my mom for patiently dissecting Gemma's actions and motivation, and my dad for fueling and informing her role as an entomologist. I knew joining you dumpster diving for cockroaches as a child would pay off someday. Okay, I didn't know that, but clearly it has, so high five for that.

To Will, thank you. To my girls, thank you. Thanks

for making this endeavor your reality as well as mine. I love you.

To you, reader, for accompanying these heroines on their journeys—thank you. Take care of yourselves. Take care of each other. Do good work. One crisis at a time.

ABOUT THE AUTHOR

EMILY B. MARTIN splits her time between working as a park ranger and an author/illustrator, resulting in her characteristic "nature nerd" fantasy adventures. An avid hiker and explorer, her experiences as a ranger help inform the characters and worlds she creates on paper. When not patrolling places like Yellowstone, the Great Smoky Mountains, or Philmont Scout Ranch, she lives in South Carolina with her husband, Will, and two daughters, Lucy and Amelia.

www.emilybmartin.me/
Facebook.com/EmilyBeeMartin/
@EmilyBeeMartin